obsession

obsession

Wanda L. Dyson

BARBOUR
PUBLISHING

Published by Barbour Publishing, Inc., P.O. Box 719, Uhrichsville, Ohio 44683, www.barbourbooks.com

Our mission is to publish and distribute inspirational products offering exceptional value and biblical encouragement to the masses.

ecpa Member of the
Evangelical Christian
Publishers Association

Printed in the United States of America.
5 4 3 2 1

dedication

This book is lovingly dedicated to Bobbi Jo Ruel—
may you follow your dream and find that it wasn't a dream at all.
It was just everything you ever wanted and
everything the Lord ever wanted for you.

And to my niece Nevaeh Murphey—
you lived only an hour but touched our hearts forever.

acknowledgments

Many thanks to my editor, Shannon Hill, and all the wonderful people at Barbour who believed in this series; Marlene Bagnull, Karen King, Sandy Cathcart, Joanie Barineau, Christi Horowitz, and all those friends who prayed me through every page; Kendra Parsons, Tully Blanchard, and Marlene for all the brainstorming and invaluable input.

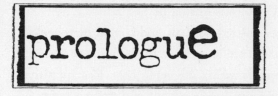

prologue

I need to go." Lori Blain laughed brightly as she pushed back from the bar and, with one artless gesture, swept her waist-long hair back over her shoulder. "I promised myself I'd get some studying in tonight."

Two hours earlier, she had entered Time Out, a trendy neighborhood bar, looking for a little diversion from a long day of college classes. Diversion had been found with this charming young man whose big blue eyes were lushly framed with long, thick lashes. Now they were framed with disappointment as the young man spun around on his barstool. "Are you sure? Maybe one more?"

Lori shook her head as she glanced down at her watch. "I really have to get back to the dorm." She picked up her drink, swallowed the last of it with one long swallow, and reached for her purse.

"Can I call you?"

The hesitation was minute. "Sure." She pulled a pen from her purse, jotted her number down on a cocktail napkin, and winked at him as a wave of mild dizziness swept over her. "I'll be looking forward to it."

As she stepped outside the crowded bar, she sucked in the fresh air. Normally, she kept close track of how much she drank on a school night, but she must have been distracted by the fun she was having with Bret. He'd been charming, funny, and a great dancer. Somewhere between the dancing and the laughing, she'd gone over her limit, and now the alcohol was hitting her.

The cool night breeze rustled her hair and cooled her cheeks. She lifted her face to it as she walked around the building to her car. Her heels clipped the asphalt with a staggered beat. Reaching the corner of the building, she put her hand out and grabbed onto a drainpipe, closing her eyes for a second.

Maybe she'd gone two drinks over her limit. She couldn't remember the last time she felt so woozy.

Taking a deep breath, she reached down into her purse and fished for her keys. Curling them in her fingers, she pushed off from the building and wove her way to the car, each step becoming more labored, more difficult.

Finally she reached the small, lime green Volkswagen her parents had bought for her when she graduated from high school. Through the windshield, a yellow daisy was visible where it sat in the vase on the dashboard.

Leaning against the car, she stared down at the keys in her hand, trying to make her brain separate the car key from the others dangling there.

"Are you okay?"

Lori looked up as he strolled over, and nodded. "Yeah."

Slowly she began to slide down the side of the car. Capable male hands reached out and grabbed her. "Easy. I think you've had a few too many."

Blinking, she looked up into a pair of blue eyes. She managed a lopsided grin. "Guesh sho."

"That's okay," he said, lifting her easily into his arms. "By the time the drug wears off, you'll wish it hadn't."

"Where. . .where you. . .are you. . .taking me?"

Juggling her in his arms, he opened the back of his van and dumped her in. "To your final resting place, my sweet."

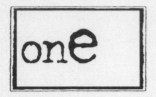

one

Friday, September 24—9:30 a.m.

I t's not like Lori to skip a meeting without calling one of us."
Kieran Jennings glanced at her watch for the umpteenth time. She'd
been accused more than once of being obsessed with time, but in
truth, she was just concerned with keeping to her tight schedule.
There was so little breathing room in it.

Trying to dismiss her concern for Lori, she looked around the
small circle. The Young Women for Professional Careers gathered
in a small circle in the campus library every Friday morning. Out of
the twenty-some members in high school, only seven were enrolled
at Monroe College. Lori Blain, Taylor Cordette, DeAnne Foster,
Pam Hamilton, herself, Dana Tappan, and Susan Wright. They
were a sisterhood among sisters—bright, ambitious, supportive, and
intelligent. She knew these girls as well as she knew her own family. Lori Blain, the starlet—blond, beautiful, and dramatic in an
easy-to-take way. Taylor Cordette, the watcher—quiet and unob-
trusive, with intelligent brown eyes that saw more than she let on.
Still waters run deep. That was Taylor. DeAnne Foster, the con-
queror—vivacious, petite, and unaffected by anyone's opinion, she
plowed through opposition and made her stand, dragging the timid

along reluctantly or otherwise. Pam Hamilton, the artist—tender, sensitive, and always handing out money to the homeless, she was quick to tears and just as quick to laugh at DeAnne's antics. Susan Wright, the dreamer—always optimistic, always seeing the gold at the end of the rainbow, always the hopeless romantic who still believed the world could live in peace if she could just get everyone to listen to her pleas.

"She didn't call me," DeAnne replied. "I haven't heard from her since Tuesday."

Dana tapped her foot impatiently. "There's a first time for everything. Maybe she met some hunk last night and figured he was more important than we are."

Kieran gave Dana a long, withering look. Dana Tappan, the princess with just a little too much attitude and none of it particularly attractive. She could be cool, aloof, arrogant, and a bit of a snob at times. Of course, she was the only one of the girls to come from a privileged background, being a judge's daughter and heir to a great fortune, raised in a house that was the closest thing Monroe County had to a mansion, with servants at her beck and call.

"I know this is hard for you to understand, Dana, but some of us actually care about the others."

Dana shot her a hot glare. "For your information, I do care about Lori, but she's an hour late and some of us have classes to get to. We can't spend the entire time talking about Lori. I'm sure she'll come bouncing in with a sweet apology and that will be that. Let's not act like it's some great tragedy."

Kieran stamped down on her temper as hard as she could. Sometimes she really wanted to slap Dana silly. But this was not the time or place for petty arguments.

"Okay," DeAnne interjected, once again taking the role of

peacekeeper. "We have to decide if we're going to do something at homecoming or not."

"Not another bake sale, I hope." Susan laughed.

"Please, anything but that." Dana grinned at Susan. "I'm never going to try to bake a cake again. What a catastrophe that was."

"We need to do something that's more in line with what we're all about," DeAnne offered thoughtfully with a faraway look in her eyes.

"Like what?" Dana asked.

"I don't know. I'm thinking." Suddenly she straightened in her chair. "I got it! How about we offer resume services? You know. . . help students prepare a resume for a really reasonable price? Give them some pointers, ideas, suggestions."

Susan wrote the idea down in her notebook. "It's a good possibility. We can set up a booth, charge maybe ten dollars, and give them fifteen minutes."

"This is homecoming, ladies." Dana stretched out her long legs and crossed them at the ankle. "Most of the kids are going to be thinking party, not prosperity."

"True," Susan acquiesced, then glanced at her watch again. She shut her notebook. "We're out of time. Let's give it some thought and discuss it more next week."

Dana shot to her feet, grabbing her backpack, hefting it to her shoulder. "We may need to think about meeting midweek. We don't have a lot of time to put this together."

The girls put their chairs back around the study table and headed out, splitting off outside and heading to their respective classes with hugs, waves, and promises to keep in touch.

Kieran fell into step with Taylor. "You were quiet today."

Taylor looped her arm over Kieran's shoulder. "Just had a lot on my mind. Family dynamics and all that."

"Your mom's new boyfriend?"

"I don't know what she sees in him."

Suddenly Kieran realized Taylor was heading in the wrong direction. "Where are you going? You don't have a class this morning."

"My dad's filling in for one of the professors, and I wanted to sit in on his class."

"Wow, really? I wish I could join you. He's so good looking."

Taylor wrinkled her nose. "I can't believe you have a crush on my dad."

Kieran laughed. "What can I say? I don't get out much."

"Still playing mommy and housekeeper? I don't know how you do it."

"You do what you have to do."

Taylor rolled her eyes. "What you have to do is take a stand, or your dad's never going to notice that you don't have a life."

"Look who's talking. And have you taken a stand and talked to your mom about all this?"

Taylor blushed lightly as she nibbled her lower lip. "It's different."

"How?"

"My dad said it's best to wait for now. I think he's working on getting my mom back."

Kieran hugged her friend. "That's great! You must be so excited!"

"I'm waiting to see it happen first. What my dad may want and what he may get could be two very different things."

Talking stopped and whispers trailed off. Chairs scraped across linoleum, and the rustle of paper increased for a moment before silence suddenly ensued.

Dan Cordette dropped his briefcase on the desk at the front of the classroom, his gaze sweeping the room quickly, taking in the body of students that were quietly waiting for him. Twenty-four males and eight females. All eyes forward.

For the most part, they were young, somewhere between eighteen and twenty, and were eagerly looking forward to careers in law enforcement. Some even had dreams of ending up at Quantico. He knew all too well that somewhere between the first time they were forced to kill and the first time they craved something to numb the pain, all that eagerness would be long dead. There was nothing glamorous about death and nothing wonderful about killers.

Turning his back to the class, he picked up a marker and wrote his name in big, loopy letters on the white board. He turned and, out of the corner of his eye, saw his daughter, Taylor, slip into the back of the class and take a seat. He shot her a quick smile.

"My name—for those of you observant enough to realize that I am not Professor Brooks—is Dan Cordette."

For most of his students, his name meant little to nothing, but at least one of the students, besides his daughter, knew exactly who he was. She stood out in the class like a dove among parakeets.

Oh yes, he knew the name Zoe Shefford. She was in her midthirties, blond, green eyes, with long, sleek lines and a killer smile. She was also infamous in law enforcement circles. For the past fifteen years, she'd been assisting police officers, parents, and the FBI to find missing and abducted children.

The last case he remembered hearing she was involved with was the Ted Matthews case last spring. Now she pops up in a criminal law class.

Why? The question plagued him as he edged his hip onto the corner of his desk.

He folded his arms across his chest and tried to keep from staring at her as he went through his opening statement. "And for those of you who don't keep up with the latest news, Professor Brooks suffered a mild heart attack a few days ago and has asked me to fill in for a couple of weeks. Or until he can figure out a way to get back to work without his doctor finding out."

There was a light flutter of laughter.

"I understand that I'm supposed to talk to you about jurisdiction and, if we have time, start on criminal liability."

Sliding off the desk, he began to pace the front of the classroom. Why would Zoe Shefford, with nearly as many years in the business as he had, be sitting in a class like this? How many cases had she worked? Sixty? Seventy? Probably a lot more. She could practically teach it.

Shuffling his curiosity to the back of his mind, he picked up the textbook and began his lecture. Ninety minutes later, Dan tossed the book into his briefcase as students filed past him. Taylor stopped at his desk. "I have to run to class. Call me later?"

"Absolutely, sweetheart. Thanks for being here today."

Taylor smiled up at him, her big brown eyes sparkling with love and admiration. He wished he could capture that look and bottle it. "Love you, Dad."

"Love you, too."

He watched her as she made her way toward the door, then turned his attention to another female.

"Miss Shefford?" he called out. "May I speak to you for a moment?"

She hiked one eyebrow in surprise as she stopped and studied him. Then she walked over.

"Yes?" She came to a stop in front of his desk, her backpack slung over one shoulder. She hadn't changed much since the last time he'd seen her. Except maybe to grow even prettier.

There was nothing but curiosity in her eyes as she stared at him.

Smiling, he zipped his briefcase closed. "You don't remember me, do you, Zoe?"

Her eyes widened just a bit. "You know me? We've met?"

Laughing, he pressed one hand to his chest. "Oh, I'm crushed. The lady so easily forgets."

She tilted her head with a smile. "I'm sorry, Mr. Cordette. I just don't recall. . ."

"New Hampshire. Nine years ago. A little boy with his parents on a camping weekend wandered off."

A light seemed to spark in her eyes as the corners of her mouth tilted up. "Evan. He was just four years old. We found him in a ravine with a sprained ankle."

"*You* found him," Dan reminded her. "Murdock was sure that he'd been abducted because someone saw a car speeding off. But you kept arguing. . .insisting that he was sitting somewhere, hurt and scared."

Actually she'd all but taken Murdock apart verbally, which stunned everyone within hearing distance. Murdock stood six-four in his socks, tipped the scales at two-forty, and was as tough as he was big. Few men had the courage to go up against him. Yet this little lady, delicate and as fine boned as china, had Murdock backing up and sputtering. When it came to Zoe Shefford, looks were very deceiving. She might seem as soft as a southern summer breeze, but underneath, she was pure steel.

"Wow. You remember all that? With all the cases you must have had over the years?" Zoe slid her backpack off and set it on the desk, resting her hands on top of it. "I'm impressed."

He smiled. "What in the world are you doing in this class?"

"I'm going for my law degree."

"Private practice?"

She shook her head. "Prosecution. I want to work for the district attorney's office putting away the guys I've been chasing all these years."

"So, you've decided to abandon fame and fortune to join the ranks of the overworked and underpaid." Dan lifted his briefcase off the desk.

"Something like that, yes."

It wasn't quite the answer he was expecting. And from everything he remembered about her, the sudden look of uncertainty in her eyes took him by surprise as well. There was a story here, and he was just intrigued enough to pursue it.

But before he could ask his next question, she asked one of her own. "How in the world did you get from the police force in New Hampshire to teaching here in Monroe?"

"Long story and best told over a cup of coffee. There's a little café across the Green. It's not Starbucks, but they have wonderful pastries. Join me and I'll tell you everything you want to know."

She hesitated a moment, then nodded. "That sounds good."

"Great! Just don't let me forget to buy a box of pastries. I have to bribe someone later."

"With pastries?"

Dan laughed as he held the door open for her. "The target in question has a real soft spot for the lemon and cherry Danishes. I never go to her for help without at least four of them to smooth the way."

"Remind me not to let you know my weaknesses."

"Oh, trust me. I'm a good investigator. I'd find out one way or another."

They stepped out into a picture-perfect day. Students ambled around them in groups of two and three, talking animatedly, still revved up by the new school year.

"You know, I feel ancient," Zoe remarked as they crossed what was commonly referred to as the "Green," a small parklike area between the school and University Road, which housed coffee shops, fast-food restaurants, taverns, bookstores, and at least two Internet cafés.

"I can imagine why you would feel that way, being older, wiser, and far more experienced than your classmates, but trust me, you are far from ancient."

Dan took hold of Zoe's elbow as they crossed University Road, dropping his grasp to open the door to a small coffee shop tucked between an Internet café and a gift shop.

"If even one of them calls me 'ma'am,' I'm gonna have to hurt them."

"If someone did, it would be one of the girls, and she'd be doing it because all the boys are too busy gawking at you to pay any attention to the rest of the girls in the class."

"What a nice compliment. You're Irish, aren't you?" She smirked up at him, and he couldn't help laughing.

"Not at all. Just speaking the truth as I see it."

As soon as they had a table and the coffee was ordered, Dan dropped the polite banter and got down to the question that had been nagging him.

"Now why don't you tell me why you feel the need to go work for the DA? The last time I checked, the police were calling *you* for help."

Zoe leaned back as the waitress set the cups down. They'd ordered simple Colombian coffee rather than opting for the fancier blends or lattes and declined any pastry.

"It's a long story. Suffice to say, I had to walk away from the work I was doing, and prosecuting criminals is something I've always felt passionate about. There are far too many of them out there getting away with murder. Literally. And when they do get caught, they manage to use the law to either get reduced sentences or off altogether."

She brushed back a lock of hair. "Well, I know this evil face-to-face, and I can make sure they don't win. I'll make sure they go away and stay there."

Dan studied her closely while she reached for the sugar, loosely measured out two teaspoons, then added cream. When he worked with her years earlier, she'd been an attractive woman with a wild mane of blond curls and big eyes that didn't seem to miss anything. She'd been focused and intense with a restlessness that gave you the impression she was moving, even when she was standing still.

She'd grown older and, without a doubt, more attractive. The long, blond hair was still curly but not nearly as wild around her face. Not only had she managed to tame the curls but the restlessness in her eyes as well. Her body was still all long, lean lines, but she appeared softer for some reason. More at peace with herself.

"Why did you have to walk away from it?"

Zoe sighed. "Because I became a Christian, and being a psychic didn't line up with scripture."

"Really? I never knew that." He scowled. "Are you sure about that?"

"Positive." She offered him the sugar. He shook his head, so she set it back on the table. "Now, you were going to tell me how you went from being on the police force in New Hampshire to teaching here in Monroe."

"I don't normally teach. I'm just filling in for Professor Brooks, who happens to be a friend of mine." He took a couple of sips while he collected his thoughts. "As for how I got here—long story short, my wife decided I loved my job more than I loved her, woke up one morning, and realized she was living with a stranger, packed up, and moved here to be near her parents, taking my two daughters with her. Six months later, I realized that I didn't want to live so far from my kids and miss out on any more of their lives, so I quit the force and moved here."

"How are things between you and your ex-wife now?"

Dan shrugged. "Better. We're actually finding a friendship of sorts. She's dating someone, and it looks pretty serious, so she's happy. That makes it easier. And as for my girls, they're thrilled that I'm actually showing some interest in their lives finally."

"How old are your girls?"

"Tanya is twenty-one and Taylor is nineteen."

Zoe raised one eyebrow, bringing his attention back to those big expressive eyes of hers. "Wow. They're grown. Somehow I pictured two little tomboys climbing all over you."

"They were when they were younger. Taylor is still pretty much a tomboy. She was in the class today. She just sat in to hear me. She's majoring in economics, not law."

"She was there?"

"The pretty brunette in jeans and a red sweatshirt."

Zoe smiled. "Ah, yes. I noticed her. She is pretty."

Dan nearly blushed with pride. "She's my baby. Tanya, however, has discovered the power of being female and is playing it to the hilt." The thought of his little girl flashing those big brown eyes at every available man in sight sobered him. "I worry about her sometimes. She goes through boyfriends at the rate of about one a week."

He stared down into his coffee, sighed, then looked up at Zoe. He was surprised to find that she was staring at him, her head tilted a little to the left, a strange little smile on her face.

"What?" he asked, more than a little curious.

The smile broadened across her face. "She's just discovering who she is. Relax, Dad. She'll be fine."

"Is that Zoe, a fellow female talking, or Zoe Shefford, psychic extraordinaire seeing something in her crystal ball?"

The smile vanished from her face as she drew back in her chair. A sudden look of vulnerability in her eyes made him realize that he'd just made a very big blunder.

"I'm sorry. I offended you. I didn't mean to."

"I know, and I'm not offended. I just wish no one knew that I'd ever considered myself a psychic." She picked up her coffee but didn't drink any. "So when you're not filling in for professors at the college, what do you do with your time?"

"I have a private investigation firm."

"A private investigator," Zoe responded softly. She wrapped her hands around her cup. "How's business?"

"Good. Busy. I now have six employees."

"And here I thought you were a one-man show."

"I was for the first year, but then the business took off, and I had to keep hiring people to handle the workload."

"It must be fascinating."

"Absolutely. And sometimes challenging and oftentimes boring. Why don't you forget the DA's office and come to work for me?"

"What?"

He set his cup down and leaned forward, propping his elbows on the table. "Start working for me at Cordette Investigations."

"You're joking."

He continued to stare at her, smiling as he watched the emotions racing across her face. Confusion, doubt, skepticism. "I'm serious. I could really use someone like you to help with missing persons investigations."

"Really?"

"Really—really."

"Wow." She stared down at the table for a long moment. Then she raised her eyes. "Sorry. I can't."

"You'd be great at it." Dan struggled with his disappointment and, determined to change her mind, he reached down and dragged his briefcase to the table. Opening it, he pulled out a file and slid it across the table to her. "I have this case. Janet Ayers. Age thirty-four. Last-known whereabouts were Monroe College. Her uncle is dying and wants to leave her his estate. She is his only living relative that he knows of. He lost touch with his sister not long after Janet enrolled here after high school. We have to find her as quickly as possible. The uncle doesn't have a great deal of time left."

Zoe picked up the file and began to read through it, turning the pages slowly. "Wow. One-point-two million. Nice inheritance."

Dan closed his briefcase and waved the waitress over. "I need two lemon and two cherry Danish to go, please."

Zoe began to tap her fingers on the table. "It's been sixteen years, and women tend to marry and change their names. This won't be fun."

"Missing persons rarely are. You know the score, Zoe. Sometimes they're cases like this. Happy ending if we find her. But sometimes the end isn't so happy." He flashed a charming smile. "First stop is Gladys Knittel. She works over in admissions. Take her the pastries. Tell her I sent them to her. Then ask her to help you go back through the records and see what you can find out."

Zoe looked up and laughed. "The bribe is for the woman in admissions?"

Dan shrugged with a sly grin. "And you thought all I had to do was flash my credentials? You'll learn. Bribery always smoothes the way. Danish, football tickets, theater tickets. You'd be surprised what you can find out after handing over a couple of passes to the hockey finals."

Slowly she closed the file and slid it back across the table. "I can't do it, Dan. I appreciate the offer, but I'm out of this business, and I'm not going back."

❖ ❖ ❖

4:27 p.m.

Kieran Jennings tossed her backpack on the kitchen table and, glancing at the clock on the wall, headed for the refrigerator. She had two hours to get dinner going, grab the laundry from upstairs, check the mail, and run the vacuum before her dad got home.

"Rachael!" she shouted as she pulled the chicken out and set it on the counter. "Are you home yet?"

There was no response from her younger sister, but that didn't mean anything. She turned the oven on, set the temperature for three-fifty, and jogged up the stairs, yanking her sweater over her head.

She knocked on her sister's bedroom door. "Rachael!" There was only a muffled response, but it was enough to prompt Kieran to open the door and stick her head in.

Fifteen-year-old Rachael was curled up on her bed, head bobbing to the music blasting in her ears through headphones while she read some textbook. Unlike Kieran, who favored their father with gray eyes and light brown hair, which tended to go blond midsummer, Rachael was a picture of their mother—black hair, dark brown eyes that hid nothing of what the young girl was feeling at any given moment, and freckles that scattered across her nose and irritated the young girl to no end.

Kieran felt the old familiar pain sweep over her. The same pain she'd felt ever since their mother had died four years earlier, leaving her to take the responsibility of raising Rachael, looking after their dad, and taking care of the house.

It hadn't been easy, and it was even harder now when she'd added college to the list of responsibilities.

Rachael looked up, smiled, and pulled her headphones off. Kieran picked up the sound of guitar and drums vibrating through the headphones from across the room.

"Hey, Kier! I didn't hear you come in."

"You wouldn't have heard a drum corps come in. Can you run the vacuum for me so that I can get the laundry and dinner?"

Rachael turned off her stereo and scooted off the bed. "Sure. I should have thought about it when I got home, but I wanted to finish this math homework before the weekend. I'll take the clothes to the laundry room for you."

"Thanks. Big plans for the weekend?"

Rachael shrugged as she started picking up the dirty clothes she had left scattered all over the room. "Maybe."

Smiling, Kieran left Rachael to the laundry and entered her room. As always, the bed was made, the drapes open, her clothes nowhere in sight. *Neat as a pin*, her mother always bragged.

At the thought of her mother, tears misted her eyes. She could still see her mother rushing out the door. . . . "I have to run and pick up your dad's stuff at the cleaners. He has a business trip tomorrow, and I've been running behind all day. I'll be right back, Kiki. Keep an eye on your sister for me." That was the last time Kieran saw her mother alive. A truck ran a red light and hit her mom's car, killing her instantly.

Kieran never allowed anyone to call her Kiki ever again.

Blinking away the tears, she hung her sweater in her closet, then changed into jeans and a sweatshirt and headed back downstairs to get dinner in the oven. Not a day went by that she didn't miss her mother. She knew her dad felt the same way. Four years, and he hadn't even started dating again. "Your mom was my soul mate," he'd told her once. "I can't believe I'd be lucky enough to have two of those in one lifetime, so why bother looking?"

After washing the chicken, she seasoned it and put it in the oven. Then she headed for the laundry room just off the kitchen. Ever since her mom had died, she'd taken care of her sister, double-checking homework, signing permission slips for field trips, playing mom as best she could. Her dad had never asked, but she had simply taken over running the house as well, making sure dinner was cooked, laundry was washed, shopping was done, and the place was clean.

Frowning, she eyed the chocolate stain down the front of Rachael's favorite shirt. Even after four years, she hated the man who had killed her mother. Dad said she shouldn't; that it was an accident. But she did anyway. And didn't even feel guilty for it.

"Kieran!"

Her dad's voice echoed through the house just ahead of the sound of the front door slamming shut. Tossing Rachael's shirt on top of the washer, she went to greet her dad.

"I'm right here," she responded, entering the kitchen from one direction as he entered from another. "What's up?"

"Have you heard from Lori?"

Kieran's brow furrowed. "No. She wasn't at the meeting this morning."

Mel Jennings frowned. "She didn't show up for work today. That's not like her."

"Maybe her class ran late?"

"She never showed up at all and never called."

"Did you try calling her?"

He nodded as he shrugged out of his coat. "No answer at home or on her cell. I just thought maybe she'd called here and left me a message."

"Nope. Sorry."

"Oh well." He reached over and dropped a kiss on her forehead. "She may be finding out that working part-time while in high school was one thing and working while in college is another."

"Yeah, but she's only putting in, what? Two days a week with you?" Kieran thought of her school load as well as the house and her sister and her dad. It didn't seem that three hours, twice a week, would be that big a deal for Lori.

"We'll see what she says on Tuesday. Maybe something came up and she just forgot it was Friday." He rubbed his hands together and inhaled with a smile. "Something smells good."

"Roast chicken."

"Do I have time for a shower before dinner?"

"Plenty of time."

He picked up his coat, draped it over his arm, and headed upstairs. "Is Rachael home?"

"In her room, I think."

She watched her father disappear up the stairs, then she sighed heavily and went back to start the load of laundry. Friday night. She should be getting ready for a date. But who had time for dating?

Just once, she wanted to cut loose and be irresponsible. Wild. Have fun. Not worry about anyone but herself.

She poured laundry detergent in the washer and shut the lid. Maybe it was time for her to break free of the restrictions she'd placed on herself and just. . .just. . .do something. Anything.

Maybe she'd get all dressed up in her sexiest outfit and go hit one of the local bars around the college. Meet some men. Dance. Laugh.

And not worry about whether her sister had clean clothes to wear tomorrow. Or if there were enough canned vegetables in the pantry to last the week. Or if the electric bill was paid on time.

Yeah. Maybe she would.

What's the worst that could possibly happen?

❖   ❖   ❖

6:19 p.m.

"I promised. I promised. I promised." Lanae Oakley kept chanting under her breath as she stepped into the dark apartment and turned on the light. A light coating of dust draped over every stick of furniture, every knickknack, every lampshade. She had never seen it like this. Never. Gammy had always kept the place spotless.

Tears welled up in Lanae's eyes as she took in the enormity of the task at hand. Sort through Gammy's belongings, pack up, toss out, save, give away. Empty the apartment, dispose of anything she wasn't going to keep, and close out her grandmother's life in a flurry of cardboard boxes and packing tape.

She hated it. She didn't want to close up the apartment. She wanted to come in on Saturday mornings to the smell of cinnamon French toast and sizzling sausage, to the sound of the classics on the radio playing softly in the background, to the sight of Gammy's smile just before she was swept into a warm hug. Who was she going to pour her heart out to? Who was she going to celebrate a job promotion with?

She didn't know where her mother was and had stopped caring years ago. She didn't know who her father was and had stopped wondering about him even longer ago. Her world had centered around Gammy. And now that Gammy was gone, her world felt upside down and tilted sideways.

And she felt so alone.

The silence seemed determined to suffocate her as surely as the grief was haunting her. She turned on the old wooden radio on the kitchen counter, took a deep breath, and began hauling in boxes from her car.

She started in the kitchen, made it through two cabinets, then shifted to the living room. After packing all the books on one bookshelf and filling three boxes, she found herself moving to the bedroom. She ran her hands lovingly over the handmade quilt on the bed and swiped at the tears.

Lanae opened one of the dresser drawers and began to lift out piles of sweaters, blouses, and floral print nightgowns in both cotton and flannel. One, a pink and white cotton nightgown, still had the price tag on it—from a store that went out of business ten years earlier.

She began to make two stacks. Things she would keep and things she would just send to Goodwill. When she finished with the dresser, she moved to the closet, her nose wrinkling at the faint odor of mothballs.

Her grandmother's fur coat and a beautiful lace shawl were set aside to keep while everything else was taken off hangers and folded into a box. When all the clothes were removed, she started on the boxes stacked in the corner on the floor. Under several shoeboxes, she found a box that was taped, tied with string, and marked with her mother's name.

Curious, she took the box out of the closet. Sitting on the bed, she untied the frayed string, cut through the tape, and set the lid aside. Peeling back the tissue paper, she lifted an infant's christening gown, yellowed with age. Was it hers? Trembling with emotion, she set it aside and continued to go through the box. A couple of pictures, mostly of her and her mother, a manila envelope full of papers, a book of poetry, a Bible, a small cheap jewelry box filled with costume jewelry, and two diaries.

Her mother had kept a diary? Somehow that surprised her. Lanae felt as if she were invading her mother's privacy, but this was all that was left of a mother she never knew.

The twinge of hurt surprised her. After all these years without her mother, she thought she no longer cared, and yet, there it was—that familiar old hurt of being left behind, unwanted and unloved by her own mother. What secrets did her mother have? And why should she even care after all these years? She didn't even know if her mother was still alive.

How old had she been when her mother had run off? Two? Three? If it wasn't for pictures, she wouldn't even know what her mother looked like. Her grandmother had tried to find her, but to no avail. The police were of little help, telling her to file a missing person's report and wait. Well, they'd waited years, and her mother had never come back.

Her mind wrestled with the emotions while her fingers moved of their own accord to turn the pages. She couldn't have stopped herself from reading if she'd wanted to. And she wasn't so sure she wanted to.

November 18, 1981. I called LT today. The creep wouldn't even take my call. His daughter is now two-and-a-half years old, and he hasn't even seen her. Of course, he's just too consumed with showing off his little prince, his precious son and heir. Well, his daughter is his firstborn, not this kid that snob he calls a wife has dropped for him! He said he loved me! Yeah! Until he found out I was pregnant! Well, he's going to pay and pay dearly for this!

Lanae's brow furrowed as she stared down at the angry scrawl. *LT*? Her father's initials were LT? And she had a half brother? Her heart began to pound as she realized she wasn't alone in this world after all. She had family. A brother! Wow. What was he like? Did they look so much alike that it was obvious they were brother and sister? Would they like each other? Become fast friends and pals?

What was she thinking? She didn't even know who LT was, much less where to find him!

She turned the page to the next entry.

January 4, 1982. Momma is really giving me a hard time about this. She doesn't think I can make LT pay up. Well, Lanae is his daughter and he deserves to pay! I sent him a letter a couple of days ago and told him that I had his precious book and that if he didn't talk to me and make arrangements for her care, then I was going to the press with the whole story. I'll bet that will bring him running. The last thing he wants are family secrets on the front page! That perfect image and his perfect family exposed as thieves and murderers. No, he wouldn't want anyone to know that, would he? He'll pay up. He'll give me anything I want. You just wait and see.

Lanae's hands shook as she absorbed the emotions flowing off the page and mingling with her own confusion and pain.

Quickly, she turned to the last page and looked at the final entry.

February 22, 1982. Tonight's the night! LT has been doing everything he can to get out of this, including siccing his bloody lawyers on me, but I held out and it worked. He's agreed to meet me tonight and give me money for Lanae. No more scrounging for every little penny. No more listening to Mom's lectures. No more wondering how I'm going to be able to pay

*the rent or buy food. I'm so tired of this life. I can't wait to get
my hands on all that money. As if LT will even miss it! Drop
in the bucket for him. He's got more money than God. And
now I'm going to have some of it. And all I have to do is hand
over that stupid book and promise to never let Lanae know
he's her father. Big deal. She doesn't need to know him and is
better off never knowing him. He'll only hurt her.*

Lanae slammed the book shut as tears began to stream down
her cheeks. It had taken blackmail to get her father to pay support.

She reached into the box and pulled out the other book. Another diary, but not the cheap dime-store variety. This one was of
beautiful leather with gold trim.

Hesitating, she took a deep breath. She hated to even think
how bad this was going to be. She slowly flipped it open and
scanned the page.

*July 8, 1951. I still can't believe it. Byron is dead. It's so hard
to grasp. He was so young and so full of life and plans and
ambitions. Another couple of months and he'd have been married and starting a family, and now he's gone. They said the
car skidded on wet pavement, but I have my suspicions.
William has been acting very strangely the last few weeks. I
hate to think this of my own husband, but I can't help it. With
Byron gone, he's going to inherit everything, the entire Tappan
fortune. Could William have hated Byron so much? Could he
really be capable of murder? Unfortunately, I know he's well
able. The question now is—did he kill his own brother just to
get his hands on the inheritance?*

Lanae shivered and closed the diary, unable to read more. Know more. *Dear Lord, what am I to do with this?* And then suddenly a thought slammed into her. This is the book that LT would have wanted back. The book he would have been paying her mother a great deal of money for. If she got the money and left town, why was the book here? Did she try a double cross at the last minute? And if she didn't give him the book, he wouldn't have paid her, and if he didn't pay her, why did she disappear?

What if. . .what if her mother hadn't come back because she hadn't been able to? What if she hadn't come back from that meeting because she was. . . ?

Lanae couldn't finish her thought as a low, keening wail crept up in her throat.

twO

Saturday, September 25—2:45 p.m.

Zoe felt the burn in her calves as her feet pounded the track pavement. Sweat rolled; muscles ached. She glanced quickly at her best friend, Daria, jogging next to her. The woman had the audacity to look like she was enjoying the torture.

"So we went out to dinner the first night and then dinner and dancing the second night. I really like this guy, Zoe. We have so much in common. I told you he was a professional photographer, didn't I?"

"Three times. Not that I'm counting."

Daria either didn't hear her or chose to ignore the little barb. "And to think we met right here at the lake. For a guy to be attracted to you when you're hot and sweaty from jogging, your hair is stringy, and you're not wearing a trace of makeup says a great deal about his character. And he has the most gorgeous pair of blue eyes I've ever seen on a man."

"You could. . .at least. . .look tired," Zoe panted as they rounded the last turn in the track that circled Sterling Lake. Up ahead, Zoe eyed the parking lot with greed. Almost done.

"I've been doing this longer than you." Daria flashed a smile as she sped up a little.

"Don't you dare pick up speed now, Daria Cicala. Don't make me have to kill you."

Daria laughed as she turned and started running backwards. "Oh, admit it. For all the moaning and groaning you did when I first pushed you into jogging with me, you've grown to like it."

"I didn't even get halfway around the first few times."

"And now you're doing the whole track with barely any effort. You're up to two miles, kiddo."

"It feels like ten," Zoe panted.

Turning around again, Daria fell into step next to Zoe, matching her stride. "Don't think about your muscles or your lungs. Think about something pleasant. Concentrate on good things."

"I'm too tired to think." Zoe could have sworn that parking lot was getting farther away. Her lungs were screaming now. How did Daria ever convince her to do this?

"Then just think what a good-looking man that new instructor is. What was his name? Dan? Now there's a man who can make you forget pain."

"He has issues."

Daria all but rolled her eyes. "Everyone has issues, Zoe. You can't keep dismissing men because they may have an issue."

"I don't date men with issues."

Daria stuck her tongue out at Zoe. "You don't date."

Daria was her best friend and had been for a long time, but the little spitfire could drive her crazy sometimes. Like a hungry dog with a good bone, she didn't give up until she got what she wanted. Hence the fact that she owned not one, but two businesses. And right now, what Daria wanted was for Zoe to find the soul mate of her dreams and fall in love.

Like that was going to happen! Dan had finally given up trying to get her to come to work for him, but he hadn't yet given up on the idea of a date. She said no three times. After the third time, he had asked her to think about it, and he'd call her in a few days. Dan was a nice guy, but she didn't think going out with him was a good idea.

"Give up, Daria. He's a nice guy, but he's still in love with his ex-wife."

Daria frowned as she reached up to wipe sweat from her forehead. "Rats. How long has he been divorced?"

"A couple of years."

"Then he's ready for someone to show him how easy it would be to forget the woman who left him. She did leave him, didn't she?"

"Yes. And no, I'm not going to go there."

"You are so stubborn, Zoe! You need to get out and date! Not every man is going to flake out on you. . . ."

Zoe came to an abrupt halt, causing Daria to backtrack. "No, Daria."

Daria bent over, hands braced on her knees as she tilted her head up and smiled at Zoe. "Okay. Got it. Fine."

"Thank you." But Zoe knew Daria too well to believe that the subject matter was closed. Daria would just bide her time and come back at it from another angle. What that angle would be was anyone's guess. Daria had tried begging, wheedling, and even setting Zoe up with a blind date while letting Zoe think that she was meeting Daria for dinner, only to arrive and find a man waiting for her. The woman was unstoppable. She wanted Zoe in love and happy.

Zoe stared at the last bit of distance to the parking lot and realized that stopping was the worst thing she could have done. There was no way her legs were going to agree to start moving again.

"I can't finish."

Daria slowly started jogging in place. "Okay, but just this once. You don't want to get in the habit of quitting."

"When have you ever known me to quit on anything?"

"Good point." Daria flashed an irrepressible grin, then looked over at the lake. Sterling Lake was tranquil, quiet. The afternoon sun glittered across the quiet water like scattered jewels. "Let's walk down by the lake."

Zoe nodded, too winded now to even bother answering, and followed Daria off the asphalt and onto the little dirt path that led to the lake's edge. The path was littered with leaves, a freshly fallen carpet of gold, brown, orange, and red.

"Are you having second thoughts about going back to school?"

Zoe was finally catching her breath. "I don't know. Maybe. I think it's just that since it's been so long, I feel like an old lady with all these youngsters. But I know I'm doing the right thing."

"You're not getting old, Zoe. You're just getting more experienced."

Zoe laughed and shoved playfully at Daria's back. "How is it that you can always narrow things down to sound so simplistic?"

"It keeps my life from overwhelm—" Suddenly Daria jerked to a stop, which caused Zoe to run into the back of her.

"Oh, no, no, no."

The panic in Daria's voice alarmed Zoe. She stepped up and looked over her friend's shoulder. It was a familiar but unwelcome sight. "Daria. . .call nine-one-one."

Daria shook her head. "I. . .I. . ."

Zoe reached into Daria's pocket, pulled out her friend's cell phone, and dialed quickly. Tucking the phone under her chin, she forced the white-faced Daria to turn around and face the parking lot, then quietly rubbed one hand across her friend's back, trying to comfort her.

"Yes. This is Zoe Shefford. I'm down here at Sterling Lake. I think you need to send a couple of officers." She sighed heavily as she stared down at the young woman on the ground. "And the coroner."

Daria doubled over and groaned.

❖   ❖   ❖

Detective Josiah Johnson felt utterly miserable. His stiff collar cut into his neck. The bow tie kept tickling under his chin. The heat coaxed a light sheen of sweat to trickle under his arms and down the side of his face. He found the smell of roses nauseating, and two of the women standing across from him kept eyeing him as if he were prime corn-fed beef. For the hundredth time, JJ wondered why he'd ever agreed to be Matt's best man.

"Do you, Matthew James Casto, take this woman, Paula Marie Horne. . . ?"

Because Matt was not only a great detective, he was the closest thing to a best friend JJ had ever had. It's called obligation. How do you tell your friend that you hate weddings, despise churches, and are deathly allergic to organdy and wedding marches?

You don't. You go ahead and get measured for a tuxedo that makes you feel like a penguin in a sideshow, laugh at lousy jokes at some inane bachelor party, make so many toasts you forget what you've already raised your glass to, and smile at so many people your face is about to crack. No wonder everyone looks happy when newlyweds take off for their honeymoon. They're glad the whole hassle is over.

"And do you, Paula Marie Horne, take this man—"

Why else is she standing there in a dress that must weigh fifty pounds with that grin on her face?

Caught up in his mental gymnastics to relieve the boredom and discomfort, JJ didn't notice the strange buzzing sound until the pastor dipped his head a little and glared pointedly over the top of his glasses.

JJ edged back his jacket and glanced down at the beeper clipped to his belt. One-eight-seven. The numbers glared up at him in an eerie green glow.

Homicide.

He shut the beeper off and shifted his weight from one foot to the other. He had to go.

Obviously dismissing JJ as a nuisance, the pastor raised his arms, the sleeves of his robes sliding down, exposing the frayed cuffs of his white shirt. "Let us pray."

I pray this is over fast. I have to go.

Someone was dead. The questions began. Who? Why? How?

The organist eased into the music, and JJ nearly bolted for the nearest exit. He was, in fact, looking for the door when the maid of honor, Charlene something or other, grabbed his elbow.

Charlene was one of Paula's childhood girlfriends, a petite redhead with freckles and a pug nose that one could only describe as elfin. He'd also spent enough time around her to know that she was mischievous, quick-witted, and possessed a delightful little laugh that could make you forgive her any prank. But at the moment, she wasn't laughing as she gripped his arm and pulled him along.

"This way, handsome."

Right. He was supposed to escort her back to the vestibule. He started down the aisle behind Matt and Paula.

"Whoa, cowboy. We're supposed to follow them, not overtake and run them down."

JJ heaved a sigh of frustration and slowed his pace. "I have to go."

"Is that why you're fidgeting? Well, the little boy's room is left and down the hall. As soon as we get—"

"Not *that* kind of go. I've got an emergency. I have to leave."

Charlene stared up at him with a look of pure horror. "Leave?" Her voice squeaked. "You're supposed to lead me in the dance at the reception."

JJ nearly rolled his eyes. Who the heck cared about a dance when someone had been murdered? "Didn't you say you had a boyfriend?"

"Well. . .yeah."

"And he's here, right? Get him to dance with you."

Charlene brightened considerably. "That'll work."

As soon as they stepped into the vestibule, JJ slipped his arm away from Charlene and grabbed at Matt. "One-eighty-seven."

Matt's eyes widened. "Go. Try to make it back for some of the reception. If not, we'll understand."

JJ nodded, pumped Matt's hand, kissed Paula's cheek, and raced out of the church, fumbling for his cell phone and keys at the same time. The phone was located first. He flipped it open and speed-dialed back to the station. "Johnson here. What have you got?"

He tucked the phone under his chin as he continued to fish for his keys.

"Young woman. Joggers found her body out by Sterling Lake."

JJ finally located his keys and pointed his keyless remote in the direction of his SUV. The dark green Jeep Cherokee chirped as the locks disengaged. He slid behind the wheel and reached for the notepad tucked down by the cup holder. "Location."

"The south park entrance, two miles around toward Nesting Point."

"I'm on my way. Fifteen minutes out." JJ closed the phone, tossed it on the seat, tore at his tie, and started the truck in smooth, quick movements. People were just starting to pour out of the church as he backed out of the parking space.

A tall blond man suddenly ran around the front of JJ's vehicle. Donnie Bevere. One of the FBI agents who had helped JJ catch a serial child killer a few months earlier.

JJ hit the brakes and watched as Donnie flung open the door and slid into the passenger seat, moving JJ's cell phone out of his way. "What's the call?"

"Young woman found out by the lake."

The agent nodded. "Let's go."

"This isn't your case, Donnie. I thought you were just here to gloat over how well you brought Matt and Paula through their breakup and into their marriage."

Donnie grinned engagingly. "I did that good, didn't I? And now it's done. As for the case, it will be far more fascinating than the reception. I've been through more of them than I care to mention." He folded his hands as if praying and fluttered his eyelashes at JJ. "Let me come with you, pleeeeeeease?"

JJ laughed. "Buckle up, and you're not officially on this, so don't take over."

"Never happen." Donnie reached for the seat belt.

"Right. And pigs fly with purple wings." JJ eyed the oncoming traffic, then hit the gas. Tires squealed as he laid a bit of rubber pulling out of the parking lot.

He hit the flashers. The siren wailed out in short staccato bursts. Traffic moved out of his way.

"How did Matt convince you to fly all the way out here from Virginia for this wedding?"

Donnie stretched out his long legs. "I was on assignment in St. Louis and passing through on my way home anyway. He asked me to stop in, and I agreed."

JJ slowed down as they approached an intersection with a red light. He put the siren on full and eased through, watching carefully for some idiot talking on a cell phone and not hearing his siren. When he saw he was clear to go, he hit the gas and sped through the intersection.

A cell phone rang and JJ glanced down. Not his. Donnie pulled his out of his pocket and flipped it open. "Special Agent Bevere." Donnie turned and looked out the window, his voice dropping a little. "Hey, babe. Everything okay?"

Grinning, JJ could just imagine the bombshell Donnie was talking to. Tall, blond, and easy on the eyes. The consensus among the other detectives when Bevere had been helping them on the child abduction case was that the agent was definitely a babe magnet.

"Yeah, I'll be catching a flight out in the morning. No, you don't need to pick me up at the airport. No need to go through all the trouble with Mandy and Cody. I'll catch a cab. Yeah. Okay, hon. Love you, too."

Donnie flipped the phone closed and shoved it in his pocket.

JJ grinned at him. "I'll bet you say that to all of them. You ever worry that all those women of yours will catch on and hunt you down?"

Perfect white teeth flashed as Donnie's eyebrows wiggled up and down. "I know how to keep the women in my life happy. There'll be no revolts."

Five minutes later, JJ slowed down and pulled into Sterling Lake's south entrance. He drove past empty picnic areas and vacant playgrounds. On a beautiful Saturday like today, it should have been bustling with families enjoying one of the few nice days left of the summer. Obviously, being invaded by police cruisers and a coroner's van was enough to send them fleeing for the safety of their homes.

One swing was swaying softly, as if the child had only run off and left it just moments before. A small shiver went down JJ's spine. The idea of a missing child still gave him nightmares.

Rounding a curve in the road, JJ spotted a cruiser and pulled up behind it. He reached down in the storage compartment between the seats and pulled out his badge, clipping it to his belt as he swung his long legs out.

JJ was surprised to see his father striding up to him, grinning like a hyena. "Let me guess. You detectives wanted to upgrade your image and this is your new uniform."

Laughing, JJ looked down at his tux. "It's the James Bond thing, Dad. We get our Aston Martins next week. They're being installed with sirens and lights."

Joe Johnson, a lifelong veteran of the force, hitched up his belt, his expression sobering. "Isn't pretty, Josiah. Young woman. You're gonna have your work cut out for you."

"Don't I always? Thanks, Dad." He started to step away, then realized Donnie was still standing there. "Oh, sorry, Dad. This is Special Agent Donnie Bevere. Donnie, my dad, Sergeant Joe Johnson."

"Calling the Feds in already, eh?"

Leaving the two men to do their meet-and-greet thing, JJ didn't bother answering, his attention already being drawn to the crime scene.

Vivian Amato, the county coroner, was kneeling over the body, carefully looking for clues while preserving any potential evidence.

JJ took one look at the long sweep of blond hair on the victim and felt his heart lurch sideways, stealing his breath.

Zoe. With those big green eyes and that incredibly long, curly blond hair. Hair that reached her waist and made a man itch to bury his hands in it.

His worst fear was finding her dead, and it had only grown worse since that afternoon Matthews had been strangling her, her face twisted with pain and desperation, her body going limp. JJ's hand had shook as he aimed the gun, knowing one wrong calculation and he'd shoot her instead of the man trying to kill her.

A firm hand came down on JJ's shoulder. "It's not her, JJ. Relax." Donnie moved his hand away. "All that blond hair. She reminded me of Zoe, too."

"Never crossed my mind," JJ replied tersely.

"Right." Donnie stepped around the body and knelt down,

looking over at Vivian. "What can you tell us so far?"

"And hello to you, too, Agent Bevere." Vivian carefully lifted one of the victim's hands and looked closely under the nails before slipping a bag over it. "Female, approximately eighteen to twenty-five years of age. Death occurred between thirty-six and forty-eight hours ago. I'll narrow that down at autopsy."

"Cause of death?"

"Offhand, I'd say exsanguinations. Multiple stab wounds. Again, I'll know more after the autopsy."

"Any idea if she'd been sexually assaulted?"

Vivian glanced up at him from under thick eyelashes. "I'll know more—"

"After the autopsy," Donnie finished her statement with a frown. "Yeah, I got that."

It wasn't Zoe. JJ took another deep breath. "Have we ID'd her?"

Vivian shook her head. "No identification so far, but we're still sweeping the immediate area. We may find something."

JJ knelt down next to Vivian, quickly scanning the immediate area. "Is this our crime scene?"

"I'm not sure, JJ, but I don't think so. There's very little indication of violence here. I'd say she was killed somewhere else and dumped here not long after death." Vivian nudged him. "Get out of my work space. I need to turn her."

JJ slowly pushed to his feet, ignoring the way his knees objected with a twinge. He stepped back a couple of feet and watched as the young girl was turned.

She was young and beautiful. Or had been. JJ shook his head. What genetic flaw in mankind could sometimes warp so severely as to breed monsters that delighted in destroying youth, beauty, and potential. . .that would give birth to soulless creatures that killed so easily with no remorse or guilt?

He couldn't understand it.

"Well, what have we here?" Vivian gently removed a piece of paper tucked in the front of the girl's tattered shirt. Her fingers carefully opened it.

JJ knelt down and reached for it. Vivian pulled it back, glaring at him. "Don't you dare touch this without gloves on!"

He yanked his hand back. "What does it say?"

"A song of death, I dream of hell, and send you to her arms."

Curling his fingers to keep from reaching for it again, JJ leaned over Vivian's shoulder.

"If this is a song, it's only the first line," Donnie said softly. He looked up at JJ. "He's letting us know he plans to kill again."

"You got all that from a few lines that say nothing?"

"A song is more than a few lines. He's on a mission, JJ."

"You're reaching." JJ stood up and stepped back, watching as Donnie did the same, leaving Vivian to bag the letter. "This could just be a few lines for this moment and nothing more."

Donnie just went on, ignoring JJ's attempt to turn the direction of his thinking. "The next victim will more than likely include the next line of the song. Each line will give us more clues."

"I don't want any more victims! We need to catch this guy now!"

Donnie took a deep breath, circling the body to take JJ by the elbow and pull him a few feet away. "You know it doesn't always work that way. Focus on your job."

"I am focused on my job, Don! I have a young girl here who had a whole life ahead of her and now—"

"And now she doesn't. Yeah, I know. Let's go talk to the joggers who found her. I doubt they saw anything useful, but it's a start."

Leave it to the Feds to always see a serial killer in everything. Some guy got mad at this girl and killed her. And now, I'm going to find him and put him behind bars. End of story.

"Have you talked to Zoe at all since last spring?" Donnie asked.

JJ shook his head as they fell in step, walking back toward the parking lot where the two joggers were sitting in the back of a patrol car. "She made it clear last time we talked that I needed to get my act together and be ready for a relationship with her. I can't guarantee her that I am."

"Then you should call and just say that you were thinking of her and wanted to know that she was doing well."

"I'm sure she's fine."

"No, you're not. You thought she might have been lying in this field."

JJ inhaled sharply. "For a minute. Just for a minute. She's not invading some killer's territory anymore. She's got a nice, safe job working at her mother's store. She's fine."

"If you say so."

"Detective!" A patrolman in his late forties with dark hair and sunglasses waved at JJ from a few feet away. "I think we found something."

Immediately, Vivian was on her feet. "Don't anyone touch it unless they're wearing gloves!"

The warning wasn't necessary. The men knew their job, and the one holding the macramé purse was indeed wearing a pair of latex gloves. He held out the wallet.

"Lori Alice Blain. Age nineteen. Lived over on Hamilton Street." He held the wallet out so that JJ could copy down the address.

"We'll check it out. Good job."

"She was a student at Monroe College," the officer added, holding up her student ID. "And I thought it would be safer for my daughter to attend college close to home." He spit on the ground in disgust. "Can we homeschool on the college level?"

"Gotta let 'em go sometime," Donnie said softly. "And then

pray like crazy nothing hurts them." He touched JJ's arm. "Let's talk to the joggers."

JJ nodded and turned to walk over to the patrol car. "Let's hope they saw something. Anything."

Donnie reached the car first and knelt down at the open back door of the patrol car. Then he looked across the petite brunette and straight into a pair of familiar green eyes. Smiling, Donnie stood up, then stepped back.

"JJ, I think you'll want to handle this."

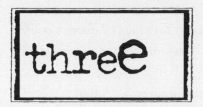

three

Zoe groaned inwardly, then climbed out of the car. After seeing the look in JJ's eyes when he realized whom he was getting ready to question, she figured the safest thing to do was keep the car between them. Folding her arms across the top of the car, she leaned forward and stared at him. He looked good. Real good.

"Well, Detective Johnson. I like your new uniform. A James Bond kind of sophistication with a Rocky Balboa kind of toughness. It works on you."

JJ's eyes narrowed as he glared at her. "What are you doing here?"

So, he was going to be nasty. Well, if that's the way he wanted to play it, so be it. "Look, I didn't ask to be here, and I sure didn't ask to see you."

JJ started circling the back of the car. Zoe pulled herself up and started backing up toward the front of the car.

"Well, Detective. I wanted to leave, but the nice officer here told me that I had to stay until they got my statement." She offered him a slow, easy smile that was anything but sweet. "I guess you're here to take my statement?"

"What were you doing here, Miss Shefford?"

"Jogging." She glanced over her shoulder, realized she'd reached the curb, and stopped. She folded her arms across her chest and lifted her chin. She wasn't going to let him push her one more step.

"Jogging?"

There was just enough of a sneer in his voice to make her lift her chin a little higher. "Yes, jogging. You know, run at a set pace for a set period of time, increasing cardio—"

"I know what jogging is. I just find it unusual to find you jogging. I didn't think you liked anything that physical. I took you more for the yoga type."

"You have no idea what I like or don't like. You never bothered to find out."

"I didn't have any reason to."

The barb made a direct hit, and Zoe felt it bury deep. "If it's a war you want, Josiah, it's a war you'll get."

JJ didn't take the bait. "Just answer my questions, Miss Shefford, and we'll get you on your way in record time."

"Yeah, I'm sure you're anxious to get back to your party. Daria and I were jogging. We came across the victim. We called the police. The police came. You showed up. Interview over."

She glanced at her watch. "You're right. Record time." Turning on her heel, she circled the front of the car. "Come on, Daria. Let's get out of here before I hit something. Or someone."

Daria scrambled out of the back of the patrol car and nearly ran to keep up with Zoe. "That went well, don't you think? Personally, I think the man is lousy at courting, but I'll give him points for trying."

Glaring, Zoe pointed at her car. "In. Now. And not another word about that man. Or any other man!"

The squeal of tires had both girls looking over at the entrance to the parking lot. Three news vans and a sedan from the local paper barreled into the lot and headed straight for them.

"Oh no. Not the press. Quick, Daria. We have to get out of here now."

Zoe barely got her car door open before Donnie was there, holding it open for her. "Will you answer some questions for me, Zoe?"

All hostility melted away at the sight of his smile. She hadn't even noticed the good-looking agent standing nearby. What in heaven's name did that say about her attraction to JJ? Better not even think about it. "Hi, Donnie."

"Good to see you, Zoe."

"It's good to see you, too. How have you been?" Suddenly it hit her. Her eyes flew wide. "Oh, no. Don't tell me we have another serial killer on the loose."

"Not that we know of."

"Donnie. You're FBI. You don't get called in just because one woman shows up dead."

Donnie leaned in close. "Don't tell anyone, but I'm not here officially. I just came for Matt's wedding."

She couldn't help smiling. "Matt and Paula got married today? That's wonderful!"

"Yep. We were hearing the 'I dos' when we got this call." His expression sobered quickly. "Did you happen to notice any strange vehicles in the parking lot? Anyone leaving? Anything that looked suspicious?"

Zoe leaned back against her car, folding her arms, keys dangling. "Any car in this lot is strange to me, Donnie. Daria and I jog here twice a week. That's not often enough to know what cars should be here. We passed a couple of joggers on the other side of the lake, but that's it. No one that I would connect to the crime. And Donnie? I'm no novice; you know that. She's been dead awhile. It's highly unlikely that she was just dumped here in the last hour."

Donnie sighed heavily, and she felt the weight of it fold over her. She knew that frustration all too well.

"I know, Zoe, but I had to ask. You never know."

"I understand." She jerked her head in JJ's direction. He was leaning against the patrol car, arms folded, eyes narrowed, staring hard at the two of them. "What's his problem?"

"Offhand, I'd say it's unrequited love."

"Oh, did some girl dump him?"

"No, she just won't acknowledge that she loves him as much as he loves her. You know how it is with the stubborn types. They dance around each other, bark at each other, dance a little more, neither one wanting to be the first one to raise the white flag, kiss, and make nice."

It took Zoe a minute to get the drift of what he was saying. She shook her head. "No. Uh-uh. Not me. You got the wrong woman. JJ is not in love with me."

"Oh, right." Donnie's head bobbed as he grinned, flashing perfect white teeth. "That's why he was so upset when he asked you out and you said no."

"I said he wasn't ready and to call me when he was. I didn't say no. He could have called me anytime over the last few months. The fact that I didn't hear from him says a lot."

"I know. It says he's really gone big-time over you. Scared stiff."

Zoe all but rolled her eyes. "Donnie, I'm the last person in the world who would ever scare JJ. The man is a rock."

"At work, yes. Love, no. Trust me, Zoe. When it comes to matters of the heart, the man is scared. He lost the woman he loved once; he doesn't want to feel that kind of pain again."

She glanced over at JJ. He hadn't moved an inch. Knowing him, he hadn't even blinked, trying to prove a point. She flashed a smile at him, blew him a kiss, and nearly laughed when his face tightened.

"You're not helping matters, Zoe."

"Good." She turned back to Donnie. "The man needs to come down a peg or two."

Donnie merely shook his head, dropping his eyes to stare down at the pavement. "You two are the most stubborn, hardheaded, mulish people I have ever met. You deserve each other."

"I know you did a great job bringing Paula and Matt together and all that, but give it up on this one, Mr. Matchmaker. It's not happening."

Zoe climbed into her car and shut the door. Donnie leaned in the window as she put the keys in the ignition. "Never underestimate the master."

Laughing, she buckled her seat belt. "Never underestimate JJ's power of denial." She dipped her head forward and eyed JJ again, then looked back up at Donnie. "Or my lack of interest."

Suddenly her car was surrounded by cameras flashing and reporters screaming questions. "Miss Shefford! Are you back working for the police?"

"Miss Shefford! Is it another missing child?"

"Zoe! Can you give a statement?"

The gold chain was woven through his fingers, the locket draped across his palm, the inscription staring up at him as if mocking him.

Lori.

She had been so very pretty in life and so ugly in death. Her sightless eyes staring up at him would haunt him for a long time.

Joey Roddy tipped his hand, letting the small, round locket fall to swing free. Like a pendulum, it swept back and forth, back and forth. *Tick-tock. Time's running out.* The little diamond chip above her name winked at him. *Tick-tock.*

He twisted his hand and let the locket fall into the wooden box. Closing the lid, he locked it, then placed it on the top shelf of the closet, where it would remain untouched until the next time he had something to add to the contents.

A pearl earring, a silver anklet, a turquoise ring, an engagement ring, a bracelet, a locket. Small treasures for his pleasure.

Pushing back the curtain, he stared out the window and watched as the traffic slowed for a red light, pedestrians hurried from place to place, and one old woman pushed her shopping cart filled with her life's treasures. He knew how the homeless old hag felt, her life reduced to an endless search for someplace safe. Some quiet spot where there were no voices, no pain, and no threat.

Stepping away from the window, he picked up his jacket from the back of a chair and slipped his arms into it.

No point worrying over what couldn't be changed. There were other things to worry about. If they hadn't found her body yet, they would soon enough. And when they did, they would do everything possible to find some trace of her killer. Some hair or fiber that could lead them straight back to him. He had been so very careful, but there was still the fear that maybe, just maybe, he'd missed something, and they would hunt him down like a dog.

Fear clogged his throat as he stepped out into the hall and pulled his apartment door closed. Immediately he flashed a bright, charming smile at one of his neighbors, just returning from grocery shopping, her bags balanced precariously in her arms as she worked the keys in the lock.

"Hi, Mrs. Gerring. Here, let me hold those bags for you."

Irma Gerring, a dainty little woman in her midsixties, was a widow with three cats and a parakeet, no family that he'd ever seen, although someone had once mentioned a daughter that lived back east somewhere. Always cheerful, she was known for spoiling her neighbors with cookies, cakes, and candy treats that she made each day, having nothing else to do with her time.

Joey liked her as well as the apple-raisin strudel she baked for him from time to time. If only he'd had a mother like her. Or a grandmother. How different things might have been for him.

"You're such a nice young man," she twittered as he set her grocery bags down on her kitchen table. "How come some sweet young lady hasn't roped you in yet?"

Joey shrugged as he smiled at her. "I guess I'm just hard to catch."

Her wrinkled hand reached out and petted him on the arm. "Oh, the right one'll come along, and you'll chase her until she catches you." She laughed at her own wit and winked at him. "I have some chocolate pie, if you have a hankerin' for some."

"I can't right now, Mrs. Gerring. I have to get to work."

Joey worked two jobs. During the week, he was employed at the Royal Car Wash from nine to four. Then Wednesday night through Sunday night, he loaded trucks at a beverage distributor, occasionally making runs with a driver to help unload stock at neighborhood bars and restaurants.

Irma walked him to the door, patting him on the back. "You take care now, Joey. I'll be making strudel sometime this week. Maybe Tuesday. I have a doctor's appointment on Monday. Those doctors must think I don't have anything better to do than sit in their office all day. They give you a ten o'clock appointment, and you're lucky if you get in before one. And then they take forever, and you don't get out of there until nearly three. A whole day wasted."

"Arrogant," Joey muttered as he tuned out her rambling.

"You are so right. Such a smart young man, you are."

Not so smart. I may have messed up big-time. I can't remember if I left any fingerprints behind. I can't be sure I didn't leave some trace for the police to find. Maybe not so smart at all.

four

Sunday, September 26—8:37 a.m.

Donnie Bevere shifted back in his chair, moving his newspaper out of the way as the waitress leaned in to refill his coffee cup. "Your food will be right up."

"Great. Thanks." As she moved away, his attention moved back to the article he was reading on the front page: YOUNG COED FOUND MURDERED AT STERLING LAKE.

It didn't tell him anything he didn't already know, but he scanned it a second time.

He and JJ had spent four hours going over preliminary evidence before handling the delicate task of informing Lori Blain's parents. Russell Blain, a tall, distinguished man with piercing dark eyes and gaunt features, remained stoically quiet, as if he were taking everything being said and felt and filing it away to be dealt with at some future time. Donnie had the distinct impression the man was doing everything in his power not to fall apart in front of them. Ginny Blain, a diminutive woman with white blond hair and china doll features, didn't have any such qualms. She collapsed in her son's arms and was eventually led away to rest. Lori's older brother, Rusty, looked like his mother, but Donnie was pretty sure that as friendly and outgoing as he appeared to be, the son was like his father, with deep emotions that were rarely given permission to surface.

The younger brother, Cameron, merely sat stunned on the edge of the sofa with tears streaming down his face. At some point, he'd slipped from the room, but neither he nor JJ could recall exactly when.

Without a doubt, Lori had been the princess of the family—the mother's shining star, the father's cherished doll. How either of the barely acknowledged sons felt about that was anyone's guess. Instincts told Donnie that the older brother harbored typical sibling resentment, while the young brother merely sought to stay close to the one so adored and feed off the residual affection.

How a parent could so obviously love one child over another was beyond him. Donnie had been one of six children, and there was no doubt in his mind that each of them had been as loved and cherished as the next. Each was prized for their own unique talents, gifts, and personality, but no one child ever rose above the others into a spotlight. It was unthinkable.

Well, whatever secrets the Blain family harbored would be dug up and chewed over and analyzed under the spotlight of an investigation that would be as intrusive to the grieving family as it was necessary. Most homicide victims knew their killers. The first suspects on any police list included family members, spouses, and significant others close to the victim. If nothing was found, the circle would move out to encompass a larger list of suspects.

And then there was the other headline with full-color photos. RETIRED PSYCHIC CALLED BACK BY POLICE? There were two pictures. One of Zoe taken awhile back, after one of her child abduction cases, and one from yesterday of her trying to turn her face away from the camera while driving out of the Sterling Lake parking lot.

It was doubtful that Zoe was too happy about being plastered across the front page as a famous psychic again. The girl was trying so hard to fade into the woodwork.

"Sir?"

Donnie folded his paper and set it aside as the waitress set a plate of scrambled eggs, bacon, and hash browns down in front of him. Reaching for the salt and pepper, he wondered if JJ had seen the headline. He had furiously denied Zoe's involvement when cornered by the press at the crime scene, but he knew the press hadn't believed a word of it. You mix a crime scene, Detective Johnson, and Zoe Shefford, and you have a headline. And the press knew it.

He took a bite of toast. It wasn't his problem. It wasn't his case. And yet he knew he was hooked. He would do whatever he could to stay around and help JJ with the investigation.

He flipped open his cell phone and made a quick call to his partner, Jack Fleming, back in Virginia. "It's me. Listen, something has come up and I need to stay here for a few days. Any chance you can clear it with the powers that be?"

Jack grunted into the phone. "And what has come up that's so important? Some pretty blond?"

"You could say that. She was found murdered, and my gut tells me it's a serial killing." He quickly filled Jack in on the details of the case. "There's going to be more. I can feel it."

"I'll cover you for a few days, but you better be right. Any trouble here, and you get back here on the double. I'm not going to risk my pension for you, got that?"

Donnie smiled. For all Jack's bluff and bluster, the man was one of the best in the business, and he trusted Donnie's instincts, as well as his expertise. If Donnie smelled trouble, Jack would go all the way to the top for him. "I got it. Thanks, Jack."

"You need help, you call me in."

"Will do."

"And watch your back, glamour boy. I don't want to have to go explaining why I wasn't there to keep you out of trouble."

Donnie laughed. "As if you've ever had to do anything of the sort!"

Ending the call, Donnie quickly dialed again. "Hi. There's a problem, sweetie. Something's come up. But I have an idea."

❖   ❖   ❖

2:47 p.m.

JJ stared down at the crime scene photos. They didn't get any better, no matter how many times he looked at them. The girl was still dead, her face swollen and disfigured in a mask of horror. She had seen evil up close and hadn't lived to tell the story afterward.

Did he have a serial killer on the loose? The prospect was chilling. Was he a local? Or just someone passing through?

Blast Donnie for raising the possibility.

She had been stabbed four times—once in the neck, three times in the torso. Brutal. Why had he targeted this particular woman? Had she just been in the wrong place at the wrong time, or had she managed to somehow anger the killer?

"Or did you know him, sweetheart? Was he an old boyfriend? Or just someone who wanted to make you his?"

"You know what they say about people who talk to themselves?"

JJ looked up as Gerry Otis tossed a file down on JJ's desk. Gerry was one of the force's best detectives with over thirty years with the department. How the man managed to work the hours he did, take care of his wife and four kids, and volunteer at some youth group his kids belonged to was beyond JJ, but it was the main reason

Gerry had turned down any promotions over the years once he'd made detective.

"No, Gerry, what do they say?"

Gerry broke out in a grin as he stroked his beard. "Come to think of it, I can't recall what they say, but I'm pretty sure it isn't good."

"And you call yourself a detective."

Gerry dropped down in a chair, laughing. "Now, that's pure rumor and speculation. I wouldn't believe any of that if I were you."

"Trust me, I don't." JJ gestured toward the file Gerry had placed on the desk. "What did you bring me?"

"Nothing. That's mine. That chop shop down on Austin? Funk took the bait. We got him cold. I'm just killing time waiting for my warrant. You working the homicide?"

JJ nodded grimly. "Young college student."

"Heartbreaking," he murmured. "Of all times for Casto to be off on a honeymoon."

"Worse happens, I get the chief to pull you and assign you to this case."

"Don't you dare! I got my hands full now." Gerry's beeper suddenly began to buzz on his hip. He glanced down. "That's it. Time to roll."

"Go get 'em, cowboy. And make it a good bust."

Gerry nodded, hauling himself to his feet. "I'll be glad to see these characters behind bars. Car thefts should drop eighty percent with Funk and his partner off the streets."

"Good collar, Gerry."

"All in a day's work."

JJ watched as Gerry left, weaving through the maze of desks. Reluctantly, he pulled his eyes back down to the crime scene photos of Lori Blain. He still couldn't believe that he'd thought she was

Zoe, even for a moment. Lori's hair was straight; Zoe's was curly. But just for that moment, his heart had skipped a little erratically. He didn't like that she had that effect on him. He didn't like that, even after all these months, she still had any effect at all.

He would prefer to have trouble picturing her face, but the truth was, he could clearly remember the way her mouth would curl up a little more on the right side when she smiled, the way her eyes would go smoky green when she was upset, the way she would fist her hands on her hips when she was angry.

The way she would push at him when she knew she was right, then laugh at his temper.

And the way she taunted him yesterday, indifference dripping off her. No, not indifference. Dislike.

She disliked him. And while he knew it shouldn't bother him, it did.

Frowning, he shoved thoughts of Zoe aside like a pesky fruit fly that would only be back later to annoy him again. In the meantime, he needed to talk to Lori Blain's neighbors, friends, and classmates. Glancing at his watch, he shoved back from his desk and reached for his coat.

"Going somewhere without me?"

Donnie Bevere strolled over, hands in his pockets, looking just as comfortable in a pair of jeans and dress shirt as he did in a suit.

JJ shrugged into his coat. "I thought you were catching a plane out of this one-horse town and heading back to the babes and the high life."

Donnie emitted something between a snort and a laugh. "And leave you to have all the fun?" His smile flattened out as he suddenly sobered. "I called my office and told them what was going on. I have permission to hang around and see what develops."

JJ picked up his keys, tamping down the irritation that surprised him. "This is not your investigation."

The words came out a little sharper than he intended, and Donnie threw his hands in the air in a quick show of surrender. "I know, JJ. I know. I'm just your sidekick for now. It's entirely your show."

"Sorry, Bevere. Didn't mean to snap." He opened his desk drawer and pulled out his weapon, slipping it into his shoulder holster. "I do appreciate any help you can offer. The sooner we get this killer off the streets, the better I'll sleep at night."

"Well, I don't mean to add to your troubles, but the press is out front in full force."

JJ closed his eyes and sighed heavily before shaking his head. "Tell me they didn't see you."

"They didn't see me."

"Let's go out the back way. I'm not in the mood to deal with the press right now." JJ headed for the back stairs with Donnie at his heels.

"Where are we headed?"

"Lori Blain's apartment. I want to check it out myself. We also need to talk to some of the neighbors; see if they noticed anything unusual."

"She have a boyfriend?"

JJ shoved the door open with his shoulder and headed down the metal staircase, his voice echoing through the stairwell. "Not that we've been able to find so far. All indications are that she was a good student, didn't date much during the school year, but was known to frequent the Time Out at least two nights a week."

By the time they reached the ground floor, JJ had warmed to the idea of having Donnie along. "And get this. She worked parttime as a file clerk."

"Worked? Her father said that he paid for everything—her apartment, her car, her tuition, and her living expenses. With Daddy picking up the tab, why would she need to work?"

"Maybe it wasn't about need." JJ hit the button on his keyless remote. His Cherokee chirped and unlocked. He climbed in and started the engine, then reached for his seat belt. "Maybe it was about striking out on her own. Doing something that wasn't controlled by Daddy."

Donnie shot him a look. "You're thinking she was rebelling a little?"

"I don't remember Daddy telling us that his little girl worked, do you? In fact, when we asked about coworkers, he specifically told us in a very snooty tone that his little girl didn't *have* to work."

In fact, Russell Blain had been more than snooty. He'd been arrogant and abrasive, treating JJ and Donnie as if they were merely ignorant blue-collar minions that he had to put up with. If he'd been Lori, he'd have rebelled, too.

Then again, for all he knew, Lori had been a snobbish little princess who had ticked off some guy with her nose so far up in the air, she couldn't see who she was talking to.

Don't go forming an opinion, old man. You know where that got you last time. Let the case unfold, then study the facts and let the facts tell you the story.

"You're entirely too quiet, JJ." Donnie drummed his fingers on the door handle. "What about this case has you bothered?"

JJ shook his head as he pulled up in front of Lori Blain's apartment. "I was thinking of something else entirely."

Donnie looked skeptical, but he remained silent as they climbed out of the car and entered the building.

It was a three-story brick building typical of the midfifties' building boom. Square, solid, brick, and boring. The staircase was gray metal, the doors to the apartments were gray metal; and from the sound of a loud conversation on one side of them, a sportscaster recapping a particularly good touchdown throw on the other side, and the sound of music—classical—from somewhere down the hall, soundproofing was simply a dream for every tenant.

JJ checked the row of gunmetal gray mailboxes and sighed when he saw L. Blain was in 306. "Third floor. It figures."

"It'll do you good. You need more exercise." Donnie slapped him on the back and started up the stairs, two at a time.

"For your information, I work out three days a week at the gym." He jogged up the stairs after Donnie.

"And eat garbage every day. Fattening, high cholesterol, bad-for-you garbage."

"I just happen to like subs."

"With extra mayo." Donnie stopped at the top of the second landing and grinned down at JJ, who was starting to breathe heavily. "That stuff clogs your arteries and makes you pant heavily when you climb three flights of stairs."

JJ struggled to control his breathing. "When you get to my age, water clogs your arteries. And I am not breathing heavily. I didn't get much sleep last night, and I'm tired."

Donnie just widened his grin and strolled down the hall to the apartment with crime scene tape stretched in front of it. "Guess your team was already here."

"Last night. They didn't find anything, but like I said, I want to look for myself."

"What do you expect to find?"

"A reason someone wanted Lori Blain dead."

6:25 p.m.

Lanae Oakley had been trying to get her mind off those diaries for two days, and it was proving to be an impossible task. Friday night, she'd brought them back to her house with a couple of boxes of her grandmother's books but hadn't accomplished much else. Saturday, she'd gone back to her grandmother's and tried to finish at least one room, but her thoughts kept drifting back to wondering about her mother, her father, the diaries, and the night her mother had disappeared forever.

She had no idea what she was going to do. It had been over twenty years. Surely if her mother was alive, her gammy would have known. Or her mother would have called or written or come back for a visit. No, she hadn't really thought about it before, but now she was fairly certain her mother was dead.

But how could she know for sure? She closed her eyes. *Please help me, Lord. You are truth and the revealer of all truth. Help me, guide me to bringing the truth to light. Show me how to find out what happened to my mother.*

When she opened her eyes, the first thing she saw was the newspaper headline and a picture of Zoe Shefford shielding her face from the cameras.

❖   ❖   ❖

9:52 p.m.

Zoe pursed her lips as she stared at the empty walls of her living room. After Matthews had burned her town house to the ground, it had been rebuilt, but it was a far cry on the inside from what it had been. Her sanctuary from the world was now barren and empty with the exception of a few necessary pieces of furniture.

The barren walls only drove home the point that she was starting over in more ways than one. A new faith, a new life, a new direction. And so far, the walls of her life, like the walls of her town house, were pretty stark.

For so long, Zoe had built tall, strong walls around her life, allowing only her mother and her best friend, Daria, to get close to her. Now, with her parents off reconciling their marriage and Daria busy with her career and new boyfriend, the emptiness in Zoe's life suddenly seemed cavernous.

True, she was involved with her church, but she still found herself keeping people at a distance. She was friendly toward them but never let them get too close. In spite of her new life in Christ, she was still relying on the old self-defense mechanisms to protect herself and her privacy. And her heart.

If they didn't get too close, if she didn't care too much, it wouldn't hurt so much when she lost them.

She and JJ were more alike than she wanted to admit.

Dropping onto her new sofa, she blew out a frustrated breath. She'd never been too good at looking into her own life and her own problems. It had always been easier to focus on everyone else's tragedy, someone else's problems, and ignore anything she was feeling deep inside. Amy, her father, her gift. She shoved it all down deep inside and concentrated on finding someone's missing child. Now, she couldn't escape the silence that led to deep introspection.

Grabbing one of the cute little pillows her mother had purchased for her in Spain, she hugged it close, trying not to think about empty walls and empty hearts.

Ah, Detective Josiah Johnson. Now there was a man with an empty heart. He was intimately familiar with logic, reason, and research and knew absolutely nothing about women, relationships, and love.

She could still see the conflict in his eyes when he glared at her over the top of the patrol car. Idiot man. But if he was such a jerk, how come she couldn't just forget him and move on? Why was she still checking her answering machine every day in hopes that he might, just might, have called?

And that poor girl. Her experienced eye had taken in more than enough to know that she'd been dead for a while; she'd been stabbed and had died somewhere else. But poor Daria. She wasn't used to such gruesome scenes and had thrown up in the bushes.

Flouncing off the sofa, Zoe headed for the kitchen and set up the coffeepot. She had to get to bed. She had a class scheduled first thing in the morning.

The phone rang a few minutes later. She glanced up at the clock with a frown. Who would be calling her this late? Her caller ID didn't help. Private number. She picked up cautiously. "Hello?"

"Zoe? It's Dan. I didn't call too late, did I?"

At the sound of Dan Cordette's voice, Zoe tensed, dropping down into the nearest kitchen chair. "No. I'm still up. Is anything wrong?"

"I meant to call you Friday, but I had to take a quick trip to Raleigh and just got back."

She stretched out her legs and propped them on the chair across from her, leaning back as she picked up the faint static that told her Dan was on a cell phone.

"It sounds like you're still on the road."

"Am I breaking up? I just left the airport."

"No, I hear you fine."

"I was calling in hopes that maybe. . . Hey, buddy, this is my lane! Get your own!" Dan huffed in frustration. "I think most of the drivers on the road got their licenses on the Internet. Okay, what was I saying? Oh, yeah. If dinner, dancing, and candlelight make you nervous, how about a play? The playhouse is doing *Fiddler on the Roof,* and I hear it's pretty good."

"I don't know, Dan. I can't help feeling that you should be asking your ex-wife."

She heard Dan grunt. "Not likely. Even if I were remotely interested, her boyfriend wouldn't take it well. Okay, you don't like plays. What about the comedy club?"

"You're not going to give up, are you?" Zoe laughed.

"Persistence is in my blood. I see a beautiful woman I'd like to know better and that's it. Can't help it. So, whatcha say?"

For the life of her, she couldn't think of a single reason to say no. He was nice. He was intelligent. He was interesting. They had lots in common. And she loved the comedy club. The problem was, she wasn't all that interested. "Let me think about it."

There was a long moment of silence, and Zoe was starting to wonder if they'd been disconnected when he suddenly spoke again. "Zoe?"

"I'm here."

"What's going on? And don't tell me nothing."

"I stumbled across a murder victim yesterday out at Sterling Lake. That's enough to make anyone feel a little off."

"Murder? Details, woman. Give me details."

Zoe stood up and began to pace as she told him everything. "It was even in the paper this morning with a big headline claiming, RETIRED PSYCHIC CALLED BACK BY POLICE. Now I'm going to have the press focusing on me."

"Wow, the front page." There was a moment of silence. "I was kidding, Zoe. I'm sorry you got caught up in that. I know you hate any kind of spotlight."

"Yes." She sank down wearily, thinking of all the calls she'd fielded for hours after she'd arrived home the night before. "And I'm not even involved. I stumbled across the body while jogging with Daria. End of story. Finding this guy before he kills again is not for me to do."

"Before he kills again? What makes you think he'll kill again? Why couldn't this just be a one-time thing?"

Mentally, Zoe pulled up short. "I don't know. That just came out. I have nothing to base that on."

There was a long moment of silence, and Zoe was starting to think Dan had been disconnected. "Dan?"

"Sorry. . .had to change lanes. I'm coming up on my exit. Did you tell the police about this?"

"No. What's to tell? I just said something, and I don't know for sure there's any fact to it. I don't even know why I said it."

"You said it because you know he will. How you know is irrelevant at this point. You need to tell the police."

Zoe laughed. "Tell them what? That I was talking to you and I slipped and said he'd kill again? You think that's going to carry any weight?"

She heard Dan hiss with frustration. "You're right."

"I just need to concentrate on school and let the police handle the Blain murder."

"The *what* murder?"

"Blain. That was her name. Lori Blain."

"Russell Blain's daughter?"

Zoe shrugged even though Dan couldn't have seen it. "I don't know her father's name. The paper said her name was Lori Blain. She was nineteen and attending the college."

"Ah, geesh. I need to call Russell. Look, I have to go. You get some rest, and I'll talk to you tomorrow."

"Okay, Dan. Drive safe." Zoe hung up the phone and stared at it for a second, then shrugged and got up. A nice long, hot bath would feel wonderful right about now. Talking about murder made her feel dirty these days.

She had just turned out the kitchen light when the phone rang again. Thinking it was Dan calling her back, she didn't bother looking at the caller ID.

"Hello?"

"Zoe Shefford?"

The voice, low and husky, was unfamiliar. "Yes?"

"Stay out of it, do you hear? Stay out of it, or you'll regret it."

five

I'm sorry, Detective." Mel Jennings leaned back in his chair, running one hand through his hair. "There's really not much I can tell you. Lori started working here part-time in high school. Three afternoons a week. When she started college, she cut that down to two. She was quiet, polite, a nice girl."

JJ's instincts were shimmering as he noted the tremor in Mel Jennings's hands. The man wasn't exactly lying, but he wasn't telling him everything. So, what was he hiding?

"What did she do for you, exactly?" JJ asked.

"Filing, typing, answering phones when I needed her to. She handled any of the overflow work that needed to be done. If my secretary or receptionist had too much to do, they'd simply hand it over to Lori, and she'd take care of it."

JJ stood up and strolled around the office. It was simple but elegant. Cherry desk, dark green leather chairs, cherry bookshelves, a few seascapes on the walls, thick carpet running wall to wall in a wash of pale green. He stopped at one wall covered in plaques and pictures. His diploma, pictures of two girls at various ages. Obviously his daughters. Mel Jennings, age fifty-one, was a family man, a successful accountant with four employees, and not so much as a parking ticket against his record.

So what was wrong?

Shoving his hands in his pockets, he turned back to Mel Jennings. "Did Lori ever talk about someone bothering her? Was she nervous or upset lately?"

The accountant shook his head. "No. Not at all. She seemed fine. Same as always."

"What about old boyfriends? Anyone calling lately? Maybe someone she didn't want to talk to?"

Again, the man shook his head. "Not that I know of. You might talk to Marta, the receptionist. She'd know if Lori received any calls while she was here at work."

He was missing something. He knew it, but he couldn't think of what to ask to get the answer he wanted. It was like fishing without any bait.

"And the last time you saw Lori was Tuesday, when she came to work as usual."

Mel shifted in his chair, running his fingers through his thinning brown hair again. "Yes. Tuesday. That was the last time I saw her."

"Is there anything else at all that you can think of that might help us, Mr. Jennings?"

Mel shook his head slowly, staring at the top of his desk. "No. Nothing." He lifted his head. "Like I said, talk to Marta. Or any of my employees. Maybe they know something that could help you."

JJ reached out and shook Mel's hand. "Well, thanks for your time. I appreciate it."

Still silent, Donnie stood up and shook hands with Mel as well, then followed JJ out.

It took them all of twenty minutes to talk to the other employees. No one saw anything strange in Lori's behavior, no one knew if she was seeing anyone, no one heard of any stalker.

"The coworkers were a bust," Donnie admitted as he climbed into JJ's vehicle. "But, Jennings was hiding something."

"I know. But for the life of me, I can't think of what—or how to get him to talk."

❖   ❖   ❖

11:30 a.m.

Zoe shoved her notebook in her backpack and slung it over her shoulder, threading her way through the cluster of students who were heading for the door. Dan had called her just before her class and asked her to meet him at noon at Geraldine's, a restaurant that happened to be located on the other side of town. She was going to have to hurry to make it on time.

He'd sounded a little evasive, not explaining why he wanted to meet, and there was something in his voice that asked her not to push for answers. So she hadn't. But his evasiveness only increased her curiosity.

Zipping through traffic, she drummed her fingers in time to the tunes from a new CD. It was a windy day, blowing those first fragile leaves from the trees, while stirring up those already on the ground, sending splashes of color in all directions.

She passed Daria's salon and wondered how her friend was feeling. Daria had called just after seven that morning, still shaky from seeing that girl's body on Saturday. Zoe had spoken to her for over half an hour, reassuring and comforting her, trying to help Daria set it aside and move on and not dwell on it, but there was no telling if Daria was going to be able to do that as easily as she could.

Heaven knows, I've seen worse over the years. And the children.

Dear Lord, the children. It still haunted her.

A few minutes before twelve, Zoe whipped her car into the parking lot of Geraldine's and spent the next five minutes trying to find a parking space. Then she nearly jogged to the front door of the restaurant.

Inside, the hushed atmosphere soothed her frazzled nerves. She took a deep breath, then stepped up to the hostess. "I'm supposed to meet Mr. Cordette for lunch."

The woman merely nodded. "Follow me, please."

Zoe trailed behind the woman as they wove through the tables packed with diners and dodged waiters and waitresses loaded down with plates of food that made Zoe's mouth water.

Finally they stopped, and the hostess pulled out a chair next to Dan, who rose to his feet along with the other gentleman at the table. Zoe smiled first at Dan, then over at the man who was staring at her with the barest hint of a smile on his face. The man appeared to be in his late fifties and had an air of success and confidence that would probably move to arrogance if it suited him. Immaculately dressed in a navy blue suit, white shirt, and red tie, his dark brown hair was still thick and wavy and sporting an expensive cut. His nails were trimmed and manicured. He would not be an easy man to know nor would he want to be.

"Right on time, Zoe."

Zoe eased down in her chair and dropped her purse under it as the two men settled down in their seats.

"Zoe Shefford. . .Russell Blain."

Zoe stiffened a bit as he reached across the table to shake her hand. His grip was firm, dry, and as no-nonsense as the man himself appeared to be.

"Mr. Blain," she acknowledged, then looked over at Dan for explanation. "My deepest condolences. I know how difficult this time must be for you."

Russell Blain merely nodded and dropped his eyes.

"Zoe, Russell and I have been talking about you."

Russell looked up at her. Suddenly Zoe felt it. The need of the parent for closure. For answers. But why come to her? She had always been the one who brought the body home. In the case of this man's daughter, she was already home. The funeral was set for Thursday, according to the paper.

Russell Blain continued to stare at her with a focused look that told her he was analyzing, judging, making decisions, and determinations.

She let him know she didn't care what he might decide to think about her by turning back to Dan. "Talking about me? Well, I certainly hope it was flattering."

"Russell is hiring us to look into his daughter's murder. I want you to be in on the case."

The waitress chose that moment to appear at the table and ask for their choices. Zoe sat back in her chair, her mind spinning. She didn't even know what she ordered. Be in on the case? Find a killer? Were they nuts?

When the waitress finally left, she draped her napkin in her lap. "Me? Why would you want me on the case? I'm not a licensed investigator."

Dan leaned forward, slid his silverware to the side, and folded his arms on the table. "You're experienced. You know this stuff inside out. You've been doing it for years. You don't need a license. You'll be helping me."

She took a deep breath, trying to grab onto the thoughts that were skittering through her mind, intent on eluding her.

Russell Blain set his water glass down with quiet deliberation. "I trust you, Miss Shefford. I know you have a focused determination that won't quit until you solve the problem and won't follow the easy path just to be done with it."

Zoe met his intense gaze head-on. "The police are on this, Mr. Blain. They'll find your daughter's killer. They're very good at what they do."

"I'm not unaware that they are overworked with only so many men and so many hours in the day. If a bank gets robbed tomorrow, my daughter's case goes in the pile with all the others. Maybe they'll find the guy and maybe they won't." He leaned forward, his eyes showing the first sign of life and passion she'd seen so far. "I want this guy found, arrested, and put in jail for the rest of his life."

She couldn't argue with his logic. He was right on target, but she also knew that Josiah Johnson wasn't going to let a killer go free just because there were only so many hours in a day. The man was relentless.

Dan leaned back as the waitress set his salad down in front of him. "Zoe, you were the one who found Lori."

"That was not my choice, believe me." She looked down at the bowl of French onion soup placed in front of her and wondered what she was thinking when she ordered it.

"Be that as it may," Dan replied, jabbing at the greens with his fork, "we both know Russell's right. We can put more time and more focus on this than the police can."

"Are you aware the FBI is here and following the investigation?"

Obviously, they weren't because both Dan and Russell Blain looked at each other in surprise.

"I know they're not advertising the fact that the FBI is here, but I can tell you that it is. I know the agent personally. He was involved in another case I worked on. And he's the one who questioned me Saturday, not the police."

Of course, JJ had wanted to, but that wasn't the point. Right now, she just wanted these men to understand that there wasn't just a lone overworked detective handling the case.

She started in on her soup, letting them digest the information.

"They must think this is a serial killer," Dan muttered softly. "There's no other reason the FBI would be called in this soon."

"The agent denied that to me and he had no reason to lie to me. He knows and trusts me." She toyed with just how much she could tell them.

"Maybe," Dan replied. "But it still makes me wonder."

"FBI or no FBI, I want you to look into this." Russell leaned forward, his voice forceful and determined. "Find the man who killed my daughter."

Zoe set her spoon down and twisted her napkin in her lap. "I'm sorry, Mr. Blain. I can't help you."

❖   ❖   ❖

3:47 p.m.

Donnie Bevere mindlessly rubbed his temple as he read. In front of him, JJ's desk was knee-deep in paperwork: contact reports, witness statements, detective activity reports, financial workups, and preliminary evidence reports. He glanced at his watch, noted the time, then went back to reading over one of the preliminary evidence reports, tuning out the ringing phones, clacking keyboards, and constant flow of uniformed officers and detectives strolling by and dropping even more reports on the desk.

An eight-inch blade, nonserrated, was used to make four stab wounds. The first, which nicked the heart, was the fatal wound. The other three stab wounds were administered postmortem.

He sat back in his chair, chewing over that piece of information.

Why bother continuing to stab after the girl was dead? What was the point? Rage? Anger? It just didn't feel right.

"What's got you looking like you're lost without a compass?" JJ lifted his coffee and took a sip.

"She was dead after the first stab wound."

That raised JJ's eyebrows. "The rest were postmortem?"

"Appears so."

JJ set his coffee down and leaned back in his chair. "Why doesn't that feel right?"

"Because it doesn't sound like something a serial killer would do."

"Unless this was his first murder and he botched it."

Donnie's brow furrowed as he thought it over. "Probable. Which would line up with his little song."

"That he's just getting started." JJ's phone rang. He held up a finger to Donnie and picked it up.

"And leaving us little to go on," Donnie murmured to himself as he stood up and started to pace.

"Grab your coat." JJ's urgent voice broke into Donnie's musings. He reached for his jacket, slung over the back of a chair, as JJ hung up the phone.

"What's going on?"

"They just found Lori Blain's car."

Excitement thrummed through Donnie's veins, warring with another obligation. He vacillated, hesitating.

"Donnie? You coming or not?"

"I have another appointment."

JJ stared at him. "Another appointment? Are you doing some side investigation and not telling me?" He took a step toward Donnie. "If you're holding back information—"

"It's personal! Geesh, JJ. Cool out." Turning on his heel, he headed for the exit.

JJ came up behind him. "What kind of personal business could you have around here? Oh, let me guess. You're off to meet some woman. Maybe a nice dinner? Take her back to your hotel room?"

Donnie pushed open the door and started jogging down the metal stairs to the first floor. "As a matter of fact, I *am* going to meet a woman. And I will take her to dinner. But the last time I checked, this is your investigation and I was just helping you out."

"Hey! Cool out! So, you've met a woman. Good for you. Just for a moment there, I thought—"

Donnie stopped at the bottom of the staircase and turned around, bringing JJ up short. "You thought I was off carrying on my own little investigation in an attempt to put you in your place. Steal your case and steal your glory. When are you going to understand that this," he swung his arms wide, "isn't the mark of who you are? When are you going to realize that whether or not you solve this case—or any other case—it's not going to alter your worth?"

JJ stood there gaping at him, something dark flashing in his eyes. "Okay, yeah. For a minute, I suspected you might be off doing something on your own, but give it a rest, Donnie. Don't make it personal."

Donnie took a deep breath, pulling the air deep into his lungs while he gathered his thoughts. JJ wasn't ready to hear the kind of truth Donnie was ready to deliver. "I'll call you later."

JJ desperately needed a life. Donnie pulled out of the parking lot and headed for his hotel. He didn't date, didn't play, and heaven knows the last time the man smiled and felt it down to his toes.

Fifteen minutes later, Donnie pulled into the hotel parking lot. He walked briskly into the building and hurried up to the front desk. The woman behind the desk was on the phone. She smiled and signaled for him to just wait until she was done.

"Don?"

He smiled and whirled around, then crossed the room at a quick lope. "Lisbeth!" He pulled his wife into his arms. Her chestnut hair was pulled back in a braid, and she was wearing jeans and a bright pink sweatshirt. It still boggled his mind that she could be a wife and mother of two and still look sixteen. "You weren't waiting too long, were you?"

Lisbeth eased out of his arms, a warm smile lighting up her whole face. "Maybe ten minutes. Mandy just fell asleep over there. You'll have to carry her up to the room for me."

He stared down at Mandy, his little blond dervish, then over at his son, sleeping peacefully in his car seat.

"You could have left the luggage in the car. I would have gotten it."

"The hotel clerk sent someone out to bring it in for me."

"How was the drive?"

Lisbeth eased the baby's car seat into her arms and carefully lifted it. "Not too bad actually. I left Mom and Dad's right after breakfast and the kids were pretty good. They watched movies most of the way."

"Movies?"

"*Sinbad* at least twice." She giggled. "Dad bought the kids one of those TV/VCR units for the car and installed it before I left. It saved my life. Remind me to pay him back big-time at Christmas."

Mandy flopped over Donnie's shoulder as he pulled her up into his arms. She felt as light as a feather and looked as soft as an angel's breath. But he knew all that would change as soon as she woke up. Where she got her energy was a puzzle to him.

After taking Lisbeth and the kids to the suite he'd moved into that morning, he brought up the luggage. By the time he got them settled and was pulling Lisbeth into his arms again, Mandy was rubbing her eyes.

"Daddy!" She scrambled across the bed and jumped into his arms, flinging her arms around his neck. "Hi, Daddy. We drove and drove and drove and we watched *Sinbad* and Pop-Pops got us a movie machine for the car and even baby Cody was watching and Grammies made us cookies and Mommy had to give a man money to drive on the road."

She made him breathless. Laughing, he tossed her up into the air, cutting off her tirade. "I missed you, too, Mandy Bear. You ready to go get some dinner?"

Giggling, she grabbed him around the neck again, holding him tight, and planted little wet kisses on his cheek. "I want chicken nubbets and flies."

"Didn't Mommy take you to McDonald's while you were at Grandma's house?"

Mandy nodded furiously, sending blond curls bobbing into her eyes. He brushed the curls back. "Then we do something different tonight. Something special."

"But Cody wants nubbets. He told me."

Donnie glanced over at his son, still sleeping peacefully in the hotel crib, his little lips puckering in and out as if he were dreaming of the moment he'd wake up and get a bottle.

"Something tells me Cody will be happy with what we have planned."

The lime green Volkswagen sat alone, looking a little forlorn and dusty in the back of the bar, a yellow daisy visible through the windshield.

JJ stood, arms folded across his chest, staring at the daisy while an officer rifled through the car. The manager of the bar had told them it had been sitting there since Thursday night. "I was getting ready to call and have it towed away."

The officer eased out of the car. "Okay, other than insurance card, the car manual, and a receipt for a car wash, the car is clean. The lady wasn't one to junk it up."

JJ reached out and took the car wash receipt, now encased in a plastic bag. It was dated for Thursday. He handed it back to the officer. "Get this car back and go over it with a fine-tooth comb."

"You got it."

Leaving the officer to take care of Lori Blain's car, JJ went inside the bar.

Time Out was a local bar that catered primarily to the nearby college students. Food, music, alcohol, and dancing in a deceptively friendly atmosphere. Other than a few couples sitting in the booths and two at opposite ends of the bar, the place was empty.

JJ worked his way through the tables and up to the bar, where a bartender was wiping down the back counters. Sandy hair, a receding hairline, a mustache; JJ put him somewhere in his midthirties. The bartender tossed his rag down and walked over. "What can I get you?"

JJ laid his badge on the bar while reading the bartender's name tag. "Bobby. How about some answers?"

Bobby's eyes widened as he eyed the badge. "What are the questions?"

"Do you know Lori Blain?"

There was a moment of hesitation, then Bobby shook his head slowly. "I don't think the name rings a bell."

JJ pulled a picture of Lori out and laid it on the bar, then slid it forward with the tips of his fingers. "Lori Blain."

Bobby picked it up. "Sure. I know this girl. She's one of the college crowd. Comes in every Thursday for ladies' night two-for-one and occasionally on the weekends."

"Was she in last Thursday night?" JJ asked, even though he knew she had to have been.

"I believe so." The bartender fingered the edge of his mustache while staring at the picture. "Yeah. Wait. She was in here. Sat here at the bar with some guy."

"Did she come in with the guy?"

Bobby shook his head. "Nah, he's a regular. Cruises for action, if you know what I mean. He was here before she was. She came in and sat down at the bar. He was down at the other end and scooted down to sit next to her. Bought her a drink. They danced a bit. Talked. You know how it goes."

Indeed he did. JJ flipped open his notebook and started writing. "Did she leave with him?"

Suddenly Bobby seemed to put two and two together. "This is the girl who was found dead at the lake, isn't it? Oh, man. What a shame. She was a nice girl."

JJ ignored Bobby's question and repeated his own. "Did she leave with this guy?"

The bartender shook his head again. "No. She left right after two-for-one ended. I think she gave him her number, though. I sorta remember her writing something down on one of the cocktail napkins and giving it to him. Then she left. He picked up his drink and headed back to the pool tables. Guess he figured there was still time to troll for more likely prospects."

JJ kept writing. "Do you remember what time she left?"

"Like I said, right after two-for-one. I'm guessing maybe quarter after ten. Twenty after."

JJ looked up. "And you're sure she left alone."

"Yep. Right out the front door."

"Tell me about the guy she was with."

Bobby shrugged. "Midtwenties. Dark hair, blue eyes, jeans, sports shirt, sweater. You know the look. Prep all the way. Like I said, he's in here pretty regular. Come back on Thursday night and you'll probably find him here."

JJ finished his notes, including a reminder to come back on Thursday night, and closed his notebook. Then he took out a business card and slid it across the bar. "I appreciate this. If you think of anything else, call me."

Bobby picked it up, looked at it briefly, then stuck it in his shirt pocket. "Sure thing, Detective. Glad to help."

JJ stood up and looked around the bar. He spotted the pool tables in the rear and started walking in their direction.

"Detective!"

JJ turned around. "Yes?"

"He had a Porsche key chain. I remember the key chain 'cause I remember thinking no way that guy owned a Porsche, but he left his keys on the bar, like he wanted the girls to see it and think he did have one. Like a lure. You know what I mean?"

JJ nodded. "Sure do. Thanks."

Making a mental note of the key chain, JJ turned his attention back to the layout of the bar. His fingers trailed across the wooden edge of a pool table, barely noting the chips in the finish. Four pool tables. Pool stick rack. Barstools. Hallway to rest rooms and fire exit.

JJ's mind snapped to attention. He strode down the short hall, passing pay phones and rest rooms, and stopped at the fire exit door. Standard metal door with panic bar. He turned and hurried back to the bartender.

"Excuse me, Bobby?"

"Yeah?" Bobby turned to face him, his rag still in hand.

"That fire door back there. If you go out, does the alarm go off?"

Bobby shook his head. "Nah. Lots of people go out that way.

Quickest way to the rear parking lot."

"And the guy who was with Lori Blain that night. You said he headed back toward the pool table."

Bobby nodded, looking a little confused. "Yeah."

"Did you see him again during the night? At any time?"

There was a long moment of silence that pulled on JJ's anticipation. Finally Bobby shook his head. "I don't know. I can't say for sure. Maybe not. Maybe. You know how it is."

"So it's possible that he walked right on past the pool tables and out the back door?"

The bartender fingered his mustache again. "Yeah, sure. I just remember him getting up right after she left and heading back there toward the pool tables. After that. . ." He shrugged.

JJ slapped his hand on the bar. "Thanks, Bobby. You've been a great help."

He watched her from the booth as she laughed at something her boyfriend was saying. He was too far away to hear what they were saying, but that was okay. He'd watched her long enough to know that she didn't suspect a thing. Never felt him watching her, following her.

There was more excitement in that than he would have originally thought. To know that he was invisible to these women, learning where they went and with whom. Learning their moods, styles, schedules, and habits. Letting himself imagine that moment when he would take them, when understanding would dawn in their eyes, and that moment later when they knew they were going to die. It was that horror and fear that he looked for. Waited for. Anticipated. Nothing else gave him such a high.

The woman stood up, leaning over to kiss her boyfriend good-bye. Knowing that it was probably the last time she would ever see her boyfriend, much less kiss him, made him grin as he stood up to follow her out.

In a few hours, my sweet DeAnne, you'll be all mine.

siX

I'm sorry for dragging you and the kids down here, but I just have a feeling about this case, so I want to hang around for a few days."

Donnie really didn't want to talk about the case. Or think about it, for that matter. Mandy was asleep in one of the double beds in the connecting room with baby Cody tucked in a hotel crib next to her. Donnie was stretched out on the king-size bed with Lisbeth nestled in his arms.

She lifted her head to stare up at him. "No need to apologize, honey. I didn't mind driving down here, and I don't mind being here. It gives us more time with you."

Donnie lifted a strand of her hair, winding it around his finger. "I'm gone so much that I just want every minute with you and the kids that I can manage. I hate thinking that they're growing up so fast and one of these days I may look back and realize that I missed so much of their childhood."

"You're a good dad, Donnie. Don't be so hard on yourself."

"This isn't exactly the kind of job that—"

There was a sudden and insistent knocking on the hotel door. Lisbeth pulled back and allowed Donnie to roll over to his feet. Out of habit, he eased his Glock out of the nightstand drawer and padded on bare feet to the door. He looked through the security eye in the door and sighed. Then he opened the door.

"What are you doing here?"

"We have a lead." JJ brushed past Donnie before he could stop him and strode into the room. He pulled up short when he saw Lisbeth curled up on the bed.

"Oh. Sorry."

Donnie opened the nightstand drawer and tossed the gun in. "JJ, I'm going to ask for your discretion."

"Sure, Donnie."

"I'm really serious about this, JJ. I'm going to share something with you that you cannot, under any circumstances, share with anyone else."

"Okay, okay."

"Promise me, JJ."

JJ shrugged. "Promise."

"Detective Josiah Johnson, my wife, Lisbeth."

JJ stared down at Lisbeth, his jaw gaping, eyes wide with amazement, disbelief, and a touch of incredibility. "*Wife*. You said wife."

"Wife. Lisbeth, this is JJ."

Lisbeth smiled and rose up on her knees to reach out and shake JJ's hand. "Nice to meet you, JJ. Donnie's told me so much about you."

"I wish I could say the same, Lisbeth."

She laughed, plumping up the pillows, then shoving them behind her as she sat back against the headboard, stretched out her bare feet, and crossed them at the ankle. "Donnie likes to protect his family. He's funny that way."

Just then, the connecting door to the second room of the suite opened, and Mandy shyly slipped into the room, rubbing her eyes. "Daddy?"

Donnie picked her up. "You're supposed to be asleep, darlin'."

Lisbeth scooted off the bed and reached for their daughter. "Let me take her and put her back down. You two talk."

As soon as Lisbeth left the room and the door closed behind her, JJ dropped down on the edge of the bed. "You're married with a kid. Wow. Talk about keeping a major secret."

"And it has to stay that way, JJ. I don't like anyone knowing I have a family."

JJ looked up at him. "Why?"

"You know this business, JJ. All I need is one criminal to decide on a little payback by targeting my family. I couldn't handle it if I lost them because of my job. As long as no one knows I have a wife and kids—"

JJ narrowed his eyes. "You said *kids*. As in plural. More than one."

"My son, Cody, is in there asleep also. He's just three months old."

"Well, congratulations, Donnie." JJ stood up, shoved his hands in his pockets, and started pacing around the room. "I will keep your secret. You can count on that. But give me a minute to alter everything I ever thought about you."

Donnie laughed wryly, pulling out a chair from the small table in the corner and dropping down into it. "Yeah, I guess it's not quite the image everyone has of me."

"Far from it." JJ strolled over to the table, pulled out the other chair, and sat down. "What are they doing here?"

"While I was in St. Louis, Lisbeth's dad was rushed to the hospital. Mild heart attack. She drove out to Ohio with the kids to spend some time with her parents. Look after things. Make sure her dad was okay. I was going to fly from here to Columbus and drive them home, but I decided to stay here; so Lisbeth drove down, and we'll drive home together."

JJ ran his fingers through his hair with a choked laugh. "I'm sorry. I'm still trying to see you as devoted husband, father, family man. Mr. Hollywood Handsome with a girl in every port is a fake."

Donnie's lips barely curled into a rough example of a smile as he toyed with a loose thread in the hem of his gray sweatpants. "It was a good run while it lasted."

JJ leaned forward, hands clasped between his knees. "I said I'd keep your secret and I will. I may not totally understand all this, but I'll respect your decision."

"Well, it may not be necessary all that much longer, anyway."

"Why?"

"I'm thinking of quitting fieldwork. Take a desk job at Quantico. Analysis. Maybe teach. Spend more time with my children."

JJ blinked. "Are you nuts?"

"Not at all. Do you have any idea how much I travel? Maybe I get to see my kids one or two nights a week. If I'm lucky. That's not fair to them." Donnie sighed heavily. "Look, I haven't talked all this over with Lisbeth yet, so there's no point in discussing it, really. Until I get her input, I'm not making any final decision."

"You really love her, don't you?"

Donnie looked up, surprised. "She's my best friend. Of course, I do." He stretched out his long legs and propped them up on the edge of the bed. "Well, you didn't come over here to meet the family, so what's up?"

"Oh. Right. I think we have a lead on the Blain case."

Donnie felt that little rush hit, thrumming through his veins. "Talk to me."

"We found latent prints in Lori Blain's car. Seems that she did us a favor and had her car cleaned on Thursday afternoon. We had a hit on one of the prints. Joey Roddy. Robbery, B&E, assault, possession."

Donnie frowned as he processed the information. "Small stuff. It's a big jump from B&E to serial killer."

"Criminals escalate; you know that."

"True."

JJ leaned forward, eyes bright. "Now, here's where it gets good. I talked to the bartender at Time Out. He remembers Lori Blain being there that night. She was at the bar talking to a guy who bought her a few drinks. When she left, he went out the back."

"Any chance it was Joey Roddy?"

"Initial descriptions match up. Midtwenties, dark hair, blue eyes."

Lisbeth chose that moment to ease back into the room. "They're asleep."

Donnie held out a hand, giving her an invitation to join them. She walked over and sat down in Donnie's lap. He wrapped an arm around her while he continued to chew on what JJ had told him.

"So are you dating Zoe yet?" Lisbeth asked JJ.

JJ glared at Donnie. "Is there anything you haven't told her?"

Lisbeth laughed lightly, leaning back against Donnie as he looked up and said, "No. It's a best friend thing."

"So are you?" Lisbeth asked again.

"No," JJ growled.

"She sounds delightful. I hope I get to meet her while I'm here. Donnie says she's not only beautiful, she's smart as a whip."

"So is Denise."

"Who is Denise?" Lisbeth linked her fingers with Donnie's.

"The woman I've been dating off and on the last few weeks." JJ stared down at the floor. "Are we talking about me or this case?"

Donnie raised an eyebrow at that. "What do you consider off and on? How many times have you gone out with her? Twice?"

"Three times, and it's none of your business."

Lisbeth leaned over and gave JJ a gentle pat on the arm. "Don't mind him. He's a hopeless romantic, always looking for everyone to find that one true love and end up happy ever after."

"Midtwenties, dark hair, and blue eyes isn't going to get us a search warrant for Roddy's place. The best we can do at this point is to have a little chat with the man and see what we can shake up."

JJ glanced at his watch. "If you want to go with me, I can pick you up here around nine."

"Nine works fine."

Lisbeth slid out of Donnie's lap and stood up. "And while you two are chasing bad guys, I'm going shopping."

"Uh-oh," Donnie laughed. "This'll cost me dearly."

9:35 p.m.

"How do you feel about that? Being asked to find the man who killed Lori Blain?"

Zoe looked over at Rene Taylor, her pastor's wife, the woman who had led her to Christ just a few months before. "I don't know. Confused, I suppose. I thought that God wanted me out of the business, so I renounced my psychic abilities and went to work full-time at Mom's boutique. Then I felt restless and decided to go back to school and get my degree. I'm not there three weeks before I'm knee-deep back in a murder case."

"And?" Rene prompted.

Zoe stared down at her cup of hot tea, slowly moving the spoon around and around. "And what?"

Rene reached over and stilled Zoe's hand. "Are you feeling negative or positive? Do you feel peace about this?"

Zoe shrugged. "I'm not sure. I'm still not on firm ground with all this letting peace rule stuff. It seems so easy for you, but. . ."

"It'll get easier with time, Zoe. No one comes into the kingdom of God and suddenly does everything right, understands everything that happens, and always knows exactly what God is doing."

Zoe coughed up a weak laugh. "No kidding. I pray, I worship, I read the Word, I go to church, and I feel like I'm groping around in the dark."

Rene's smile was both indulgent and sympathetic as she reached for another brownie. "Ah, you're just like the rest of us then."

"So, how do I know this is what God wants me to do?"

Rene shrugged as she finished chewing and swallowed. "Let me ask you something. Just for argument's sake, let's say you've decided not to work this case."

She paused, staring hard at Zoe.

Zoe finally set her spoon down. "And?"

"Just do it. Decide that you're not going to work this case. Tell me you're not going to work this case."

"Okay," Zoe replied. She was extremely confused but willing to play along. "I'm not going to work this case."

"Quick, tell me what you feel deep inside."

"Bereft."

Rene threw her hands up with a wide smile. "There ya go! See? No peace. Take the case, Zoe. It's what you love and what you're good at."

"I don't know how, Rene." Zoe scrambled to put her thoughts into words her friend and mentor could understand. "Daria says I'm always complicating things rather than taking it to the lowest common denominator."

A deep furrow creased Rene's forehead. "Lowest common denominator?"

"Keep it simple."

"Ah!" Rene's face cleared as she set her brownie down on the plate and began to pick at crumbs with her finger. "She's right.

Although the truth is, most of us don't do that. We run around, fretting ourselves into a frenzy trying to pinpoint exactly what it is that the Lord wants us to do with our lives instead of realizing that as long as we always maintain an attitude of submission to His leading, He'll make sure we get where He wants us to go."

"So, when I met Dan. . .and Daria and I found Lori Blain. . .and Mr. Blain asked me to help his family find his daughter's killer. . .I should just see these as the Lord orchestrating everything to bring me into the place He wants me to be?"

Rene licked the crumbs off her finger. "That's a good way to put it, Zoe. Before the foundation of the world, the Lord called each of us to a specific time and place in history to accomplish the work He's called us to do. Billy Graham, Martin Luther, John Wesley, me, you. Every single one of us has been gifted to accomplish that work."

"But what are *my* gifts?"

"Well, I know you have been gifted with incredible discernment. Use that gift, sweetheart, and see where the Lord takes you with it."

Rene reached out and took Zoe's wrist. "Come on. We'll pray and ask the Lord to confirm that this is all by His hand. And if it is, we'll ask that He work mightily through you to bring this killer to justice."

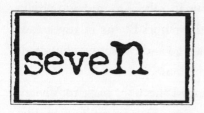

seven

Tuesday, September 28—5:08 a.m.

To sing hell's praise and then rejoice in all of evil's charms." JJ shivered as much from revulsion as the early morning chill. He stood up and handed the note to Donnie. "This guy is really starting to tick me off."

The body had been found by a sanitation employee on early morning rounds, emptying Dumpsters at local businesses. According to her driver's license, she was twenty-year-old DeAnne Foster, five-foot-five, brown hair, hazel eyes, one hundred and four pounds.

What the driver's license hadn't told JJ was how long she'd been dead. He'd have to wait for Vivian Amato to tell him that. All he knew was that she had been stabbed four times, just like Lori Blain, and the killer had left a note, just as he had with Lori Blain. And chances were, she hadn't been sexually assaulted. Just like Lori Blain.

So the focus of the investigation would change now. The press would be all over this like flies on day-old garbage, and the chief would be screaming for results. The last thing the political players would want would be press and hysteria over a serial killer.

Bad for reelections. Bad for fund-raising. So, the chief would assign him a few more detectives and shove him in a small conference room with promises of anything he needed and expect miracles.

"Your suspect list just got cut dramatically," Donnie said wryly as he handed the note back to JJ. "All of Lori Blain's relatives and close friends just got permission to pass go and collect two hundred dollars. You've got a serial killer on the loose, JJ."

"We knew that, Donnie." JJ handed the note back to Vivian and stepped away from the crime scene. Donnie walked beside him, hands deep in his coat pockets, shoulders hunched against the cold wind.

"We did; we just couldn't act on it as a sure thing until now."

"I guess that means you'll be officially here."

"I can call Quantico and tell them what's going on. As for whether or not they'll want to jump on this right away is another matter. They may feel you can handle this without us."

JJ ran his fingers through his hair, wrestling with frustration. "Let's work on this another day or so. See if we get any leads from this victim before I make that decision."

"Fair enough," Donnie replied. "Are we still going to talk to Roddy today?"

"Yeah. But first, I want to see what we can dig up from this crime scene. I'm hoping he left us something we can use to nail him."

Donnie's cell phone rang, interrupting their conversation but not JJ's frustration. He continued to chew on it while Donnie stepped away and carried on his conversation with someone.

Two girls, both stabbed. So far, the only link they had were student IDs from Monroe College. Was someone targeting the college? Or was there something else that had made both these girls come to the attention of a killer? Had he approached them and been turned down? Had they reminded him of someone he hated?

"JJ. I gotta go."

JJ glanced at his watch. "Okay. I'll pick you up—"

"No," Donnie jumped in, cutting him off. "That was my partner. We have a sniper targeting the I-95 corridor in Georgia and South Carolina. I'm leaving now to head back to Quantico."

He reached out and gave JJ a pat on the shoulder. "Call me if you need anything."

"Will do. Stay safe."

Donnie flashed a toothy smile and winked. "Always."

As JJ turned to head back over to Vivian Amato and the crime scene techs, Donnie called out. "JJ?"

JJ stopped and looked over his shoulder? "What?"

"Get this guy."

"I will."

❖   ❖   ❖

7:30 a.m.

Daria Cicala was on her second cup of coffee when the phone rang. She stared at the caller ID, surprised that her sister would be calling so early. Noreen was a notoriously late sleeper.

"Hello?"

"Daria?" Hearing the shaky tearfulness in Noreen's voice immediately put Daria on edge.

"What's wrong, Nora?"

There was a hitch, then a long, mournful sob. "Nora, talk to me."

"It's DeAnne."

Daria felt the cold chill go right down her spine. Of her seven nieces and nephews, DeAnne was her favorite. It might have been because DeAnne had been the first niece or because she was so like

Daria in temperament and style, but Daria wasn't into analyzing the reasons too closely. From the moment Noreen had placed the child in Daria's arms, Daria had been a goner.

"What's wrong with DeAnne?" Daria reached out and grabbed the back of a chair, leaning against it for support. She wasn't sure what was coming, but Noreen wasn't a whiner or a crier. For her to be in all-out hysterics meant this was bad. Really bad. A car accident? Some horrid disease? Leukemia, maybe?

Noreen started sobbing again, and there was a muffled noise that had Daria nearly jumping out of her skin. "Nora! Talk to me!"

"Daria?" Suddenly Noreen's husband, Frank, came on the line.

"Frank, what is going on?"

"The police were just here. DeAnne. . .Dee was—" His voice broke in a sob. "She's gone, Daria. They said someone killed her."

Daria's knees gave out, and she sank to the floor in one crumbling move. "No. No." Not DeAnne with the big, laughing brown eyes and the serious attention to detail. Not DeAnne, who thought the world revolved around her aunt Daria. Not little DeAnne, who would skip in Daria's shop and jump up in a chair, demanding that her aunt Dee give her a haircut. Or years later, all grown-up, asking Aunt Dee to make her look wonderful for her high school graduation. Her prom. Her first homecoming.

"Daria?"

Swiping at the torrent of tears streaking down her face, Daria could barely croak out an audible, "Yes."

"I hate to ask you this, but Noreen needs me. Can you call your brother and let him know? And your parents?"

"Sure." As much as she hated to even think of making those calls, she had to do something. Anything. She couldn't let Noreen and Frank down. "What about Hannah? Is she okay?"

"We haven't told her yet. Noreen's in the bedroom, and I'm just going to try and get Hannah off to school before she realizes what happened. I don't think I can handle telling her about her sister just yet."

Hannah was only twelve, the latecomer in the family whom no one was expecting, least of all Noreen, who had been so sure she was going through menopause. Surprise. And along comes Hannah, a sweet but sensitive child who would take this very hard.

"If you need me to pick up Hannah after school, just let me know."

"Would you? Could you do that? I would so appreciate it."

"I'll pick her up and bring her home. By then the whole family will be there and we can tell her together."

Frank seemed to sigh in relief. "Thanks, Daria. I'll talk to you later on then."

Daria hung up the phone and reached for a dish towel. Tissues weren't going to do the trick today. Suddenly she lunged for the phone and dialed quickly.

"Zoe!" She knew Zoe had been asleep, but it was one of the rare times when she didn't care. "Zoe, it's me. It's bad."

Zoe's voice sounded muffled. "What's bad?"

"Zoe, I need your help."

"Anything, Daria. What do you need?"

"I need you to find the man who just killed my DeAnne."

Zoe's voice suddenly went fully alert and sharp as a tack. "DeAnne?"

Daria started sobbing again. "My DeAnne, Zoe. He killed my girl. You find him, Zoe. You find him for me. And when you do, give me five minutes with him."

"Daria. . ."

"No. No excuses. I don't want to hear you're *not* in this anymore, you're *not* doing this anymore, it's not your job anymore. You find him, Zoe. You do what you have to do, and you find that monster. And then I'm going to cut his heart out."

❖ ❖ ❖

Zoe sat on the edge of her bed, face buried in her hands as the pain washed over her. It was, on some level, like losing her sister, Amy, all over again. She couldn't bring herself to resent Daria's snippiness, as rare as it was. She understood all too well what Daria was feeling.

It was hard enough to lose someone you love, but when it came suddenly and for no reason that made sense to your mind, it ripped at the heart, leaving gaping wounds in your soul that bled anger and cried out for vengeance.

It was only natural that Daria would turn to her for help. The problem was, Daria was going to expect her to make things right.

Oh, Lord, what am I going to do?

Anger swelled like a hurricane-swept ocean, crashing down on her grief and burying it in a turbulent, churning swell of resentment. She was trying so hard to be a good Christian, to avoid the temptation to use her old psychic powers, and to do things the way she thought God wanted her to do them. But now what? She couldn't let Daria down, and she couldn't turn her back on the Lord.

Where were You, Lord, when DeAnne needed You? How could You let this happen to her?

She had met DeAnne many times over the years and knew how much Daria loved her. Daria was being ripped apart, and now Zoe was caught in the maelstrom.

Well, enough was enough!

Zoe grabbed the phone and made a quick call. "Dan? It's Zoe. I'm in."

❖   ❖   ❖

9:08 a.m.

The pounding in his head was confined to his temples and the back of his neck, but it felt as though it was shooting pain through his whole body. JJ turned the key in the lock and pushed open the front door of his town house.

As if sensing that JJ was not going to be in the mood for playful shenanigans, Zip sat patiently in the foyer, his feathered tail slapping the rug in a gentle reminder that JJ had not walked him before running out of the house just after four in the morning.

"Hey, Zip." JJ gave the golden retriever a quick pat on the head as he headed down the hall. Zip followed close at his heels until JJ entered the kitchen, then the dog pushed by JJ, bounding toward the back door. He stood there, looking out the sliding glass door, tail swishing rapidly in anticipation of being let out.

JJ unlocked the door and slid it open long enough for Zip to shoot through, then closed it and headed for the bathroom. He found the aspirin and swallowed four of them before jumping into the shower.

Another serial killer. He lifted his face and let the hot water pound down on him. How many women would die before this creep could be found and locked up? The answer would be his responsibility. The sooner he found the guy, the sooner the killing would stop. As the highest-ranking detective in the department, task forces were always his to form and lead. The pressure would be overwhelming. Nothing he hadn't faced before, but he didn't welcome it.

And the longer it took him, the more the chief would lean on him, the press would hound him, the families would question him, and the faces of the victims would haunt him.

Why did he want to be a police officer again? Oh, right. Because he wanted to make a difference in the world. He could have done that painting houses.

Zoe shot a glance at the clock as she hopped on one foot, trying to simultaneously put her other shoe on, grab her jacket off the bed, and check her hair in the mirror. It would have to do.

Dan asked her to meet him at his office at nine-thirty. She'd be lucky to get there by nine-forty-five.

Of course, now she was wondering if she was making the right decision in getting involved in the case!

The parents were grieving. They would want her to touch their daughter's belongings, delve into that strange world of mystical knowledge, and suddenly produce the closure they needed, the justice they felt they deserved, and the vengeance that ate at their souls.

And she wasn't the one to give it to them. So, what in the world was she doing? *Lord, please let me know that this is what I'm supposed to be doing. I need some kind of confirmation. And make it too big for me to miss, will You?*

She kept the radio on low as she drove, letting her thoughts dominate. How tempted would she be to drift back and use her old powers? She'd tried so hard to stay away from any situation that might tempt her. And tracking down a killer could be extremely tempting.

About the fourth time she looked in the rearview mirror, she took notice of the little blue car that was following her. Or maybe it was just heading in the same direction she was.

One day, and she was already starting to see boogeymen in the shadows.

By the time she arrived at Cordette Investigation's parking lot, she was running on a full head of steam. The little blue car had been behind her the whole way. When she parked, she had watched as it slowed down, then turned the corner.

"I'm here to see Dan," she told the receptionist as she rushed into the lobby.

The young woman, a cute little redhead with freckles across her nose, used her pen to point down the hall. "You can go on back. Dan's office is the first on the left."

"Thanks."

Zoe stepped up to Dan's door, took a deep breath to calm her nerves, knocked once, and opened the door.

Dan was tilted back in his chair, his feet on the corner of his desk, a newspaper in his hand.

"Sorry I'm late."

"No problem," a man replied from a chair next to the desk. "We were waiting for you." He lifted his coffee cup. "Kyle Chelan."

Zoe sat down into a chair. "Nice to meet you."

"Okay," Dan said. "Now that we're all here, let's get started."

No matter how she looked at this, it was going to be a delicate balance. Russell Blain was a friend of his. Daria was a friend of hers. The pressure would be on to give their friends what they were looking for, and that pressure would trickle down to her. Dan would expect her to do whatever she could, even delve into her old abilities to close this case satisfactorily. And that, she couldn't do.

"Zoe?"

"I want to help, Dan, but I'm not a psychic anymore, and I'm not going to do what I feel is wrong just because they're friends of yours or mine or because you expect it. I'm sorry, but it's just—"

"Whoa, slow down!" Dan swung his feet to the floor and

straightened. "No one is asking you to do that, Zoe. And I certainly don't expect it."

"Then exactly what *do* you expect from me?"

"I want you to examine the evidence, ask questions, and look at the case with the practiced eye of a woman who has seen this kind of thing up close and personal many times before. You know how they think. How they operate. Why they do it. I need that part of you."

"I don't know why they do it other than there is something vital missing from their souls."

"If they even have souls." Kyle snorted.

Dan folded his arms on his desk and leaned forward. "I take it you're concerned about how this affects your faith?"

She nodded slowly. "I renounced my psychic abilities, Dan. I won't use them. And as far as I know, that's the only thing I had that would have been of any use to you at all."

"You're wrong, Zoe." Dan gave her an encouraging smile. "I know what you can do. I've seen you work, remember? I want your insights."

"My insights." Zoe took a deep breath. "You want *my* insights."

"Yes." He leaned back in his chair. "Look at this case from every possible angle. Use your instincts. Your experience."

It took a minute to realize that she'd panicked for nothing. All the tension seemed to be draining right down through her fingertips, making them tingle. "Okay. I'll do what I can."

Dan grinned at her. "Great! I'd like you to start at the crime scene, then head over to Lori's apartment. Russell gave me the keys for you." He opened a drawer and pulled out a set of keys. "In the meantime, Kyle is going down to get copies of the autopsy and police report."

Zoe leaned forward and picked up the keys. "Okay."

Dan shut the desk drawer. "I'd like to meet you both back here around four. We can go over everything we have and talk about a plan of attack."

Zoe nodded as she climbed to her feet. "Guess I better get started."

Dan stood up. "I'm going to go out and talk to her friends. See if they know anything."

"And Zoe?" he added just as she reached the door.

She turned, clutching her coat in her hands. "Yes?"

"This has really upset you, hasn't it?"

Leaning back against the door, she shifted her coat while gathering her thoughts. "Another girl was killed this morning. She happens to be my best friend's niece. I knew this girl, Dan. It just got personal. The problem is, I know everyone is going to want more from me than I can give them."

Circling his desk, he leaned back against it. "We're talking about people who just lost a child to a violent crime. You are more than familiar with that. You've come across it too many times over the years not to know what they're feeling."

"And too many times not to know that I can't give them what they want."

"Nobody can, Zoe. They want something to alleviate the grief. Someone to take away the pain of having that child suddenly cut out of their lives but not their hearts. Right now, they think that catching the killer will do that. We both know better."

Daria's words came back loud and clear. *You find that monster, then I'm going to cut his heart out.* He was right. Not that it made her feel a whole lot better, but he was right, and that forced a deep sigh out of her. "Just do what you can, Zoe. That's all."

"Thanks, Dan." Zoe pulled Dan's door closed and slid her arms into her coat, heading for the front door. As she entered the reception area, a young woman stood up, clutching a package to her chest. Zoe may not have noticed her if it hadn't been for the woman's hair. It was short, softly feathered around big, light brown doe eyes, and so blond it was almost white.

Zoe shot her a quick smile as she headed for the door.

"Miss Shefford?" the receptionist called out, then pointed her pen at the blond. "This young woman wanted to talk to you."

Surprised, Zoe turned and nearly bumped into the woman, who was now fidgeting nervously. "I'm sorry, Miss Shefford. I just really need to talk to you."

Zoe motioned in the direction of a small grouping of chairs and sofas in the corner of the reception area. "What can I do for you?"

"I'm sorry. I just want you to know that I wasn't stalking you or anything, I just need to talk to you and—"

"Stalking me?" Zoe draped her coat over a chair, pulled out another one, and sat down.

"I went to your house, but you were just leaving, so I followed you here." She slowly lowered herself into a chair, still clutching her purse and package. "I was hoping you could, well, maybe. . ."

"The blue car." Zoe felt a shiver of relief. "Why don't you just take a deep breath and start from the beginning?"

The young woman laughed nervously. "I know. I'm so wired I'm not making any sense. This whole thing has been a nightmare. Anyway, I found these diaries in my grandmother's dresser, and it's been driving me crazy. And I kept praying that the Lord would show me what to do, then there was your picture; and I just felt you were the one the Lord wanted me to turn to, which sounds crazy, I know, but I'm not crazy. Really, I'm not. I'm not some weird fanatic who goes around hearing strange voices or anything like that. It's just that I really felt that He wanted me to talk to you."

Zoe held up a hand, the woman fell silent, then Zoe reached

forward. "My name is Zoe Shefford, and your name is?"

"Oh." The woman reached out and shook Zoe's hand. "Lanae Oakley."

"Nice to meet you, Lanae. Okay, now forget following me, calm down, and tell me what has you so upset."

Lanae leaned forward, still clutching her package tightly and staring at Zoe with a desperation that Zoe felt all the way to her toes. "I think my father killed my mother, and I need you to help me prove it."

eight

By the time he'd showered and changed clothes, Zip was standing at the door waiting expectantly for food. JJ slid the door open and allowed Zip to trail his heels while he pulled out the bag of food and filled the bowl.

"Too bad you aren't a bloodhound, Zip. I could use one right about now."

Zip's response was merely a soft whine as he sat down, his tail sweeping the floor. JJ had found Zip as a puppy, abandoned and hungry, and had brought him home intending to feed him, then find him a home somewhere. Within a matter of hours, JJ had resigned himself to keeping the puppy that had curled up in his lap after eating and roughhousing with JJ until dropping in exhaustion.

While Zip was no bloodhound, he was completely devoted to JJ and a pretty good watchdog. But, even if Zip had been worthless as a watchdog, JJ would have kept him. Zip was the only one, other than his mother, that he knew loved him completely and unconditionally. That kind of love was hard to reject even though it meant sometimes sending someone over to feed Zip when he was knee-deep in a demanding case.

"Come on, boy. Out you go. Hopefully I won't be too late tonight. And no digging around the shrubs, you got that?"

Zip barked and ran for the door. JJ set the food and fresh water bowl outside on the deck, locked the door, and watched Zip dive into the food. Then, JJ grabbed his keys and headed out.

"Hey, Mr. Johnson."

JJ paused halfway into his Jeep and looked over at the next yard where eleven-year-old Josh Cameron was standing with his skateboard under his arm. The Camerons had moved in next door about two months earlier, and Josh had immediately adopted JJ as his favorite neighbor and Zip as his favorite neighborhood dog.

"Hi, Josh. Why aren't you in school?"

"Teacher's conference. You gonna work late today?"

"Maybe." JJ smiled, knowing what was coming next.

"You need me to walk Zip before dinner?"

"If you wouldn't mind. His leash is hanging in the garage. You know where to find it."

"Yeah." Josh grinned. "Thanks, Mr. Johnson. I'll walk him good. And I'll take his ball, too. He likes to play fetch."

"He only likes to play fetch with you, Josh. Make sure you lock the gate when you put him back in the yard."

"I will, Mr. Johnson. I'm always real careful."

"I know you are. I'll see you later."

JJ climbed into his Jeep and started the engine. Josh tossed his skateboard to the sidewalk and jumped on, waving as JJ backed out of the driveway.

At first, JJ hadn't known quite how to react to this kid following him around the front yard, asking a million questions, knocking on his door wanting to take Zip out to play, offering to mow the lawn, rake leaves, or help him wash his Jeep. But the kid grew on him, even as the kid's boundless energy wore him down and made him feel old. Josh was an only child, and that was something that JJ could relate to. Once the boy made a few friends at school and around the neighborhood, he'd probably slowly forget about him and Zip.

In the meantime, Zip loved the attention, so it worked out well for everyone.

Sitting at the intersection of Prospect and Route 32, JJ saw a familiar car pass by, heading in the direction of Sterling Lake. If she was going back out there to the crime scene, he'd be tempted to choke her. It was a secluded area and, since the news broke about Lori Blain, deserted by joggers. No one was taking a chance on being the next victim by being caught alone out there near the lake. But you couldn't count on Zoe to be smart and play it safe.

The light changed and, instead of going straight, JJ quickly turned left and headed out toward Sterling Lake. If she did turn into Sterling Lake, he was going to make sure she found a new place to jog. The woman obviously needed a keeper!

❖   ❖   ❖

11:04 a.m.

Zoe stepped out of her car, locked it, and headed down the path to the lake. She wasn't going to have a hard time finding the exact area where she and Daria had found Lori Blain—the entire area was cordoned off with crime scene tape.

She stepped up to the tape and eyed the chalk outline on the grass. Lori Blain didn't die here; this was merely where the killer chose to dump her body. So, where did he actually kill her? And why? What was it about Lori that made her a target?

Fingers trailing the tape, Zoe walked the perimeter of the crime scene, taking in the surrounding area. The lake, the jogging trail, the little patches of woods, a few cottages on the far side of the lake, the roof of a couple of commercial buildings just beyond the park. . .

He would have waited until after dark to bring her here. Probably after midnight, just to make sure he didn't run into the occasional teenager who ignored the park closed-at-dusk rule to party at the lake. More than likely, he had parked right where Zoe had parked, the closest space to the trail leading from the parking lot down to the lake. If he'd been in a van, he'd have backed it up to the curb, opened the doors—

"Would you care to explain why you're invading a crime scene?"

Zoe nearly screamed as his voice cut through the silence and her thoughts. Whirling around, her hand slammed against her chest.

JJ stood there, his fists on his hips, his brown leather jacket unzipped, his face hard and unrelenting.

"You scared the daylights out of me, JJ! What were you thinking?"

"That you're an idiot to be hanging around down here when you know as well as I do that killers like this love to revisit the scene and relive their glory. Wouldn't he just love to find another young woman waiting, all alone and helpless?"

Between the truth of his words and the chill in his voice, Zoe felt herself tighten up and prepare for battle. "I'm not exactly helpless, JJ, and you know it."

"Yeah, I noticed that a couple of months ago when you were in the process of being strangled."

"That was different!"

JJ jammed his hands down in his jacket pockets. "I'm not even going to waste my time asking how it could possibly be different. You obviously don't have enough sense to come in from the rain, much less avoid making yourself a target for a killer."

"I'm not even going to go there with you, JJ." She started to brush past him. He grabbed her wrist.

"I asked you why you were here. You know this area is off limits. I could arrest you for this."

Zoe merely stared at him. Arrest her? Was he nuts?

"Why are you here, Zoe? What are you looking for, more bodies?"

"You really know how to aggravate me, JJ, you know that? Well, it's none of your business what I'm doing here." She jerked at her hand. It didn't budge. "Let me go, JJ."

"Don't push me, Zoe. I've been up since four this morning, I have a serial killer on the loose, and I'm not in the mood to dance with you."

Zoe glared up at him, ignoring the glint of steel in his green eyes. "I don't care what time you rolled out of bed."

"We found his second victim in a Dumpster this morning. And he made sure we knew he wasn't done killing."

Zoe tried to pull her hand from JJ's once again. This time he let go. "I know that."

"How? That is not public knowledge yet. At least, I hope the press hasn't caught wind of it yet."

"It was DeAnne Foster. Daria's niece."

"Ah, geesh. I'm sorry." He took a deep breath. "In the meantime, I'm going to ask you one last time, what are you doing here?"

"I wanted to see the crime scene."

"Why? I thought you were done with this kind of work?"

"Maybe I'm not, after all."

"Oh, yes you are, Zoe Shefford. You're going to walk away, drive home, work at your mom's little boutique, and never look back."

Zoe knew her temper was spiking, but she couldn't help herself. The man was insufferable! "You don't have the right to tell me what I can and cannot do, Josiah Johnson, and you certainly won't be patting me on the head and sending me home like a good little girl!"

"You're going home and forgetting all this, or I'm arresting you for trespassing on a crime scene!"

Zoe erupted into laughter. The man really was incredible. "Right. Arrest me."

JJ stepped forward and snapped a handcuff on her wrist, cutting off her laughter as quickly as a hatchet chopped through drywall. "You can't be serious, JJ."

He grabbed her other wrist and cuffed it. She stared down at her wrists in horror. "Josiah Johnson, this isn't the least bit funny."

"I'm not the one who was laughing."

12:30 p.m.

Chief Harris peered over the top of his glasses. "You got Cole, Chapman, Barone, and McClellan. Otis is working on the chop shop case, and I'm not pulling him off it. And you got Casto when he gets back from his honeymoon. What else do you need?"

JJ tapped his pen against the arm of the chair. "More men, more hours in a day, more leads, and less hassle from the press."

Harris laughed, leaning back in his chair. "Oh, and you want miracles."

"Would be nice, Chief."

"What about that psychic we used last spring? Shefford? You're friends with her, right? She did well for us on the Matthews case. Maybe she can help you out a little with this."

JJ thought about Zoe sitting down in a holding cell and frowned grimly. "I don't think she'll be too cooperative. She told me after we closed the Matthews case that she was quitting the business."

Harris shifted in his chair, a clear indication that JJ's allotted time was coming to a close. "Shame. Well, you have a press conference at five. Any idea what you're going to tell them?"

"I'm going to do everything I can not to let the term *serial killer* get out, but somehow I don't think I'll be successful."

Harris grunted. "Not since they found out about the second vic." He slapped the arms of his chair, JJ's cue to leave. "Keep me posted."

JJ rose to his feet. "Will do, Chief."

Closing the chief's office door behind him, JJ headed toward his desk to gather all he would need to move into the conference room, where the new task force would be set up.

"Hey, JJ."

JJ turned and watched as Denise McClellan made her way through the maze of desks. "Hey, Mac."

"I got word you wanted to see me?"

Denise McClellan was a short woman, barely hitting five-foot-five, with short, curly brown hair, big brown eyes, and a thousand-watt smile. She'd disarmed many a perp with that smile. Cute, petite, and spunky, she made JJ think of a Meg Ryan with brown hair and a badge.

"Ditch the uniform and get into civvies. I got custody of you to work on the task force to find a killer."

That smile notched up a few watts. "Yeah? Fantastic! I am so bored working domestics. If I have to calm down one more drunk beating on his wife and convince the guy I'd find him far more attractive if he'd drop the baseball bat. . .I'm going to start using one myself."

JJ chuckled. "You sweet talker, you. How fast can you get back here?"

Denise looked at her watch. "Hour?"

"Works for me. We'll be in conference room three. Have you seen Chapman?"

"Last I heard, he was on his way out to lunch."

"Okay, thanks. See you in an hour."

Denise nodded and headed off, leaving JJ to watch her go. It had been a major exaggeration to tell Donnie that he'd taken Denise out three times. Denise was engaged to be married to an airline pilot. The three times he'd taken her out were all police functions, and they had merely gone together. Neither of them had considered it a date by any means. He'd never been to her home, didn't know her home phone number—although he would before this day was out—and had never thought of her as anything more than a coworker. But it had kept Donnie and his wife from hassling him about Zoe.

Zoe! She was still down in holding! JJ dropped his files off on his desk and headed for the stairs. He hadn't meant to leave her down there this long, but Harris had called him in and given him orders to set up the task force to handle this killer, and JJ had forgotten all about her until Harris had mentioned her name. She was going to be spitting bullets.

He jogged down one flight of stairs and opened the dented metal door. A man was pacing the floor and looking fairly aggravated.

Ignoring the man, JJ walked over to the desk. "Hey, Ira? You got paperwork for me?"

"Yeah, yeah. Where have you been? This guy's been waiting to spring the Shefford woman and you haven't even filed the charges yet."

"Forget them. It was all a big misunderstanding. You can release her."

Ira growled under his breath and disappeared through a door to get Zoe.

"You Detective Johnson?"

JJ turned around. "Yeah. So?"

"Dan Cordette. Cordette Investigations. You want to explain to me why you're hassling one of my employees?"

1:15 p.m.

He sat, his legs stretched out along the low block wall around the fountain, a book open in his lap, his dark sunglasses hiding his eyes. To anyone walking by, he was just another student taking advantage of the bright sunshine, which had burned off the early morning chill and provided a warm fall day to study outside.

Oh, he was studying, all right, but it wasn't the book in his lap. It was the blond walking across the green, heading toward the campus library, a blue and orange backpack slung over her shoulder.

He'd been watching her for over a week, getting her class schedule down, finding out where she spent her spare time, looking for the perfect time and place to strike.

She wouldn't be an easy target. She lived on campus in one of the girls' dorms and didn't hang out at the local bars or clubs. She rarely went out at night, and if she did, it was usually just to grab food or do laundry. And she tended to do laundry on Wednesday nights.

It was a shame, really. She seemed like a nice girl. He could almost like her. But he had his agenda, and he couldn't lose sight of that for a moment. The means would justify the ends. And, oh, what ends they were.

He smiled as she pulled open the big, heavy doors and disappeared inside. *Sorry, sweetheart, but you have to be sacrificed for the greater good.*

Zoe knew her temper was on a short leash as she stomped into the conference room with Dan and JJ behind her.

"Would you like to explain to me exactly what is going on here?" JJ slammed the conference room door closed as she and Dan pulled out chairs and sat down.

"I'd like to know that myself." Dan looked from Zoe to JJ and back to Zoe again. "I gather the two of you have worked together before?"

Zoe glared up at JJ, her temper held in check only by Dan's presence, and then, only barely. "Yes, we've worked together before."

"I see." Dan leaned back in his chair.

"I doubt it," JJ shot back. He turned to Zoe, slamming his hands down on the conference table and locking his elbows as he leaned forward. "Why didn't you tell me you were working for him? You were almost killed the last time! Haven't you had enough of this?"

Zoe held his steely gaze. "I'm not Macy, JJ. I don't need you to protect me."

She watched as the muscle in his jaw clenched. "You know something, Zoe? I'm getting tired of you throwing Macy in my face. She's gone. She's been dead for years, and I've long since come to terms with the fact that I couldn't have saved her. This isn't about Macy. This is about you."

"I can take care of myself."

"And pigs fly with purple wings. If a killer decides to strangle you, he might have to stand in line right now, but let's get something straight, lady, you cannot take care of yourself if someone decides to kill you. If I had been the perp today out there at the lake, you'd be dead right now. You never heard me coming."

She couldn't argue with that, even though she wanted to. Besides, she was still dealing with his insistence that he had dealt with his guilt over Macy's death. It had been the barrier between them, keeping them apart. So, if he'd dealt with it, why hadn't he called her?

Dan smiled. "I think I'm beginning to understand now."

She turned away from JJ and looked over at Dan, embarrassed that he'd been caught in the middle of one of her and JJ's little battles. "It's not what you think."

"I think it is." Dan leaned back in his chair, the smile tugging at the corners of his mouth fading quickly. "But regardless of what the two of you may feel for each other, we have a killer to catch."

"We?" JJ straightened. "I don't think so. This is a police matter."

"Zoe and I have been hired by Russell Blain to look into his daughter's murder."

JJ threw his hands up. "Great. Now I have this to deal with on top of everything else."

Zoe lifted her chin defiantly. "We are not something you have to deal with, JJ!"

Dan held up one hand, drawing the attention back to him. "I hate to interrupt this pleasant exchange, but I'd like to go back a bit and find out exactly why Zoe was arrested in the first place. There was no violation, so what were you thinking, Detective?"

"He wasn't thinking; that's the whole problem."

Color crept up JJ's neck so fast, even his ears turned red. "You told me that you were out of this business. No more chasing killers, no more crime scenes, no more putting yourself in danger!"

"I don't owe you any explanations! I was asked to help on this case, and I'm helping!"

"So you've gone back to your old crystal ball and voodoo magic, I guess." JJ lunged to his feet and began to pace.

Zoe slapped the table with the flat of her hand. "I have *not* gone back to anything, you oaf! Has it ever *once* occurred to you that I happen to have a brain? That maybe, just maybe, all these years helping the police do their job that I might have learned a few things!"

"Excuse me, people." Dan raised a finger.

"I don't want you putting yourself in the line of fire again, Zoe!

Do you know how close you came to being killed the last time?"

Zoe came to her feet. "You don't have to remind me that if you and Donnie had taken one more minute, I'd have been dead right now, JJ. I'm well aware of that. Things went bad. But that was the first time in all the years I've been in this work that my life was in that kind of danger!"

JJ walked over to her, crowding her space. She didn't back up. His nose came down close to hers, so close she could smell the coffee on his breath. "And I don't want you in that kind of danger ever again!"

She lifted her chin a little higher. "It's not your call! I make the decisions for my life, and you have nothing to do with it!"

"Hello?" Dan coughed.

"No, but I'm the one who will have to be impartial when I investigate your murder, right? I'll just identify your body, send it to the morgue, and treat it like any other murder investigation. Is that what you expect me to do?"

"I'm not going to end up dead, JJ!"

"You don't know that!" JJ's voice whipped out high and sharp.

"And I now pronounce you husband and wife. At least I now understand your hesitation to go out with me."

Dan's words weren't very loud, but both JJ and Zoe turned to stare at him. "All you had to do was tell me that you were in love with someone, Zoe. I had no idea."

"I'm not in love with anyone, Dan." Zoe stepped back from JJ as if it would burn her to stand that close much longer. "You misunderstand. We just have a tendency to fight, that's all."

Dan chuckled as he leaned back in his chair, looking from Zoe to JJ and back again. "You just happen to be fighting because the man is scared spitless that you're going to end up getting hurt. I'd say that speaks volumes."

"You couldn't be more wrong," JJ interjected with a trace of sarcasm. "We've never even been out on a date."

Zoe whipped around again and jabbed JJ's chest with her finger. "Because you never called!"

"You told me you weren't interested! Why would I call you?"

"For heaven's sake," Dan mumbled and rolled his eyes.

She jabbed him again. Wounded rage pooled in her throat. "I didn't say I wasn't interested! I said you weren't ready!"

Dan rapped his knuckles on the table, getting their attention once again. "Can we get back to talking about the case? You two can kiss and make up later."

Zoe quietly eased back down in her chair, embarrassed that she'd let JJ rile her in front of Dan. "I'm sorry, Dan."

Dan waved away her apology. "I can understand the man's need to protect you, but in the meantime, we have a case to worry about."

"I don't want her pursuing this guy," JJ repeated stubbornly. "He's a serial killer and, while he seems to be targeting college students, we can't assume—"

"Zoe is a college student."

"What? Since when?"

"I started taking classes this fall."

JJ ran his fingers through his hair. "Great. You just love putting yourself in the crosshairs, don't you?"

"Oh, like I was supposed to know that someone would start targeting college students?" Zoe leveled her voice and prayed for patience. The last thing she wanted was to lose it again with Dan watching her with an expression that was part impatience and part amusement.

"Well, you're the psychic." JJ's lips curled in a mocking snarl.

"I'm not a psychic!"

"Well, finally!" JJ threw his hands up. "You admit the truth!"

"Oh, stop it!" Zoe's temper snapped. "I am not a target, I am not making myself a target, and I am working on this case whether you like it or not! We have a man out there who is trying to confuse you, and you're following his little trail without one question!"

"Oh, so now you know the mind of the killer!"

"Stop putting words in my mouth!" She jerked to her feet. "Let's go, Dan."

Dan didn't budge as he leveled those all-knowing eyes on her. "Please sit down, Zoe," he said quietly.

Zoe hesitated, torn between wanting to appear rational and wanting to get as far from JJ as she possibly could as fast as possible. Slowly she sank into the chair.

Dan turned to look at JJ, his voice soft and level, rational and inquisitive. The kind of voice that made you want to respond to it. "You said the killer was targeting college students. I gather there's been another victim?"

"Yes," JJ admitted, adding nothing.

"If this is a serial killer, where's Donnie?" Zoe asked, biting back the impulse to add a little bite to her words just for principle.

"On his way back to Quantico." JJ pulled out a chair and dropped down into it.

"Doesn't he know there's been another victim?"

"He knows. He was there this morning." JJ rubbed his face wearily. "There's a sniper in Georgia or South Carolina or something and he had to respond to that."

Dan folded his arms on the conference table and leaned forward. "Our involvement could be a real help to you, Detective. Zoe and I will be turning over every rock in Lori Blain's life, which leaves you free to concentrate your manpower on other areas of this investigation."

JJ stared down at the table for a moment, then lifted his eyes and turned them on Zoe. "I'd like you to tell me what you know about this perp we're looking for. You said he's trying to confuse us. What do you mean?"

Zoe rubbed at the back of her neck. "I can't explain it, JJ. I just know that he's not out killing women because he likes killing. There's another motive at the heart of this. I don't know what it is, so don't ask me."

"And you got this information. . .where?"

Zoe shifted in her chair and licked her lips. "You're not going to believe me."

JJ snorted. "Another one of your psychic visions? The tarot cards told you? Or better yet. . .the spirit of Lori Blain told you this."

She really wanted to slap him silly. "This has nothing to do with anything psychic, JJ. Will you please get off that merry-go-round?"

"Then what is it I'm not going to believe?"

"You're not going to believe that I think God is showing me."

JJ stared at her for a long, uncomfortable moment, then. . .he burst out laughing. Slowly he rose to his feet. "God told you. Yes, well. . .I think that explains everything nicely. I'm done here. Mr. Cordette, I suggest you take this flake and get out of here."

Zoe lurched to her feet and stepped in front of JJ as he headed for the door. "Don't you dare talk like that, Josiah Johnson. I know what happened out there at that storm shelter, remember? You heard from God. You believed. How can you laugh in my face now?"

"I don't know for sure it was anything more than good instincts, Zoe. That was a long time ago. I told you then and I'll tell you now, I don't believe in the supernatural."

"You knew it was God, JJ!" Her voice trembled with emotion. "You knew. Don't rationalize that away."

He shook his head at her, stepped around her, and opened the door. "I have an investigation to see to. Please don't get in my way."

She stared at the door as it snapped closed behind him.

"Why don't you tell him how you feel, Zoe?"

She turned back to Dan. "What?"

"Tell him you love him. That's what he needs to hear from you. He's worried sick about you and is irritated at himself for caring about someone who doesn't care about him. He needs to know that you *do* care—that you care very much."

"I can't."

"Why not?"

"Because I'm afraid of what will happen if I do."

"And what do you think will happen?"

Zoe shoved her hands in her pockets and stared at the door. "He'll have the power to hurt me."

"You're right. Can't trust a man like that." Dan threw his arm over her shoulder and grinned. "If I promise to never hurt you, will you go out with me?"

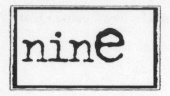

nine

I'm going to be late for work." Joey Roddy stared at the floor, shuffling his feet as the two detectives stood in the doorway.

"This won't take long," Detective Chapman insisted for the second time. "We just want to ask you a few questions."

"I told you, I don't know any Lori Blain."

"Then why are your fingerprints on her car?"

"I work at a car wash! My fingerprints are on cars all over town, but I'm no killer and I don't know this girl."

He took a step forward, but Chapman didn't budge. She didn't like the way his eyes were everywhere but on her, his hands were trembling, and he wouldn't stand still. The kid had so much guilt showing, you couldn't miss it if you tried.

She was trying to look inside his apartment, just on the off chance that some incriminating evidence might be laying out in the open, but Roddy was doing his best to block the door and keep her out.

"Why don't we go inside and take a seat? You can answer a few questions for me, and I'll be on my way."

"I have to go to work."

"I'll clear this with your boss." She tried to edge forward, hoping to back him into the apartment, but either the kid was dense, or he'd tangled with the law enough to know his way around investigations. He wasn't obligated to let her into the apartment. He didn't have to answer any questions.

"I didn't kill this woman, I don't know who did, I didn't know her, and I have nothing to tell you."

Stymied, Denise had to back off and give up for now. "If you're innocent, you'd go a long way to proving that to me by cooperating."

Roddy eased forward and closed the apartment door behind him. "I have nothing to tell you. Now leave me alone."

"Why not start by telling me where you were last Thursday night."

"Where I am every Thursday night. Working. From six to three at Tri-State Distributors."

He sidled around her and walked quickly down the hall, then disappeared down the stairs. Denise blew out a heavy breath. The smell of his guilt still hung in the air like smoke after a fire. When JJ had given her the assignment to talk to Roddy, she had been sure it was a dead end. Like the kid said, he worked at a car wash; his fingerprints would be on cars all over the city.

It wasn't until she'd knocked on Roddy's door and showed him Blain's picture that she'd felt that first tingle as her instincts started kicking. From then on, she'd known that she was on to something, but Roddy was too slick to hand her any answers.

He was evasive, nervous, fidgety, and lived within blocks of Lori Blain's apartment. It had the marks of a suspect. Except that he supposedly had an alibi. She'd check with Tri-State, but if his alibi squared, why was he so nervous?

❖　❖　❖

"I guess you want me off the case now." Zoe looked across the table at Dan, who appeared to be more interested in his plate of ribs than firing her.

"No. I want you to tell me what you think his motive is." He lifted one brow as a grin spread across his face.

"Greed."

"Why both these women?"

Zoe looked down at her plate, her appetite fleeing. "I don't know."

Dan pointed at her plate with his fork. "Eat that chicken before it gets cold."

"I'm not sure I'm hungry."

"Eat it anyway. You'll need all your strength to go the next round with your detective."

Zoe soothed her throat with a sip of her tea. "He's not my detective."

"Eat."

Zoe reached for her fork. "Why do you believe me?"

His shoulders lifted in a shrug. "Why wouldn't I? I know what you can do, Zoe. I've seen it for myself. You say you aren't a psychic anymore." He shrugged again. "Okay. But my grandmother once told me that all good gifts come from God. So, just because you're not a psychic doesn't mean that God hasn't given you a gift for knowing things that other people don't know; the ability to see what everyone else misses."

Zoe was impressed, even if she wasn't sure she could agree with his theory. Yes, all good gifts came from God, but it was what you did with them and who they were submitted to that made the difference.

"Greed, huh?"

"I think so. I'm not entirely sure, so don't go hanging any arrest warrants on it, but I met this woman this morning. She wants me to help her, and she gave me some diaries to read. It was like a novel—love, hate, intrigue, mystery, and greed. It was the greed that kept resonating with me, and every time it did, I would think of Lori Blain. I think it was God getting my attention and trying to point me in the right direction."

Now the look on Dan's face was that of a man who not only needed a little more convincing but wanted more.

"I know, Dan. It sounds a little out there, but I feel so sure of this."

He waved his fork on his way to his plate. "No, it's okay. I don't have to understand everything to accept it. I'll work this case my way and let you work it your way, and it will be interesting to see how the team works out."

"Tell me about this woman you met."

"Lanae?" Zoe leaned forward. "Get this! Her mother disappeared in 1982, and Lanae was raised by her grandmother. As far as Lanae knew, her mother had run off with some man and abandoned her. Her grandmother just died, and while packing up her grandmother's apartment, she finds these two diaries. One belongs to her mother and the other belongs to a very wealthy, very prominent family. Her father's family."

"Did she know who her father was before she found these diaries?"

Zoe shook her head. "Nope. Anyway, she starts reading her mother's diary and finds out that the man wanted nothing to do with Lanae. So the mother somehow gets her hands on this family diary, which, by the way, implicates one of the family members in the death of his brother in order to get his hands on the family inheritance."

"Greed."

"Exactly."

"What prominent family? Would I know of them?" Dan pushed his empty plate to the side and reached for his coffee.

"Tappan."

Dan's jaw dropped as he stilled, his eyes growing wide. "As in Judge Leonard Allen?"

Zoe nodded. "Yep."

"He's Lanae's father?"

"Looks that way."

He slumped back in his chair. "Talk about opening a can of worms, that will do it."

Zoe's lips flatlined. "I know. I haven't finished going through all the material, but it's explosive, no doubt about that. I'm just not sure why she felt I was the person to deal with this. I have no clue as to how to go back twenty years and find out what happened to Lanae's mother."

Dan reached forward and patted Zoe's hand. "You'll figure it out. You went back over twenty years and found your sister's killer and found her body."

At the thought of Amy, Zoe's heart contracted. Yes, she had found Amy's killer and had nearly died at his hands, as well. Amy was now at rest in a memorial grave next to so many other children murdered by Ted Matthews. A marble angel looked down on them, watching over them.

Dan angled his head, keeping his eyes locked on hers. "But, Zoe. I would advise you to be very careful. Judge Tappan is not a man you mess with lightly. If he thinks you're looking to rattle the skeletons in his closet, he will bury you."

8:24 p.m.

"Where is that ambulance?" Dana Tappan screamed over her shoulder at her brother, then leaned down close to her father's face. "Hang on, Dad. Help is coming."

Her father's face was pinched and gray, his eyes barely focused, and his labored breath came in shallow gasps. Dana clenched his hand in hers, rubbing gently, trying to offer comfort, encouragement, trying to will life into his body.

Her ears strained to hear the wail of sirens, but there was only the incessant ticking of the grandfather clock in the corner of the library, the shifting of melting ice in the ice bucket on the side table, the shuffle of her brother's pacing from oriental carpet to highly polished hardwood floors.

And that ragged gasping for breath.

That was the worst sound of all. It made the fear claw at her throat like a hungry animal.

"Daddy, please hang on. Please. Help is coming."

He merely stared vacantly beyond her. Swiping at the tears streaming down her face, she turned to her brother. "Marcus! Call them again! They should have been here by now!"

Marcus stared blankly, his arms clasped around his stomach. He was as pale as their father. Concern for him flooded Dana. "Are you okay?"

"He's. . .he's dying, isn't he?"

It was supposed to have been a celebration of sorts, the family coming together to celebrate Dana's birthday. Actually, her birthday was still four days away, but their dad was going to be away on a trip, so they decided to have the birthday dinner a few days early.

Dinner had been excellent as always. Cook had prepared a delicious prime rib for dinner and strawberry shortcake for dessert, Dana's favorites.

After dinner, Marc, Dana, and their father had retired to the library for champagne. Halfway through the first glass, their father had clutched his chest, turned pale, and collapsed to the floor.

Sirens suddenly ripped through Dana's panic, and her head jerked up. "Let them in, Marcus! Quick!"

Marcus jumped as she yelled, spun on his heel, and rushed from the room as if demons were hot on his trail. Dana knew he was upset, but she didn't have the energy to coddle him and worry about their father, too.

"Daddy? The ambulance is here, okay? You just hang in there, please? Come on, Daddy. Look at me, look at me." She framed his face in her hands, trying not to let the gray pallor spook her. He'd be okay. He just had to be. She couldn't lose him yet. Not yet. "Daddy? You're going to be fine, do you hear me?"

Marcus suddenly rushed into the room, the EMTs right behind him with a stretcher. She reluctantly rose to her feet and backed away, allowing them unfettered access to her father. "He just clasped his chest and went down. It might be a heart attack."

One of the EMTs was listening to her father's heart with a stethoscope while the other checked for a pulse. "Does he have a history of heart problems?"

Dana shook her head, then realized he wasn't looking at her. "No. He's always been in great health."

Marcus moved in close to her as if seeking comfort. She wrapped an arm around his waist. "He'll be okay, won't he, Dana?"

"I'm sure he will, Marc. The doctors will take care of him."

A few minutes later, the two EMTs lifted her father onto the stretcher and carried him from the house. She grabbed her purse and car keys as she followed them out the door.

"I'll ride with you, okay, Dana?" Marcus slipped his coat on.

"Sure." Dana broke out into a run toward her car. She nearly dropped her keys trying to get in and fumbled twice putting the key into the ignition.

"Dana?" Marcus pulled his door closed and reached for the seat belt.

She backed out of the driveway, blinking away the tears. "What?"

"What are we going to do if we lose him? I mean. . .what if he dies?"

"Don't, Marcus." She let the tears stream as she concentrated on staying right behind the ambulance through side streets, stop signs, and red lights.

"He didn't look good, Dana."

"He's not going to die, Marc. He's strong. He's tough. You know he's tough." She felt a small tremor of relief as they pulled into the hospital drive.

"You're right. He's tough. He'll be fine." His voice shook with emotion. She reached over and clasped his hand, squeezing it.

"We won't lose him, Marcus."

She whipped her car into the first parking spot she came to and jumped from the car, practically running for the emergency room door where the ambulance was backing up.

The back of the ambulance was pulled open and an EMT jumped out. He looked over at her and something in his eyes spoke volumes.

"No," she whispered. She brushed past him and looked inside the ambulance. Her father lay there, covered in a white sheet. "No."

"I'm sorry, miss. We did everything we could, but we just couldn't save him."

The emergency room doors swung open with a *whoosh* and a doctor hurried out, followed by two nurses. "What have we got?"

The EMT turned away from Dana. "DOA. Massive coronary. Fifty-nine-year-old male."

"What was his name?" one of the nurses asked, jotting down the information on a clipboard.

Dana looked over at the nurse as her heart began to break. "Leon."

The nurse looked up at her. "Full name?"

"Judge Leonard Allen Tappan the third."

Zoe kept reading as she reached over and picked up her mug of herbal tea. For the past hour, she'd been sitting in bed, pillows propped up behind her, reading Leona Oakley's diary. Slowly she sipped, never taking her eyes from the page.

It was like reading a good suspense novel. A woman, tired of living in poverty, meets a wealthy young lawyer from a prominent old family while working as a waitress at the local country club. She flirts, he responds, they have an affair. He gives her the standard line—that he loves her and is going to leave his wife (who happens to come from a wealthy political family) and marry her. She believes him. Then she finds out she's pregnant, and he demands that she get an abortion. She refuses. He stops seeing her. She gives birth to a beautiful daughter. He refuses to acknowledge the child. She gets herself hired as a waitress at a big political fund-raiser at his house and sneaks into his library, hoping to find something she can bargain with. She hits the jackpot with a diary in the bottom of his desk drawer. She demands money in exchange for the diary, and he agrees to pay her. She goes to meet him, without the diary, and is never seen again.

Zoe closed the diary, tapping the cover of the book with her fingers. What happened to Leona Oakley? Had she panicked at the last minute and left town? Had she met with Tappan? Had he been angry when she didn't show up with the diary? Had he threatened her? Withheld the money? Killed her?

The police should have been called. Why hadn't Leona's disappearance been reported? What had the grandmother been thinking?

Or what had she known?

Zoe sipped her tea, her mind racing. What happened to Leona Oakley?

ten

J J grimaced as he slowly lifted the bar above his head, sweat trickling down the side of his face as he fought to hold the weights.

"What have I told you about having a spotter, JJ?" Carl Fenlowe, the owner and manager of Weigh It Out, scowled at JJ.

"That I should always have one when working the weights."

"Do I see a spotter?" Carl ran a hand over his bald head, the tiny diamond stud in his right ear twinkling.

"You're here, aren't you?" JJ grinned at him as he dropped the weights into the rack.

"One of these days, JJ, I'm going to revoke your membership."

"Nah. You like me too much." JJ swung his feet to the floor, grabbing the towel and wiping the sweat from his face and neck. "Place is slow this morning."

"About usual. You just don't tend to be here in the morning. Working on a bad case?"

"Yeah."

"Must be those two women found stabbed." Carl leaned against one of the treadmills, keeping an eye on two men over at the punching bag. One man was steadying the bag for his friend.

"Hey!" he yelled over to them. "Stand back from that bag unless you want one of those jabs to end up on your face!"

He turned back to JJ. "Any theories yet on who is doing the killing?"

"We got a couple of people we're looking at, but no one is exactly jumping up and confessing." JJ looped the towel around his neck.

"You hear the morning news?"

JJ shook his head as he came to his feet and stepped onto the treadmill. "Nope."

"Judge Tappan died last night."

JJ glanced over at Carl. "Another one bites the dust."

"Yeah, well, I think a lot of people over at the prison are celebrating today."

JJ tossed his towel aside. "How did he die?"

"Heart attack is the unofficial cause of death."

Turning on the machine, JJ began to jog in place. "He was one nasty man. He didn't care who he decided to dislike—drug dealer, prostitute, cop. If he didn't like you, you were in trouble."

"He didn't like you, did he?"

JJ grinned. "Hated my guts. I arrested one of his buddies for drunk driving. He didn't take it well when I refused to drop it and make the arrest go away."

"You always were a political animal, Johnson. It's a wonder you're not a senator by now."

After forty-five minutes of hard workout, his legs were starting to feel the burn, his arms ached, and he was tired. But he laughed anyway. "I got my eye on the White House. None of that little Senate and Congress stuff for me. I'm going straight to Pennsylvania Avenue."

There was a sudden loud thump, then an even louder voice. "Ouch! What are you trying to do, kill me?"

Carl growled under his breath and stomped over toward the two men at the punching bag, one of whom was now sprawled on the floor, holding his nose, which was bleeding. "Didn't I warn you? I'm not cleaning up that blood, you got that!"

JJ shook his head, laughed, then turned his attention back to his running.

A few minutes later, Carl tapped JJ on the shoulder. "You got company."

Curious, JJ turned off the machine and turned around.

Zoe stood there, her long blond hair draping over one shoulder in a braid. He let his eyes drift down over her, taking in the blue silk shirt beneath a blue plaid shawl, the dark blue skirt that ended mid-calf over tan suede boots. She had every man in the place drooling.

"Miss Shefford. I'm not sure you're aware of this, but this place really doesn't cater to women."

"Cut the Miss Shefford routine, JJ. It's getting tiring. I really need to talk to you. It's important."

JJ lifted one eyebrow. "Are we calling a truce?"

"Call it anything you like. I need to talk to you."

There was something in her eyes that made him swallow the smart remark waiting on the tip of his tongue. He nodded. "There's a diner across the street. Go on over and get us a table. I'll get cleaned up and join you in about fifteen minutes."

Zoe nodded silently before turning and walking out. No. She floated out. The woman couldn't walk like other women; she had to drive him crazy by moving as if she walked on air.

Shaking his head at his own stupidity, he headed for the showers.

Zoe slipped into the booth and unwrapped her shawl, folding it next to her on the seat. Clasping her hands on the table, she looked around. Most of the tables were occupied with men and women on their way to work, stopping in for a quick breakfast, which in some instances was just coffee and a Danish. Four waitresses rushed between tables, booths, and the kitchen, making most of their stops at the coffee machine.

She was still second-guessing her decision to talk to JJ about the diaries, but after hearing about Judge Tappan's death when she woke up, she knew time was running out. Maybe it had already run out. Without Tappan, how could she ever find out what happened to Leona Oakley? He may have been the only person with the answers to Lanae's questions, and he was gone.

But JJ had his hands full with the death of two college girls. He didn't have the time to be concerned with one young woman's search for her long-lost mother. Still, he would understand justice.

JJ slid into the booth, his hair still damp and curling at the ends from his quick shower. "Did you order me coffee?"

"The waitress hasn't even stopped by here yet."

JJ lifted a hand, signaling a waitress. Within seconds, she was sidling up to the table. "What can I get ya?"

"Two coffees to start with. By the time you get those here, we'll be ready to order breakfast."

The woman nodded and hurried away.

Zoe leaned forward. "How do you know I haven't already eaten breakfast?"

JJ shrugged as he slid the silverware aside and reached for one of the menus tucked behind the condiments. "I hadn't thought about it, to be honest. I'm hungry. You want something?"

Zoe didn't know whether to laugh or be insulted. Since she was hoping to get his help, she decided just to laugh it off. She reached for a menu. "Then you're buying."

"I never doubted that for a moment," JJ replied with a wry twist to his lips.

Zoe slapped the menu down on the table. "You never ease up, do you? Just once, do you think you could manage to be pleasant? I know it might be a stretch to think you could actually act human, but maybe pleasant isn't out of the question."

"Just maintaining the image you have of me." JJ kept on perusing the menu.

Zoe reached up and snatched the menu out of his hands and tossed it down. "What did I do to you to make you hate me?"

"I don't hate you, Zoe. I'm just fed up with your arrogance."

"Arrogance? Me? You're the one with the attitude!"

JJ folded his arms on the table in front of him, his green eyes cool with pride and temper. "You've made it perfectly clear that I'm not good enough for you. That you don't think I'm smart enough. I'm just some ignorant cop."

Zoe clenched her teeth. If he'd been any closer, she'd have punched him. "I've never thought of you as stupid, you ignorant oaf!"

JJ raised one eyebrow. "Like I said."

"Stop it, JJ! You are deliberately twisting everything I say!"

"Doesn't take much twisting, Zoe. If you like me so much, why wouldn't you go out with me?"

"Because you were still hung up on Macy! You had this crazy idea that it was your fault that she died. Because you were always so busy running around trying to prove that you had some sense of self-worth when you were wonderful just the way you were!"

The waitress set two mugs of steaming coffee down in front of them. "Decided yet?"

JJ turned to look up at her, flashing a charming smile that had Zoe seething. "I'll have two eggs over easy, bacon, wheat toast, and hash browns well done."

The waitress nodded and turned to Zoe. "How about you?"

"I think I've lost my appetite."

JJ shook his head. "Bring her a strawberry waffle; hold the whipped cream."

The waitress nodded and hurried away.

"I don't recall ever telling you that I liked strawberry waffles."

JJ shrugged as he added cream and sugar to his coffee. "You'd be surprised what you can find out about someone without ever having them tell you a thing."

"I'm surprised you cared enough to remember anything about me." She wrapped her hands around the coffee mug, trying not to feel pleased.

"Yeah, well, don't take it too seriously. I tend to remember odd details about all sorts of things."

"Trust you to ruin any idea of being friendly."

JJ leaned back, stretching out his long legs. "Not me, Zoe. You. I distinctly remember every one of your little barbs. I'm nothing, just like my dad said. That I was ignorant, insufferable, with a misplaced-hero complex. Oh, and let's not forget that criminals are so much smarter than I am that they have me chasing any direction they want like. . .what was it you said? A puppy running after its momma's milk?"

"Oh, like you never got in a few of your own? What did you call me—decked-out demagogue of deceit?"

"Why did you come to see me this morning? To review every sharp thing we've ever said to each other and compare scores?"

"No. I needed to talk to you about a missing woman. To get some advice from you on how to handle this. Stupid of me, wasn't it?" She reached into her purse, pulled out a ten-dollar bill, and tossed it on the table. "Thanks, anyway."

As she stood up, JJ reached out and wrapped his fingers around her wrist. "Don't storm off. Sit down and eat your breakfast; tell me what you're talking about."

"I wouldn't want to bother you, Detective. I know how busy you are."

He tugged on her arm, exhaling with a bone-weary sigh. "Sit down, Zoe. I don't have the patience right now to argue with you."

She stared at him for a long moment, then slowly eased back down, sliding into the booth. "Why can't we have a civil conversation without going for each other's throats?"

She wasn't sure she actually expected an answer, but her thoughts had tripped out before she'd had a chance to stop them. JJ seemed to be thinking it over and on the verge of some kind of answer when the waitress returned with their food.

"Here ya go, folks. Can I get ya anything else?"

JJ shook his head, flashing her a quick smile. "We're fine, thanks."

Reaching for the salt and pepper, he glanced over at Zoe. "Why don't you tell me about this missing person?"

The rest of the meal went pleasantly enough. She told him about Lanae's diaries, and he told her how to go about looking up old records at the police station.

"I know it's not all that you were hoping for, but you're going to have to start at the beginning. Find out if anyone did file a missing person's report, find out if there were any Jane Does showing up at the morgue about that time."

Zoe blew out a heavy breath. "Sounds tedious."

"Most detective work is." He stacked his silverware on the empty plate and moved it aside. The waitress took that as her cue and returned with the coffeepot, refilling both mugs. Then she stacked the dishes and whisked them away.

"And Zoe?"

She lifted her head and looked across the table at him.

"Be very careful. Tappan just died, and no one is going to be too thrilled at someone coming in and defaming his character when he is no longer in a position to defend or explain himself."

"You don't believe these diary accounts?"

"I'm not saying that. I think Tappan was an overbearing, arrogant, and ruthless man, but I don't know for a fact that he ever cheated on his wife, much less fathered a child by some waitress. And I sure can't say whether or not he is capable of murdering a woman to keep her quiet about his affairs." JJ took a sip of his coffee. "And no one is going to be anxious to hear anything bad about the illustrious Judge Tappan right now."

"But, if Lanae is Judge Tappan's daughter, doesn't she have a right to a share of the estate?"

"Now you're opening a whole new can of worms. If I recall correctly, he has two grown children who will inherit. I doubt they're going to let a strange young woman waltz in and take a third of the estate without a fight. That means paternity tests, DNA, yada, yada. And that means holding up the distribution of the estate until this is settled one way or another." JJ glanced at his watch. "As much as I'm enjoying this, I have two murders to solve."

He picked up the check and slid out of the booth. "How about I call you later, and we'll see what you've found out?"

She couldn't help the little spark of pleasure that ran through her. "Sure. Later."

JJ's brow furrowed a bit as he dug for his wallet. He tossed a couple of bills down on the table, then headed for the register.

Zoe stared after him. "Yeah. Later," she whispered to herself. Then she whipped out her cell phone and the little slip of paper with Lanae's phone number. "Lanae? It's Zoe Shefford. I think what you need to do next is find an attorney and put a claim against the Tappan estate."

❖   ❖   ❖

9:35 a.m.

JJ tossed his leather jacket over the back of a chair as he eyed the stack of files on the conference table. Denise was stirring powdered creamer into her coffee, Chuck Barone was reading a computer printout, and Pat Chapman was sprawled back in his chair, his feet propped up on the conference table, eating a donut with one hand and holding a cup of coffee with the other.

"Where's Cole?"

Denise tossed the plastic stirrer into the trash can and pulled out a chair. "Coroner. Picking up the autopsy on DeAnne Foster."

JJ leaned back against his desk, crossing his feet at the ankles. "Okay, who wants to go first?"

Barone never looked up from the report he was reading. "I've checked both girls' school and work records. So far, no common denominator. One was an English major; the other was math. Blain was from a fairly well-to-do family; Foster was strictly blue-collar middle class. Her dad was a truck driver for Guaranteed. Foster worked her way through high school and college at a music store in the mall. Blain was working for an accountant. There's always the off chance the two girls met at the music store or passed each other on campus, but all indications are they didn't know each other. My guess is our un-sub targets the campus."

JJ turned to Chapman, who was brushing chocolate flakes off his chest. "Chapman?"

Chapman looked up at JJ. "No steady beau for Blain. She dates from time to time, but no one steady relationship. The guy she went to the prom with was a guy from her history class. They went out three times before the prom and twice after. The girl was obviously more interested in studying than dating. All the guys I did talk to said that she was friendly, fun to be with, but not interested in a long-term relationship. They were lucky to get a kiss good night."

JJ frowned as he rubbed his cheek. "According to the autopsy on Lori Blain, she was not a virgin, so there had to be a lover somewhere along the line."

Chapman shrugged. "So far, I haven't found anyone who will admit to it. Like I said, they all claimed to have gone no further than hand-holding or a kiss good night."

Denise looked from Chapman to JJ. "That doesn't fit. You know how guys are at that age. They would be more inclined to say they were getting it on with her, even if they weren't."

Chapman eyed the donut box in the center of the table. "Which tells me the girl wasn't making the rounds. If there is a guy, she kept it discreet."

"What about Foster?" JJ asked as Chapman honed in on a glazed donut and plucked it from the box.

Chapman set the donut down on a napkin in front of him and licked his fingers. "DeAnne had three boyfriends. First one was in tenth grade." He flipped open his notebook. "Johnny Kline. Puppy love. Then in her senior year, she started up with the center on the basketball team. Steven Taylor. Went to the prom with him. They broke up halfway through the summer when DeAnne found out he was also dating a girl he worked with at a local restaurant. Six months later, she started dating Lee Wheeling, a guy she met on campus. I talked to Lee, and he said that they're still dating, still in love, and he's devastated by DeAnne's death. According to Lee's roommate, that jives. He claims that Lee and DeAnne were inseparable, and there have been no fights or disagreements lately."

"Anything on family members?" JJ pushed off the desk and pulled out a chair at the conference table. He sat down, eyeing the donut box for himself. There was a cinnamon twist there with his name on it.

Denise looked surprised. "I thought we had a serial killer on our hands? Why would we be investigating the families?"

JJ hooked the donut box with his finger and dragged it closer, lifting the donut out. "Doesn't hurt to at least look. I know it's a long shot that these two murders are unrelated, but it's something we have to at least consider for the time being."

Denise and Chapman exchanged a look.

"I'll make it easy on you," JJ interjected into the silence. "It's yours, Chapman."

Chapman frowned but nodded.

Then JJ looked over at Denise. "What happened with Roddy?"

"The guy is guilty of something but wouldn't give me the time of day. He does have an alibi, and I checked it out. He was working at the time that Lori Blain was killed."

"What about Foster?"

"I didn't have a time of death on Foster, so I didn't ask, but he wouldn't have been working. He was nervous, shaky, and had his eyes everywhere but on me. The guy is definitely not comfortable around cops."

She angled her head and shrugged. "But he wasn't going to let me into that apartment, and he isn't going to cooperate without a search warrant. The kid knows his way around the legal system and plans to use everything he knows."

"Gut reaction?" JJ bit into the donut and nearly moaned in delight. It was ultra-fresh and melting in his mouth.

Denise frowned, staring down at her notes. "I don't know, JJ. He was definitely uneasy, and I think he was hiding something, but I can't say for sure he's our man."

JJ nodded. "Stay on him. If he had an alibi, he's not the same man who was seen with Blain at the bar. We're going to need some-one to check that out."

"Let Cole do it. He loves working nights."

JJ glanced over at Barone and laughed. "I'd think you'd jump at the chance, what with your wife being away."

Barone not only came from a large Italian family, he was rais-ing a large Italian family. He and his wife, Maria, had seven chil-dren. Their house was always busy, always noisy, and always loaded with laughter, bickering, and love. His wife's father had died, and Maria had taken all the children back to Brooklyn for the funeral.

Barone grinned. "Are you kidding? No one reaching for the remote, no one hogging the chips, no one complaining that I'm sleeping with the window open. I'm getting the best nights of sleep I've had in years."

"Is your mother-in-law going to be moving in with you?" Denise asked with a wicked grin.

Barone growled and muttered something in Italian. "Don't even raise the suggestion. I'm hoping that Maria's sister will offer first. She lives there in Brooklyn, so Momma Carmen can stay around her friends, her church, and her neighbors."

JJ reached for a napkin, wiping his fingers clean. "Do we have anything back from forensics?"

Denise leaned forward and started going through the stack of files in the center of the table. "I don't think we've gotten Foster back yet. Nothing new on Blain."

JJ stood up and walked over to the bulletin board where he had the main points of the investigation lined up for easy reading under the pictures of the two girls.

He turned around and glanced at each member of his task force. "We have a serial killer on the loose, and he's killed two women in less than a week. Let's find him before he kills again."

Zoe reached down and tied the laces on her white sneakers. If she was going to have to do a lot of walking today, she wasn't going to do it in those pumps she had on earlier when she went looking for JJ. Jeans, sweater, and sneakers. Much more comfortable.

She ran a brush through her hair quickly, then tied it back with a scrunchie. The curly blond strands nearly reached her waist. Everyone she knew had warned her that they would kill her if she ever cut it, but they weren't the ones who had to wash and condition it, much less dry and brush it.

The phone rang, and she walked over and sat down on the edge of her bed, picking up the receiver. "Hello?"

"I understand you didn't take my warning seriously. I told you to stay away and keep your nose out of things that don't concern you. This is your last warning. Next time, you'll meet with an unfortunate accident."

"What. . ."

The dial tone cut into her question. Slowly, she replaced the receiver. This has to be about Lori Blain's murder. No one could possibly know about Lanae and the diaries yet.

Unless. . .

Zoe dumped her purse on the bed, scrambled through the contents until she found the scrap of paper with a phone number on it, then picked up the phone and quickly dialed.

"Lanae? It's Zoe. You didn't tell anyone about the diaries, did you? Or that you had given them to me?"

"Zoe? Wow. Umm, no. Oh. Wait. I mentioned it to my friend, Annette, but that's it."

Zoe's foot started tapping. "Would she mention it to anyone? Is there any way this information would have traveled back to the

Tappan family so fast?"

"No way. Annette knows this is a big secret for now. She wouldn't tell anyone, and even if she did, she doesn't know anyone who moves in those circles. Why?"

"I just wanted to make sure we have the element of surprise, you know? Keep this all under your hat, kiddo."

"Okay. I can do that."

Zoe hung up the phone. Okay, so if this wasn't about the diaries, then it was definitely about the two murders. The killer must have seen her picture in the paper and figured she had been called in by the police. That's right. The first time he called was the same day that her picture was in the paper.

Shoving everything back into her purse, Zoe's mind raced. *Okay, Father. You got me into this, so You've got to protect me, guide me, then get me out in one piece.*

The doorbell rang, chiming through the house. Zoe abandoned her purse and went to the door. Daria came storming in like a soldier hell-bent to rescue a hostage. Her hair, usually so perfectly groomed to look casual punk, was lifeless and flat. Her eyes were red rimmed and swollen, and her hands were shaking.

"Since when do you ring the bell?" Zoe asked.

"Sorry. Not thinking. Here." Daria shoved a stuffed bear into Zoe's hands. "It's been on Dee's bed since she was a baby. She always sleeps with it."

Zoe stared at the bear with dawning horror. "I can't do that, Daria." She handed Daria the bear, but Daria refused to take it.

"Are you telling me you won't help us? You're my best friend! How long have we been friends, Zoe? Twenty years? Twenty-five? How dare you turn me down?"

Zoe took Daria's hand and pulled her over to the sofa. "Sit."

Daria balked.

"I said, sit." She gently pushed. Daria plopped down with a huff.

"Yes, Daria, we are best friends. Yes, I love you. You have been closer than a sister to me. I would do anything for you. But not this. And it's not fair to ask me. You know I won't go back to using psychic powers."

Daria glared up at Zoe, folding her arms across her chest with a childish pout. "If you were my friend, you would do this. It's important. That monster killed my DeAnne. Do you understand that?"

Zoe sat down next to her friend. "Oh, Daria. You know I understand. A monster killed my sister. How many years did you stand by me while I was trying to find her body?"

"Then how can you tell me no?"

"Because it's wrong, Daria. Nothing I do is going to bring DeAnne back."

Daria flew up off the sofa, stomping through the room, her arms flailing. "You think I don't know that! DeAnne is gone. I'll never see her or talk to her ever again. I won't see her graduate from college or get married or have a baby. That monster stole all that from me! I want him to pay!"

"And I want him to pay, not only for what he did to DeAnne, but also for causing you this pain. I love you. I hate seeing you in pain."

"Then do what you do. I've seen you do it a hundred times."

"Not to find a killer, Daria. To find a child who was missing. It's not the same thing at all." She honestly didn't know if it was or not, but she really didn't care. She had to find some way to calm Daria down and get her to back off from insisting that she try and revive her old psychic powers.

"You could try."

Zoe sighed heavily as she stared down at her hands. This was the hardest thing she'd ever done. And it hurt.

"No, Daria."

Daria snatched up the bear and stomped to the door. "Then we are no longer friends. Don't ever call me again."

"Daria, don't do this!" Zoe came to her feet in a rush of emotion, but the only response was the slamming of the door.

eleven

Wednesday, September 29—2:47 p.m.

Mel Jennings jumped when the phone rang. He took a deep breath and picked up the receiver. "Yes?"

It was the receptionist. "I'm sorry, Mr. Jennings, but Mr. Hornsworth called. He had to cancel his three o'clock with you. His wife just went into labor."

"Okay, thanks." He hung up the phone with a sigh of relief, then stood up and began pacing around his office. He needed to tell the police the truth about Lori but couldn't bring himself to admit the truth. Once told, it would never be a secret again, and everyone would know.

It wasn't everyone he was all that concerned about. It was his daughters and Lori's family that he wasn't ready to face. Russell Blain would want to kill him, and his Kieran would probably never look at him the same way again.

It was an accident, but would anyone believe him? Of course not. And he could swear from here till kingdom come that he hadn't meant for it to happen, that things just got carried away, but it wouldn't stop the landslide of trouble from tumbling down on top of him and ruining his life.

He had tried to be cool when those detectives had questioned him, but he could see in their eyes that they knew he was lying. They were probably digging into every aspect of his life. They'd question Kieran. Rachael. His sister.

Sweat began to bead on his forehead as nervous fear eased through him. How could this have happened to him?

❖　❖　❖

Dan twirled his gold pen through his fingers as he read over the autopsy reports. Kyle was sprawled in the chair across the desk from him, sipping on iced tea. Motown played softly on the radio sitting on the file cabinet.

Finally Dan leaned back. "Well, nothing we didn't already know. No surprises. And no clues. What about forensics?"

Kyle gave him a pointed look. "The police don't even have all the forensic reports back yet, so how did you expect me to get them?"

"It was worth asking." Dan tapped his pen on the blotter. "What about this guy at the bar?"

"Yeah. The bartender's name is Bobby, and he was a fountain of information. The guy that was with Lori Blain usually comes in on Thursday nights, but I thought I'd drop in there tonight anyway and see if he happens to come in. What about the Foster girl?"

Dan shook his head. "I haven't been able to find anyone who saw her after she left class at three-thirty. I'm still trying to get in touch with some of her neighbors in hopes that someone saw her come in or go out. And I've got calls out to three of her girlfriends. Maybe one of them knew something or was with her."

"Has Zoe checked in yet?"

"Not yet. I'm sure she'll call when she has something to report."

Kyle slapped the arms of the chair and stood up. "Well, I'm

going to go change into something that looks more like I'm out to impress a woman and less like I'm a Fed about to arrest someone and head for the Time Out."

"Let's hope our guy decides to drop in tonight."

❖ ❖ ❖

Zoe sat down on the steps outside Lori Blain's apartment and buried her face in her hands. She had been running all day, talking to classmates, friends, neighbors, and she had nothing. Zip. Nada. She was no closer to finding Lori's killer than she had been the day she found Lori's body.

"Oh, Father. I have no idea what to do. I've done everything I know to do, and I'm getting nowhere. Help me, please!"

Tears welled and spilled over, running down her cheeks. She swiped at them, frustrated with herself. "This shouldn't be so hard! Father, please help me. Tell me what to do!"

You have all that you need. It's in the book.

Zoe felt a small tremor of adrenaline run though her. "What book, Lord? The Bible? It would take me weeks to go through that book for clues. You can't mean that book, so what book are you referring to?"

The diaries came to mind, but she discounted those as well. They were diaries, not books, and she was asking about Lori Blain, not Lanae Oakley.

"What book, Lord?"

She lifted her head and stared down the street. The sun was low in the sky. It would be getting dark soon. Frustrated, she rose to her feet and headed for her car. She was going to have to call Dan and tell him she didn't have a single thing to contribute.

Other than a death threat, that is.

7:54 p.m.

Kyle was on his third club soda and starting to believe he was wasting his time. He glanced at his watch. Almost eight.

Bobby came up, his towel flung over his shoulder. "You okay?"

"Another one and I'll be able to float out of here."

"How about some coffee?"

Kyle thought about it for a minute. "You know, that sounds good. Cream, no sugar."

Bobby smiled and gave a quick nod. "Comin' right up."

Kyle spun around on his bar stool and watched the dance floor. Girls in tight jeans or tight skirts with men that were draped all over them. Men that more than likely wouldn't remember the girl's name tomorrow. He couldn't help feeling a little sorry for them. They had no idea that they were desperately trying to find something and going about it in the worst possible way. What man truly wanted to marry a woman, the future mother of his children, knowing that she went home with a different man every weekend?

Bobby came back with his coffee, and Kyle turned around. "Thanks."

"He's here," Bobby said softly. "At the far end of the bar in the black jacket."

Kyle picked up his coffee cup, his eyes cruising down the bar until he spotted the man in question. Kyle smiled, pulling a couple of bills out of his pocket and sliding them across the bar. "Thanks, Bobby. You're a gem."

"Glad to help. Having girls abducted from this establishment is bad for business."

Bobby wandered off to take care of other customers. Kyle

picked up his coffee and moved down the bar to sit down next to the man he'd been waiting for.

The man didn't look too thrilled when Kyle slid in next to him. "I was saving that seat," he said with a strong trace of sarcasm.

"Really? Saving it for whom?" Kyle took a sip of his coffee and eyed the man's car keys. Sure enough, there was a Porsche key chain.

"Look, I asked you nicely."

"No, you didn't. You merely mentioned that you were saving the seat." Kyle reached into his pocket, pulled out his ID, and flashed it. "We need to talk."

Immediately, the man slid off the bar stool and reached for his car keys. Kyle snatched them up and shook his head. "Now, that's not nice. I need to ask you some questions, and you need to answer them. Be a good boy, and you'll be cruising this joint and lying to women in no time. Give me a hard time, and I'll call Detective Johnson, who is also looking for you, by the way, and he'll slap on the handcuffs first and ask questions later."

The man sank back down, but the belligerent look on his face never faded. "I have no idea what you want to question me about."

Kyle pulled out his notebook and clicked his pen. "Let's start with your name."

"Leland. Bret Leland."

"Address?"

"None of your business."

"You know, I really despise someone giving me a hard time." He looked over at the bartender. "Bobby. This guy doesn't look twenty-one, does he?"

Bobby sauntered over, staring hard at Bret Leland. "Come to think of it, nah. I need to see your ID. Gotta card you."

Leland looked like he was going to explode as he glared at Kyle, but he pulled out his wallet and tossed his driver's license down. "I drink here all the time. You know I'm not underage!"

Kyle wrote down the address on the ID, then slid it back to Leland. "Thanks for being so cooperative."

Bobby was called away to another customer. Kyle pulled out a picture of Lori Blain and slapped it down on the bar. "Have you ever seen this woman before?"

Bret slowly moved his eyes from Kyle's face to the picture, then back again as he put his license away and slid his wallet back in his pocket. "No. Why?"

"Try again."

"Maybe."

Kyle stared hard at Bret. "Could we be a bit more definite here?"

"Yeah. I think so."

"When?"

"Last week."

"Where?"

"Here. Would you tell me what this is about?"

Kyle ignored Bret's question. "So, tell me how the evening went. You said. She said. You did. She did. You left. She left. Give me the details."

Bret's eyes shifted to his drink. He turned around on the barstool, facing the bar, and picked up his drink. "I have no idea. I meet women all the time."

"Try again, Mr. Leland. I'm not playing with you, and the police won't, either. I suggest you jog your memory and tell me what I need to know."

"What is this about? If she's accusing me of something, she's lying."

"She came into this bar. You met her. What happened?"

"Nothing."

"Be a little more specific."

"She came in last week. I don't remember what time. We had a few dances and a few drinks. I think her name was Lisa or Lara or Lori. Something like that. Anyway, she said she was a student at Monroe." He took a gulp of his drink as if needing the fortification. "We seemed to hit it off, then all of a sudden, she says she has to leave. I asked for her number, and she gave it to me and then left. That's it."

The fact that Bret wouldn't look him in the eye bothered Kyle. "What time did she leave?"

Bret shrugged. "I don't remember. Wasn't all that late. Ten. . . maybe eleven. Look, what's this about?"

"Okay, she left and then what?"

Bret shrugged again. "Then I met a cute little brunette, and we played some pool, danced a little."

Kyle finished jotting down his notes. "Does this little brunette have a name?"

"Monica."

Kyle looked up. "Just Monica? The girl doesn't have a last name?"

Kyle rolled his shoulders. "Look, man, you know how it is. You pick them up, spend some time, drop them off. I'm not looking to marry any of them, you know? It's just about having a good time for the night."

"You tell these girls that? You know. 'Gee, babe, come home with me, we'll hit the hay, and then I'll forget you tomorrow, whatcha say?' That sort of come-on wouldn't go over well, I guess."

"Don't bust my chops, man. It's the way it is."

"Right." Kyle wrote a few more things down. "So what time did you leave the bar that night?"

"I don't know. One, maybe."

"With Monica."

"Yes."

"Where did you go?"

"Her place."

Kyle looked up again. "Do you happen to remember where she lives?"

"No." Bret took another sip of his drink.

"Did you ever call Lori?"

"Who?"

Kyle tapped the picture. "Lori. Lori Blain. Did you ever call her? You said she gave you her number."

Kyle shook his head with a leering grin. "Nah. Didn't get the impression she was looking for quick and easy, if you know what I mean. But I may call her if things get slow."

Kyle wanted to shake Bret's teeth until they rattled. "You ever read the papers, Mr. Leland?"

Bret lifted his glass, stared at the contents, then looked over at Kyle. "Not very often."

"Too bad. If you'd bothered to read the papers, you'd know that Lori Blain walked out of this bar last Thursday night, headed for her car, and never made it. She was found murdered, her body dumped like garbage. I don't think she'll be taking your calls."

Kyle was pleased that he'd put a look of total panic on Bret's face. He closed his notebook and shoved it in his pocket as he stood up. "You were the last person to see Lori Blain alive, Mr. Leland. The police are looking for you. They'd like to talk to you. It might behoove you to contact Detective Johnson."

Bret's face had completely drained of color, and his hands were shaking as they held his drink. "I didn't hurt that girl. She walked out that door, and I stayed here. I didn't kill her."

"You were the last person to see her alive, Mr. Leland. You're going to have to do better."

Leland suddenly seemed to find his backbone and turned belligerent. "You can't prove anything. If you could, the police would have arrested me already. You got nothing. Now leave me alone."

"You know, it's a shame that being a total jerk isn't against the law." He tossed his business card down on the bar. "If you think of anything else, call me. And do yourself a favor. Call the police before they have to track you down. They aren't nearly as nice as I am."

❖   ❖   ❖

Dana stood in her father's closet, deciding, rejecting. Grieving. Should she choose the navy blue pinstripe, the black, the gray? White shirt? Blue tie? Red tie? Her aunt had offered to do this, but Dana had politely turned her down. It was her father; she would make the funeral arrangements, choose his suit, order the flowers, contact friends and colleagues, and take care of the thousand little details that came with a life ending.

"Why don't you let someone help you?" Marcus leaned on the doorframe, folding his arms across his chest. "You don't have to do this all alone, you know."

"It's our responsibility, Marcus."

"Is that a reprimand, dear sister?"

Dana lifted the gray suit from the bar, walked past him into the bedroom, and laid it across the bed. "You've been drinking again, haven't you?"

Marcus shot her a cold glance as his mouth twisted in a crooked smile. "We all grieve in our own way, Dana. Don't judge me."

Guilt pricked her gently. She had always been the strong one, the smart one, the ambitious one. Marcus, sensitive and quiet, had been the creative one, which did nothing to earn their father's respect. Oh, their father had loved Marcus, but he had never understood his son. Marcus had tried so hard, always looking to do something that would make their father proud of him and never quite succeeding.

It was Dana who had been the clear and undisputed favorite. She was the one who always got good grades and went on to college, majoring in law and walking in her father's footsteps. Marcus had barely made it through high school, went to three different colleges, never graduated, and changed majors so often, she never could keep up with them.

In the end, it hadn't really mattered. Marcus lived at home, took over their mother's potting shed, and converted it to a studio. He'd tried writing the great American novel but gave up after ten months and thirty pages. Then he decided he was supposed to be writing music but gave up on that in a record four months. After his brief flirtation with music, he moved over to painting. This new passion had lasted the better part of a year and a half. Fortunately for him, the family was wealthy enough to support his search for talent along with his lack of ambition.

"I'm sorry, Marcus. I know you loved him. I know this is as hard on you as it is on me."

"You have no idea," Marcus replied caustically. Then he shook his head and sank down on the bed. "I'm sorry, Dana. I just can't believe he's gone. I didn't know he was sick."

"None of us did."

"What are we going to do now?"

"Do?" Dana perched on the edge of the bed. "I don't know. Get through the funeral. Lewis says we'll do the reading of the will on Saturday. I'm sure Dad left everything in perfect order."

"I'm sure he left everything to you. Let's face it. If you wanted it, they bought it for you before you could finish asking for it. If I asked for something, I got a dirty look and a lecture on the value of money."

"Don't, Marcus."

"You won't throw me out, will you?"

The question stunned her. At first, she wasn't sure if he was serious or not, but when she looked into his eyes, she realized he truly questioned whether or not he would still have a home on Sunday. She reached out and grabbed his hand. "Oh, Marcus. This will always be your home. You have to know that."

He squeezed her hand. "I guess I do. I'm just—" He blew out a heavy sigh, rank with alcohol.

"We'll be fine, Marcus. It'll be okay. We'll miss him, just the way we missed Mom when she died, but we'll go on and it'll be okay."

"What do we know about running his affairs? There are business interests and trust funds and stocks and bonds and stock portfolios."

Dana smiled. "It'll be fine. There are lawyers and financial advisors and accountants. We won't have to handle all this alone."

A tear ran down her brother's cheek. "I miss him, Dana. He could be so cold sometimes, but I loved him. I don't even remember the last time I told him that."

"He knew, Marcus. And he loved you, too."

"You should move back here, Dana. The house shouldn't sit empty."

Dana stood up and headed back for the closet. "You live here. It won't be empty."

"I live in the guest house out back. I don't want the house."

Dana returned with a white shirt and two-tone gray striped tie. "I'll think about it, but right now, it's just too soon for me to think that far ahead. I just need to concentrate on getting through the funeral."

"I'm sorry, Dana. I haven't been much help to you, have I?"

He looked so sad that her heart broke for him. Even though he was twenty-three and she was twenty-one, she'd always felt as if she were the older sibling and he the younger.

He'd be lost without her.

"I'm okay, Marc. Honest."

"You always are, Dana." He bounced up off the bed and gave her a quick hug. "I need a drink."

"Marcus! No! You've had enough today. Please."

He gave her a look she couldn't interpret. "I haven't had nearly enough."

twelve

Thursday, September 30—12:06 p.m.

Y ou want something from the deli?" Denise picked up her coat while she waited for JJ's answer.

"Yeah." He leaned back in his chair and stretched out his legs, trying to work out some of the kinks from sitting too long. "Get me ham and Swiss. You know how I like it."

"On rye with mustard, pickles, and chips." She hooked her purse strap over her shoulder. "And iced tea."

"Either get me an extra large one, or make it two of them. I am so tired of coffee, I can't see straight."

"I'll take care of you."

Denise disappeared through the door. JJ stood up and walked over to the file cabinet, where he searched through the stack of files to find the one he wanted.

He'd no sooner found it than Marsha stuck her head in the door. "JJ? DeAnne Foster's parents are here."

JJ closed his eyes briefly as he took a deep breath and geared himself mentally for the second victim's family.

"Send them in."

He'd only spoken to them once, so far, and that was late

Tuesday afternoon. They were the kind of people you couldn't help liking. Frank Foster was a big man, easily standing six-foot-five in his socks, while his wife was a petite five-two. He was a truck driver. She was a teacher at a local middle school. Frank was on a bowling league. Noreen volunteered at the hospital pediatric ward. Both were kind, decent, hard-working people who had been completely devastated at the loss of their firstborn child.

The door opened again, and the Fosters slowly walked in. Frank had one arm draped over his wife's shoulders as if holding her up. "We're sorry to bother you."

JJ waved to a couple of chairs at the conference table. "No, please don't apologize. Have a seat. Can I get you something? Coffee? Soda?"

Both the Fosters shook their heads and sat down gingerly, as if they weren't sure the chairs would hold them.

JJ pulled out a chair across from them and sat down. He smiled at Noreen. "You know I know your sister, Daria? It's not hard to see that you're sisters. You look a lot alike."

Noreen's lip barely curled in a ghost of a smile. "We took after our mother."

"I can't tell you how sorry I am about DeAnne. I know this is extremely difficult for you."

Noreen merely nodded as she dabbed at her eyes with a balled-up tissue that looked like it desperately needed to be replaced.

"What can I help you with?"

Frank Foster leaned forward, his hands clasped on the table in front of him, his eyes glistening with unshed tears. His wife placed her hand gently on top of her husband's. They linked fingers. "We were hoping. . .is there any news at all? I mean. . .we can't even plan—"

His voice cracked, and he bowed his head.

Tears began to streak down his wife's face, but she kept her head high as she spoke. "We need to think about a funeral. There are relatives to contact. Our pastor asked what funeral home. We don't even know when. . ."

"I'm sorry, Mrs. Foster. They're still collecting evidence, but we should be able to release the. . .release DeAnne to you within another day or two."

Frank Foster hitched a harsh breath, as if sucking in all the pain and burying it as deep as he could. "Have you found the animal that did this to her?"

JJ shook his head. "Not yet. We've been able to track her activities up until around nine that night. After that—" He shrugged. "We just don't know. If there's anything that you can think of to help us. . ."

"We've told you all we know," Frank said softly. "She said she was going shopping and would be home by nine. She had to study. She had classes in the morning. But she never came home."

Noreen Foster reached for a tissue and dabbed her eyes. "Have you found her car?"

JJ shook his head. "Not yet, but we are looking for it. We'll find it."

"Detective," Frank Foster interjected softly, "I know how busy you are, and I know that our DeAnne wasn't this animal's only victim, but please. . ." He leaned forward, the intensity of his emotion hitting JJ like a douse of cold water. ". . .Find him before I do."

❖　　❖　　❖

Zoe turned on the tap, filled the glass with water, then tossed three aspirins in her mouth and washed them down. She turned off the tap, clutched the edge of the sink, and lowered her head, willing the nagging headache and the frustration away.

She hadn't expected this kind of struggle. It had always been relatively easy. The police would call and she'd go running. She would meet with the parents or the detectives or the FBI. They would give her something that belonged to the child—a coat, a toy, a shoe, a shirt, a favorite blanket. Most of the time, the information would start coming the minute she reached for it.

Now, she'd been on the case for four days and didn't have a single thing. Nothing.

It was time to admit that she'd blown it. She had misunderstood the Lord. She wasn't supposed to be working on the murder case at all. Or Lanae's case, since she wasn't getting anywhere with that, either.

Maybe she was supposed to be working at her mother's boutique, just the way JJ had said. Pushing off from the sink, she marched into the living room.

What had she expected, anyway? She wasn't a psychic anymore. She'd renounced all that when she became a Christian. She should have understood that renouncing one part of it was renouncing all of it. No more finding missing persons. No more delving into crimes and helping solve them. No more police investigations, forensics, and crime scenes.

But everything in her wanted to help. She wanted to give Daria the answers and the closure she needed. It was breaking her heart to know that her best friend was hurting and she wasn't doing a thing to help.

Sinking down on the sofa, she picked up Lanae's mother's diary and let it fall open. What happened to Leona? Did she meet with Leonard Tappan that night? If she went to meet him, why didn't she take the diary with her? Why leave it behind? Or did she decide at the last minute not to meet him? And if she didn't meet him, then where was she?

She'd checked and found that there had been no activity on Leona Oakley's social security number, so she hadn't relocated somewhere else and gotten a job. She could have relocated and changed her name, but she would have had to change her social security number, and that's not as easily done as it sounds.

Okay, it was possible, though. There were people who dealt in that kind of business. For a fee, Leona could have a whole new identity, complete with social security, driver's license, and credit cards. But supposedly, Leona didn't have that kind of money. Which is why she wanted money from Tappan.

Could it be that she got the money from Tappan, left town, and assumed a new identity? Maybe. But why? Why leave her mother and child behind? Why disappear completely? Unless she was afraid of Tappan, but if she was, she would have been afraid to blackmail him in the first place.

Nothing added up, and the endless circle of questions was getting Zoe nowhere.

You have all you need. It's in the book.

The words kept echoing in her mind. *It's in the book.* But what book? She'd read both diaries twice. She knew the story, the players, and the plot. Two brothers stand to inherit a fortune, but one brother isn't into sharing, so he arranges for his brother to have a little accident, and voila! He inherits everything.

But it wasn't Lanae's case she was worried about. It was Lori Blain. And DeAnne Foster. To find their killer before he struck again was imperative.

So what was this cryptic message about a book?

Lord, You know I'm only human. I can't understand what it is You're trying to tell me. Forgive me, but I just don't get it. You're going to have to make this a whole lot clearer for me.

Suddenly she glanced up at the clock. She'd completely lost track of time. She was supposed to meet Rene in fifteen minutes. It would take her at least twenty to get to the diner. She tossed the diaries into her purse, grabbed her keys, and hurried out the door.

❖   ❖   ❖

It actually took her twenty-five minutes but only because they were tearing up Crum Drive due to a water main break, and she had to detour out of her way and back again.

Rene was sitting in a booth, chatting with their waitress when Zoe shrugged out of her jacket and slid into her seat.

"Sorry I'm late."

Rene merely smiled. "Not a problem. The Lord always knows." She looked up at the waitress and winked. "Two iced teas, Alice. Thanks."

The waitress nodded and hurried away.

Zoe looked from the waitress to Rene. "What did I miss?"

"Alice is having some problems and needed some ministry. Your being late just gave us the opportunity to talk a bit."

Zoe unrolled her silverware and placed her napkin in her lap. "You never miss an opportunity to share the love of God, do you?"

"My dear, there are so many hurting people, it's hard not to find opportunities. Most of the time, however, we stay so self-absorbed, we miss them." Rene folded her hands on the table. "How is it going with your case?"

"Cases," Zoe corrected and held up two fingers. "I now have two cases, and neither is going anywhere at all."

"Well, when you do something, you do it right, I'll say that for you." Rene leaned back as Alice returned with their drinks.

After ordering their sandwiches, the waitress hurried off, and

Rene jumped right back into the conversation. "Okay, I know you are looking into the murder of that poor college girl, so what's the other one?"

Zoe added a sugar to her iced tea and stirred as she explained about Lanae Oakley and the two diaries. "I have two women from the college and one woman from over twenty years ago that might or might not be dead, and I haven't a clue where to start."

"The Tappan family is a pretty big deal around here, Zoe. They own two of the mills and heaven knows how much property, not to mention their political connections."

"Don't I know it." Zoe went to sip her tea when a cold shiver when up her back, settling at the base of her neck. Her hand began to shake. She set her glass down quickly before she dropped it.

"Zoe?" Rene leaned forward, concerned.

She didn't know what she felt, but it was strong. There were no words to describe it, which was fine, because she couldn't find her voice anyway. Everything inside her was humming, vibrating.

Rene grabbed her hand. "Zoe, don't be afraid."

Zoe shook her head. She wasn't afraid. It didn't feel *bad* exactly. Just different.

Suddenly Rene's eyes went wide, glancing over Zoe's shoulder. Curious, Zoe slowly turned her head, knowing that whatever she was feeling was connected to what she would see.

But all she saw were people. Businessmen hunkered over cell phones, businesswomen with laptops next to their salads, mothers and children and couples and waitresses and waiters.

Confused, she looked back at Rene.

"The couple that just walked in. It's Judge Tappan's children. I can't remember their names, but I've seen their pictures enough to know that it's them. The young couple at the table in the corner, both dressed in black."

Zoe looked around, zeroing in on the young man, then the young woman. And she felt it again, staring at the girl.

Whipping around, she looked at Rene. "That girl. I felt it. Rene, that girl."

Rene grabbed Zoe's hand. "Calm down. Take a deep breath and explain."

Zoe inhaled and slowly let it out. "The guy that's killing the girls at the college?"

"Yeah?"

"He's targeting that girl."

"What girl?"

"Tappan's daughter. He's already decided that he's going to kill her."

Lanae's knees were like Jell-O as she sank down in the chair, clasping her hands in her lap. "I want. . .I want to thank you for seeing me."

Wes Branson sat stiffly in his chair behind an immaculate desk, a gold pen in his hand, his glasses perched on the end of his nose. "Well, I must admit, your call intrigued me. So, you believe that Judge Tappan was your father."

"I know he was. It's all in my mother's diary."

His lips quirked in a smile of pure indulgence but remained friendly. "Just because it was written in your mother's diary doesn't make it fact, and the courts aren't going to take that diary as fact. There will have to be paternity tests. Worse, Judge Tappan is now deceased, so your timing is going to be suspect."

"I just found out myself," she insisted.

"I understand." He set the pen down and steepled his fingers. "But I need you to understand what you are in for. The judge was a powerful man. There are people who will want to keep his reputation spotless. You come out with these allegations, and they will try to bury you in the press and turn public opinion against you."

"I can handle it." Lanae leaned forward a little. "Are you going to help me? Will you take my case?"

"The first thing I'm going to suggest is filing a lien against the estate for back child support."

Confused, Lanae tipped her head and stared at him. "Child support?"

"It's just to start the ball rolling. First, we have to establish you as the judge's daughter. Once that is done, then we can go for your share of the estate."

"It's not about the money, Mr. Branson. I just want to prove that he was my father. And I want to find out what he did to my mother."

"One thing at a time, my dear. One thing at a time." He picked up the phone and called in one of his paralegals. After hanging up, he leaned back. "First, let's rattle the tree and see what falls out."

❖   ❖   ❖

Dan Cordette glanced at his watch again as he parked in front of the police department and climbed out of his car. The last time he'd been here, Detective Johnson hadn't been particularly hospitable. He doubted it was going to be any better today.

Upstairs, he knocked on the conference room door and, when he heard JJ call out, went in, dreading what he was about to face but knowing he had to do it.

JJ nodded toward a chair as he closed a file on his desk. "Have a seat. What can I do for you?"

"I just wanted to share some information."

JJ leaned back, hands resting on the arms of the chair, his manner cool and remote. "What kind of information?"

Dan tossed a file folder down on the desk. "We found your mystery man at the Time Out. His name is Bret Leland. I ran a background check on him. He's a player, but there's no record of violence. His address is current. He works as a regional sales rep for a local bakery."

JJ opened the file and read it over. "He knows he's a suspect now."

"Yes. Not much I could do about that, but the good news is, he hasn't gone into hiding."

"Let's hope I don't have to hunt too hard for him."

Dan recognized the reprimand, but it was far less harsh than he'd been expecting. Detective Johnson had been pretty upset on Tuesday when he came down to bail Zoe out, so he had been fully expecting the same treatment today. Other than being a little cool, Johnson wasn't being too difficult.

JJ turned a page. "He swears Blain left alone and he stayed at the bar."

"We've been trying to verify his alibi, but so far, no luck."

"Somehow that doesn't surprise me. Do you honestly believe that this mystery woman exists?"

Dan smiled at the term *mystery woman*. He'd referred to her the same way about three times in an earlier conversation with Kyle. "Monica. No last name. No known address. Sounds hokey to me, too, but he doesn't seem to be too upset by any of this, either."

JJ closed the file and set it to the side. "I appreciate you sharing this with us, but I guess it wouldn't do me any good to ask you to stay out of my investigation?"

"None whatsoever." Dan slapped the arms of his chair and rose to his feet. "But I won't hold it against you for asking."

JJ stood. "Dan? Can I ask you a question?"

"Yes. And no, I'm not."

"Yes and no. . .what?"

Amused, Dan opened the door with a grin. "Yes, you can ask, and no, I'm not dating Zoe. But, I haven't given up trying."

He walked out of the office and pulled the door closed before JJ could answer. Still grinning to himself, he checked his watch and jogged down to the lobby of the building.

thirteen

J J reached out and rang the doorbell. Hearing the faint chimes echo inside, he shoved his hands into the pockets of his jacket as he waited. A moment later, she opened the door, nearly taking his breath away. Her hair was loose around her shoulders, tumbling in waves and curls that had no pattern, just beauty. She was wearing a dark green velvet jogging suit, or at least he assumed that's what it was. Could have been some fancy lounging outfit, for all he knew. Women's fashions were never his strong suit. He just knew she looked wonderful.

It took him a few seconds to realize that he had to find his voice in the midst of his scattered emotions. Taking a deep breath and trying to keep his tone level, he finally said, "You called?"

Zoe stepped back and opened the door wider. "Come on in. I appreciate you coming."

"Must be really important for you to actually invite me over."

"It is."

He heard her close the door as he sauntered into her living room. It looked nothing like the room she'd had before the fire. Something else Matthews had stolen from her.

Unzipping his leather coat, he slid it off and took a chair next to the sofa. "So what's this all about?"

"I know who the next victim is going to be."

Her words slammed into him, nearly taking his breath away again, only this time in a bad way. "Explain."

Zoe sat down on the sofa, leaning forward, her hands clasped between her knees, a frantic light awash in her eyes. He'd seen that light before and knew all too well exactly what it meant. Zoe was on a mission. She had the scent of the killer, and she would be going after him with a vengeance. This stubborn, headstrong woman would be determined. Well, if she was going to go after this killer, regardless of what he said, then he was just going to have to find another way of protecting her.

"I was having lunch with a friend, and this young couple came in. I didn't see them at first, I just felt it. It was so strong, JJ. I've never had anything quite like this happen, but when I turned to look at them, I saw the girl and I knew. I just knew that the killer had targeted her."

"And who is this girl?"

"Her name is Dana Tappan."

"Tappan? As in Judge Tappan's daughter?"

"Yes." Zoe's face sobered quickly. "She was there with her brother. I guess they had just come from the funeral home or something, because they were dressed all in black. JJ. We have to warn her. She needs to know that the killer has his eye on her."

JJ leaned back in his chair, folding his arms across his chest. "Do you have any idea of how much security will be at that funeral? We're talking about a judge, Zoe. The killer would be a fool to try and target her."

"Fool or not, he has, and he wants her dead." Her hands fluttered. "I could feel that so strongly. It was overpowering."

"Coffee?"

The sudden change in subject threw Zoe off, which is exactly why he did it. He needed time to think. "Do you have any coffee?"

Zoe slowly rose to her feet, confusion shadowing her face. "Sure. I'll be right back."

JJ watched her head for the kitchen. He'd love to rip her theory to shreds, but he knew that Dana Tappan was a law student at the college. Heaven knows, there had been enough publicity about it in the papers. Young woman following in her father's footsteps and all that. The fact that the judge had died suddenly might mean a slight delay in the killer's plans, but if he was targeting Miss Tappan, he'd wait and strike later, after the funeral.

The funeral was Friday. That didn't give them much time to find him.

Zoe stepped into the doorway between the kitchen and the living room, leaned against the doorframe, and folded her arms across her chest. The steely look she gave him let him know that she wouldn't be dismissed. "Coffee's brewing."

"What else have you picked up, Zoe? Besides the Tappan girl being a target?"

Zoe shook her head. "Nothing concrete. I still don't have a firm grip on any of this. It's all shadows and shifting thoughts. He's illusive. And very crafty. I get the sense of a chameleon, changing his looks, attitude, and behavior as it suits him. He may look completely different each time he kills, disguises that would keep eyewitness accounts from being worth much."

"Not that we have any witnesses."

"Exactly. But he's not taking any chances. He knows you're coming after him. He knew that before he started, but the need to do this was greater than his fear of you."

"He needs to kill?"

Zoe nodded, pushing off from the doorway, moving slowly into the room. "The need is obscure. I can't get any real sense of it, only that I know it exists."

"He's insane."

She shook her head as she perched on the arm of the sofa and crossed her legs. "I don't think so. Not in the way you mean."

"Why this girl? Why any of these girls? What made them targets?"

She stared at him for a long moment, but he had the oddest sense that she wasn't seeing him at all. Her voice, when she finally spoke, seemed distant and focused somewhere else. "They simply were the means to an end. They did nothing specific except catch his eye. They serve a purpose and help to deceive."

JJ leaned forward, elbows on his knees as he watched her. "What purpose?"

"To get what he wants, and he wants it very badly. It gnaws at him day and night, stirring up his anger, his rage. He can barely think for it anymore. Each kill brings him closer to peace."

JJ's head fell forward, and his fingers combed through his hair. "How many girls will die before we catch this guy?"

"I don't know. The Tappan girl is not the only one he's got his eye on."

JJ's head shot up. "That's two more."

Zoe nodded soberly. "At least. There could be more. I just don't know."

"How do you know this, Zoe?"

She blinked and her eyes bore into his. "My sheep know My voice." A smile broke across her face so bright it nearly blinded him. "God told me."

Kieran Jennings turned the ignition off and flinched as the radio and heater went as silent as the car engine. There was no reason to feel nervous. It was just a local hangout. There were tons of students in there, and she probably knew some of them by face if not by name. So why were her hands shaking?

Because she wasn't used to getting out. It was guilt, that's what it was. Usually, on a night like this, she'd be home doing laundry, paying bills, picking up after her father, doing something for someone else and nothing for herself.

Why did she feel as if she was walking into danger?

Okay, so two of her friends had been murdered, and the killer might still be in the area. But she was going to be careful. She wasn't going to let her guard down. She wouldn't let any strange man walk her to her car or get her alone. As long as she stayed in a crowd, she'd be fine.

Tonight was her night. Tonight, she was going to dance and laugh and flirt and have fun. Tonight, she wasn't going to think about the house or her sister or her father or a killer on the loose.

Taking a deep, fortifying breath, she climbed out of the car and locked it. Squaring her shoulders, she made her way across the parking lot and into the club.

The pulsating music immediately assaulted her ears. She wove through the press of the crowd and made her way to the bar.

A young man turned on his barstool and looked at her with cool blue eyes. Then he slowly smiled. "Hey, doll. Can I buy you a drink?"

"This is crazy." Denise McClellan turned down the radio and glanced over quickly at Zoe as she stared out the window. "You realize that we have no idea where to start looking."

"I'll know it when I see it."

They had been driving around for the better part of an hour, trying to find some trace of the killer. JJ had called Denise and asked for a favor. Foolishly she'd jumped to say yes before she even asked what the favor was.

Naturally she'd kept the smile plastered to her face when she arrived at Zoe Shefford's to find out she would be playing escort to the woman.

JJ owed her big-time! And she intended to collect.

She pulled up to an intersection, trying to decide which way to go. There were four bars down to the left and a nightclub and two taverns up on the right. Her fingers drummed on the steering wheel while she waited for the light to change.

"Go right," Zoe interjected quietly.

Checking the traffic behind her, Denise turned and eased over into the right lane. When the light changed, she turned, driving slowly, every nerve on edge, waiting for Zoe to speak.

JJ had to be losing his mind. There was no other reason for actually believing that this Zoe Shefford was sensing God leading her, showing her, directing her. . .talking to her.

She could have sworn that JJ had never put much stock in the supernatural. Ghosts, witches, psychics, mediums, tarot cards. . .even God—it just didn't work with his philosophy of life. What you saw was what you got. All the rest was slight of hand, cons, lies, and superstitious nonsense.

Denise understood some people's need to believe in something outside of themselves. Life could be cruel and hard, and heaven knows, there were so many events in a person's life that could break them if they didn't have something else to lean on, to trust. God's will. The fates. Destiny. Karma.

But from what little she knew of Zoe, she wasn't weak, and she didn't need something to lean on. She was one tough cookie who could take anything the world dished out and still be standing. So why did she need all this religion and supernatural stuff?

"Turn in here." Zoe's voice cut through her thoughts, and the authoritative tone grated along Denise's nerves. She spun the wheel and pulled into the parking lot of X-treme, one of the new clubs that had popped up over the last two years.

When they climbed out of the car, Denise leaned against the hood and folded her arms across her chest.

"Problem?" Zoe raised an eyebrow.

"I think so, yes."

"And that would be?"

"Your attitude, for one."

Zoe looked surprised as she tilted her head. "My attitude?"

"I'm not one of your flunkies, so don't toss orders around at me as if you had the right."

"I wasn't aware that I was tossing out orders, but if it came across that way, then I'm sorry." Zoe stared at her for a long moment, and Denise found herself actually tempted to wilt beneath that probing gaze. "You're attracted to him, aren't you?"

"Who?"

One of Zoe's eyebrows lifted, annoying Denise further. "Okay. Yes. I'm attracted to JJ, but the last time I checked, he wasn't involved with anyone."

"And if he's not involved with anyone, why do you look at me as though you'd like to hang, draw, and quarter me?"

"I have no idea what you're talking about."

Zoe laughed, straightening. "I see. We're back to that again. Well, let's clear the air and make sure we both understand each other. If you want him and you can get him, you can have him. Now, can we just get inside and see if the man we're looking for is in there?"

As Zoe walked past her, Denise reached out and grabbed her arm. "And just so we do understand, you aren't the woman for him, so stay out of my way. How's that?"

Denise could have sworn the woman all but looked down her nose at her and sniffed.

"Like I said, if you can get him, you can have him."

❖ ❖ ❖

Dreading the loud music, Zoe marched into the club, trying to curb her temper and ignore the woman following her. Sure enough, the bass was loud enough to confuse a cardiac beat, and the volume made her flinch and wish for earplugs.

It didn't seem to bother the good Detective McClellan at all, as she wandered about the club. She stayed right behind her as they wove through the crowd.

Finally Denise tapped her on the shoulder. "Anything?"

She nodded. "He's here. I just can't get a good fix on him."

They circled the room twice, then sidled up to the bar, where Denise ordered them both orange juice on the rocks.

A table opened up and Denise claimed it. Zoe sat, still searching the room.

"He's gone." Zoe frowned, rubbing her temples with her fingertips.

"Did he leave with a girl?"

"I have no idea, but I don't think so. I'm feeling peace."

"Feeling peace," Denise muttered as she slid back her chair and stood up. "Yeah, we close investigations on peace all the time. Sure. And the DA and the judge have no problem with that. Yes, Your Honor, I have total peace that this man is a killer. Lock him up? Absolutely."

"I just love sarcasm," Zoe told her. "We were close. He was here, but something ran him off."

"God?"

Zoe rolled her eyes, yanked the car door open, and climbed in. Attitude was rolling off Denise in waves, which was just fine with her because she was feeling a little attitude herself.

There was nothing but silence in the car on the drive back to her town house. Denise pulled up in the driveway, Zoe climbed out, and neither woman even said good night.

Fuming, Zoe opened the door just as her answering machine picked up. "This is Zoe, and it's entirely possible that I'm not in the mood to answer the phone right now, but if you leave a message, I'm sure I'll be in the mood to call you back as soon as I can. *Beeeeep*."

Zoe heard a man's voice. "It's me again, Miss Shefford. I saw you at the bar tonight. Did you think you could catch me that easily?" There was the sound of amused laughter. "I warned you to stay out of this, but you aren't listening to me. Listen to me now, Miss Shefford. Stay. Out. Or. Die."

181

fourteen

Friday, October 1—8:20 a.m.

Dad, this is so not fair!" Kieran Jennings slammed the cabinet door closed. "I take care of everything around here. You go to work, you meet with your friends, you have a life. Rachael has her friends and her school activities. She has a life. But me? My life is taking care of you and Rachael."

Mel Jennings set his plate in the sink. "Kieran, you are exaggerating. You go to school. You have your friends."

"Really, Dad? Name one."

"DeAnne."

"Yes, and I'll be going to her funeral next week. Who else?"

"What about Pammy? Isn't she your friend?"

"Sure. I see her once a week for an hour. You know what all my friends are doing? Dating. I haven't had a date since my high school prom."

Her father poured coffee into his travel mug and secured the lid. "Kieran, I don't object to your dating. I have a problem with you hanging out in bars. Especially right now. There's someone out there targeting young girls from your school. If I had my way, you wouldn't even go to school."

"I can believe that! You'd rather I stay home and play wife and mother!"

He spun around, his face red with fury. "I think you've said enough."

Any other time, Kieran may have backed down from that anger. Her father's temper wasn't released often, but when it was, it was uncontrollable. . .but not this time. "The laundry, the shopping, the cleaning, the cooking. When do I have time for me? You can't bury me in this house and keep me to yourself forever!"

"You are out of line, young lady!"

Kieran grabbed her pack and headed for the back door. "No, I'm just out of here."

She slammed the door behind her, ignoring her father's booming demands that she get her backside back in the house. She wanted her freedom, and she didn't know any other way of getting it.

11:30 a.m.

Dana stepped out of the limousine, keeping her head down as cameras flashed all around her. She couldn't believe that they were hounding her on this, of all days. Forget respecting her privacy or respecting her grief—get that picture. What were they hoping for? A smile?

She felt Marcus's hand on the small of her back and hurried up the walkway and into the church. Fortunately the police had kept the press from invading the sanctuary.

They had chosen St. Michael's for the service because it was the largest church in Monroe. Her father had been a well-known and highly respected judge; so the most influential, the most powerful, the most wealthy, and all those who just wanted to be seen with the influential, powerful, and wealthy were expected to attend.

Even so, Dana wasn't prepared for the church to be so crowded. It didn't look as though there was an empty seat to be found. She recognized some of the other judges, lawyers, and the mayor. There were police officers, business owners, movers and shakers. And very few of them really knew her father at all. This was more show than funeral, and that irritated her even more. She wanted to toss everyone out except the few close friends and family members she knew her father liked and respected.

Of course, if she'd used a smaller church, she would have had a great excuse to do exactly that. Wouldn't that have brought down the wrath of Monroe on her head?

It was bad enough the service was being held in a church. As far as she knew, her father hadn't stepped foot in one since the day he married her mother. He always said that he couldn't trust his future to some object of mythology or tradition. The Tappans had always made their own way in the world, plowing through obstacles as if they weren't there and leaving their mark, and their fortune, to the generations of Tappans behind them.

Dana swallowed the grief that swelled up in her throat and made her way up to the front of the church, trying not to make eye contact with anyone. She couldn't handle it right now. Everything was just too raw.

She sat down in the pew reserved for immediate family. Marcus sat down next to her, immediately reaching out to take her hand and clutch it tightly. She could feel the tremor of emotion through the tips of his fingers, and it comforted her to know she was not alone in her grief.

Finally it took every ounce of strength she had to raise her eyes to gaze over at the coffin. The loss slammed into her, bringing a fresh round of tears to her eyes.

Her daddy was gone forever.

❖   ❖   ❖

JJ eased back the edge of his suit coat, revealing the badge hanging on his belt. The officer nodded and stepped aside, letting JJ and Zoe proceed into the church.

"I still have a hard time believing the killer could get in. Security is too tight."

"He's here," Zoe whispered softly as they found seats in the back of the church. "I know he's here."

"Any idea where?"

Zoe shook her head as she crossed her legs and straightened her skirt. Clasping her hands in her lap, she began to look around.

JJ didn't actually believe that Zoe was getting any feelings or information from God. That was beyond ridiculous. He just knew that either he went along with her and let her think they were working together, or she'd be off trying to catch a killer by herself and more than likely get herself into trouble. He was going to send Denise with Zoe this morning, but for some reason, Denise told him she'd rather have her fingernails removed with a pair of pliers. Women. There was no figuring them out.

Maybe, like him, Denise had a problem with all this God stuff, too.

Sometimes he felt a little guilty about not believing in God after what had happened in the Matthews case, but mostly he was just confused. Religion, God, faith—these weren't concepts he'd been raised with. It was hard to suddenly discount everything he believed and take on a whole new philosophy of life. Besides, if he suddenly took God seriously, there was no telling what he'd have to give up.

God had a lot of rules and regulations that had to be followed.

Okay, that wasn't the primary reason. Rules and regulations were something he was raised with and was comfortable with. It was this trusting something bigger than himself. Trusting someone else with his life, his future, and his heart. He couldn't see where God gave Christians an edge in life. Their lives appeared to be just as messed up and filled with problems as everyone else's. So, what was the point?

He leaned in close to Zoe, trying to ignore the soft scent that filled his nostrils and made him want to lean in closer. "Anything?"

"He's definitely here. I can feel his hatred. He thinks he's close. He's going to finish this soon."

"God is letting you read his mind?"

Zoe slanted him a glance that was anything but friendly. "Don't, JJ."

"What do you expect from me?"

The look on her face softened. "I know it's hard for you to understand. I'm not sure I understand completely myself, but I just *know* what he's feeling. It's not a voice in my head or anything."

"But God isn't holding a light over the guy's head or anything. He could help us out a little more, you know."

"He has a reason for doing things the way He does."

"And heaven forbid we mere mortals question His methods? Or His timing?"

Zoe's hand covered his, and he came close to wrapping his fingers around it. "JJ, I don't think He's bothered by our questions, just our impatience."

"Impatience?" JJ couldn't keep the sharp hiss out of his voice. "We have two girls dead and who knows how many more on his list and your God may be bothered by my impatience?"

"We have to trust what He's doing."

"Oh, right. Back to that old adage. Just trust God."

Zoe moved her hand back to her lap, and JJ could have kicked himself. This wasn't the time or the place to antagonize her or get into some debate over God's way of running the universe.

He turned his head to the front and straightened as the service started and the wonderful things done by Leonard Allen Tappan the Third were touted.

JJ let his mind wander back to DeAnne Foster. They had managed to narrow her time line a little more. She had been seen at a ladies shop at the mall at eight-forty-five, where she bought a pair of jeans and a sweater. Then she was seen at the drugstore on University a few minutes after nine and, according to the store records, bought a tube of mascara and a can of hairspray. She'd walked out of the drugstore, and from there they lost track of her movements. It might help if they found her car, but so far, it hadn't turned up anywhere.

Barone had run a background check on the boyfriend, Lee, but the kid was clean. Good grades, one parking ticket, and plenty of friends vouching for the fact that he was a good guy and would never hurt DeAnne.

Well, someone had. And that someone could very well be seated in this church right now. JJ gave the room a good once-over, but no one stood out in his mind as being a killer.

Denise had her eye on Roddy, checking out his alibi. The fact that his job at the distributor was a short distance from the lake was interesting but hadn't become relevant yet. They somehow had to figure out how he would have left work without anyone knowing, gone to the bar, abducted Lori Blain, dumped her body, and returned to work with no one the wiser. It was tough to put together, but if there was anything there, she'd find it.

And while Denise was following up on Joey Roddy, Cole was looking into Mel Jennings. There was more there than met the eye, but so far, they hadn't found a connection between Mel Jennings and DeAnne Foster. Cole had gone to the Time Out on Wednesday night, but their suspect hadn't shown up. Right now, all he had on his suspect list, besides Bret Leland, the man in the bar, were Mel Jennings and Joey Roddy.

But neither Mel Jennings nor Joey Roddy were in attendance, and Zoe was insisting that the killer was here. So where was he going wrong in the investigation? There was only one connection so far, and if Zoe was right, and Dana Tappan was a target, then the connection was still the college, where Dana was also a student.

JJ's cell phone suddenly started vibrating. As he reached for the phone, Zoe glanced over at him and raised an eyebrow in question. He jerked his head, indicating that he was going outside to answer it. Zoe slid out of the pew to allow him to pass.

He flipped the phone open as he headed for the doors, speaking softly. "Johnson."

"Hey, partner. I hear you need me."

JJ pushed open the door and stepped outside. "Matt? Where are you?"

"Straightening up the kitchen."

"You're supposed to be on your honeymoon!" He heard the door open and looked over his shoulder. Zoe stepped out, buttoning her coat.

"I heard about the case and insisted on coming back to help you."

"You give up laying on the beach in Key West to work on a murder case? Yeah. Right. Now tell me the truth."

JJ smiled when he heard Matt's laugh. "Okay. Truth? Paula had an allergic reaction to a bee sting and was feeling so bad she wanted to come home. She took her medication and is sleeping. I thought I'd call in and see how the case is going."

JJ couldn't help laughing again. It was good to hear Matt's

voice. Even better, it was good to have Matt back. "Yeah, partner. I need you. Get caught up on the case. All the files are in my office."

"Whoa, cowboy. I'm on my honeymoon and my wife is sick. I can't just drop everything and come running."

"I need you, Matt."

There was a long moment of silence. "Let me see to Paula. If she's going to sleep for a while, I'll come in for a little bit and see what I can do."

JJ grinned. "Great. I'll check in with you as soon as the funeral is over."

"What funeral?"

"Judge Tappan."

"No kidding. I didn't know he was sick."

"Neither did anyone else. He died of a heart attack on Tuesday."

"Okay, I'll bite. Why are you at Tappan's funeral? You didn't even like the old coot."

JJ looked over at Zoe. "Zoe feels that the killer has targeted Tappan's daughter. We're here in hopes of getting a bead on the guy."

"Zoe? As in former psychic extraordinaire?"

"One and the same."

"How is she?"

JJ glanced over in Zoe's direction and was surprised to find her standing right next to him with her hand out. "Ask her yourself." He handed Zoe the phone.

JJ shoved his hands in his pockets as he listened to Zoe.

"Matt! How are you? Congratulations, by the way. Yep. Sure, that would be great. So, you're back? Great. Oh, poor Paula. Yeah, tell her I said to get plenty of rest. See you then." She closed the phone and handed it to him. "The funeral's about over. Did you want to go back in?"

JJ shook his head. "No. If I hear one more person ramble on and on about what a wonderful, kind, giving, and saintly man Tappan was, I may get sick."

"He wasn't a very good man, was he?"

JJ shrugged lightly as he leaned back against the black wrought iron railing. "He was a ruthless, manipulating, and greedy man, and in my mind, unethical on the bench."

"Well, I'm glad you thought so highly of him." Zoe's eyebrow rose as she gave him a twisted smile.

❖   ❖   ❖

As everyone stood to leave the church, he stood with them, watching Dana as she walked up to the coffin and placed her hand on it, bowed her head, and prayed.

If she only knew how soon she would be following her father, she would be praying for her own soul, as well. The thought made him want to smile, but this was a funeral, and he couldn't allow his anticipation to draw attention to the fact that he wasn't here to mourn.

Oh, he would be kind and not kill her today. Let her bury her father and grieve with her family; then, when she least expected it, he would strike.

❖   ❖   ❖

Dana eased into the limo and scooted over to let her brother in. Lost in thought, she was caught off guard when her brother nudged her, then took the seat across from her. She was counting on holding his hand, leaning on him.

She looked up and started to ask him to remain beside her when she realized that her father's lawyer was climbing in beside her.

"We need to talk and this is more private."

"Talk? Can't this wait? We just buried our father. We'll be back at the house in less than half an hour."

"This can't wait." Morton unbuttoned his jacket. "There's been a suit filed against the estate."

"What!" Marcus all but shouted. "Why?"

"It's a paternity case. A young woman claims that the judge was her father. She's suing for back child support."

Stunned, Dana stared at him. "This is ridiculous! Dad never cheated on Mother. There are no other children."

"Can't you dismiss this as the nonsense it so obviously is?" Marcus reached over and took Dana's hand, giving her a reassuring squeeze. "And to dump this on us now. It's incredible."

"Supposedly, she has some evidence to support her claims. I'm meeting with her attorney on Monday to find out exactly what we're facing and I'll keep you posted, but I wanted to give you a head's up just in case this girl goes to the press. I wanted you to hear it from me rather than the six o'clock news."

Dana moved across the seat and curled up next to her brother, letting him wrap his arms around her. "I can't believe this. I just can't."

"It'll be okay, Dana. Morton will expose her as a fraud and we'll be fine."

Not if I get to her first, Dana thought bitterly.

Denise McClellan stared down at the map in her lap and nearly cried. It couldn't be this easy. She picked up her notebook from the passenger seat and went over it again.

Joey Roddy *had* been working that night, but not loading trucks the way he claimed. His night supervisor suddenly remembered that one of the drivers had called in sick at the last minute and he'd given the run to Roddy, something he did from time to time. No big deal to him, but it could be a very big deal to the investigation.

One of the bars on the route was the Time Out.

According to the delivery report for the night, he would have been there a little after ten.

Denise started the car and pulled out of the parking lot, racing back to the station.

Matt Casto felt bombarded from the moment he stepped foot in the station. He was welcomed, pounded on the back, kissed on the cheek, and peppered with questions about his early return.

He finally made it to the conference room, where the task force was already in full swing. He walked over to the board and studied the faces of Lori Blain and DeAnne Foster. Two pretty girls whose lives were snuffed out because someone decided that it was okay to kill them. Sick.

He glanced over the evidence, leads, forensic highlights, and suspects, trying to get a quick overview of the case and the progress that had been made. So far, it didn't add up to much.

Chuck Barone rushed into the room. "Matt! Welcome home! Have you seen JJ? Is he back from the funeral yet?"

"Not yet. He'll be here soon. What's up?"

"I think I found a connection to the girls." He walked over to the conference table, laid a file down on top, and flipped it open. "All three girls belonged to a—"

"Three girls?" Matt looked back over his shoulder at the pictures on the board. "We have three?"

Barone shook his head. "No, but Miss Shefford believes that Dana Tappan is a target, so JJ asked me to keep her in the equation, and sure enough, she's on the same list."

"What list?"

"This list." Barone tapped the printout. "Lori Blain, DeAnne Foster, Dana Tappan. They all belonged to Young Women for Professional Careers in high school. It's a highly selective group run by professional women who help mentor these young women going on to college."

Matt snatched up the list and went over the names. Abbot, Banning, Blain, Brenner, Cordette, Corvasce, Eyler, Foster, Frank, Hamilton, Jennings, Kensington. He stopped reading and looked over at Barone. "How many of these girls are at Monroe College?"

"Seven." He picked up another list and handed it to Matt. "Lori Blain, DeAnne Foster, Pam Hamilton, Kieran Jennings, Taylor Cordette, Dana Tappan, and Susan Wright."

Matt felt the kick that came with a strong lead and the gut instinct that he was on the right track. "Get that list out to the other colleges. Find out if any of these other girls have been killed."

"Already in the works." Barone looked grim. "And you should know that Lori Blain worked for Mel Jennings."

Matt shook his head and shrugged in silent question.

Barone nodded to the list. "Mel Jennings has a daughter, Kieran Jennings. She's on the list."

Before Matt could frame a response, Denise McClellan rushed into the room. "Matt! You're back! Where's JJ?"

"Not back from the funeral yet. What's up?"

"One of our prime suspects. Joey Roddy. He was supposed to have had an alibi for the night of Lori Blain's murder, but come to find out, he was there. At the bar. And he was there at the right time."

"What do we know about him? Have you interviewed him?"

McClellan nodded. "He was secretive, uncooperative, and definitely nervous. He also has a record."

"We need to bring him in for questioning, and we need a search warrant for his place." Matt circled JJ's desk, dropped down in the seat, and picked up the phone. After he found JJ, he would have to call Paula, make sure she was okay, and let her know he was going to be working late. He just hoped he could keep the excitement out of his voice, or she might think he was excited to be away from her, and nothing could be farther from the truth.

Steve Cole stopped taking notes and lifted his gaze to look Mel Jennings in the face. The poor man was practically squirming in his chair, and Steve knew another minute or two of silence, and the man was going to either jump out of his skin or confess to anything and everything he ever did in his life.

Cole kept his face impassive, his eyes steady, and his demeanor as intimidating as possible. He was very good at the art of saying nothing and shouting that he knew everything and was just waiting patiently for them to go ahead and get it off their chest.

Mel jerked up out of his chair and began to pace his office. "I swear to you, I have no idea who hurt Lori."

"Killed," Cole corrected coldly.

Mel swallowed hard, his Adam's apple jumping up and down hard and fast. "Right. I don't know. I don't."

He sank back in his chair and ran his fingers through his thinning hair. "I can't help you. Now, if you don't mind, I need to get back to work."

Cole tried another tack. "Did you know DeAnne Foster? Did Lori ever mention that name to you?"

"No. But my daughter did. DeAnne was a friend of hers from high school. They were in a group together."

"What kind of group?"

"Women for Professional Careers, or something along those lines."

Cole's phone rang, and he stepped back to answer it. "Excuse me just a minute."

Jennings nodded with obvious relief and busied himself at his desk.

"Hello?"

He listened for a moment, responded with a few affirmative responses, then slowly closed his phone, disconnecting the call. Cole turned back to Mel Jennings. "Mr. Jennings, do you know where your daughter is?"

"Probably at school. Why?"

"She's been placed on a possible target list."

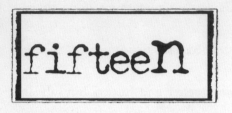

fifteen

The conference table was crowded with files, notes, reports, file folders, napkins, coffee cups, pens, pencils, laptops, and dinner left-overs. Every chair was occupied as the task force prepared themselves for a long night of brainstorming and strategy planning.

JJ was sitting behind his desk, feet propped up on the corner, his shirt unbuttoned at the collar, his tie tossed over the file cabinet with his coat, a container of General Tso's chicken in his lap. He waved his fork in the air. "Has there been any word on Roddy's warrant yet?"

Denise shook her head. "Not yet. The DA said he'd call as soon as he got it signed."

Frowning, JJ toyed with a piece of broccoli. "What about Roddy himself?"

"We have a man keeping an eye on him. He's at work right now and doesn't seem to suspect anything." Denise studied her notes. "The minute we get the warrant, we'll pick him up and send a team over to take his place apart."

Barone hung up the phone, leaned back, and stretched, his arms nearly reaching the wall behind him. "Okay, we've got Dana Tappan and Susan Wright covered, but we can't find Kieran Jennings and

Pam Hamilton. And I can't get any information at all on this Taylor Cordette."

Zoe perked up. "Taylor Cordette?"

"Yeah. You know her?"

She shook her head. "Not specifically. She's Dan Cordette's daughter. Are you saying she's on the killer's list?"

"Yep."

Zoe dug out her cell phone and left the room.

JJ watched her step out into the hall, the stress of the day drawing dark circles under her eyes. He'd tried to send her home twice, but she'd refused. She was drawn in emotionally now, and, as always, she'd keep her nose to the ground and pursue this to the end regardless of what anyone said. Especially him.

"She has no business being here," Denise said quietly, perching herself on the corner of his desk, keeping the conversation between the two of them.

"If I don't keep her close, she'll be chasing down the killer all by herself."

"You're not her keeper, JJ."

"I know, Denise. It's complicated."

Denise surprised him by reaching out and touching his hand lightly. "JJ, she's not interested in you. Get the hint. There are tons of other women out there who are, and they're standing around waiting for you to notice."

JJ laughed at the picture of women lining up outside his door, taking a number. "Right."

"JJ, I'd really like to talk to you. Privately. Maybe we can go get some—"

Zoe came back into the room and JJ looked up at her. "Did you contact Dan?"

She nodded, looking down pointedly at his hand linked with

Denise's. Then she stiffened and picked up her purse. "He's on his way to his ex-wife's now. He'll be staying with her. I have to go."

"Wait. Zoe." He went to stand.

Barone, lost in his world as always, spoke up. "He'll be going after Hamilton. We have to find her."

JJ disengaged his hand from Denise's. He'd have to deal with Zoe later. "We have an APB out on her. Her parents have been notified, and we've left messages at her apartment." He knew there was a sharp edge to his voice, but he couldn't help it. "In the meantime, the other girls are being warned. There's not much else we can do."

Denise walked over to the coffeepot and poured herself a mug. "If it's Roddy, he won't be getting anyone tonight. He won't be able to make a move without us seeing it."

The phone rang and Barone picked it up. JJ swung his feet to the floor. "Okay, we need some ideas, people."

There was a loud groan through the room. He understood how they felt. They'd been going over every detail for the past four hours and hadn't come up with anything solid.

Barone hung up the phone and raised his voice above the groans. "We got the warrant. They're bringing Roddy in as we speak."

JJ felt a surge of relief. Roddy may not lead anywhere, but at least he felt like something was progressing. "Denise, head over to Roddy's. I want you there supervising the search."

Denise nodded, set her coffee down, and grabbed her coat.

Matt raised his hand. "Can I beat up the suspect, huh-huh, can I?"

JJ rolled his eyes. "And to think I missed you."

❖   ❖   ❖

Dana Tappan stared at the police officer in total disbelief. "That's impossible."

Her brother came up behind her, placing his hand protectively on her shoulder. "Are you sure?"

The officer nodded grimly. "Sure enough to be giving you some warning. We can't provide you with round-the-clock protection, but we will be increasing patrols on this street."

"Patrols?" Marcus laughed mockingly. "Like that's going to do any good. We'll hire a bodyguard. Bring in extra security. No one is going to get anywhere near my sister."

Dana finally made her way through the emotion to find her voice. "I just buried my father. We have some woman making claims about my father. And now you're telling me that some serial killer is stalking me. Could this day get any worse?"

She felt her brother's hand squeeze her shoulder. "It'll be okay, sis. We can afford the best security available."

"I don't need extra security," Dana said wearily. "I need some peace and quiet."

Climbing to her feet, she headed for the stairs. "I'm going to bed. Please see the officer out, Marcus."

"I'll call and see about getting a bodyguard here for you."

Dana nodded as she leaned heavily on the railing and began to climb the stairs. "Fine. I'm too tired to think straight. Tomorrow I'll come up with a battle plan. Tonight I'm just going to forget how I spent today."

❖   ❖   ❖

Denise leaned against the two-way mirror and studied Joey Roddy as he sat squirming in his chair across from Matt and JJ. So far, he hadn't asked for an attorney, but she didn't doubt he was building up to it.

Most of the past hour had been spent watching JJ. Whenever she was around him, all her senses seemed to go on high alert, as if she were suddenly on the edge of danger. Not in danger for her life, maybe, but she knew the danger was to her heart. She could close her eyes, put headphones on, and blast the music, and she'd still know when Josiah Johnson walked into a room. He had an effect on her that no man had ever had.

She wasn't sure when she'd first realized that she was falling in love with him, but being around him, working with him on this case, only intensified it.

She'd called Lenny the night before and broken off the engagement. Obviously she couldn't marry one man while pining away for another.

Now all she had to do was get Zoe Shefford out of the picture.

The door to the interrogation room opened and Cole strolled in. *Here we go.* She leaned forward, bracing her hands against the glass, and waited for the fireworks.

Cole bent down and whispered something in JJ's ear, and Roddy nearly came out of his seat with jitters. His eyes were darting all over the room as if every exit had just vanished into thin air.

"I didn't kill that girl! I don't care what you say, I didn't kill her!"

Cole pulled out a small evidence bag and tossed it down on the table. The impact on Roddy was unmistakable.

"I want my lawyer. I'm not saying another word."

Knowing that nothing more would be accomplished by trying to talk to Roddy, Denise headed back to the conference room with JJ and Matt.

"For whatever it's worth, I don't think Roddy is going to be very cooperative."

JJ opened the conference room door and waved her in. "For whatever it's worth, finding Lori Blain's necklace in Roddy's apartment combined with his fingerprints on her car and his botched alibi pretty much seals his fate."

"He could have stolen it out of her car when she had it washed."

"He could have." JJ dropped wearily into his chair. "But it's too strong a link to ignore. He was at the bar at the time the suspect disappeared. Her necklace was found in his apartment. His fingerprints were on her car. He lied about his whereabouts. He works close to where the body was dumped."

"Circumstantial. We can't stop looking at other suspects. We haven't connected him yet to DeAnne Foster." Denise stood, her hands resting on the back of a metal chair.

"We're working on it."

Matt leaned against the corner of the conference table. "Have we found Pam Hamilton yet?"

"Yes." The voice in the doorway had everyone turning. Steve Cole looked furious as he stood there. "We just got the call. Pam Hamilton's body was found out by the lake."

"What about Kieran Jennings?" JJ asked as he stood up and reached for his coat.

Cole shook his head. "Nothing so far. Mr. Jennings is out looking for her. He'll call if he finds her."

"*When*, Cole. *When* he finds her. Let's try to stay optimistic here, okay?" JJ opened his desk drawer and pulled out his badge and weapon.

"What do you want to do about Roddy?" Matt asked as he followed JJ out. "If we were watching him all day, he couldn't have gotten to the Hamilton girl."

"We'll hold him anyway until we know for sure what we're dealing with."

❖   ❖   ❖

Zoe tucked the phone under her chin as she opened the refrigerator and pulled out the juice container. "Rene, I can't help feeling as though I've missed something, but for the life of me, I don't know what it is."

Using her hip, she pushed the refrigerator door closed and headed for the sink. "I've gone over everything two or three times. It just doesn't make sense to me. I keep sensing that the motive is greed, but since when are serial killers motivated by greed? It's about power, anger, revenge. Things like that."

She poured half a glass of juice. "And this is definitely a serial killer, Rene. I didn't think it was at the beginning, but there's no doubt about it now. All the girls he's going after are members of a club in high school for women going into professional careers."

"So you think this is about some kind of twisted hatred for intelligent, ambitious, or at least on-their-way-to-being-successful women of influence?"

Zoe swallowed some juice and set the glass down. "That's what it looks like."

"But couldn't that be a form of greed? Wanting to keep that power within the male realm?"

She leaned back against the counter and considered the new angle. "It makes sense in a twisted kind of way."

"You're dealing with a serial killer, Zoe. It's always going to be twisted, evil, and diabolical."

But it still didn't feel right. No matter how she moved it, shaped it, flipped it, and looked at it again, it still seemed wrong. "Maybe I'm not even supposed to be involved. Maybe that's why I don't feel right. This could be the Lord's way of telling me to get my nose out of it and leave it to the experts."

"Zoe, don't ever forget that we have an adversary. Do you really think that he's going to step aside and let you serve the Lord without trying to stop you? What better way than to confuse you and make you doubt that you're doing what the Lord called you to do?"

"So that I get paralyzed with fear and do nothing," Zoe added, repeating what Rene had told her before.

"Exactly. I'm glad to see you've been listening. Honey, you're moving by faith, and anything we do in faith, believing that we're doing what the Father has called us to do, He will honor."

Zoe returned the juice to the fridge and rinsed out her glass. "This isn't the same thing as whether or not he called me to give forty or a hundred and forty to the building fund. There are girls being killed here, and so far, I haven't been able to do a single thing to stop it from happening."

"How do you know?"

"How do I know what?"

"How do you know that you haven't done something to stop it? For all you know, you've slowed him down or stopped him. For all you know, you have said something or done something that will keep him from being able to kill again. Stop looking at what you think is success by your terms, and trust that the Father has this under control. He knows what He's doing and why He's doing it."

"And in the meantime, I haven't the slightest idea what to do next." Frustrated, Zoe grabbed the sponge from the sink and began to wipe down the counters.

"And you're not used to that, are you, Zoe? You've always been in control of your life. You knew what you were doing and how to do it. You felt comfortable and efficient. You were successful, and although you may not have sought notoriety, you received it anyway, which only served to reinforce everything you believed about yourself.

"Now you're learning a whole new way to work with your talents, and it isn't comfortable at all, is it? It's like groping around in the dark."

Frowning, Zoe tossed the sponge back into the sink. "Not to

mention being blind, deaf, and dumb at the same time."

Rene laughed, and the sound of it pulled a reluctant smile out of her. "You're doing fine, Zoe. I promise you are. You have to learn to trust these new instincts. The Father doesn't operate the same way the enemy does, so it's going to be new territory for a while, but you will come to understand what He's doing through you and why."

"But, Rene—"

"Listen to me. Take everything He's told you or showed you or you've picked up through feelings and instincts, and look at it again. They are all pieces of the puzzle."

"It is the glory of God to conceal a thing: but the honour of kings is to search out a matter."

"Proverbs twenty-five. You've been studying."

Zoe pulled out a chair and sank down in it, toying with a place-mat. "Rene, what if I'm wrong?"

"Zoe, are you the only chance these girls have?"

"No. The police are looking into it. So is Dan Cordette. And the FBI is aware."

"So quit thinking all the responsibility is on your slender shoulders. You're not alone in this."

"And what do I do about Daria? She's been my best friend for so long, I can't remember a time when she wasn't in my life. Now she won't even speak to me."

She heard Rene sigh. "That's a tough one, Zoe. I won't deny that. She's hurt and grieving. A volatile combination. Right now she needs someone to be the scapegoat, and you're it."

"I don't want to lose her friendship, Rene."

"How far are you willing to go to keep it?"

Zoe closed her eyes, swallowing the lump in her throat. "I don't know."

❖ ❖ ❖

JJ raced back to the station after just fifteen minutes at the crime scene. Pam Hamilton's body was found in the east parking lot at Sterling Lake, dumped near her car in tall grass. She probably wouldn't have been found at all if hadn't been for the APB they'd put out on her. A patrol car had spotted her vehicle and called it in.

And a note had been pinned to her chest. "To kill, to die, to bleed, to honor hate and greed, I plunge my knife deep."

He felt like punching something. They had been so close to saving her. Well, there were still four more girls on the list, and he was going to do everything he could to keep them alive if he had to lock them up and put them in jail until he caught the maniac behind this.

His headache was back, moving up the back of his neck in a slow, steady crawl. Rolling his neck, he pulled into the parking lot and cut the engine. He sat there for a moment, knowing that once he stepped through those doors, there would be nothing but chaos and ringing phones and a million demands on him. Forget peace and quiet. Forget being able to think beyond any given moment.

Seven girls on a list. All attending Monroe College. All once members of an elite group. Why? Because he didn't like women in powerful positions? Women in authority? But these girls weren't. They were just students. Was it about stopping them before they became successful? Why not just go after women who already are successful?

Joey Roddy had Lori Blain's locket, but like Denise said, he worked at the car wash and could have picked it up. There was Bret Leland, the man in the bar and the last man to see Lori alive. So far, he was laying low, calling in sick to work, and staying who knew where.

His cell phone rang, interrupting his thoughts. He climbed out of his vehicle, flipping the phone open. "Johnson."

"It's Donnie Bevere. How's it going?"

"Three girls dead, two suspects, and nothing."

"I can be back there tomorrow if you need me."

JJ wrestled with his feelings. He could use Bevere's help and expertise. At the same time, he had always felt resentment over the FBI's habit of taking over an investigation.

Did it matter? Four girls were still on the killer's list. Would they really care who it was who saved their lives?

"I need you. We have four more girls on the killer's list."

"The killer's list? What list?"

JJ yanked open the front door of the department and explained as he made his way through the lobby, up the stairs, and into his office. By the time he reached his desk, he was ending his call. Matt was the only member of the task force still awake and in attendance. He was on the phone with Paula. "I'll be home within the hour, honey. I'm really sorry, but this case is critical."

JJ shrugged out of his coat, wishing he could be home within the hour. He'd be lucky if he caught a few hours of sleep on the sofa.

Matt hung up the phone and looked up at JJ with expectation. "What do we have?"

JJ sank down in his chair. "Bevere will be here in the morning. Amato will be working overtime tonight processing the crime scene. Cole has a lead on Leland and is bringing him in for questioning."

Matt grabbed the phone and hit redial. "Paula? I hate to say this, but go on to bed, and I'll try not to wake you when I come in. We have a possible break in the case."

sixteen

Saturday, October 2—7:30 a.m.

*D*id I not warn them that the iniquity of the fathers would be visited
upon the children unto the third and fourth generation?

*I'm sorry, Byron. You understand, don't you? I just don't feel like
sharing.*

*The car spun around and around and around. Byron screamed. There
was the sound of screeching tires, twisting metal, and shattering glass.*

*I'm sorry, Byron. I just don't feel like sharing. I'm sorry, Lori. I just
don't feel like sharing. I'm sorry, DeAnne. I just don't feel like sharing.
I'm sorry—"*

Zoe jerked awake, her heart pounding, the sound of shattering
glass still echoing in her mind, and an irritating sound demanding
a response. With a ragged breath, she reached for the alarm clock,
groaned when she saw the time, hit the OFF button, and fell back
into the pillow.

The dream came back in disjointed bits and pieces, and she
chewed on them while dressing. None of it made much sense. She'd
been dreaming about something in Lanae's diaries, and somehow it
had twisted, the way dreams often do, into bits and pieces of things
she'd been worrying over all week.

Picking up her Bible from her nightstand, she headed for the kitchen, where she turned on the television and started coffee.

"After burying their father yesterday, Judge Tappan's children were expected to stay out of the public eye for a few days, but they were both on their front lawn this morning with this to say to the press. . . ."

Zoe turned and stared at the television as the news report ran.

Lanae stared at the television with disbelief and mounting horror.

"We don't know yet who this woman is, but I find it utterly despicable that some greedy, money-grubbing con woman has chosen this time to try to besmirch our father's name and demand money from our family."

Wide-eyed with indignation and anger, Dana Tappan stood in front of her home, microphones shoved in her face. It looked like every news service in the state was there and maybe even a few from out of state. "She is a liar. She is not related to us, she is not entitled to any part of our father's estate, and she will not get away with dragging his name through the mud and making such outrageous accusations."

Lanae felt a cold chill run down her spine. What had she done?

Dana lifted her chin and looked directly into the camera. "I have instructed my attorney to dig into this woman's background and show her for the cheap, insensitive lowlife she really is."

Lanae grabbed the remote and hit the OFF button. Dig into her background? Expose her? Dear heavens, they were going to twist everything they could find and make her look like some terrible person. She wouldn't be able to show her face in this town when they were done with her.

She reached for the phone, but it rang before she could pick it up to dial. "Hello?"

"Lanae? It's Wes Branson. I gather you've seen the news?"

"They're making me look horrible!"

"It will only get worse from here, but you can't let this bother you. We have a long battle ahead, and they're just letting you know they're not going to roll over and play dead on this."

Lanae shuddered. "They've convinced me, all right."

"Don't worry. We'll counterattack when the time is right. They want to win this in the public opinion arena, but that's not where the real war is fought. Keep that in mind."

"I just didn't expect this."

"Take a deep breath and stay focused on the goal."

Lanae dragged in a lungful of air. The goal. *Find out what happened to my mother.*

❖   ❖   ❖

"JJ?" Matt nudged his friend, who was sprawled on the sofa in the department lounge.

"Hmmm?"

"Wake up."

"Mmmmm."

Matt shoved at JJ, smiling at the scowl that immediately showed up on JJ's face. "What?"

"It's noon. You need to get up."

JJ sprang upright, the scowl replaced by disbelief. "I couldn't have slept that long." He glanced at his watch, then turned to glare at Matt. "It's only quarter after eight."

Matt ignored the reprimand, grabbed JJ's ankles, and swung them around to the floor, dropping next to his friend on the sofa. "What time did you finally get to zonk out?"

"About four." JJ rubbed his eyes with the heels of his hands. "Cole called in a little before that to say that Leland may have skipped town."

"Did his background check bring anything to light?"

"Not a lot. Raised by his mother, who was a politician. Has an older sister, a doctor, who is also married to a doctor. His father left right after he was born." JJ stretched. "A few scrapes with the law when he was in his teens, but nothing more than most boys his age. Shoplifting, drinking, speeding tickets."

Matt watched as JJ lumbered unsteadily to his feet and headed for the coffeepot. "That's a strong background for a serial killer, JJ. A successful mother, a successful sister, no father, and he ends up a salesman for a bakery company. That's gotta hurt."

"But why these girls?"

"Why any victim? We know he was the last one to see Lori Blain alive. We have the bartender who can place Leland there at the club with Blain. And if he's innocent, why did he disappear on us?"

JJ stirred his coffee, then tossed the stirrer in the overflowing trash can. He took a sip of the coffee, grimaced, then shuddered in revulsion and poured it out in the sink.

"Has anyone called in yet?" JJ grabbed his shoes.

Matt hauled himself up and followed JJ back to the conference room. "Not yet. At least not that I've heard."

Just as they entered the conference room, Denise showed up with huge cups of gourmet coffee.

JJ grabbed one eagerly. "I love you. Marry me."

"Name the day," Denise quipped back with a grin and offered Matt a cup.

"I'll check my calendar and get back to you."

Matt noted the look on Denise's face, and it made him wonder. She laughed as if she understood JJ's joke, but the laugh never quite reached her eyes.

He was wondering whether to bring up the subject with her when Barone strolled through the door. "Morning, all."

Barone had barely taken his usual seat behind the computer when the phone rang. "Homicide."

Matt turned his attention back to JJ. "You need to go home, shower, and shave. You look like death warmed over and reheated in a microwave."

"It may have to wait." Barone hung up the phone and spun his chair around to face the others. "That was Cole. He found our illusive Mr. Leland. They're on their way in. And there's one small detail he thought you all might be interested in."

"What's that?" Denise asked.

"They found a knife hidden in the wheel well of his trunk. It is consistent with the type and style of knife Amato feels was the murder weapon. I think we've found our killer."

Kieran pulled up into her driveway, eyeing the police car parked in front of her house. She felt a sense of panic and doom. She quickly parked and ran into the house. Something must have happened to her father! Or Rachael!

She burst through the door. "Dad!"

"Kieran!" Her father sprinted into the foyer and pulled her into a rib-crushing hug. "Oh, thank God. I've been so worried! Where have you been?"

"I was with some friends. What is going on?"

Her dad stepped back, holding her at the end of his arms,

looking over her as if trying to reassure himself that she was truly there and unharmed.

"Is Rachael okay?"

"Rachael's fine," he assured her, taking her hand and leading her into the family room, where a police officer was standing, waiting. "She's upstairs."

"Then what is going on?"

"Sit, honey."

Kieran could feel that sense of uneasiness growing stronger, and she struggled not to fall into a full-out panic. Her father had dark circles under his eyes, and the lines in his face appeared deep enough to walk through. His clothes looked as if he'd slept in them, and for a clotheshorse like her dad, that was almost considered sacrilege. "Dad. Talk to me."

He sat down next to her, holding her hand in both of his. "This officer will explain everything."

"Can I take my coat off?"

Her dad blinked at her, not quite focused. It was the officer who broke through the tension. "Please forgive us, Miss Jennings. We've been so caught up in all of this, we've quite forgotten that you're a little in the dark here. Would you like something to drink?"

"Oh. Yes. I made some coffee, Kieran." Her father bolted to his feet. "Do you want some?"

"You made coffee?" Kieran unbuttoned her coat, surprised at the giggle that bubbled up. Had to be nerves. Her father never made coffee. "I think I'll pass."

"Hot tea? Chocolate?"

Kieran shook her head as she slid her coat off and tucked her feet beneath her. "I'm fine, Dad. I just really want to know what this is all about."

The officer, a uniformed policeman she guesstimated to be in his late forties, had deep brown eyes, curly brown hair, and a long thin nose that gave the impression of aristocratic blood, but his demeanor couldn't have been friendlier.

"I apologize again that you've been unduly distressed, Miss Jennings. But we have reason to believe that you may have been targeted by a serial killer, and we need to keep you safe until we know for sure."

If he'd told her that a nuclear bomb had exploded and the world was ending in three minutes, she didn't think she would have been any more stunned. *A serial killer? Targeting me?*

She threw her hand up as if to ward off the danger his words implied. "Wait a minute. Why would a serial killer want to target me?"

The officer looked down at his hands, then lifted his eyes to meet hers. "You know about Lori Blain and DeAnne Foster?"

Slowly she nodded.

"And Pam Hamilton?"

"No! Not Pam, too." Suddenly the pattern began to emerge, and she felt the panic begin to swell again. "The group."

"Yes, ma'am. One by one, three of you at Monroe who were members of Young Women for Professional Careers have been killed. You're on the list."

Kieran felt the blood draining, taking her breath with it. She knew her father had his arms around her now, but she couldn't feel the comfort or support they were supposed to bring. Someone wanted her dead. "Why?" she whispered, not entirely sure she'd said it loud enough for anyone to hear, but obviously she had.

"When it comes to the sick mind of a serial killer, Miss Jennings, you can't always pinpoint something so obvious. He has some demented reason, and until we catch him, we won't know or understand."

"I just saw Pammie the other night."

The officer shifted forward in his chair. "What? Where?"

"At X-treme. She was there with some guy. I talked to her for a little while."

"By any chance, did you get the guy's name? The one that was with Miss Hamilton."

Kieran frowned, thinking. "Bart? No. Wait. Brent, Bret, something like that."

He jumped to his feet. "I need to use your phone."

❖ ❖ ❖

11:35 a.m.

Dana paced the length of the room, her temper simmering just below the surface, barely held in check. "This woman has to be stopped. How dare she do this to our family?"

Marcus was sitting in their father's chair, his long legs stretched in front of him, his tie loosened, his big brown eyes fixed on her. "She won't win, Dana. We have the finest attorneys on retainer. They'll make mincemeat out of her."

"What about this proof she's supposed to have?"

Marcus shrugged with just a subtle lift of his shoulders. "If it exists, it's fabricated. There's no way Pop had another kid. Don't you think we'd know if he did?"

"How can you be so calm?" Dana flounced down on the chintz sofa.

"If this woman was for real, why didn't she come forward while Pop was alive? Why wait until he couldn't defend himself? Because she isn't for real, that's why. She thinks she sees a chance to get rich quick. We'll be too buried in our grief to fight. Too devastated to object. We'll want to take the easy way out, and paying her off would be the easiest way to make it all go away."

"Well, she's got another thing coming if she thinks I'm just going to roll over and play dead."

Dana looked around the room, a room her mother had taken such great pains to decorate. Everything was tasteful, expensive, and old-fashioned. "I'm thinking about having this room redone."

Marcus's eyes widened. "What?"

"I've hated this room for so long. All pink and mauve and green. Yuck. I want to redecorate it. Something tasteful and understated."

"Do you really think you should? Mom did this room before she died. Pop always made sure everything stayed exactly the way she left it."

Dana tilted her head and gave her brother one of those I-can't-believe-you-said-that looks she was famous for. "It's just you and me now, Marcus. Our house. Our furniture. We can do whatever we want with it."

"So that means you're going to move back in?"

"Yes. I think I will. Seems stupid to pay rent on an apartment when we have this house."

Marcus glanced at his watch. "What time are we supposed to meet with Morton?"

"At two. Relax. We have tons of time." Dana bounced to her feet. "I'm going out for a while. I'll be back way before Morton is due."

"Where are you going?"

"Out."

"Wait a minute! The police told you not to go out alone. You said you were going to get a bodyguard."

"I haven't had time to worry about it." Dana slid into her camel overcoat. "I'll be fine. Don't be such a worrywart. If there is a serial killer out there, he's not going to try and hurt me in the middle of the day where he could be spotted."

"I'll go with you."

"No. You need to stay here in case I'm not back before Lewis arrives."

"Then why can't you just wait until later, when I can go with you?"

"Because I have something important to do, and it won't wait." She picked up her purse and sailed out the door.

❖ ❖ ❖

Donnie dropped his luggage off at the hotel, changed shirts, then headed over to meet with JJ and Matt. His mind was already switching gears from the seventeen-year-old who had been terrorizing travelers on the I-95 corridor to a serial killer terrorizing Monroe.

He'd been listening to the news on the radio, and the town was in full-scale panic. Women were talking about buying guns, men were talking about not letting their women out alone, parents were talking about keeping their kids home from school, and the local pound said that they didn't have a single German shepherd, Rottweiler, Doberman, or pit bull left for adoption. In addition, most of their large-breed dogs were now flying out the door, regardless of their temperament.

Three girls were dead. The town now knew they had a serial killer in their midst. No one would be sleeping peacefully until he was caught.

The stress level for law enforcement would be at an all-time high.

Well, here comes the cavalry, he thought with a wry smile.

He found JJ on the phone trying to convince the press that there was no reason to raise the panic level.

"Too late," Donnie whispered with a grin as he tossed his jacket over a chair and started going through the files, catching up on the investigation.

JJ hung up the phone. "Too late for what?"

"Panic. I was listening to the radio on my way over here. Guns, big dogs, and deadbolt locks are in high demand."

JJ's lips twisted. "Figures. Well, welcome back to hell week. I gather you caught your sniper?"

"The FBI always gets their man. In this case, a teenager with a hunting rifle and a grudge against his father who made him get a job because he was no longer in school." Donnie sat down on the edge of the conference table as he perused the interview with Bret Leland.

"Leland is swearing he didn't hurt anyone, doesn't have any idea how the alleged murder weapon ended up in his car, and was only avoiding the police for fear of being arrested for something he didn't do."

JJ's chair squeaked as he leaned back. "You buy that?"

"I don't buy anything unless it's on sale. You haven't charged him yet?"

"We're waiting for forensics to give us a positive ID on the knife. If it doesn't fit, we must acquit."

Donnie laughed. "You're sharp today. You got the other girls covered?"

"Done. We don't have enough men to put round-the-clock guards on them, but we beefed up drive-bys and encouraged them to stay home and indoors."

"Looks like you may not have needed me after all." Donnie closed the file and tossed it down.

"One can only hope."

Lanae zipped up her coat, slung her purse over her shoulder, and pulled her apartment door closed behind her. If she was going to have to go into hiding—namely, staying in her apartment until this all blew over—she was going to need to stock up on provisions.

It had taken her fifteen minutes to make an extra-long shopping list. All things considered, it would probably take three hours just to buy it all.

It was ridiculous, of course, but she couldn't help herself. The idea of people pointing at her, whispering about her, telling each other stories about her over the dinner table.

She lifted her face to the sun. The weatherman promised a beautiful, partly cloudy day in the midfifties with increasing cloudiness after sunset and a 90 percent chance of rain tomorrow. She wouldn't mind staying indoors tomorrow. Maybe it would be cold and rainy and miserable every day of reclusion. By the time this was over, she'd be a world champion solitaire player. Or in a straitjacket from too many soap operas.

The squeal of tires penetrated her self-pity. She lifted her head and looked in the direction of the sound. The car was coming at her! Straight at her!

And it wasn't stopping.

Lanae tried to jump out of the way, but the bumper of the car clipped her on the hip, sending her tumbling head over heels.

She slammed down, her mind registering pain, asphalt, and someone screaming in terror. Or maybe that was her own voice.

Then. . .nothing registered at all.

Zoe took a deep breath before knocking loudly on the front door. It had taken every resource Dan could put at her disposal, but she'd finally tracked down a woman named Corinne Hearn, a friend of Leona Oakley's. According to the diary entry, Corinne knew about

Leona's affair with Tappan and the subsequent blackmail attempt.

Zoe could only hope she knew even more.

The door opened, and a tall, stocky woman with gray hair and a weathered face eyed Zoe warily through a pair of thick glasses. In spite of the fact that it was the middle of the afternoon, she was wearing a tattered blue bathrobe and fuzzy slippers. A cigarette dangled from her thin lips. "Yeah?"

"My name is Zoe Shefford. Are you Corinne Hearn?"

"Ellis."

"I beg your pardon?" Zoe's heart began to fall. Another dead end.

"Ellis. My name is Ellis now. Why are you looking for me? If you're looking for money, you're out of luck."

"No," Zoe assured her with a smile. "I'm not some kind of bill collector. I'm a friend of Lanae Oakley's. I'm looking into some things for her and was hoping you could help."

"Little Lanae?" Corinne grinned, showing a few missing teeth. Those that weren't missing were stained from too many cigarettes and too little money for a good dentist. Or maybe any dentist at all. "Guess she ain't so little anymore, is she? All growed up. How she doin'?"

"She's good, but she wants to know what happened to her mother."

Corinne Hearn Ellis suddenly looked resigned and defeated all at once. She stepped back from the door. "Come on in. You want a beer?"

"No, thank you. I'm fine."

The house, such as it was, was shabby, but it appeared to be clean. The tiny living room was dominated by a yellow floral sofa, a blue plaid chair, and a green recliner. Zoe chose the plaid chair, tucking her purse next to her feet.

Corinne settled down in the recliner and kicked it back. "I

always figured someone would come looking someday. Just figured it would be the law and didn't figure it would take this long."

Zoe knew then, as clearly as she'd ever known anything. "Leona Oakley is dead, isn't she?"

Corinne snorted in a distinctly unladylike manner. "Well, of course she is. Heavens. If she were still alive, she'd be with that kid of hers. She sure did love that little Lanae. Nothing she wouldn't a done for that kid."

She picked up her beer bottle and took a long swig as if seeking fortification. "I warned her, I did. Told Paulie that Leo was no good. Couldn't be trusted. Mean as a snake, that man was. But you think Paulie would listen? No sirree. Not that gal. She was all-fired sure she had a way to beat him at his own game."

"Leo, as in Leonard Tappan?"

"Yeah. He's dead, I hear." She snorted again. "Devil finally came for his own. Took 'im long enough."

Zoe clasped her hands together and leaned forward, eager to hear it all. "What happened that night, Mrs. Ellis?"

Corinne waved her hand. "Corie. Just call me Corie. Lordy, I ain't thought about that night in a long time. I never been so scared in my life."

"You were there?" Zoe wasn't sure why she was surprised, but she was.

"Oh, yeah. I saw it all."

"What happened?" Zoe pulled out her notebook and started taking notes, wishing she'd thought to bring a tape recorder.

"I was hiding in the ditch. Plan was for me to witness it all so she could feel safe. I was supposed to be her ace in the hole, I guess. We was young and so stupid."

She took another swig from her drink and tucked the bottle in her lap. "He showed up, all brash and sass, demanding she give him that book back. She told him she didn't have it with her and she wasn't going to give it to him until she got all the money she wanted." Corinne stopped for a second, taking a deep breath.

"Then he shot her."

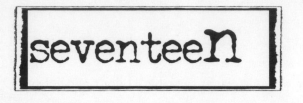

seventeen

Saturday, October 2—2:47 p.m.

Dan Cordette couldn't believe his ears. He stood in the hall of his ex-wife's home and listened to Taylor whine about not being able to go to a football game with her friends.

"Let me get this straight, Taylor. We have a serial killer who has brutally murdered at least three of your friends, and you don't understand why we're being so mean and making you stay home?" He looked over at his ex-wife, hoping she could make sense of their daughter, because he sure couldn't.

"Taylor, your father is not being unreasonable. We are concerned for your safety."

Taylor stomped her foot, her eyes flashing with indignation, acting the tortured victim. "I can't believe this! We're talking about a football stadium. Thousands of people. No one in his right mind is going to try to hurt me in a place like that!"

"He's not in his right mind," Dan snapped. "That's the whole point!"

Taylor fumed, folding her arms across her chest. "So, you're not letting me go."

"Absolutely, utterly, and completely not."

Growling under her breath, Taylor spun on her heel and ran up the steps. A few seconds later, Dan and his ex-wife heard a bedroom door slam shut.

Jeanine Cordette shook her head. "Well, that was pleasant."

"Is she always like this? So. . .volatile?"

"She's a teenager. It goes with the territory." She headed for the kitchen. "I need to start dinner."

Dan followed her, taking a seat at the table. "I don't remember Tanya being so hard."

Jeanine pulled a sack of potatoes out of a bin and started peeling. "You were never home, and when you were, she was always looking to get you on her side so she could override my rules."

"I'm sorry, Jeanine."

She cast a look over her shoulder. "For what?"

"For not understanding how hard it was for you to raise them alone. I didn't make it easy for you."

She resumed scraping the potatoes over the sink. "No, you didn't."

"Where's Peter?"

"Pete. And I have no idea. We aren't seeing each other anymore."

That surprised Dan. "No one told me."

Jeanine shrugged as she set a peeled potato aside and started another one. "I'm sure no one thought it mattered to you."

"I thought you were happy."

"It was good for a while."

"I'm sorry." Dan picked at the place mat, trying to find some other topic of conversation. So far, he hadn't been doing all that well.

His cell phone rang, giving him a reprieve. "Hello?"

"Dan? It's Zoe. I got good news and bad news."

"Give me the good news first."

"Fatalist. The good news is I found an eyewitness who saw Leonard Tappan shoot and kill Leona Oakley."

Stunned, Dan shook his head as if to clear it. "Say that again."

"I didn't stutter. And she's willing to come in for a formal deposition."

"Then what's the bad news?"

"I just got a call. Someone struck Lanae in a hit-and-run. She's at the hospital. Critical condition. I'm on my way there now."

"So am I." Dan closed his phone and jumped to his feet. "I have to go."

"I'm not surprised," Jeanine responded.

"This isn't me just running off because work calls. Someone is killing young girls—"

She placed two fingers over his lips. "Go. You can eat when you get back."

"Thanks, I may even be back before you set the table."

JJ leaned back against the wall, his arms folded across his chest, and studied the man being processed.

Bret Leland, with hands cuffed behind his back, looked mad enough to split wood with spit. "I didn't kill anyone. I don't know how that knife got in my car, and I'm not saying another word without an attorney. I know how this works. You need a scapegoat, and anyone that you pin this on will do. Well, I'm not going down for something I didn't do."

Matt pushed Leland down in a chair. "I'm hurting for you, Leland, I really am."

"May I?" Donnie asked JJ.

"Be my guest."

Donnie strolled over and took a chair across from Leland. "I'm Special Agent Donnie Bevere—"

"FBI?" Leland's expression went from anger to fear in a split second. "Why are you here?"

"We have three dead women, Mr. Leland. That makes it a serial killing. That means I get to step in and take over." Donnie leaned forward with a grin that was far from pleasant. "Lucky you."

JJ grudgingly had to admire Donnie's style. That grin was pure malice and intimidation. He had to see if Donnie would teach him how to do that. Leland was turning to jelly.

"I didn't kill those women."

"Really? Well, I'm so glad to hear that. But I have a problem, Mr. Leland."

"What's that?" Leland asked warily.

"I have a murder weapon in your car." Donnie ticked off on his fingers. "I have you connected to two of the three victims. I have you positively identified as the last person to see at least one of them alive and with one of the others hours before she was killed. I have you avoiding us and refusing to come in voluntarily to answer some simple questions."

"I was scared."

"Understandable, Mr. Leland, but it also makes you look suspiciously guilty."

Denise slipped into the room and took a spot next to JJ. "How's it going?"

"He's not admitting to anything and yelling for an attorney."

She grimaced. "Figures."

"You got anything for me?"

Denise gave him that thousand-watt smile and winked. "I thought you'd never ask."

JJ laughed, shaking his head.

"Oh," Denise continued. "You meant business. Yeah, your guru just called in. Seems some girl got clipped in a hit-and-run. I told her we were homicide and directed her down to traffic. And Amato called."

JJ felt that adrenaline rush and straightened. "What did she have to say?"

"We may have a murder weapon."

"May?" JJ squawked.

"She says she can't make it a positive ID until she has it tested for possible trace fluids, but it is a positive for size and style of blade."

"We need more."

Denise shrugged. "Looks that way."

"You have the search warrant for his house. Find more evidence."

"I'm on it." Denise disappeared through the door.

Matt nudged JJ's shoulder. "She's so stuck on you, it's not funny."

"What are you, nuts? She's engaged. We're just friends, that's all."

"That's not what the gossip line is buzzing with. Seems she told Marsha that she broke off her engagement."

JJ went to deny it again, then remembered the way Denise was suddenly touching him far more than she ever had before—a pat on the shoulder, a stroke on the arm, holding his hand a little too long. And there were the suggestive remarks. "You think?"

"I know." Matt dropped his hand on JJ's shoulder. "And I don't imagine Zoe is too happy about it."

"Zoe? What does she have to do with any of this?"

Matt shook his head. "Thou art so blind, so deaf, and so utterly dumb. I'm going to go call Zoe back and find out what's going on. It's not like her to call us over a hit-and-run. Something else is up."

JJ grabbed Matt's arm. "No. You stay here and help Donnie. I'll go see to Zoe."

"About time."

❖ ❖ ❖

Zoe paced the length of the room again. She was probably driving some of the people in the waiting room crazy, but she didn't care. She had a witness to a murder, someone had tried to kill Lanae, who was now fighting for her life, and that Denise woman wouldn't put her through to JJ.

"He's interrogating a suspect, Miss Shefford. I'm sure you think that he should just drop everything and be at your beck and call, but it doesn't work that way."

Someone needed to give that woman an attitude adjustment.

And okay, maybe she did think of JJ as hers, and maybe that was a bit presumptuous, but this wasn't about losing a set of car keys. It was about murder. JJ would *want* to know.

She started to think about sitting down when Dan rushed into the room. "Zoe! Let's take a walk."

He took her arm and led her down the hall and outside the emergency room. Dropping her arm, he buttoned up his coat. "Okay, from the top."

Step by step, Zoe went through the facts for him, from tracking down Leona's friend, to everything Corinne said, to getting the call about Lanae.

"Why would they call you about Lanae?"

"She had my number in her wallet. They didn't have any other contact information, so they called me." She shoved her hands down in her pockets. "I think someone wants her dead, Dan."

"It could have been an accident."

Zoe shook her head. "I don't think so. She reveals she's Tappan's illegitimate daughter, and the next day she gets hit by a car? A little too much for me."

"It was deliberate?"

"A witness saw the whole thing. Said the car accelerated when Lanae crossed the parking lot and deliberately hit her."

"Okay, sounds like attempted murder to me. So, who would stand to benefit from Lanae's death?"

Zoe looked up at him. "Tappan's kids."

"Or someone who thought so highly of the judge that he couldn't stand someone dragging the judge's good name through the mud."

"Maybe, but you gotta love the judge an awful lot to attempt murder just to protect his good name."

"Good point."

Zoe reached out and touched Dan's sleeve. "By the way, I heard that your daughter is on that list. I'm sorry. She's safe, isn't she?"

"I practically have her locked in her room." Dan frowned. "And she's hating it."

"Well, of course she is. You would, too, if you were in her shoes."

"I guess. She just doesn't understand how worried I am."

Zoe laughed. "That's because she isn't a parent. She's a teenager. Teens have this philosophy that lasts until they're in their late twenties, and it affects everything they do."

"What's that?"

"They're invincible."

Dan tipped his head back and laughed. "You know my daughter."

"I've had my share of dealings with teenagers and I was one. . . *long* ago."

"Zoe, I hate to do this, but I need to ask you for a favor."

"What do you need?"

Dan stopped and stared down at her. "I know I said that I understood about your abilities and that I wouldn't pressure you. That was then. It was my friend's daughter. Your friend's niece. But. . ."

Zoe closed her eyes briefly, then opened them again. Perhaps it had been inevitable from the start. She started walking, not wanting to see that look in his eyes. "But, this is *your* daughter."

"I'm sorry."

"Dan, I'm doing all I can."

"Zoe, maybe God wouldn't be all that upset if you just did a little bit, you know? Just this once. We have to stop this man before he kills again."

She really didn't know what to say to him. The desperation in his voice pulled at her. The look in Daria's face had, too.

"Zoe?"

"Let me think about it, okay? No promises. Just give me some time to think."

Dan's face lightened, and he smiled. "Fair enough."

She stopped and turned. "We need to get back and see if there's any word on Lanae."

"We need to talk to. . .well, speak of the devil."

"What?"

"I was about to say that we needed to talk to Detective Johnson, but there he is."

Zoe looked up and saw JJ standing at the door to the emergency room, watching them approach. Denise must have given him her message after all.

"Detective." Dan shook hands with JJ. "Boy, are we glad to see you."

"What's going on?"

"Color me surprised. You mean your girlfriend let you out?"

JJ's mouth flattened, and his eyes took on a dangerously hard glint. "Don't even start with me. She's not my girlfriend."

"Maybe you need to tell her that. I think she has a different perspective."

"Are you just going to stand here and act like a jealous wife, or are you going to tell me what's going on?"

"Jealous wife!" Zoe choked out a weak laugh. "Oh, please. In your dreams. I only called you because someone tried to kill Lanae."

❖ ❖ ❖

"Where have you been?" Marcus hissed at Dana when she came breezing through the door. "We've been waiting twenty minutes for you."

Dana ignored the censure in his voice as she draped her coat over a chair and headed for the library. "I told you I had some errands to run."

Stepping into the library, she sank quickly in the nearest chair. "I'm sorry to keep you waiting. Traffic was worse than I expected."

Morton, her father's attorney, came to his feet. "Dana. Are you okay? You look a little shaken."

"I'm fine." Dana managed a weak smile.

"Nothing happened, did it? I did ask you not to go out alone."

Dana shook her head. "I had some things to take care of and, really, I'm just fine."

Kicking off her shoes, she tucked her feet beneath her. "Marcus, be a dear and get me a drink, will you?"

Marcus, who had barely sat down, got back up and headed for the bar in the corner.

Morton sat down behind their father's desk and picked up his glasses. "I guess we can begin."

"What about this woman making claims against Dad?" Dana asked. "How does she affect the estate?"

"She is claiming to be his illegitimate daughter and suing for eighteen years of child support. Her attorneys haven't given us a final amount yet, but they're talking into the millions, based on your father's income."

"Millions?" Marcus gasped as he handed Dana a glass of wine. "Is she crazy?"

"Like a fox," Morton told him. "Eighteen years plus interest. It's hefty. Now, here's where it gets tricky. In order for her to collect on the child support, she will have to prove that she is Leo's daughter. If she does—"

"She can't!" Dana interjected sharply. "She isn't, therefore she can't."

Morton held up one hand. "Bear with me. If she proves that she is his daughter, she not only collects the child support, but she is then eligible for one-third of the entire estate."

Dana couldn't believe her ears. To pay this woman child support was one thing, but to welcome her as a full heir and hand over one-third of the estate was another matter altogether. "How can she? She isn't mentioned in the will."

"Neither are you and Marcus."

"What?" Marcus barked. "Of course we are!"

Morton shook his head. "No. You have to understand. Your father's will was set up right after you were born, Marcus. He fully expected that there might be more children to follow. The will states that everything will be equally divided among *all* his children."

"So, if this woman proves that she is one of Dad's children, she gets a full one-third of the estate."

"Yes." Morton took his glasses off and polished them with his handkerchief. "She is older than you, Marcus. That would make her the firstborn child. There is a provision in the will that the firstborn will inherit the house."

Dana couldn't believe what she was hearing. It was unbelievable. Her home. Her father's estate. The money. "But Dad fully expected that to be Marcus!"

She knew all too well that Marcus didn't want the house. He'd told her that on more than one occasion. He considered it a monstrosity. In her mind, the house was hers. To think that some stranger could just waltz in and take it away from her was beyond taking seriously.

Morton shrugged. "Doesn't matter what he expected. The courts will only go by the wording of the will."

"And there's nothing we can do?" Dana asked.

"Prove she's a fraud. That's the only option you have."

"Or make sure she knows not to mess with us," Dana said with cold calm.

5:02 p.m.

Zoe sat curled up in one of the most uncomfortable chairs she'd ever encountered, staring down at her hands, picking at her nail polish. JJ was outside, talking to Matt and Donnie on his cell phone, and Dan was sitting quietly next to her.

Dan slapped his thighs and stood up. "I'm going to go. Jeanine and the girls are expecting me for dinner. Call me and let me know when you find out about Lanae?"

Zoe looked up at him. "Sure. I'll call you later."

"I'd stay, but you're in good hands with Johnson."

Zoe laughed lightly. "I'm not in his hands, but I'm fine. Go. Enjoy time with your family."

A few minutes after Dan left, JJ came in and sat down. "Explain your theory to me again."

Taking a deep breath while gathering her thoughts, Zoe leaned her head back against the wall. "Tappan kills Lanae's mother and buries the body. Corinne is too afraid of Tappan to say anything. Lanae finds her mother's diary as well as a Tappan family diary that implicates William Tappan—"

"The judge's father."

"Yes. William Tappan kills his brother, Byron, and inherits the entire estate. Judge Tappan wants the diary, but he kills Leona before he can find out what she did with it. Now, Lanae steps forward, claiming to be the judge's firstborn child. We haven't even mentioned the diary or her mother yet, and already there's an attempt on her life. The way I see it, one or both of the Tappan heirs are trying to get rid of the competition. Namely, Lanae."

JJ rolled his shoulders. "History repeats itself."

His words, spoken so casually, punched through her, flipping switches she hadn't known existed. "Say that again."

"What? History repeats itself?"

"That's it!"

"I'm lost."

Zoe started bouncing in her seat as it all started coming together for her. "When I was reading the diary, the Lord kept giving me this scripture about the iniquity of the fathers becoming the sins of the children into the third and fourth generations! That's what He was trying to show me!"

"Would it surprise you to know that I have no idea what you're talking about?"

She reached out and slapped his thigh. "No, but that's okay. Look how long it took me to figure it out."

JJ smirked. "Just tell God to get better communication skills."

"Miss Shefford?" A doctor in green scrubs, his facemask pulled down around his throat, looked over in her direction from the doorway.

Zoe stood and hurried over to him. "How is she?"

"Concussion, skull fracture, three cracked ribs, collapsed lung, and a fracture in her right leg. She's stable, but we have her lightly sedated right now while she's intubated."

"Can we speak to her?" JJ asked.

"And you are?"

JJ pulled out his badge and held it out for closer inspection. "Detective Johnson. Homicide."

The doctor gave him a speculative look. "Homicide? Was someone else killed?"

"Someone tried to kill her."

"I'm sorry. I thought it was just an accident." He folded his arms across his chest. "I don't see a problem with you seeing her, but she won't be able to answer any of your questions, Detective. Like I said, she's intubated. It will be another day or two before the lung is inflated and we can take the breathing tubes out."

JJ put his badge away. "Not a problem. I'm going to post a guard outside her door and restrict visitors to Miss Shefford and members of my team."

"What about her relatives?"

The force of JJ's answer set Zoe back on her heels.

"It's entirely possible that her relatives are trying to kill her."

eighteen

Sunday, October 3—11:27 a.m.

Donnie still couldn't make the pieces fit. He'd gone over the evidence, the files, the interviews, the forensic reports, and the autopsy findings, and it just wasn't coming together for him the way he thought it should.

In some respects, it seemed like a slam dunk.

But the knife didn't fit. What was it JJ had said? If it doesn't fit, you must acquit. Corny and overdone, but there was a grain of truth there that was throwing a real wrinkle in the fabric of this case.

Why would Leland keep the knife that close? They had gone over his car with a fine-tooth comb and the latest in forensic equipment. Not one hair, not one fiber that would put the girls in his car.

Pacing the room, he walked it out in his mind. Leland goes to a bar and picks up the girl, possibly drugging their drinks to make it easier to abduct them. He puts them in a vehicle and takes them somewhere to kill them. Then he transports them to another location to dump them. That would explain why there were no fibers in his car. He used another vehicle—a van perhaps. Leland worked for a bakery, and while he was a salesman, it's entirely possible that he would have access to one or more of the company's delivery vans.

That lined up with the fact that Amato agreed that they had a separate crime scene out there somewhere.

So why was the knife in his car? Why wasn't it hidden somewhere in the transport vehicle?

Okay, if it was one of the company trucks, he wouldn't want to take a chance on one of the drivers finding it. Or maybe he used a different truck each time.

A small detail, but it bothered him anyway. It was just the kind of thing that a good defense attorney could rip to shreds.

They needed to find the crime scene. They had to connect the girls to Leland through forensic evidence that would nail the prison door shut behind him.

"You look like a man with a problem." JJ walked into the room, taking long strides as he headed for his desk.

"Did you just come from the hospital?"

"Yeah." JJ tossed his leather jacket over the filing cabinet and dropped down in his chair. "Lanae isn't awake yet, but even if she was, she still has those breathing tubes in, so she wouldn't be able to answer any questions."

Donnie eased a hip onto the edge of the conference table. "Do you find it odd that we have two very distinct things going on at this exact moment and one common denominator?"

"What's that?" JJ flipped through his messages, making two piles.

"Case number one—we have this Lanae Oakley woman making claims against a powerful but now deceased judge, and an attempt is made on her life. Case number two—we have three girls killed and a list of girls who are possible targets."

JJ leaned back in his chair, narrowing his eyes. "And?"

"And what is the common denominator that links these two cases?"

"Zoe Shefford has her nose in both of them?"

Donnie shook his head as he laughed. "Try again."

Drumming his fingers on the arm of the chair, JJ pursed his lips. "Dana Tappan."

"Bingo." Donnie pointed a finger at JJ. "Give the man whatever is behind door number one."

"So, what are you thinking?"

Donnie sobered quickly. "I have no idea, but it's bugging the daylights out of me. Things don't work this way, and you know it. Two apparently unrelated cases that have one name popping up on both cases? Uh-uh. Something is fishy and it ain't Willy."

"Who?"

"Willy. Orca. Whale." Donnie waved a dismissive hand. "Forget it. You have to have kids to understand. Has anyone been down to Leland's place of employment and checked out the company trucks?"

"For what purpose?"

"Not one fiber or hair showed up in his car. He used a different vehicle to transport the bodies. If he doesn't own a van or truck, it's possible he used one or more of the company delivery trucks."

JJ picked up the phone. "I know Chapman is checking to see if he owns another vehicle or property. I'll tell him to check on the company trucks."

Donnie continued to think while JJ tracked down Denise and gave her more work to do. When JJ got off the phone, Donnie was back to the other puzzle he was working on.

"I think we need to go have a chat with Miss Dana Tappan."

JJ lumbered to his feet. "Okay by me."

"Do we have anyone out talking to this Corinne Ellis about Lanae's mother?"

JJ nodded as he hooked his badge to his belt and slid into his shoulder holster. "I sent Denise and Steve. They're going to see if she can take them to the spot where Tappan buried the woman. If she can, they're going to call in a crime scene team to start digging around."

"And to think I only came for a wedding."

JJ rolled his eyes as he climbed into the Jeep. "And to think I actually like a Fed."

Zoe opened the screen door and knocked again. Louder. The door slowly opened, and Zoe smiled down at Hannah. "Hi. Do you remember me?"

Hannah nodded solemnly. "You're Aunt Daria's friend."

"Is she here?"

Hannah nodded again and stepped back, opening the door a little wider. "She's in the family room with my mom."

"Thanks."

Daria was sitting on the sofa, her arm around her sister's shoulders as the two women sobbed. Daria's brother-in-law, Frank, was on the phone. He saw her before Daria did and waved her in.

Then Daria lifted her head and stared up at Zoe. "Did you find him?"

"The police have him in custody." Which wasn't quite what Daria meant, but did it really matter at this point? The important thing for the families was that someone went to jail for the crime, not who specifically found him.

"Why haven't we heard that on the news yet?"

She sat down on the edge of a chair. "Because they haven't officially charged him yet. There is some forensic evidence they're waiting for. Some loose ends to tie up. They want to make sure that they don't make a single mistake that a defense attorney could use to get the guy acquitted."

Noreen merely sat there, staring off into space, tears streaming down her face. Zoe wasn't sure she was hearing anything being said.

Turning back to Daria, Zoe tried to swallow her own nervousness. She couldn't ever remember being nervous around Daria. They never fought, never screamed at each other, never ignored each other.

Until now.

And Zoe didn't know how to bridge the air of tension between them. "Daria."

Daria sniffed, waving her hand. "No. I'm the one who needs to apologize. I should have realized that when I needed you, you'd come through for me."

Guilt poked at Zoe, making her practically squirm as she sat there staring at her best friend. She'd never lied to Daria. Why was she even considering it now? Because it wasn't the time or the place for coming clean.

"Daria."

"No, really. I can't believe I talked to you the way I did. I mean, how can some religious beliefs compare to a lifelong friendship?" Fresh tears welled up in Daria's eyes. "The funeral is set for Tuesday."

"I'll be there." Zoe rose to her feet. "I need to go. I just wanted to stop in and let you know that the man is in custody."

Frank, now off the phone, moved forward. "I'll walk you to the door."

Zoe leaned down and gave Daria a hug. "I'll call you later."

Daria nodded, swiping at tears.

At the front door, Frank stepped outside with Zoe. "They really have him?"

"They believe they do."

He took a deep, rasping breath, tipping his head back. The struggle to keep from breaking down emotionally was etched on his face.

Then he lowered his face and gave Zoe a look that sent a shiver down her spine.

"Make sure he stays locked up."

❖　❖　❖

Denise keyed her mike and spoke to her partner, Steve Cole. "Anything?"

"Not yet," he responded.

Denise ducked beneath a low evergreen branch and stopped to look around once more. After twenty years, it was like trying to find a needle in a haystack.

Specifically, it was a small outcropping of rocks that resembled the head of a horse. That was the best Corinne Ellis could remember after so many years. Go out the old logging trail to the wooden bridge. Pull over. Walk down to the ditch. Turn right. Walk about fifty yards and look for the horse-head rocks.

Denise would like nothing better than to be able to call JJ and tell him she'd found the body of one Leona Oakley. *Let's go out for dinner tonight, JJ, and celebrate.*

But first she had to find the rocks.

Another ten minutes passed, and Denise was getting increasingly frustrated. She keyed her mike again. "Steve? I've gone nearly a half mile. I'm turning back."

"Ten-four. I've gone nearly that far myself. I'll meet you back at the car."

"Ten-four."

Rather than walk back in her tracks, she chose to move up from the ditch another ten yards, then start back. She was nearly back to the bridge when she noticed a pile of rocks half-buried under leaves and fallen tree limbs.

Dragging some of the limbs aside, she stood staring down, hands on her hips, laughing. Give that woman the prize. Even after twenty years, she'd described the pile of rocks perfectly.

Denise keyed her mike. "Steve. I got it."

"Where are you?"

Looking around, she answered. "About seventy-five yards down from the bridge and about twenty yards up from the ditch."

"Be right there."

"I'm calling in the CSI boys."

"Ten-four."

After calling the crime lab, she called back to the station. Steve appeared just as she got through to Matt. "Matt? Where's JJ?"

"He's out with the Fed following a hunch. What's up? You find something down there?"

"Sure did. Found the rocks, anyway. She described them perfectly. I called the lab. They're on their way to start digging up the area."

Denise stepped back as Steve started clearing the area around the rocks.

"I'll let JJ know if he calls in. In the meantime, keep us posted."

Denise swallowed her disappointment that JJ wasn't around to talk to. "Will do."

She ended the call, closed the phone, and stuck it back in her pocket. "We got about twenty minutes until the shovels get here."

Vivian Amato loved her job as a coroner. Most of her friends thought she was absolutely nuts, but she'd always loved puzzles. And her job was one of the most fascinating puzzles she knew of. How did they die? When did they die? Why did they die? And sometimes. . .who made sure they died?

Done with the day's work, she bought a soda from the vending machine, then sat down behind her desk to start going through the mail and faxes that were piling up.

Twenty minutes later, she opened one brown envelope from the state lab and started reading it. She nearly spit a mouthful of soda all over the report when she read the findings on one tissue sample.

Grabbing the phone, she called upstairs. "Matt? Is JJ around?"

"No. He's out on a call. What's up?"

"Are you sitting down?"

"No, but give me a second and I will be. Okay. Give it to me."

Vivian leaned back in her chair, staring at the report in her hand. "Judge Tappan died of a heart attack."

"News flash, Amato. Even I know that."

"Yeah, big boy, I'll bet you do. But, I'll bet you didn't know it was induced by GHB. The judge was murdered, Matt."

nineteen

J J and Donnie waited until the two nurses stepped into the elevator before following. The ride up to the fourth floor of the hospital had been quiet—neither man felt inclined to discuss what was on their minds in the presence of strangers.

They had gone to the Tappan home, only to be turned away by the housekeeper. Neither Miss Dana nor Mr. Marcus was home, but both were expected home for dinner at six. Disappointed, JJ opted for running by the hospital and seeing Lanae before heading back to the station.

Hopefully, she was awake and able to give them something about the driver.

JJ showed his badge to the guard, then pushed open the door.

The drapes were opened, letting sunlight flood the room, and the television was muted. Even so, it felt dark and depressing. Zoe was sitting in a metal chair next to Lanae, holding her hand, talking softly to her.

As JJ and Donnie stepped into the room, Zoe stood up. "She's still out of it. The doctor suspects possible swelling in the brain from the head injury."

"What now?" JJ asked.

Zoe shrugged. "He says not to be too concerned yet, that sleep is just her body's way of healing. They took her for X-rays earlier. If the brain is swelling, they'll take her into surgery. But they're keeping a close eye on her."

Donnie rubbed his jaw, looking concerned. "We need to know if she saw the driver at all."

Suddenly JJ's phone rang. In spite of the no-cell rule in hospitals, he opened it quickly. "Johnson. Talk fast."

Donnie and Zoe huddled over Lanae, trying to give him some privacy as he took the call.

"I'm on my way." JJ snapped the phone closed. "They found Leona Oakley's body. And the coroner called. Judge Tappan was murdered."

"Killing a judge is a federal offense." Donnie gave JJ a pointed look. "You know there's nothing I can do. I have to call Jack, and we have to take over."

"It's yours with my blessing. I got enough on my plate right now without investigating that murder, too."

As they hurried out of the room, Zoe was hot on their heels, slipping her arms into her coat. "They found Lanae's mother?"

JJ nodded as he hit the elevator button. "Exactly where your witness told us she was. Good job, Zoe."

"Then the judge did kill her. Lanae is going to be disappointed. I think she was still holding out hope that her mother was out there somewhere, maybe afraid to come back."

The elevator doors opened, and the three of them stepped in. Donnie hit the LOBBY button. "Proving that Judge Tappan killed her is a moot point. He's dead, so he can't go to trial."

"No, but it gives Lanae closure." Zoe dug through her purse for her keys.

JJ looked down at the keys in Zoe's hand. "Where are you going now?"

"I don't know. Where are you going?"

"Back to the station."

Zoe flashed him one of those grins that told him she was up to something. "Then I'm going to the station, too."

"And why is that?"

"Because I haven't bugged you nearly enough yet today."

"And pigs fly with yellow wings."

7:10 p.m.

JJ didn't know whether he was coming or going. After leaving the hospital, Donnie had called Vivian Amato, questioned her for nearly ten minutes, then called his partner, Jack Fleming.

Within two hours, the FBI had descended on the station like a swarm of flies on a picnic. They took over two conference rooms and half the bull pen. Then they confiscated every file JJ had on Judge Tappan.

Zoe hadn't shown up at the station, and it took awhile before JJ stopped expecting her to walk through the door every time it opened. She hadn't been serious about coming to the station to bug him. He didn't know if he was disappointed or not.

Denise had called in to report that a body had indeed been found near the rock formation. Vivian Amato was onsite and promising to have some answers for him within forty-eight hours. Not nearly fast enough. Chapman had a team down at the bakery, going through the trucks, looking for evidence. Barone was hunched over his computer, looking for information on Leona Oakley. Matt was interviewing Corinne Ellis.

And the press was howling on the front steps, hungry for sound bites and meaty stories.

Donnie rapped on the doorjamb, breaking into JJ's mental gymnastics. "You busy?"

"Just juggling a million and one details. What do you need?"

"We're on our way to the Tappans' place and thought you might like to come along."

JJ grinned like a little boy offered a new bike. "Can I, huh-huh?"

"Let's roll, dude."

"Donnie." JJ grabbed his jacket. "I think it only fair to tell you that I think you need a life. You watch entirely too many movies."

Donnie staggered back, dramatically throwing his hand over his chest. "It's all those stakeouts. They warp you."

Grinning, JJ just shook his head and followed Donnie out.

Twenty-five minutes later, JJ watched as Donnie knocked on the front door of the Tappan house. When Marcus Tappan opened the door, Donnie flashed his badge. "Special Agent Donnie Bevere, FBI. I'm sorry, Mr. Tappan, but I'm going to have to ask you to step aside."

Marcus Tappan slowly turned white, staring in disbelief as Donnie turned and waved to other agents. Then Marcus spoke up. "You can't just come barging in here! What's this all about?"

"I'm afraid I can, Mr. Tappan. This house is a crime scene. Now if you'll step aside."

JJ herded Marcus back into the dining room, where his sister was in the middle of dinner. When Marcus and JJ entered the room, she slowly stood. "What's going on?"

"The FBI is here," he told her, his voice shaking with disbelief and confusion.

Dana looked from her brother to JJ. "I demand to know what this is about."

"Your father was murdered, Miss Tappan. When a judge is murdered, it becomes a federal matter."

Glaring, Dana tossed her napkin down, shoving back her chair. "This is ridiculous. No one murdered my father. I want you people out of my house immediately."

JJ stepped in front of her as she attempted to storm past him. "Let me give you a polite warning. The FBI isn't nearly as nice as I am. You go out there spouting your indignation and getting in their way, and they're liable to just toss you in handcuffs, haul you off, and ask questions later."

Dana's eyes narrowed with a dangerous glint as she stared up at him. "I have never been so insulted!"

"Oh, it's no big deal, Miss Tappan. Getting insulted is just part of life. You'll get used to it eventually."

She nearly hissed in his face, but to give her credit, she backed up. JJ breathed a sigh of relief. He expected more fireworks than this. The woman had a reputation for being nearly as tough as her father.

"Why don't you just have a seat?" he suggested.

Donnie walked into the room with two other agents. "I'm going to ask each of you to go with one of these agents. We need to ask you a few questions."

Marcus was visibly shaken as he slowly followed one of the agents from the room. Dana, on the other hand, lifted her chin, walked back to the table, and took her seat. With careful deliberation, she picked up her napkin, shook it, and placed it in her lap.

The agent looked at Donnie, who looked pointedly at Dana. "You can question the princess here in the dining room."

The agent nodded and headed over to take a chair next to Dana.

"JJ, I could use you in the library."

"I'm calling my attorney!" Dana's head snapped up. "And you

better not touch anything that belonged to my father!"

Donnie ignored her as he walked out of the room. As soon as they left the dining room, JJ erupted into laughter. "*Princess.* I like that. The woman has an attitude big enough to drive a tanker through."

"She'll be singing a different tune by the time Harry is done with her. He comes off quiet, but he's a brutal interrogator." Donnie pushed open the door to the library, where another agent was already going through the filing cabinet.

"Where do you want me?"

"Go through his desk. Look at personal papers, appointment books, files. We need to find something that will give us an idea as to who killed him and why."

JJ chuckled. "Everyone he ever sent to jail. Everyone he ever strong-armed. Everyone—"

"I got it, I got it."

JJ sat down in the leather chair and sighed heavily as his muscles cried out in gratitude. "Oh, man. I want this chair."

Donnie laughed as he opened a cabinet. "And you wonder why the rich are always smiling."

There was very little talking over the next half hour as they tore the room apart. JJ had the beautiful mahogany desk covered with three distinct piles of papers: IRRELEVANT, IMPORTANT, and NOT SURE BUT SURE LOOKS QUESTIONABLE.

"Looks like he has a lot of business dealings with Lewis Morton."

Donnie looked over from the book shelf. "Who?"

JJ tossed a file into the IMPORTANT stack. "Lewis Morton. When Tappan was the district attorney, Lewis was the assistant district attorney. Everyone thought Morton would go for Tappan's job when he made judge, but instead, he quit and went into private practice. He's handling the Tappan estate. And it looks like they had a few fingers in each other's pies."

"Any reason Lewis might want the judge dead?"

Donnie shook his head and opened another drawer. "Not that I can see so far."

"Knock-knock." Matt stepped tentatively into the room. "JJ?"

"Over here."

Matt whistled as he looked around the room, moving slowly toward the desk where JJ waited. "So this is how the upper crust layers their bread."

"Cute. What are you doing here? I thought you were interviewing Corrine Ellis."

"Done. I'll fill you in later. Got something more important." He looked over at Donnie. "Hey, Hollywood. You may want in on this."

Donnie merely smiled, shaking his head as he set down the box in his arms.

Matt eyed a leather chair in front of the desk, moved a stack of files off it, and sank down in it. "I may never move again. You think the chief would let us order a couple of these?"

"No. Now what's so important?"

"Amato called. Leona Oakley was shot at close range with a .32 caliber. Two shots to the chest that she knows of. Could have been more, but after so many years. . ." He shrugged.

"Okay, so we now know Leona was shot. I don't see why you had to come running over here for that."

"I'm getting there," Matt quipped, running his hands over the buttery-soft leather. "She was shot with a Colt .32, and not just any Colt .32. Specifically, a Colt Police Target Revolver."

Donnie whistled. "You're kidding."

JJ looked from Matt to Donnie and back again, feeling a little lost and not exactly liking it. "Okay, somebody tell me why this is earth-shattering."

Donnie glanced at Matt, then answered JJ. "This was a gun

manufactured in the early 1900s. Colt had two versions of this pistol. A .32 caliber and a .22 caliber. The .32 was discontinued in 1915. We're talking about a gun that is relatively rare and mostly owned by dealers or collectors."

JJ caught on to what had put the sparkle in Matt's eyes. "And the judge was a collector. You need to see if he has one of these in his gun case."

"Bingo."

❖   ❖   ❖

Zoe stood up with the rest of the congregation, collecting her coat, Bible, and purse before making her way out of the pew.

"Hi, Zoe." Mrs. Pollock smiled and nodded in her direction, clutching her walker tightly.

"Hello, Mrs. Pollock. How are you doing?"

"The arthritis has been particularly nasty this year. I should have gone to Miami with my sister. I can be so stubborn sometimes."

Zoe laughed. "Well, it's not too late to catch a plane and join her on the beach. I hear there are some really good-looking hunks hanging out down there."

Mrs. Pollock's laugh was belly deep. "Oh, dear. You are too funny. Could you see me trying to walk along the beach? My walker would keep getting stuck in the sand."

"Perfect excuse for some hero to come rescue you."

"Posh." The woman took another few steps with the walker, then stopped and looked back over her shoulder at Zoe. "With my luck, his wheelchair would get stuck, and I'd end up having to save him."

Zoe laughed. "You have a good evening, Mrs. Pollock."

"There you are."

Zoe turned around to see Rene approaching. "Hey, Rene."

Rene took Zoe's hand and pulled her to the front of the church, taking a seat in the front pew. "Now. Tell me."

"Tell you what?"

"Tell me how it's going."

Zoe blew out a heavy sigh. "Oh, man. Well, there are times when I think I know exactly what the Father is doing, then five minutes later, I'm completely clueless."

Rene laughed. "So, you're making progress."

"Is that what you call it?" She took a deep breath, trying to organize her thoughts. "When I was a psychic, I knew how to sort of reach out to the children for whatever information or feelings or impressions I could get. This is *so* totally different. Now, I have to pray and ask for guidance, but I'm not always sure I'm going to get it. Then, I'm not always looking for anything specific when I *do* get it. It's like not knowing one minute, then a few seconds later, just knowing. And it comes in bits and pieces."

"That is progress."

Zoe toyed with the strap on her purse, struggling to find the words to describe something illusive. "You know that scripture about His Word being a lamp unto my feet and light unto my path?"

"Yes. Psalm 119, I think."

"It's kind of like that. Father gives me enough information to move forward, but so little, I have to stay dependent on Him."

"He likes to keep us focused on Him, lest we think that we can do it without Him."

"Oh, I know I'm not doing this without Him."

Rene patted Zoe's arm. "I'm glad it's getting easier. I've really been praying for you this week. I know it's been hard. And I called the prayer team to let them know we needed the Father to help you and the police find this killer."

"He's in custody," Zoe told her, grateful and oddly touched that people had been praying for her. "And they found Lanae's mother's body. I haven't been able to tell her yet because she's still in a coma, but hopefully this will help bring her some closure."

"I'm sure it will." Rene slapped her thighs and stood up. "Well, now that I know you're doing well, let's go down and see if anyone left us any cake."

❖　❖　❖

Lanae felt the edges of awareness dragging at her—pain was growing stronger, people were hovering, something was beeping. She wasn't sure what it all meant, but she resisted it as best she could. It was the pain she wanted to avoid. The more awareness there was, the greater the pain.

She knew there was something she was supposed to be doing, but she couldn't remember what. There were little flashes—like movie clips—of a car speeding toward her, or someone screaming, or a face, partially obscured by the glare on glass.

There was one voice that penetrated deeper than the others. There was something familiar about the soft cadence of her words and the way she kept assuring Lanae that it was going to be fine.

What was going to be fine? And what did she mean when she said they had succeeded? That they'd found her? Found who?

The questions seemed to come at her faster and faster; and the irritation of not knowing made Lanae pull away again, to retreat farther into the nothingness until, once again, there was only silence.

❖　❖　❖

The press had descended on the Tappan home in full force. Satellite vans lined the street, reporters gathered in groups to discuss theories or hound every official-looking person available, and cameramen wandered through the melee looking for that once-in-a-lifetime shot.

While Donnie and JJ remained inside the house, overseeing the gathering of evidence, a special agent-in-charge from the state office prepared and delivered occasional press conferences.

Dana and Marcus had been questioned by three different agents each before finally being allowed to leave with instructions to stay available for further questioning.

Marcus had been sullen but cooperative. Dana, on the other hand, had ranted and railed, called her attorney, and balked at every opportunity. The agents, used to dealing with far worse, showed endless patience and steely determination. They never budged an inch, and eventually she stomped off to her apartment, angry but compliant, while her brother checked into a hotel.

They had found a Colt Target Revolver, circa 1913, locked in a velvet-lined box and hidden in the back of the gun cabinet in the master bedroom. It had been removed for a ballistics test. In the spirit of cooperation, the FBI was expediting the tests using their own labs.

In the meantime, JJ helped Donnie in trying to reconstruct the judge's last evening. The cook had told them that the judge had been home all day and only had two visitors late in the morning. One was his attorney, Lewis Morton, and the other was one of his golfing buddies, Judge Martine. Marcus had been in and out, and Dana had arrived just after five.

After cocktails in the library, dinner had been served promptly at six-thirty. She had served the Tappan family broiled fish, steamed vegetables, and rice pilaf. The judge was watching his health, she told them. He was concerned about his heart.

That had been news to JJ. "Miss Tappan told us that the judge was in perfect health," JJ had replied.

The cook had leaned forward conspiratorially. "The judge didn't want the kids to know. He figured they were already counting the days to his death." She had clucked softly in disgust. "Never seen such a family."

She went on to tell them that she had retired to her room after cleaning up dinner and didn't know anything was amiss until she heard the sirens out front. By then, the judge was being taken away in an ambulance.

Donnie suspected that either something in the dinner or something in the liquor cabinet had been used to administer the drug that had so increased the judge's heart rate that it had brought on a heart attack. It was too late to test any of the food, but everything in the bar had been taken away for toxicology analysis. JJ wasn't too optimistic. It had been too long since the night of the incident. The killer would have come back and replaced the contaminated bottle, hiding his tracks.

It was nearly eleven, and JJ was ready to fall asleep on his feet. Thank goodness, Josh was taking care of Zip for him or the guilt would have been overwhelming.

"You look like you're ready to call it a night."

JJ rolled his head, then his shoulders. "I was ready two hours ago. You guys are relentless." He looked around the room, which was a shambles. "I'm not cleaning this mess up."

Donnie laughed. "I wouldn't ask you to."

"Excuse me, Detective Johnson?" An agent came running into the room. "I think you need to come with me. We discovered something you might find interesting."

The excitement in the agent's voice gave JJ a shot of adrenaline.

On the other side of the pool, they entered a small guesthouse being used by Marcus. The living room was fairly neat and decorated in dark green plaids and stripes, trimmed in gold and burgundy.

The kitchen was pristine. Appliances were stainless steel, counters in pewter gray, and the walls wallpapered in green, gray, and white. JJ admired the man's taste.

"In here." The agent motioned them back to the small bedroom.

At first glance, it was a bedroom like most—a bed draped with a dark green comforter, two nightstands in light oak, a dresser, and a small desk. Books, candles, and collectibles were scattered around, adding the personal touches expected.

Then JJ saw what wasn't expected. Handcuffs latched to the headboard, a curl of rope, and a roll of duct tape tossed under the bed and just barely visible.

With latex-covered hands, Donnie's partner, Jack Fleming, picked up a small bottle and held it up. "GHB. And over there on the desk is a picture of the murdered girls. And several more he must have had his eye on."

JJ felt the shudder right down to his heels. He walked over to the desk and stared down at the picture album. Photographs of the girls had been lined up. Three girls had black cross marks over their faces.

"Marcus Tappan?" JJ turned to look at Donnie and Jack. "Marcus Tappan killed those girls? But why?"

"That's what you need to find out," Jack replied grimly. "We're only here to cover the judge's murder."

JJ pulled out his phone and called the station, ordering three of his men to go pick up Marcus and bring him in for questioning.

❖   ❖   ❖

Dana Tappan slammed the car door, then started stomping across the parking lot. It was insufferable! To be removed like a servant, to be questioned like a criminal. She was Judge Tappan's daughter. When her father was alive, no one treated her like this! No one dared!

"Dana?"

Surprised to find him outside her apartment, she turned around. "What are you doing here?"

"I needed to talk to you." He stepped closer.

"I'm not in the mood to talk. You know how difficult this evening was on me. I need a long, hot bath and a good night's sleep. We can talk tomorrow."

She turned her back to him. Suddenly he grabbed her around the waist, pinning her up against his body while putting his hand over her mouth.

Outraged, she tried to struggle, but his arm was like a vise, anchoring her, making her attempts to get away futile.

He began to drag her backward. "Would have been easier if you'd had that drink I offered you, but oh, no. Not Miss Priss."

He opened the van door and threw her down inside, pinning her with his body while he pulled out duct tape and covered her mouth. "Just in case you decide to get mouthy with me, because I am really so tired of hearing your voice."

She kept trying to wiggle out from under him. It just didn't make sense, and her mind struggled to accept that she was actually in danger. She managed to get one hand free and swung back to punch him, only to have him wrap his hands around her throat and begin to squeeze.

Starved for oxygen, she slowly stopped struggling as she felt her strength fading away.

"Much better."

He taped her wrists, then her ankles. Then he pulled the tarp up. Just before he covered her face, he leaned down close, so close she could smell the alcohol on his breath. "I've been waiting a long time for this. Oh, and in case you were wondering, yes. . .I killed your friends, and now. . .I'm going to kill you."

❖   ❖   ❖

"I don't buy it!" JJ insisted for the third time as he and Matt dug into hot roast beef sandwiches. While heading back to the station to wait for Marcus Tappan to be brought in, JJ and Matt stopped for a quick bite to eat.

"What's not to buy? No, you're right, I wouldn't leave drugs and ropes and pictures of dead girls lying around in the open at my house for someone to find. But Marcus thinks he's in the clear. Why would the police be searching *his* house?"

JJ shook his head. "I still don't buy it. It's too convenient. Just like the knife in Leland's car. Too easy, too obvious. This killer has been three steps ahead of us all along. I don't see him making such a classic mistake now."

"Three steps ahead of us?" Matt nearly spat out his iced water. "We've been on this guy's heels every step of the way! How long did it take us to get to Matthews? A month?"

JJ waved his fork at Matt. "Five weeks, but that's not the point. We stepped into this only because we found out, through a mistake at the lab that didn't send everything back at the same time, that Tappan was murdered. If that hadn't happened, we'd still be chasing Joey Roddy. Or Bret Leland."

"He was young, rich, arrogant, and didn't think the law applied to him. He got too arrogant. It backfired on him."

JJ poked at his mashed potatoes. "Okay, tell me this. You're Marcus. You're a killer. The Feds have just invaded the house. You know that just a few hundred yards away, in your bedroom, is enough evidence to get you convicted for at least three murders and possibly even the murder of your own father. Now, the Feds, nice guys that they are, let you know that you have to leave the house because they consider it a crime scene. They let you go back to your lair and pack a bag before leaving for a hotel. Do you leave the evidence out and about?" JJ leaned forward to press his point home. "Or do you take it with you?"

"You're good, you know that, JJ?"

JJ shrugged and lifted his glass of water in salute. "Now, your turn. Convince me I'm wrong."

"Okay, so who planted the stuff on Leland and then planted the stuff in Marcus Tappan's room?"

"Got me."

Matt laughed as he pushed his empty plate aside. "Great. Now you run out of ideas."

"Who knew we were there?"

"The whole neighborhood, the press, anyone who saw the eleven o'clock news. . ."

JJ shot him a scornful look. "Who had access to the property?"

Matt ticked them off on his fingers. "The FBI, some of our men, a couple of reporters managed to get in and were escorted off, Dana Tappan, Marcus Tappan, Lewis Morton, the cook, the housekeeper."

"Forget the cook and the housekeeper. I can't see them cruising bars at their age."

Matt narrowed it down as he waved to the waitress and raised his coffee cup. "Suspects. Dana. Marcus. Lewis."

"Lewis has no motive for killing three innocent women."

"And Marcus does? Or Dana? You want coffee?"

JJ eyed the pot in the waitress's hand. "Decaf, yes. Maybe Dana didn't like the girls in her group."

"So quit the group."

JJ laughed. "Not everyone takes the easy way out, especially if they think they're so much better than everyone else. We really don't know what went on in that group. Maybe they were all giving Dana a really hard time. Maybe she snapped and decided to get even with them."

"And Marcus? What's his motivation?"

The smile vanished from JJ's face as tension-relieving bantering turned serious again. "That's tougher. He has no connection with those girls that we know of."

The two men fell silent as they doctored the coffee to their individual tastes.

JJ lifted his mug, took a sip, then stared over the top at Matt. "I keep thinking about something Zoe said."

"What was that?"

"That this was about greed."

Matt yawned. "Greed? As good a motivation as any. It could work for killing the judge. Either one of the kids or even both of them could have killed him off to get their inheritance sooner."

"What about the girls, though?"

When the cell phone rang, JJ groaned. "Hello?"

"JJ? It's Chapman. We got a problem."

"Do I really want to hear this?"

"Probably not, but you're going to anyway. Marcus Tappan is gone."

Every nerve in JJ's body suddenly went on high alert. "What?"

"He's gone. We can't find him anywhere."

JJ gave up the idea of getting any sleep. "Did you check his sister's apartment?"

"Her car is parked outside her apartment, but she's gone, too. We can't find her."

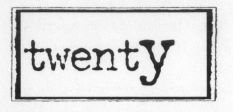

twenty

Monday, October 4—3:47 a.m.

Zoe went from being sound asleep to being wide awake so fast, she wasn't even disoriented. Glancing at the clock, she wondered what it was that could have awakened her, but the house appeared quiet.

Punching her pillow, she turned over, burying her face, closing her eyes, and trying to go back to sleep. Her eyes popped open. She flipped over again and sat up.

Something wasn't right, but she didn't know what it was. "Okay, Lord, what's wrong?"

Maybe it was Lanae. Zoe had dropped by the hospital after church to check on her, but Lanae had still been in the coma. Zoe kept trying to talk to her, reassuring her that everything was going to be fine, that they'd found her mother, that she was going to get better, but Lanae never responded.

Zoe wasn't sure if Lanae was aware of her or not.

Dan had called not long after Zoe got home. With Leland in jail, he'd felt Taylor was safe and had opted to go home. He had asked Zoe if she'd seen the news, and when finding out that she hadn't, he told her about Tappan being murdered and the FBI descending on the Tappan home.

Swinging her feet to the floor, she reached over and turned on the lamp next to the bed. JJ would be there. It might be federal jurisdiction, but that wouldn't stop JJ from wanting to be there to see it all go down.

Picturing JJ, his pale green eyes watching every step and sticking his crooked nose into every little thing, made her smile. If only things could have worked out differently between them. Her heart told her they would have made a good team.

❖   ❖   ❖

JJ was too wired to sleep. He drove around the quiet streets of Monroe, his mind jumping from Tappan's heart attack, to the bodies of Lori Blain, DeAnne Foster, and Pam Hamilton, to a bloody knife in Leland's car, to Lori's locket in Roddy's apartment, to pictures and drugs in Marcus Tappan's bedroom, to Lanae Oakley in a coma, to her mother in a shallow grave, to a rare gun in the judge's gun case.

There were too many pieces to this puzzle, and they all seemed to revolve around the Tappan family. That they were connected, he had no doubt. *How* they were connected was driving him crazy.

He pulled into the driveway and, for a long moment, stared at the car parked in front of him, scratching his head. Then he realized what he'd done.

Maybe he was crazy, so far gone from lack of sleep that he was losing his mind, but in a way, it made perfect sense. He needed to hammer this out, and he needed someone with a fresh perspective to take it all apart with him and put it back together.

And he knew exactly the person he needed.

That she might slam the door in his face was a distinct possibility.

Pulling out his cell phone, he decided to call first. If the worst happened, she'd hang up on him.

She answered on the first ring, which surprised him. "Did I wake you?"

"No, actually I was already awake. What's going on?"

"Just driving around, trying to figure some things out. I need to talk to you if you're up for it."

"Sure. Where are you?"

He stared up at the house. "In your driveway."

"Good grief. Come on in." She hung up, and he tucked his phone away before climbing out of the Jeep. By the time he reached the front porch, the light was on, and she was opening the door.

Zoe ushered JJ in. "You want some coffee?" she asked as she turned on lights and took JJ's coat.

JJ shook his head as he dropped onto the sofa, stretching his legs out. "I just had something with Matt. He was the smart one and went to get some sleep."

Zoe curled up in the chair across from him. "And you've got too much on your mind to sleep."

"Exactly," he responded, scratching his day's growth of beard. "I notice I didn't wake you. Worried about Lanae?"

"Actually, I'm not. I feel positive she'll be fine. When she's ready to wake up, she will. I was sound asleep and then woke up about ten minutes before you called. Then I couldn't get back to sleep."

"How's Daria holding up?"

Zoe frowned as she toyed with a throw pillow. "Barely. This has hit her whole family pretty hard."

"Is she still angry with you?"

"No. She thinks I had something to do with Leland being taken into custody, so she's okay with me. I don't know how she'll feel when she finds out that I didn't."

"Don't tell her."

"It's a lie, JJ. I have to tell her eventually."

JJ smirked. "Always honest and morally upright."

The sarcastic response was right there on the tip of her tongue, but it suddenly felt as though she were choking on it.

Be silent, child, and listen.

The request surprised her, but she was willing to try. So instead of snapping back at him, she just tucked the pillow in her arms and looked at him. Really looked at him. The fatigue grooved into his face. The dark circles under his eyes, making the pale green look even lighter. The stress was getting to him.

JJ lifted one eyebrow as if waiting for her to launch a counter-attack. Finally he stared down at his hands. "Sorry. You didn't deserve that."

Still, she didn't feel free to comment, so she just waited patiently. A minute passed. And then another. Finally JJ rubbed his eyes with the heels of his hands. "The gun that killed Lanae's mother was found in Tappan's gun collection. Or at least, there's a ninety percent chance it's the same gun. Donnie sent it off for a ballistics check, but it's a rare gun, so he's pretty confident. We found evidence in Marcus Tappan's room that indicates he was the one who killed Lori, DeAnne, and Pam Hamilton."

Zoe nearly jumped out of her seat. "Leland isn't guilty?"

"We're thinking the knife may have been planted."

"Holy cow."

"It gets worse. If the judge was murdered, the suspect list is fairly small at the moment. Other than the cook and the house-keeper, there were only four other people around that day. His son, his daughter, his attorney, and his golfing buddy."

Zoe started feeling nervous energy building. Tossing the pillow aside, she stood up and began to pace the room as JJ went through everything point by point. By the time he finished twenty minutes later, she was back in the chair, her feet propped up on the coffee table, her sock-covered feet crossed at the ankles.

JJ was sprawled across the sofa, his head resting on the arm. "So, I'm not sure where to pull the first thread to see where it leads. It's like all those tangled strands of Christmas lights and you start working on one strand, only to have to keep stopping at little dead ends to go work on another strand until you finally free one."

Zoe pointed her finger at JJ. "Right from the beginning, I kept getting the sense that this whole thing was about greed. I'll bet you anything that the judge was killed for money. Either his kids killed him to get their hands on the inheritance, or one of his buddies killed him for financial reasons. Either way, it will come down to the almighty buck."

"I'll agree that Tappan was probably killed for money. And Lanae's mother was definitely killed over money. But what about the girls, Zoe? What does any of this have to do with them?"

Zoe pouted. "I don't know that part yet. Give me time. Go on to something else and we'll come back to it."

"Okay. Did you find anything at all in those diaries that could help us?"

"I'm not sure. Leona wrote that she kept going to Tappan for child support and he kept putting her off. So, she stole the Tappan diary and was blackmailing him with that. We know she went to meet him to pick up money but didn't take the diary with her. And we now know for sure that she didn't leave the meeting alive."

JJ toed his shoes off, propped his feet on the arm of the sofa, and closed his eyes. "No, she didn't leave alive, and we know, or at least we're pretty sure, she was killed with Tappan's gun."

"What if. . .someone else was there that night?"

JJ opened one eye and looked at her. "Say what?"

"Just put yourself in the judge's shoes. He has a new wife and a new baby. He's the district attorney, and that's an elected position.

Being a political animal, the man ain't dumb, and he sure isn't going to put himself in the middle of a scandal. So, if you were the judge, would you have gone out there to meet some woman you had an affair with who was now demanding money for a kid you weren't even sure was yours?"

The other eye popped open. "He didn't know whether Lanae was his or not?"

"I don't know. Leona merely wrote that she wanted child support, and the judge wasn't acknowledging Lanae, so it's possible. Just play with me here."

Ignoring the sudden twinkle in his eye, she went on with her scenario. "So, the judge has a little affair, and now she's coming after him—blackmailing him, actually—for a lot of money. Is he going to lower himself to deal with this alone?"

JJ smirked again. "The judge? Not likely. He had flunkies to handle the unpleasant side of life for him."

"So what are the chances that he got one of his flunkies to deal with Leona? To go get his family diary back? To get rid of this little problem?"

"Pretty high, actually. So, going with your theory, the judge gave the order and someone else pulled the trigger. Too bad we have a witness that said Tappan pulled the trigger."

"It was the middle of the night, out in the country. How can she be absolutely positive it was Tappan and not someone else?"

"Zoe, it's a dead end. We can't prove it."

Zoe started tapping her bottom lip with her finger. Something about their scenario felt so incredibly *right*. Well, it might feel right, but proving it would be impossible.

Nothing is impossible for Me.

Suddenly JJ shot upright, his feet hitting the floor with a distinct thud. "The gun!"

"What?"

"If I were Tappan and I'd just gotten someone to do my dirty work, I'd want to make sure it could never come back on me. It's my gun, after all."

"Yeah?" Zoe struggled to follow him.

"So, the killer brings the gun back to me. I'd lock it away, which is exactly what Tappan did. It was in a locked box inside the gun case."

"JJ?"

He whipped out his cell phone and dialed, grinning at Zoe. "You are brilliant, you know that?"

"Yes, but I didn't know you realized it."

JJ laughed. "I didn't want your head to swell."

He turned his attention back to the phone. "Donnie? I'm sorry for waking you, but I need you to listen. Call the lab where the ballistics check is being done on Tappan's gun. Have them check that gun for fingerprints. Yes! Fingerprints! It's a hunch, but will you do it? And the bullets, too!"

❖   ❖   ❖

6:20 a.m.

Matt rolled over and kissed his wife gently on the cheek, trying not to wake her.

"I gather you're claiming the shower first?" Paula opened her eyes and smiled softly.

"I'm sorry. I didn't mean to wake you."

"I have to go to work today, remember? Honeymoon is over. Back to reality." She stretched, making little mewing sounds that reminded him of a kitten.

"I love you."

Paula reached up and cupped his cheek. "I love you, too. But, if you're not in the shower in thirty seconds, I'm taking the shower first and you'll just have to wait."

Matt bolted out of bed and ran to the bathroom. "I win. I win!"

By the time he got out of the shower, Paula had his coffee and breakfast waiting. He inhaled the wonderful aroma of bacon and coffee. "Oh, marry me."

Paula handed him a mug of coffee. "I already did. That's why you get breakfast. But you have to eat alone. I need to get in the shower and see if you left me any hot water."

Matt piled his plate and sat down at the breakfast bar to enjoy his breakfast. And to think he had avoided getting married. He must have been crazy. Paula had retrieved the morning paper and set it on the counter. He yanked off the rubber band and shook the paper open to the front page.

JUDGE TAPPAN SUSPECTED IN MURDER OF MISTRESS.

Dropping his fork, Matt grabbed the phone and dialed the station. "JJ around? Okay, thanks."

He hung up, wolfed down another bite of toast, and hurried into the bedroom to retrieve his jacket. He stuck his head in the bathroom. "Paula! Something's come up. I have to run."

"Love you," she yelled above the sound of the shower. "See you tonight for dinner."

"Love you, too." He pulled the door shut and rushed out.

Where had the Tappan siblings run to? And why had they killed so many innocent girls? And why leave a trail so easy to follow? Questions tumbled and nagged during his fifteen-minute drive to the station. When he finally got upstairs, JJ was moving around the conference room like a dervish, demanding answers, calling for files, giving orders.

"Matt! Good. I need you to help Chapman dig into Marcus

Tappan's life. Find everything you can on him. Denise and Barone are looking into Dana's life. They have to have someplace to run to."

Matt tossed his jacket across the back of a chair. "Anyone checking airlines? Bus stations?"

"Chapman is on it."

Lanae felt as though every breath was drawing fire into her chest. She wanted to bury herself in the darkness again, but it was receding, and she couldn't bring it back.

Little by little, she became aware of pain. Her head, her chest, her shoulder. Then there were the voices, slowly becoming distinct.

"Her vitals look good. She should be coming out of this pretty soon."

"Her color looks better, that's for sure."

"She's a very lucky lady."

"Keep the drip going and check her BP and temp again in two hours."

"Yes, Doctor."

"Will she remember?"

"Hard to say, Miss Shefford. We won't know anything until she wakes up and talks to us. I'll be back to check on her later."

"Thank you, Dr. Aaron."

Lanae felt someone take her hand. "Lanae? Come on, sweetie. Open your eyes. We need you to wake up."

She remembered that voice. It was that nice lady who was helping her find her mother. What was her name again? Lanae struggled with her memories. She could see bright green eyes and long blond hair. The woman had a warm smile and a gentle touch. Her name, however, remained elusive.

"Lanae? I need to run. There is so much going on, but the important thing is for you to get better, okay?"

Suddenly the woman's hand was gone, and Lanae desperately wanted to reach out and grab it, hold on to it for a little while longer. Her body, however, didn't want to obey what her mind was struggling to command. It seemed as if her mind and her body had been disconnected.

She heard a door close, and the silence made her want to cry.

7:30 a.m.

Kieran reached up and pulled two mugs out of the cabinet, then set them next to the coffeepot. It was in the last stages of brewing, sending up an incredibly eye-opening aroma.

Her father shuffled in, tossed the paper down on the table, then headed for the coffee. When he saw that it wasn't ready yet, he went back to the table and sat down.

Kieran couldn't remember the last time she'd seen her father come to the kitchen on a Monday morning dressed in jeans, pullover, and socks. He looked as if he hadn't slept all night.

She probably looked as bad as he did.

"Aren't you going to work today?"

Mel shook his head as he stared down at the table. "I can't. Not today."

The coffeemaker sputtered to let them know it was finished. Kieran filled two mugs and set one down in front of her father. "Are you going to Lori's funeral this afternoon?"

His hand was shaking when it reached for the mug. "Are you?"

"Yes."

When she'd first decided to break free of the responsibilities of taking care of him and her sister, she hadn't imagined the kind of tension it would cause. The walls that would appear. The difficulty of having a normal conversation with her own father. They'd always been so close. Now, she struggled to find something casual to say.

"I need to talk to you, Kieran."

"I have to make breakfast for Rachael."

"Rachael can make her own breakfast. Please sit down."

Surprised, Kieran picked up her coffee and sat down at the table across from her father.

"You were right. I didn't want to admit it, but the truth is, I have put everything on your shoulders since we lost your mother. It was just easier, I guess. It was also incredibly selfish of me."

There were tears in his eyes, and it broke her heart. "Dad, it wasn't—"

"Yes, it was," he insisted, cutting her off. "I know this might be hard for you to understand, but your mother was everything to me. My first love, my only love. And then she was gone, and I couldn't cope. It was so much easier for me to just bury myself in my work and let you take care of everything else."

"I didn't mind, Dad."

He took her hand and clasped it. "I know. You've grown into an incredible woman, Kieran, and I'm not sure I can take any credit for that at all. But you did grow up, and now you want a life of your own, and I wasn't ready for that to happen. I didn't want you to force me to step back into my role as a parent."

Kieran didn't know what to say, so she just sipped on her coffee.

"Sweetheart, I need to confess something to you, and I don't know how you're going to take it."

Wrapping her hands around her mug, Kieran steeled herself for whatever was coming. It wasn't often that her father's voice shook. This was going to be bad.

"You don't have some serious disease, do you?"

Mel shook his head. "No, honey. It's nothing like that. Kieran, you know that ever since Lori was killed, I've been acting a little strangely."

Confused, Kieran merely stared at him, willing him to just get it over with.

"I didn't mean for it to happen. I was just so devastated by your mother's death. Work became my whole world; then Lori was there, and she was so sweet and so understanding and so concerned."

Kieran shook her head. "What are you saying? Please, tell me you didn't. . ."

"I'm sorry, honey. I know she was your friend, but you have to understand. I didn't mean for it to happen. She didn't mean for it to happen."

Kieran jumped out of her chair, moving around the room, agitated and downright angry. "You were having an affair with my friend, and you both lied to me! You hid this from me! And you know why you hid it? Because it was wrong! Maybe if it had been someone your own age, I could understand, but Lori? What were you thinking?"

"Kieran. . ."

"No. You weren't thinking. That's the problem. Having an affair with a woman the same age as your daughter? Sneaking around behind everyone's back? Is that the way you'd have me act, Dad? How would you feel if my boss suddenly started having an affair with me, and we were hiding it from the world?"

"I wouldn't like it." Tears glistened on his cheeks as he reached out, trying to take her into his arms.

She pushed him away and continued to pace. "No. You wouldn't like it. And you'd be tempted to go after my boss, too, wouldn't you?"

He hung his head. "It was wrong. I know it was wrong."

Kieran whirled around, eyes blazing with temper. "And you know what else bothers me? *I* couldn't date, *I* couldn't go out, I couldn't have a *life* because you were too busy making sure *you* had a good time. Making sure *you* had a life. And you were doing it with *my* friend."

Kieran shook her head. "No, she was *not* my friend."

"Kieran." He reached out for her again.

She backed away, unable to look at him, turned, and ran from the room.

8:05 a.m.

Joey Roddy glared as JJ kicked the metal cot where Joey was trying to sleep. "Get up, Roddy. We need to talk."

"I've said all I'm going to say."

"Well, if you want to go home this morning, you'll answer one more question to my satisfaction."

Slowly Joey rolled to sitting position. "What question?"

"How did you come to have Lori Blain's locket?" JJ leaned down so close he could smell Joey's sour breath. "I need an honest answer for a change, Joey. This is no time to play with me."

Joey eyed JJ warily before he finally dropped his head. "I took it off her."

"Lori Blain? You took it off Lori Blain?"

Joey nodded as he sighed heavily. "I was taking a smoke break at work and saw these funny lights down by the lake. Sometimes kids go down there to get stoned and sometimes if I go down there, they give me some, ya know what I mean?"

JJ was sure he did. "Go ahead."

"So I wandered down there, and by the time I got there, the lights were gone. That's when I saw her laying there. I thought she was passed out. Drunk, you know? But when I came up close to her, I saw the blood. And I knew she was dead. Then I saw the locket and I took it."

"Did you see the man who dumped Lori's body? Or his car?"

Joey shook his head. "But I'm pretty sure it was a van that pulled outta there. White or light gray."

JJ backed up a step, keeping his eyes on Joey while his mind raced. "Did you see anything, Joey? Anything at all that might help us?"

Joey looked up at him. "I don't think so. It was kinda dark out there, ya know?" Suddenly Joey's head snapped up a little. "Wait. Maybe."

"What, Joey?"

"He was playing a song on the radio. Or maybe a CD player. In the van. I heard the song 'cause it's one I hear on the radio a lot."

"What song, Joey?"

"*The Song of Death*. It's a new one by that heavy metal group, The Lords of Hell, or something like that."

"A song of death, I dream of hell and send you to her arms?"

"I stand in your shadow and wish you dead." Joey grinned. "Yeah, man. You know it? Didn't figure you for the heavy metal type."

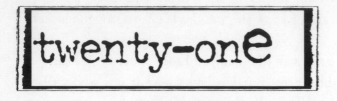

twenty-one

Zoe climbed into her car and pulled the door closed. As she put the key in the ignition, she had the strongest sense of another presence there with her. At first, everything in her went still as her mind caught up and reassured her that the car had been locked and no one had been in the car when she climbed in.

Taking a deep breath, she slowly looked over her shoulder into the backseat, just to make sure.

No one was there.

Hands gripping the steering wheel, she stared through the windshield, trying to understand this overwhelming feeling that she was not alone in the car. Warm and comfortable, it was so tangible, so real. She felt as if she could reach out and touch someone. But no one was there.

"This is crazy."

Will you trust Me?

Zoe felt reassured as the voice echoed through her with power and authority. "Yes. . .Lord."

You must find the daughter. He seeks to kill her. JJ will need your help, and I will show Myself to him through you. Trust Me.

Suddenly, the sense of presence was gone. She needed to find JJ, then they needed to find Dana. She wasn't entirely sure who the "he" was that the Lord had been talking about, but it didn't matter. What mattered was finding Dana before it was too late.

Dana slowly opened her eyes. They felt heavy, as if she'd only been asleep for an hour. She went to roll over to check the alarm clock, only to find that she couldn't move. Confused, she blinked, looking through the darkness at why she felt anchored to her bed.

Then it came back to her. The horror. The confusion. The truth.

Tears welled up in her eyes as she wrestled against her bonds, only to find them completely secure. Anger began to take hold as her eyes began to adjust to the darkness and she could make out bits and pieces of her surroundings.

He'd left her alone, but for how long? Was he really going to kill her? Had he really killed the girls from her group? Why? How could she not have seen this in him? How could she not have known? Or even suspected? Surely, to do these things, he had to be completely insane. Couldn't she see the insanity?

Obviously not, because she hadn't suspected a thing—had never seen it in his eyes, never heard it in his voice.

She looked at the dresser, the walls, the window boarded over. The hunting cabin. She was at her father's hunting cabin. It had been years since she'd been here. Her father used to come here all the time to get away on weekends but slowly lost interest. It had been sitting, empty and abandoned, for at least five years or more.

Or so she'd thought.

She pulled on her wrists again, trying to loosen the bonds, but there was no give at all. Dropping her head back down, tears welled up and began to stream. It couldn't end like this. She had so many dreams. So much she wanted to do. How could he just end her life with no more thought than stepping on a bug?

Where was he? Off sleeping peacefully, dreaming of her funeral? He'd probably attend, weeping with just the right amount of grief. He'd put just the right amount of tremble in his voice when he mentioned what a shame it was that she had to die so young.

Well, she wasn't going to go easy! She was a fighter, and by golly, he was going to find out just how hard she could fight!

With renewed determination, she began to twist her wrists again, working against the rope, ignoring the burn and the tearing flesh.

❖ ❖ ❖

Zoe purposefully wove through the desks in the bull pen, never slowing down until she reached the conference room. JJ wasn't there.

Denise was. "What can we do for you, Miss Shefford?"

"I'm looking for JJ."

"He's out doing his job. Would you care to leave a message?"

Zoe gritted her teeth and stepped farther into the room. "No, I do not care to leave a message. I need to talk to Detective Johnson. Now, you can either cooperate or get out of my way. Either way, don't mess with me."

Denise raised one eyebrow, her mouth twisting into a smirk. "Is that a threat, Miss Shefford?"

Zoe folded her arms across her chest and lifted her chin. "Unlike you, I'm not threatened when I perceive a little competition on the field. Winner takes all, Miss McClellan. Can you handle that?"

"You're a flake, Miss Shefford. He needs a woman who has both feet on the ground. Someone who respects him."

"If you truly respected him, Miss McClellan, you would respect the choices he makes in his life, and you would respect his ability to know what he wants and what he feels is best for him."

Denise's face flushed red with temper, and her eyes flashed with far more than mere annoyance. "You don't have a clue who Josiah Johnson is."

JJ's voice suddenly cut through the room and startled both women. "You're wrong, Denise. Shouldn't you be following up on something?"

Denise mumbled something under her breath and made a quick exit, shooting a lethal, hot glare in Zoe's direction as she passed.

"You needed to see me?" JJ dropped wearily into a chair.

Zoe pulled up a chair and sat down, her knees nearly touching his. "JJ, I know you don't trust me or my instincts or my abilities, but I need you to listen to me."

He pulled at his tie, undoing the top button of his shirt. "I'm listening."

"Marcus and Dana aren't on the run."

"Could have fooled me."

Zoe leaned forward a little. "I know what it looks like. JJ, I believe that Marcus has taken Dana, and he's going to kill her. I think that was the plan all along."

She could see the thoughts tumbling through his mind as he stared at her. Finally he spoke.

"Marcus decides to kill his sister and kills a couple of her friends first to make it look like a serial killer."

"Something like that, yes."

"And now, knowing that we know. Knowing that we're on to him, he's taken his sister from her apartment, taken her somewhere, and he's still going to kill her?"

"Yes."

"Zoe, the jig is up for him. He can't win, and he knows it. Why would he keep going? It's over. He'll spend the rest of his life in prison."

"He doesn't know that, does he?"

She saw it cross his face, a mixture of disbelief, understanding, questioning, and skepticism. "He's on the run."

"For the death of his father."

JJ shook his head. "It doesn't fly, Zoe. I'm sorry. He has no reason to kill her. They're in this up to their eyeballs, and they've run. Even if your theory is right, why would he kill her now?"

"Because he doesn't believe it's over. I don't know why, JJ, but I'm sure of this. Dana Tappan is going to die if we don't find them."

"JJ?" Matt stuck his head in the door. "Sorry to interrupt, but Chapman says he got a hit on the Tappan siblings. Two airline tickets from Pittsburgh to Cancun. Flight leaves this afternoon."

JJ jumped to his feet, glancing up at the clock on the wall. "They must have figured we have the airports around here being watched. Okay, call the Pittsburgh police. Tell them the situation. See if they'll help us out by covering the airport. Tell them to detain until we get there."

Matt nodded and ran for the phone. JJ went to his desk and opened the drawer, pulling out his badge.

"I appreciate you trying to help, Zoe."

Zoe slowly rose to her feet. "This is all wrong, JJ. Please listen to me. They're not getting on any plane in Pittsburgh."

As he passed her, he reached out and squeezed her arm gently. "Trust me, Zoe."

Then he was gone.

Dan stood at his office window, hands in his pockets, staring out at the traffic. When he'd found out that his daughter might be targeted by a serial killer, he knew he had to protect her, no matter what. Even if that meant staying in his ex-wife's house. At the time, he thought it would end up being one of the most uncomfortable, most miserable times of his life.

He couldn't have been more wrong. They had been a family again, just for a little while. He'd helped with dinner dishes. Had been there at the table discussing his daughters' lives. Had played some ridiculous board game with them and had never laughed so hard in his life. Had built a fire in the fireplace and enjoyed the quiet of ending the day stretched out in a recliner while Jeanine worked on some sewing project and they talked about their lives, their daughters, their day.

And now that he'd returned to his own place, he just wanted to go back home. Because that's how he felt now. Home was where Jeanine and the girls were.

Somehow, he had to get Jeanine to fall in love with him again and give him another chance.

His phone rang, interrupting his thoughts. He walked over to his desk and picked it up. "Cordette."

"Dan? It's Zoe. I need information, and I need it quick."

Pulling out his chair, he sat down behind his desk. "What do you need?"

"When we gathered all that information on Tappan, did we find out if he owned any properties in the area? Not the commercial properties. Maybe something secluded? Out of town?"

"Hold on, hon. Let me check."

Dan set the phone down and went to his filing cabinet. He rifled for a few minutes, pulled out the file he was looking for, and returned to his desk.

Flipping the file open, he picked up the phone. "While I'm

going through this, you want to tell me what's going on?"

"Marcus has taken off with Dana. I believe he intends to kill her."

"Did you tell Johnson?"

"I told him. He doesn't buy it. He doesn't feel that Marcus has anything to gain by killing her. While I was there with him, he got information that Marcus and Dana had booked a flight to Mexico, flying out of Pittsburgh. And that was it, Dan. He shut me down and ran off to Pittsburgh to catch them."

Dan stopped flipping through the pages. "Wait a minute. I don't understand. Why would Marcus want his sister dead? I thought she was one of the targets for the serial killer?"

"Marcus is the serial killer, Dan! He killed those girls to cover up killing his own sister for the inheritance. Just the way his grandfather killed his own brother for the same reason."

Dan felt something bitter churn in his stomach. "That is so sick."

"I know. Are you finding anything?"

"I'm looking. I'm looking." He started going through the reports faster. "Yeah. Here. Tappan owns a lodge out. . .holy cow."

"What?"

"It's out on Old Logging Trail Road. That's where Leona Oakley was killed. Ah, geesh. It was right there in front of us the whole time."

"Dan! Where on Old Logging Trail?"

"Oh. Right. Cross the bridge. The trail bends to the right. Go to the end. The cabin is there, overlooking the river."

"Thanks, Dan!"

"Wait! I'll go with you! You can't go out there alone!"

"I don't have time to come pick you up, Dan. He's going to kill her. I have to get out there now."

"Where are you? I can meet you. Zoe? Zoe?"

Dan slammed the phone down, grabbed his jacket, and ran out of the office.

❖   ❖   ❖

"Hello, sis."

Dana opened her eyes and looked up at Marcus. His hair was in disarray, his clothes wrinkled, his eyes wild with madness. "Why are you doing this?"

Marcus grinned down at her as he jumped up to sit on the dresser. "Because I want to."

"I'm your sister. Why would you want to kill me?"

"Because you're my sister." He picked up the knife and lifted it up for her to see. "I can't let you take half of what's mine."

Tears started welling up in her eyes again. "If you want the whole estate, I'll give it to you, Marcus. Just please don't kill me. It's not worth dying over."

"Oh, easy for you to say." His laugh was brittle as he winked at her. "You know, the first time, that girl, Lori? I didn't like the killing part very much at all. But after DeAnne, it got easier. By the time I got Pamela, I was almost enjoying it. Now, you are going to be the best fun yet."

Fear clawed at her, scraping her soul in desperation. Cold terror paralyzed her, racking through her emotions. Her voice cracked as she struggled to buy time. But buying time for what? No one knew where she was. No one knew to come looking for her. No one was going to rescue her. She was going to die here today.

And she didn't want to die. God, she didn't want to die. *Please, God, save me. If You're really capable of all things, do this one thing for me. Save me. Get me out of this alive. Please, God.*

"What's the matter, Dana? Afraid? All the other girls were. You should have seen how afraid they were."

"Did. . .did you kill Daddy?"

"Of course I did. I knew he had a heart condition, even though he tried to hide it. He wasn't as smart as he liked to think he was." Marcus began to dig into the wooden top of the dresser with the point of the knife. Gouging.

Fresh waves of grief welled up inside her. "Oh, Marcus."

His head shot up. His eyes narrowed. "You stupid little idiot! You think he was so wonderful? So perfect? You have any idea of how many mistresses he had? Mom was the saint, always having to put up with his drinking and his lying and his cheating."

"That's not true!"

"It is true! I even saw him once, sneaking a woman into the pool house when Mom was in the hospital. He was a pig!"

Dana shook her head, refusing to believe what her brother was saying. He was mad. Insane.

"That girl who's suing for child support? She probably is our sister."

"No! It's a lie!"

"Oh, please, Dana. Wake up and smell the coffee. Dad was crooked, on the bench and off. Why do you think the police hated him so much? They'd go out and find a criminal and dear old dad would take a payoff to let him go on some technicality. What? You think judges make the kind of money dear old dad made just from their salary?"

Dana began sobbing as she struggled between wanting to keep her brother talking and hating every word he was saying. "He wouldn't."

Marcus laughed again. "He would and did at every opportunity. You are so naïve, Dana. He was a lying, mean, arrogant old man who thought he could buy and sell the world. You remember that guy you were dating two years ago? The one you were *sooooo* in love with?"

"Dylan?"

Marcus nodded. "Yeah. Dylan. You know why he broke up with you and left town? Because your wonderful daddy paid him to go away. Said he wasn't good enough for his little princess. Wasn't ambitious enough."

Marcus jumped down off the dresser. "I'm tired of talking. I need to kill you and get back. Lewis is supposed to be covering for me, and I need to make sure we have our stories straight."

"Lewis?" Dana screeched in disbelief. "Lewis knows what you're doing?"

"Criminy, Dana. Are you really that stupid? Lewis has been helping me. In fact, some of this was his idea."

He strolled over toward her, the light in the room dancing off the blade of the knife. Dana felt her throat go dry. "Don't, Marcus. Please. For the love of God, don't do this."

"Sorry, Dana. God never did anything for me, so I can't see doing anything for the love of Him." He stood over her, grinning. "Bye, sis."

He raised his hand.

And then plunged downward.

Dana screamed.

❖ ❖ ❖

"I don't like the feel of this." JJ was practically squirming in his seat as Matt sped up the Interstate.

"The feel of what?"

"I don't know. Zoe tried to tell me not to go to Pittsburgh, but I wouldn't listen, and now it's driving me crazy. Either I'm losing my mind, or she was on to something."

Matt glanced over at JJ quickly, then sifted back to watch the road. "We can turn back, JJ. It's not too late. If the Tappans show up at the airport, the Pittsburgh police are going to detain them for us anyway, so it won't matter when we get there."

"I don't know. What do your instincts tell you?"

"You really want my opinion?"

"Yes, I want your opinion."

"I've never known Zoe to be wrong."

"I was afraid you were going to say that. Turn the car around." JJ pulled out his cell phone and dialed Zoe's number.

Zoe reached the end of the driveway to the cabin far sooner than she thought she would. Pulling over, she cut the engine as she looked around. She spotted the rear bumper of an old van parked on the far side of the cabin.

The ring on her cell phone had her nearly jumping out of her skin. She pulled it out and flipped it open. "Hello?"

"Where are you?"

"JJ? I'm at Tappan's cabin down on the Old Logging Trail."

"Get out of there right now. I'm on my way. Fifteen, maybe twenty minutes out."

Suddenly Zoe heard Dana scream, a high-pitched wail that sent shivers down her spine. "I can't. He's killing her."

Closing her phone, she shoved it back in her pocket. Taking a deep breath, she climbed out of her car. "Lord, I really, really need You right now. Protect me, guide me, give me wisdom, give me strength, and anything else I need. And a diversion would be nice right about now."

Ideas came and went as she circled around to the back of the cabin. A gust of wind lifted the corner of a tarp, snapping sharply before it drifted down again. Zoe hurried over and lifted the tarp. A riding mower sat parked, key in the ignition. Her mind racing, she looked around until she found a large rock. Then she started the mower, turned the steering wheel away from the house, and put the rock on the foot pedal. It shot forward. She jumped back and raced around the house as the mower set off across the backyard.

She stopped and peered around the corner of the cabin in time to see Marcus come bolting out the back door, stop, and look at the mower.

As he jumped off the back porch and took off after the mower, Zoe raced to the front door.

Bursting through the door, she blinked, trying to adjust to the dim light. "Dana!"

A sudden noise to her right had her wheeling around and heading down the hall to a rear bedroom. She saw the bed. Then she saw Dana. And the blood.

"Dana?" She rushed forward.

The mower was still running as she lifted a sluggish Dana. "You've got to help me, Dana. I can't carry you."

Dana moaned softly as she leaned against Zoe and tried to stand up. Zoe pulled her forward, and the two girls stumbled toward the door.

The sound of the lawn mower motor going silent made Zoe's heart slam against her ribs.

"We have to hurry, Dana! Hurry!"

Reaching the front door, she tried to push Dana to run. "Hurry!"

Dana mumbled something that Zoe ignored as she pushed Dana. Reaching the car, she took one hand off Dana to open the car door. Dana slid to the ground and collapsed at Zoe's feet.

"Not now, Dana." As she reached for Dana, a hand grabbed her arm, whirling her around. Marcus stood there, a bloody knife in his hand, poised to strike her.

"You had no business coming here, lady. Guess it's your day to die, too."

Zoe shook her head. "No, Marcus. I don't think God is going to let you kill me." *Right, Lord? I'm right, aren't I?* "I need you to put the knife down now."

"You know, I'm really getting tired of people telling me what to do." He lifted the knife, extending his arm a few inches.

Zoe backed up a step. "You won't get away with this, Marcus. The police are on their way."

Marcus laughed as he stepped toward her, waving the knife. "Then we just won't be here when they get here."

He grabbed Zoe's arm and yanked her nearly off her feet. "You won't get away, Marcus. They're going to be crawling all over this place in a matter of minutes."

"Then we better hurry, huh?" He shoved her toward the van. "Get in."

Zoe opened the van door and crawled up in the passenger seat. Marcus grabbed duct tape and quickly bound her hands. Then he ran around, got behind the wheel, and started the engine.

"You can't get away, Marcus."

"Shut up! I am so tired of women running their mouths." Marcus stomped on the gas. The van lurched forward, throwing Zoe back, then sideways against the window as he drove like a madman through the brush and away from the house.

"Only God can fix this mess, Marcus. And you have to stop now if you want His help."

"I don't need His help!" The van bounced, creaking and groaning over ruts and rocks, careening across the field.

Zoe kept her voice low and calm. "Marcus, you need to listen to me."

"Shut up, or I'll kill you right now!"

He slashed out with the knife. Zoe yanked back, but not far enough. The knife sliced into her.

Dan tried dialing his cell phone again and, when it still wouldn't dial, threw the phone across the front seat of his car. No service. He was only eighteen miles from town. *How can there be no service?*

He looked down at his speedometer. He was pushing eighty, and still not one police car had made an appearance. *Where is a cop when you need one?*

When he reached Old Logging Trail Road, he gave up all hope of taking the cavalry in with him. He reached across the front seat, opened his glove compartment, and pulled out his 9mm. He laid it across his lap and concentrated on his driving. *Okay, Zoe. I'm on my way. Just stay cool until I get there.*

JJ paid little or no attention to Matt's driving as he coordinated efforts by cell phone. Donnie was sending reinforcements to the cabin. Denise was setting up for the helicopter in case Marcus tried to run. Chapman was making sure a medical team would be standing by.

Then right in the middle of confirming Donnie's ETA, the cell phone went dead and he couldn't get service back. "Blast it!"

"Lost service?" Matt asked.

"Yes. How far are we from the trail?"

"Three minutes. Maybe four."

JJ rubbed his jaw. "Let's hope I haven't lost my mind. If we get out there and Marcus isn't there with Dana, I am going to have such egg on my face. Calling in the FBI, calling in a helicopter. I mean, could I get more out on a limb for a woman who swears she hears from God?"

"Have you ever considered that maybe, just *maybe*, Zoe does hear from a Higher Power?"

JJ shot Matt a withering frown. "God? Talking to people? A little farfetched, don't you think?"

"I don't know. Maybe. Maybe not. I mean, if there is a God and He created people, why wouldn't He want to talk to them? Why bother creating all these humans, then ignoring them like they don't exist?"

"Well, if there is a God, Matt, why is the world in the mess it's in?"

Matt shrugged lightly. "I think it's called free will."

"What *are* you talking about?"

"I don't remember a whole lot, JJ. I haven't been to church since I was a kid, but I do remember that God was real big on choices. Something about choosing between life and death. Choosing between Him and some other gods. Choosing good over evil. That kind of stuff. Like, okay, people, here's the deal. I want you to do good, but I won't make you. It's your choice. Well, most people in this world choose to go their own way and do what they want. Even if it hurts other people."

Suddenly Matt slammed on the brakes. "Here's our turn."

JJ grabbed the strap above the door and braced himself for the sharp turn. "Well, if Marcus hurts one hair on Zoe's head, I'm going to choose to put a serious hurting on him."

Matt laughed and shook his head. "I wish you'd just admit that you're in love with her and get it over with."

"I'm not ready for that yet."

"Take it from me, JJ. You can't always be ready for love."

twenty-twO

Monday, October 4—11:47 a.m.

Zoe fought not to pass out as blood ran down her arm and the front of her shirt, dripping onto her lap. Lightheaded, she kept blinking, trying to watch where Marcus was driving. Every time he hit a rut, her whole body vibrated with pain. She clenched her teeth to keep from screaming.

Lord, help me. Help Dana. Get someone out here fast, please.

Sirens punched the air, and Marcus slammed his foot on the brake. Zoe lurched forward, putting out her hands to keep from flying through the windshield.

Marcus rolled down his window halfway and listened carefully. "They're going down the driveway. They'll pass right by and not even know we're here."

Staring through the woods that separated them from the driveway, Zoe couldn't see anything but trees. And if she couldn't see the police, they couldn't see her.

Marcus laughed, slapping the steering wheel. "I did it. I did it. They'll never get me now."

"They know you did it, Marcus," Zoe said softly, her strength draining with each drop of blood. "They found the drug and the girls' pictures in your room."

Marcus turned to stare at her, confusion pulling his brows together into one line across his forehead. "What are you talking about? What pictures? What drug?"

"There was rope and handcuffs and duct tape under your bed. They know you killed those girls."

He shook his head, a grin breaking out. "Oh. You're messing with me. I get it. Make me think. But see, I never kept anything at my house." He pointed his finger at her. "Nice try, though."

As the sirens faded, Marcus eased the van forward, cautiously emerging from the woods and out onto Old Logging Trail.

"Her mother was killed out here. Did you know that?"

"Who?" Marcus carefully checked both directions before pulling out onto the trail and heading back toward the bridge.

"Lanae Oakley's mother. She met your father out here to get money for their child, and he killed her."

"Oh. Her." Marcus slowly accelerated. "Well, the judge was there, but it wasn't the old man who killed that woman. It was Lewis."

"Lewis?" Zoe felt the beads of perspiration on her forehead. Her fingertips were tingling. She had to stay awake. She had to.

"He always cleaned up the judge's mess. Made the judge a success. Took care of all the dirty little details. And you know what the judge did for him? Nothing."

There was a swooshing *whomp-whomp-whomp* sound that kept getting louder. Zoe wondered if it was something inside her own head, warning her that she was about to lose consciousness.

Marcus slapped the steering wheel again as he stared up through the windshield at the helicopter. "Cops!"

He pressed down harder on the accelerator, pushing the old van to the limits. They sped down the road toward the bridge. "If I can just get to the other side of the river, we can lose them in the woods again."

Zoe's head began to drop. She jerked it up, staring out the windshield, trying to ignore her body's insistence on shutting down. If she could just close her eyes and sleep.

Flashing lights appeared on the other side of the bridge. Marcus slammed on the brakes and tried to execute a fast U-turn at the edge of the bridge. The van fishtailed, swerved. The rear bumper slammed into a bridge girder, and the whole van shuddered in protest.

Then suddenly, the side of the old wooden bridge gave under the impact, and there was a thundering bellow of splintering wood as the van crashed through it.

Marcus screamed. Or was it her? Zoe felt the van pitch, rolling over on its side as it slid down the embankment toward the water.

Bracing herself, she closed her eyes and waited for the inevitable plunge into the icy water.

❖   ❖   ❖

Dan knelt beside Dana, pressing his shirt into a particularly nasty knife wound, trying to staunch the bleeding. "Hang in there, sweetheart. Help is on the way."

"My brother. . ."

"We know. Just save your strength, okay? You don't need to tell us anything. We know."

"He. . .took. . .her."

Dan's breath caught in his throat as his already racing heart skipped a beat. He'd seen her car but had been hoping that she was playing it smart, hiding somewhere in the woods, keeping her head down until it was over. He should have known better. Zoe Shefford never kept her head down except when she was charging in like a bull.

"He took Zoe? She was here?"

"Yes," Dana whispered softly. "He'll. . .kill. . ."

"It's okay. The police are on the way. They may have found her already. Just relax and save your strength. Hang in there, Dana."

Suddenly in a cloud of dirt, a patrol car came barreling down the driveway, skidding to a halt a few feet from Dan.

Two uniformed officers exploded from the car, guns drawn. "Police!"

"Cordette! Cordette Investigations! The killer got away. He has a hostage. This girl needs medical attention immediately!"

One of the police officers aimed his gun at Dan. "Step away from the girl. Keep your hands where I can see them."

Dan stood up, raising his hands. Arguing with them would only waste more time. Time Dana didn't have. "Please let Detective Johnson know that I'm here and that Marcus has Zoe Shefford."

The officer holding him at gunpoint merely stared unrelentingly at Dan while his partner patted him down, looking for weapons. He found the 9mm tucked in the back of Dan's waistband and confiscated it.

"It's registered, and I'm licensed to carry it. Get Detective Johnson or Detective Casto!"

The police officer pointed to the ground with the barrel of his gun. "Down on your knees, hands behind your head."

"Detective Johnson needs to know."

"We'll notify him as soon as we know this area is secure."

Dan sank to his knees, complying quickly, hoping that the sooner he convinced this cop that he was no threat, the sooner they would bring in a medical team for Dana and JJ would be notified that Zoe was out there somewhere in the hands of a killer.

Zoe gasped as the cold water rushed in and surrounded her. The rising water moved up her legs. Hands bound, she struggled to get the seat belt unbuckled. Next to her, Marcus was groaning, holding his head, blood trickling through his fingers.

Ignoring him, she went back to the seat belt. The water quickly moved up to her waist. The buckle finally gave way beneath her trembling fingers. Grabbing the door handle, she tried to push it open. It wouldn't budge.

The water was now up to her chin. She lifted her face, trying to keep from going under while continuing to push on the door.

The water kept rising, cold and unrelenting.

"Cordette? Yes, he's one of us. Let him go." Matt passed the handset mike back to Cole, then waved an ambulance forward. When the driver of the ambulance pulled up, Matt told him, "We have an injured girl. Knife wounds. Sounds critical. Get her out of here."

The driver nodded. "We have a medivac ambulance waiting back up the road. We'll airlift her out."

Matt looked around for Donnie. The agent, along with his partner, leaned on the hood of his car, pointing to a map spread out in front of him and giving out directions in a rapid-fire manner worthy of a general going into battle.

Matt hurried over. "Have we found Zoe?"

Donnie lifted his head, and the look in his eyes was enough to send a chill down Matt's spine. "I just got word from the helicopter. The van crashed through the bridge and is in the river. We've got men on the scene, and I'm on my way out there now."

"Was she in the van?"

"We don't know." Donnie slid behind the wheel and pulled the door closed.

Matt leaned down in the window. "Donnie, I suggest you find her alive or leave town before JJ finds you."

Donnie turned the key. "Where is he?"

"Searching the woods with a team."

"He may have heard by now then."

Matt stood back as Donnie executed a three-point turn and drove back up the driveway, leaving a trail of dust in his wake.

Cole waved to Matt from the front porch. "Matt!"

"Yes?" he responded, jogging over to the porch.

"We need you in here." Cole led him back inside the cabin, then down a flight of narrow stairs to the basement.

It was cold, damp, and poorly lit, but Matt could see two uniformed officers standing in the corner with flashlights. They stepped back as he approached.

He looked down and felt a cold chill run down his back. "Someone tell me this is not what I think it is."

JJ ran to the edge of the bridge and looked down. The old van had disappeared beneath the dark water, leaving only ripples in its wake.

"We've called for divers, sir."

"They'll be dead long before those divers get here."

Toeing off his shoes, JJ steeled himself not to think of Zoe in that river, trapped, running out of air, running out of time.

He slipped and slid down the embankment, ripping off his coat as he went. Then, taking a deep breath, he dove into the icy, black water.

The cold hit his skin, then sank right down to the marrow of his bones as he groped in the underwater darkness. His fingers touched metal, giving him renewed hope even as the cold sapped at his strength and threatened to pull him under.

A panel. A tire. A window. He groped along, trying to find a door handle even as he listened for some sound inside the van. It was so very quiet. So still.

His hand touched, then gripped the handle and he pulled, trying to open the door. The force of the water against the door held the door against his best efforts.

His lungs screamed for air, but he was afraid to waste time going back to the surface, then starting all over again.

Fisting one hand, he pounded on the glass, trying to break through it. It was like punching through cotton, his blows barely putting any force at all against the window.

He pressed his face against the glass and saw her, pale as a ghost floating in the dark water, her blond hair reduced to murky tendrils floating eerily around her face.

She was going to die inside that van, and there was nothing he could do about it. If only he'd listened to her when she'd begged him to take her seriously.

As always, he'd been far more inclined to trust facts and figures than Zoe's instincts, and once again, she'd proven that sometimes facts and figures must give way to something far more intangible. Truth.

Unable to hold his breath one more second, he reluctantly kicked upward, bobbing to the surface, gasping for air, spitting out water, and praying for more time.

He heard someone yell at him from the bridge above, but he couldn't make out the words. His ears were ringing and his heart pounding far too hard for sound to penetrate. Taking two more deep breaths, he flipped and dove once more.

❖   ❖   ❖

Kneeling down, Matt pulled a pair of latex gloves out of his pocket and slipped them on. "Anyone tells Amato I did this, I'll deny it and have you busted down to parking meters."

He carefully slipped his hand under the skeleton and eased out the wallet from the tattered remnant of jeans the corpse was wearing. Easing the wallet open, he looked at the driver's license. "Dylan Copeland."

Rising to his feet, he looked over at Cole. "Call in Amato, then let's see if we can find out who Dylan Copeland was and what the poor guy was doing here. I need to get up to the bridge. Cole. . . take over."

Denise hated this. She really hated this. "Hold this." She handed her holster and gun to a uniformed officer standing next to her. "Call that medivac and have them land as close to this location as possible. Tell them we have three, possibly four people who will need attention from hypothermia and at least two from serious injury."

She reached out and pulled the nightstick off the officer's belt. "Remind me to return this."

Then she climbed on the rail of the bridge, took a deep breath, told herself she was an idiot, and dove.

Rene calmly rolled out the dough for her piecrust as she talked with the Lord. "All the prayers have gone up, Father. We've covered this as best we can; now it's up to You. I know You'll protect Zoe. There's still so much that You've called her to do, so You're not going to let the enemy take her yet, but give her that understanding, will You? At times, it's terrifying to serve You. We humans don't do well not having all the answers before we begin, and Zoe is so new at all this."

She carefully placed the crust into the pie pan and set about the fluting process. "I don't know what's happening or where, but I can feel the unease and the tension, so I know something is going on. But You know and You're there with Zoe. Let her feel Your presence, Father. Reassure her that You're right there with her, watching over her, keeping her safe, holding her in Your arms."

Reaching for the apple filling, she began to pour it into the pie pan. "And while You're at it, Father, I'd really appreciate it if You could let that man of hers know that You are in control. Help Him find You in all of this."

Covering the pie with another layer of crust, she sliced a few holes in the top, then slid it into the oven.

Now, all she could do was wait.

❖   ❖   ❖

JJ felt someone nudge up against him. In the murky water, his vision was blurred, but he saw something dark moving against the glass, then, suddenly, the window was breaking away.

Ignoring the jagged remains of the window, he reached in and felt around for Zoe. His fingers tangled in long, flowing hair. Urgency pounded against his temples as he struggled to get a firm hold on her, then slowly lift her, pulling her through the window.

The person next to him had disappeared, but he had no time to wonder who it was or where they went. It could have been an angel for all he knew, but he didn't care. Getting Zoe out of the van and out of the water were all he could concentrate on.

Finally Zoe's feet came through the window. With one arm securing her against his body, he kicked upward with all the strength he still had left. It was feeble at best, but it was enough.

As soon as his face broke the surface, he greedily pulled air into his lungs. Hands reached out and grabbed him. Zoe was pulled from his arms. He wanted to hold onto her but didn't have the strength.

Panting, gasping, trying to get enough air into his lungs to stop the burning need, he allowed himself to be pulled from the water and stretched out on the bank. Blankets were draped over him, and someone came down over his face with a mask. Oxygen rushed into his lungs, and he closed his eyes, blissfully grateful.

Somewhere nearby, someone would be taking care of Zoe. He didn't know if she was alive or not and desperately wanted to ask, but he had no voice, no energy. Slowly, he felt himself drifting off as he was lifted up.

As soon as JJ appeared with Zoe, Barone turned to watch for Denise. Precious seconds ticked by. "Where is she?" he yelled to a man watching from the bridge above them. "Do you see her?"

The officer shook his head.

"Come on, Dee, come on."

He glanced over to see an EMT slipping an IV into Zoe's arm. Quickly, he turned back to the water. She wasn't coming up, and it had been too long. *Where was she?*

Barone toed off his shoes and was about to dive in when he saw her head hit the surface. Breathing a sigh of relief, he waded in. Reaching into the water, he grabbed under her arms and lifted her up.

Her head lolled over against his chest, and he saw the blood. "Help! I need help here!"

❖❖ ❖❖ ❖❖

Donnie slammed on the brakes, cut the engine, and jumped out of the car.

"Help! I need help here!"

Donnie ran to help Barone as he struggled to bring someone out of the water. Sliding sideways down the embankment, he reached out to Barone to get his balance.

"She went to get Tappan out," Barone said as they carried her up the bank.

"Where is Tappan?"

Barone sank to his knees, holding Denise and shaking his head. "He didn't come up."

Donnie turned around, ready to dive in, when one of his men appeared in the water. "He's gone!" the agent yelled up to Donnie. "No sign of him."

Donnie turned to the young agent standing by. "I want two teams scouring the riverbank to the south and two teams to the north. He's going to want to get out of that water as quick as he can. Find him."

"Yes, sir."

Donnie signaled a police officer standing nearby. "Get that chopper back over the river. See if he can spot our fugitive."

"Done."

Jack lifted his head, signaling Donnie. "I'll take the team heading south on the other side of the river."

"Okay."

If Marcus Tappan was in the river, he'd be going downriver. It was unlikely he'd have the strength to fight the upstream current to go north, but Donnie couldn't take any chances.

Donnie was betting on south. He took off into the woods with his team. Marcus was out there somewhere, and he was determined to find him.

❖ ❖ ❖

Marcus clung to a branch, gagging water, sucking air, and heaving with exertion. The sound of a helicopter approaching was enough incentive to force him to set aside his throbbing head and burning lungs to drag himself out of the water.

These were his woods. He'd played here as a child and knew them far better than a bunch of dumb cops. They'd never find him now.

Crawling, he grabbed a tree and hauled himself up to his feet. Staggering, he took a moment to get his bearings. There was a cave nearby. He and Dana used to play in it when they were children, pretending to explore new worlds and uncharted territory.

The helicopter drew closer. Marcus pushed off the tree and hurried through the brush. He just needed five minutes. That's all. Five minutes and he could disappear forever.

❖ ❖ ❖

JJ opened his eyes. It took a minute to realize that he was inside a helicopter and an EMT was checking an IV drip. "Zoe?" His teeth chattered, slurring his words. "The girl? How is she?"

The EMT looked down at him. "Which girl, sir?"

The question confused JJ. *Which girl?* "She's blond. Beautiful."

The EMT nodded. "We're taking care of her. I don't know what her condition is, but she is alive."

While JJ still wanted to know who the other woman was, he couldn't find the strength to ask. Cold chills still had him shaking uncontrollably, sapping every ounce of energy he possessed.

Zoe was alive. It was going to have to be enough for now.

Marcus shivered, his wet clothes clinging, dragging at his limbs as he jogged through the woods. He had to get away as fast as possible. He didn't know how close the cops were, but he wasn't taking any chances.

It was hard to pinpoint where things had started going wrong, but now they were out of control. It had been such a simple plan. A little GHB to speed up the judge's heart and, *poof*, he was out of the picture. In the meantime, he would hide his sister's murder by making it look like she had just been one more victim of a serial killer.

It should have gone as smooth as silk. He'd planned everything so well. Every step had been thought out over and over again. How did the cops find out about his dad? He must have overlooked something critical. He'd been assured that GHB wore off in about twelve hours and left no trace. There was no way they did an autopsy that fast, right?

Somehow, they must have tested his blood before the twelve hours had passed, and that had messed everything else up.

Marcus stopped, looking around. The cave should be right here in this area. Brush had grown up thick and heavy. It took Marcus a few minutes to find the mouth of the cave, well hidden behind a thicket. If someone didn't know it was there, they'd never find it. Taking one last look over his shoulder, Marcus crawled into the cave, disappearing from view.

Curling against the wall of the cave, Marcus reached up and wiped his forehead. It surprised him to find blood on his hand. He must have hit his head hard when the van went into the river.

Hopefully the girl died in the van.

Something that girl in the van had said still bothered him. About the cops finding that stuff in his room. It had to be a lie. She was just trying to trap him into confessing. That's it! It was all a setup.

But what if it wasn't? How did stuff like that get there? Of course, there was only one person who had access, but Lewis wouldn't betray him. Not in a million years. There was too much money at stake.

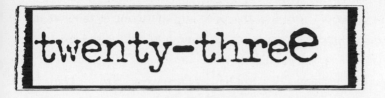

twenty-three

Monday, October 4—8:15 p.m.

I'm sorry, Detective, but we need to keep you overnight for observation." The doctor gave JJ one of those no-nonsense looks that might have withered a lesser man.

"I'm fine, and I have a job to do. A little cold water isn't going to stop me. Now, if you don't mind, I'm going to get dressed and get back to work."

"You're not going to be any good to anyone if you're sick. Do we understand each other?"

"And you're not going to be good to anyone if you're in jail for assault on a police officer."

The doctor's eyes went widened. "I have not assaulted you."

"Your word against mine. I'm sure one of those needles could pass for a deadly weapon. Then again, maybe not, but I won't have any trouble waiting until morning to figure it out. Do we understand one another?"

"Fine, but I assume no responsibility for your health."

JJ slid off the gurney and reached for his pants. "I'm so glad we see it my way."

The doctor stormed out in a huff. Matt, leaning against the wall with arms folded across his chest, had a smirk on his face almost deep enough to pass as a laugh.

"It's not funny." JJ held up his pants. Besides being wet, they'd been cut off him.

Matt shrugged. "You had the poor guy sputtering. I thought it was amusing. Besides, if you're ornery enough to fight with a doctor, then you're feeling well enough to walk out of here."

"I want to check on Zoe and Denise. Then we need to see Dana."

"I'll see about getting you some clothes."

"We have to call it off, Donnie. We're not going to find him in the dark." Jack leaned back against the car.

"We were so close! Do you know how much it bugs me that he got away?"

"We'll get him, Donnie. But not in these woods and not tonight. I'd bet my dinner bill that he's long gone." He pushed off the car and opened the door. "Let's go get some dinner, regroup, and see if we can't figure out where he'd go hide."

Donnie called in the men, told them to go eat and get some rest. "We'll start again first thing in the morning."

Climbing in his car, he slapped the steering wheel. "We were right there!"

Jack buckled his seat belt. "It's not the first time we've been close enough to smell them and had them slip away. He won't get far."

Donnie bit down on his frustration as he drove back to town. Had it been up to him, he'd have tracked through those woods all night, but Jack was right. It was so dark, they could have walked within feet of Tappan and not even seen him. On top of that, the men were tired and hungry.

Tomorrow was another day.

"Where are we going to eat?" Jack asked.

"You call it."

"Denny's."

"Done." Donnie slowed down at a red light. "Have we heard anything from the hospital?"

"I heard one of the girls died, but I don't know which one."

JJ slowly eased down into the nearest chair, his heart falling to his feet. "Dead? You're sure?"

The surgeon, who hadn't even bothered to change out of his blood-spattered scrubs, offered JJ a look of compassion. "I'm sorry. The knife wound nicked an artery. She bled to death in that water, even though the cold slowed the flow of blood. We did everything we could."

Matt shook hands with the surgeon. "Thank you, Doctor. I'm sure you did."

Silently Matt took a seat next to JJ. "You okay?"

"She didn't deserve this, you know?" JJ closed his eyes for a moment, shoving his feelings down deep. He needed to call her parents and let them know. They were going to be devastated.

"No, she didn't."

"She shouldn't have gone in there."

"Standing around and doing nothing was never her style."

"He's going to pay for this."

Dan Cordette took a deep breath, then knocked on Jeanine's front door.

She looked surprised when she opened the door. Then a little panicked. "Dan? Are you okay?"

"It's not my blood. I'm fine."

Jeanine ushered him into the kitchen and pushed him down in a chair. "Are you sure you're not hurt anywhere?"

"I'm solid. Just tired."

Jeanine brushed her fingers through his hair as if to reassure herself that he was in one piece. "Are you hungry? Do you want some dinner?"

"I could eat."

She hurried to the refrigerator. "I'll make you something. Leftovers okay? Meat loaf?"

"If it's your meat loaf, it's more than okay."

Busying herself with heating up dinner, she kept stealing glances at him.

"I'm really okay, Jeanine. I promise."

She turned around, facing him, tipping her head in that little gesture that he'd memorized a hundred times in his mind. "Why don't you go take a shower? I'll have dinner ready when you get out."

Wearily, Dan hauled himself up and headed for the bathroom.

Two hours later, showered, fed, and wearing one of his old football jerseys he didn't know she'd kept, he was tucked in the guest room, fast asleep.

JJ stood over Dana's bed, listening to the rhythmic bleeping of the machines. Matt stood quietly nearby. They'd been sitting for what seemed like hours waiting to see her, only to have the doctors keep them at bay. Finally JJ had just barreled into her room.

"Like I told you, Detective. She lost a lot of blood and her body went through an incredible trauma. I expect her to sleep a little while longer."

"We have a man out there who's killing people left and right, and this woman may be able to help us. I can't afford to wait."

"Well, unless she can talk in her sleep, I don't see how she can help you."

Matt reached out and touched JJ's arm. "Let's go. We'll try again first thing in the morning."

JJ was ready to agree when Dana's eyelids flickered, then slowly opened.

She licked her lips. "Stop him."

JJ leaned down. "We're trying, Dana. He has to be hiding somewhere. Do you have any idea where he might have gone?"

"Lew. . .in on it."

JJ took her hand and squeezed it gently. "I don't understand what you're trying to say."

"Lew. . .helping. . .Marc."

"Lewis Morton? Are you sure?" But even as he asked, he had no doubt she knew what she was talking about. "Dana, I have to ask you this. Did you know what your brother was doing?"

She softly shook her head as a tear trickled down her cheek.

"Thank you, Dana. Now get some rest and get well."

JJ turned to Matt and jerked his head toward the door. As soon as they were out in the hall and the door was closed behind them, JJ spoke. "You think he'd have run to Lewis?"

"I don't know, but it's worth a look."

"JJ, you're tired, you're angry, and you're more than a little on the edge. Call Donnie and let him follow this up."

"If you don't want to come with me, Matt, that's fine. Go home to your wife. But I'm going after Marcus Tappan, and God help him when I find him."

Matt sighed heavily. "Fine. Let's go."

❖   ❖   ❖

After stopping by JJ's to change clothes, they headed for Morton's. Matt knew better than to even try to reason with JJ. He sat quietly in the car, merely bracing himself when his partner took a corner a little too fast.

He followed JJ to Lewis Morton's front door. All the lights were out in the house, but obviously, that wasn't going to stop JJ.

They stood on the front porch for nearly five minutes, ringing the bell and pounding on the door before Lewis Morton finally answered it. Dressed in a bathrobe over dark blue pajamas, his hair sticking up, and his eyes heavy with sleep, he glared at JJ and Matt. "May I ask what this is about?"

JJ shoved him back into the house, stepping inside without any invitation. "Where is Marcus Tappan?"

Looking more than a little outraged, Lewis gripped the belt on his robe. "How should I know?"

"He's your client, or should I say your partner? Now, where is he?"

"I have no idea. And what do you mean, partner?"

JJ looked around. "Is he hiding in one of your rooms?"

"No! And you can look if you want. Now what are you talking about?"

"Marcus told his sister that you were helping him kill those girls."

Either the lawyer was a masterful liar, or he was truly stunned, because Lewis's face showed nothing but shock and outrage. "Helping him? Helping him kill what girls?"

JJ must have started to have a few doubts himself because he stared at Lewis for a long moment, then started backing up. "Marcus Tappan is wanted for murder. He's on the run. You are an officer of the court. You see him, you best make sure he turns himself in."

Matt almost had to run to keep up with JJ all the way back to the Jeep. "What now?" he asked as he climbed in.

"I don't know. I underestimated Marcus, that's for sure."

"Why would he implicate his attorney in his crimes?"

JJ pulled away from the curb. "Wild goose chase. While we're watching Lewis, he's off on another trail completely."

"We've got men watching his house, and we'll put one on Morton's place. He'll surface eventually."

"You want me to drop you off?"

"Where are you going now?"

"Back to the hospital."

❖ ❖ ❖

JJ didn't bother to turn the lights on as he moved softly through the hospital room. Pulling up a chair, he sat down beside the bed and picked up her hand.

She looked so frail, like a piece of fragile glass that would shatter if you touched it too hard. He knew those looks were deceiving. She was a tough lady; brave, compassionate, stubborn, and strong enough to survive so much in life.

He had wanted to date the woman, not fall in love with her. After Macy had been ripped out of his life, he'd sworn he'd never let himself get that close to someone ever again. Never allow himself to be vulnerable to loss and pain. He was supposed to be careful and practical and smart enough not to fall in love.

He'd always analyzed and dissected every woman from the first date on, picking at every flaw until he'd unraveled it. And the fact that

309

he'd been so successful, or that it had been so easy, had convinced him that none of them had been right for him. But he couldn't dissect Zoe. No matter how hard he picked and pulled, the threads of attraction wouldn't give.

And now, she had woven herself into his life. And his heart.

He rubbed his thumb over her white knuckles. "You knew I didn't want you rushing into a situation like that, but you wouldn't listen, would you? Once again, you put yourself in the line of fire, and look what happened."

Forcing himself to look into her pale face, he clenched his jaw. "I was on my way to Pittsburgh, so convinced that I knew what I was doing, then there were all these little doubts. It was like you were right there in the backseat, poking at me with your little theories and feelings and instincts. The next thing I knew, we were turning around and coming back.

"You're one in a million, you know that? You drive me crazy, but I'm finally beginning to understand that it's because you challenge everything I believe and make me think, and that scares me, lady. What if God really does talk to you? I've chewed that one down to a nub, and I gotta tell you, I can't find any other explanation for what you do and how you do it. You were right, even though it didn't make sense. And only God could have known. Now, what am I supposed to do with that?"

"Stop denying Him," Zoe whispered softly, her lips curling in a ghost of a smile.

"You're awake."

"Couldn't miss you finally seeing things my way. It may never happen again."

JJ laughed as he lifted her hand to his lips and kissed her fingers. "Ain't that the truth? How are you feeling?"

"Like I've been in a car accident, sliced with a knife, dumped in a river, and nearly frozen to death. Other than that—I feel fine."

Caressing her fingers, JJ took a deep breath. "I was so scared when I saw that van go off the bridge. I thought you were gone."

"So did I. How did I get out?"

"Denise and I dove in after you. She broke the window and I pulled you out."

Zoe squeezed his hand. "I'll have to thank her."

JJ bowed his head, pressing her hand to his forehead. "Marcus killed her, Zoe."

"What?"

"After she broke the glass on your side, she went back to get Marcus out. When she pulled him out, he cut her throat and swam away."

"Oh, no." A tear drifted down Zoe's face. "I'm so sorry."

"Denise died doing her job. She would have wanted it that way."

She squeezed his hand, and while it didn't have much strength to it, it seemed to touch him right down to his toes. "It's still hard on you. She was one of your officers."

"Yes. I know the two of you didn't like each other, but she was a good person and a good cop."

"It wasn't a matter of not liking her. It was just a bit of female rivalry. Nothing I would take personal."

JJ chuckled. "Confident, aren't you?"

She opened her eyes and looked at him for a moment before they slipped closed again. "It's taken me awhile to understand that most of our bickering is our unique way of flirting."

"I should let you get some sleep."

"Don't change the subject. Not this time."

"It scares me, Zoe." He dropped his eyes to her hand, staring at it while he gathered his thoughts. "I don't know how to handle it."

"I know. Me, too."

"You? Afraid? I didn't think you were afraid of anything."

She gave him another weak smile. "I'm afraid of my feelings for you."

"What do you think we should do?"

"Argue until we get so aggravated we kiss?"

JJ laughed, dropping his forehead to the bed. "I think I'll wait until you feel better." He lifted his head, still grinning. "It wouldn't be a fair fight right now."

He watched her for a moment, then realized she'd fallen asleep.

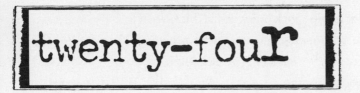

twenty-four

The old logging trail was closed from Highway 16 all the way out to Miln Creek Road. Fifty yards from the logging trail bridge, a mobile command center had been set up to house local, county, state, and federal law enforcement. Thanks to some of the procedures set in place by the Homeland Security Agency, coordinating the efforts of the different agencies and jurisdictions had been relatively easy compared to past efforts.

The river was being searched—by air with helicopters, by foot along the riverbanks, and by motorboat. So far, Marcus Tappan's body had not washed up, but the search continued.

The woods, pastures, and fields were being covered grid by grid on foot, horseback, and four-wheel all-terrain vehicles.

Showered, shaved, and fed, JJ sat in the trailer parked on the logging trail and went over the day's reports while Donnie continued to coordinate search teams. For once, JJ wasn't concerned with who would put the handcuffs on Marcus Tappan. The man would be caught and would go to prison for a very long time. It didn't matter to him if it was a state prison or a federal one.

Right now, JJ's focus was on just catching Marcus so that

everyone in Monroe County could breathe easier.

When his phone rang, he reached over and picked it up, never taking his eyes off the report he was reading. "Johnson."

"Hi, Johnson."

JJ smiled, leaning back in his chair. "Hey, Shefford. You're awake."

"Yes. Sorry I missed you this morning when you came in. But thank you for the flowers. They're beautiful."

"You were sleeping so peacefully, I didn't have the heart to wake you."

"Busy day?"

JJ snorted. "To say the least. Meetings with the press. Meetings with the chief. Meetings with the FBI. Meetings with the search teams. If I never have to go to another meeting in my life, it will be too soon."

She laughed, and he closed his eyes, absorbing the warmth of it. "I didn't get a chance to thank you last night, but I want to make sure you know how much I appreciate you jumping into that river to save me."

"All in a day's work."

"Josiah?"

"What?"

"Just say you're welcome and leave it at that. It was no small thing. Quit making it sound as if it were."

JJ picked up his pen and began twirling it through his fingers. "It was no small thing, Zoe. I thought I'd lost you."

She was silent so long, he wondered if she'd hung up on him. "Zoe?"

"You can't shake me that easily, Detective. You need someone to keep you on your toes."

"Promise?"

Zoe laughed again, this time a little brighter, and it made him smile, imagining the sparkle that was probably alight in her eyes. "Did you get any sleep last night?"

"A few hours. I feel like one big ache, but I have survived worse."

Matt appeared in the doorway with food. JJ waved him in.

Zoe spoke but sounded distracted. "JJ? The doctor is here. He wants to check my stitches."

JJ tossed his pen on the desk, then cleared a spot on the table serving as a desk while Matt emptied the bag. "I'll come by later. Do what the doctor tells you. Wait! On second thought, *don't* do whatever the doctor tells you."

"Why not?"

Bracing the phone under his chin with his shoulder, he peeled back the paper on his cheeseburger. "Because if I tell you to do something, you're guaranteed to do the opposite. So, don't listen to the doctor."

Zoe laughed again. "You've figured me out. I'm in trouble now."

He hung up the phone and bit into a French fry. "Took you long enough."

Matt pulled up a chair and dropped into it. "The roach coach was packed. Some of the teams are starting to come in to eat. Was that Zoe?"

"Yes."

"How is she?"

"Feeling better." JJ eyed Matt's food. "You got onion rings?"

Matt popped one in his mouth with a grin. "Yep."

"And you got me French fries? You know I love onion rings."

Matt waved one under JJ's nose. "You have too many one-on-one meetings today to risk it. But I promise to enjoy them for you."

"You're a real pal." Sulking, JJ picked up his cheeseburger.

"I have to admit you're handling all this remarkably well."

JJ frowned, his brows drawing tight over the bridge of his nose. "Handling what?"

Matt waved around them. "All this. You've never been big on sharing. And while we've been out there involved in the search, you're content to coordinate from in here. Not exactly the hands-on fanatic I am so familiar with."

JJ shrugged. "Guess I'm getting old."

The door flung open, and Donnie burst into the room in a swirl of energy. "Peace and quiet. I'll take it." Pulling out a chair, he dropped into it, digging into his food as if he hadn't eaten in days.

"Be our guest," JJ replied. "We're willing to share."

"Any progress out there?" Matt asked.

Donnie shook his head as he checked the inside of his turkey on whole wheat. "It's like he vanished into thin air. If it wasn't for the fact that he hasn't washed up in the river, I'd swear he drowned."

Marcus huddled in the small barren cave, feeling like a caged animal. He was cold, damp, hungry, and tired. This wasn't the way it was supposed to work out.

He desperately wanted to call Lewis but wasn't sure how to manage it. The cops were crawling all over these woods, and his cell was in the van at the bottom of the river. And even if he called Lew, he wasn't sure it was safe. They were probably watching Lew's every move, figuring he'd run to his attorney.

Why couldn't his sister and that nosy woman have died when they were supposed to? They'd more than likely told the police everything by now. That is, if they survived. He smiled as he remembered the look on his dear sister's face when he stabbed her. But the warmth of that memory quickly faded.

It was cold in the cave. He wanted his home, his bed, his coat. His car. If he had his car, he could blow this town and go anywhere. But his car was back at the house.

He needed to get to Lew. Lew could get him out of town and provide him with enough of his money to live comfortably somewhere until this blew over.

There was the sound of conversation outside, followed by snapping branches and radio chatter.

Quiet! He had to be quiet. *Don't move. Don't breathe. They'll walk right on by and never know I'm here.*

But they didn't walk right on by. Footsteps had stopped outside the mouth of the cave. Voices continued, but he couldn't make out what they were saying. He wanted to creep closer to listen but was afraid they'd hear him.

Someone yelled, "Over here!"

Panic surged through him, rising up like bile in his throat. His heart started pounding so hard it almost hurt as he tried to figure out a way to crawl farther back in the cave.

They'd found him!

Lanae heard someone rustling around in her room and slowly opened her eyes. A nurse was checking her IV.

"You're awake." The nurse smiled warmly as she set her clipboard down on the edge of the bed. "Would you like some water?"

"Yes, please." Lanae's voice was little more than a raspy whisper.

"I'll get you some water and let your doctor know that you're awake."

"What happened?"

The nurse picked up the yellow plastic water pitcher. "You were hit by a car. You don't remember?"

"I'm not sure."

"Don't worry. You're fine, sweetie."

Lanae wasn't so sure how fine she was. Her whole body ached, and her head felt like it was hosting an entire college drum corps.

While waiting for water, she licked her dry lips and tried to remember a car accident, but nothing came to her. She remembered feeling humiliated and wanting to hide from the world. And she could recall wanting to go to the store for groceries, but after that, there was nothing at all.

"Well, it's good to see you awake, Miss Oakley. I'm Dr. Borden."

He was tall and thin with short brown hair and deep chocolate brown eyes that seemed too big for his face. Gracing her with a warm smile, he pulled out a small flashlight and proceeded to check her eyes.

"Have a bit of a headache?"

"Pounding."

"I'll bet you do. We'll give you some Tylenol for that and order you some food. How will that be for starts?"

"Good."

Dr. Borden gave her an approving nod before launching into the details of her injuries. While her head was still spinning, he was headed to the door. "Well then, let me go see to some dinner for you, and I'll be back to check on you a little later."

And then he was gone.

The sudden silence seemed overwhelming. Picking up the remote, she turned on the television.

"The manhunt continues. Law enforcement teams from the local, state, and federal level are scouring the area for the suspected killer. If anyone sees Marcus Tappan, they are instructed to call law enforcement immediately, but do not try to apprehend the suspect.

He is considered armed and dangerous."

Lanae stared at the television screen as emergency numbers flashed under the picture of the man she believed to be her half brother.

Suspected killer?

"FBI special agent Donnie Bevere spoke to us just an hour ago. Here's what he had to say."

"Marcus Tappan is suspected of killing his father, launching a killing spree that took the lives of three young coeds and a police officer. He also attempted to kill his own sister, Dana Tappan, and Private Investigator Zoe Shefford."

Zoe? He'd tried to kill Zoe? Dear heavens, what had been happening? What had she gotten Zoe into?

"Agent Bevere! Is it possible Marcus Tappan drowned and that's why you haven't found him?"

Agent Bevere turned to the reporter. "It is possible, and we are sweeping the river by boat and helicopter. If he's out there, we'll find him."

"Agent Bevere! What about Dana Tappan? Has she given any indication why her brother has done this?"

"No comment."

"Was the sister in on it?"

"There is nothing that would lead me to make that conclusion at this time."

Another reporter jumped into the fray. "How is local law enforcement feeling about you taking over their case?"

"To be honest, we have been involved since the murder of Lori Blain, working closely with Detective Johnson as he built his case. It wasn't until Judge Tappan was murdered that we became fully involved, and we are still working closely with Detective Johnson and his team. We may come from different arenas, but we all have the same goal. Bring Marcus Tappan in and see justice served. That will be all for now."

The news anchor returned. "So, to recap. . .Marcus Tappan, son of the recently murdered Judge Leonard Tappan, is wanted for the murder of his father and four women. Law enforcement is asking for your help. If you see this man, please call the emergency number flashing on your screen."

Lanae watched, stunned, her mind spinning in a hundred different directions.

"I heard you were back with us."

Lanae nearly jumped out of her skin as a rough-looking man with a crooked nose and pale greenish-gray eyes walked toward her bed. "Who are you?"

"Detective Johnson. Monroe County Police. I've been here to see you often. It didn't even dawn on me that you didn't know who I was." He pulled up a chair and sat down. "How are you feeling?"

"Rough. Did someone try to kill me?"

"That's a distinct possibility. Is there anything about the hit-and-run driver that you can remember?"

Lanae felt sideswiped again. "Hit-and-run?"

Detective Johnson sighed wearily. "I guess you don't remember anything."

"Not really, no." Lanae chewed on her lip. "Excuse me, Detective?"
"Yes?"

"I was watching the news. I heard about this man, Marcus Tappan. They say he killed some people."

"Marcus Tappan. Your half brother."

Lanae felt her heart jump with nervous tension. "You know about that?"

"I do. And I'm worried that he may have been the one who tried to run you down."

"Oh, my gosh. I never thought. . ." She swallowed hard. "I was concerned about my friend. They said that he tried to kill her."

"Zoe?"

"Yes, do you know her?"

He smiled at her then, and she felt the tension begin to flow out and dissipate. "I know her very well. She's in this hospital right now. Two floors up. And she's fine. He cut her shoulder, so she had to have a few stitches, and they took a dive into a river, so they were watching her for hypothermia. But she's fine and should be released sometime today."

Lanae sighed in relief. "I'm so glad. I was so worried that it was all my fault."

Detective Johnson leaned forward and took her hand in his. "None of this is your fault, Lanae. Marcus killed his father, then tried to kill his sister. He may have tried to kill you, too."

"But why?"

"We can't say for sure, but it looks like he was obsessed with money and power. It was all about greed. He wanted it all for himself, and not only was he not willing to wait to inherit, he didn't want to share."

Detective Johnson stood up. "I'm going to leave you my card. If you remember anything, will you please call me?"

Lanae took his card. "Of course. And will you tell Zoe I was asking about her?"

"She was in and out of here constantly until she got hurt. I can pretty much guarantee she'll be down here before she goes home, but just in case she isn't, I'll tell her."

"Thanks." She watched him walk to the door. Another thought came to mind. "Excuse me, Detective Johnson?"

He turned around. "Yes?"

"If Marcus is still out there somewhere, are we still in danger?

Dana, me, Zoe? Will he try to come after us again?"

"There has been a police officer outside your door since this all started. There's one watching your sister. We'll keep you safe."

But Lanae couldn't help wondering how safe any of them really were if Marcus was determined to kill them.

Marcus heard the voices move off into the distance and nearly threw up in relief. Doubling over, he gasped and heaved as the panic slowly receded. They had been too close. Nearly on top of him.

Come nightfall, they'd have to call off the search until morning. He was going to have to get out and make his way to Morton's.

Wiping at the sweat beading on his forehead, he rocked on his knees, trying to tamp down the fear and anger. It was all their fault. If they'd just minded their own business, this would have been all over. They had no business in his house.

Then again, there shouldn't have been anything in there for them to find.

That question still nagged at him. Why had they found anything in his place? Or had she been lying?

One thing was for sure. As soon as he got out of here, he was going to find out, then someone was going to pay. And pay dearly.

Zoe winced as the nurse checked the bandages. "They're looking much better."

"How soon can I get out of here?"

The nurse shook her head as she rewrapped Zoe's shoulder.

"Itching to get away from us? Well, I think you'll be with us another day. Maybe two."

"But, I feel. . ." Zoe erupted in a spasm of coughing that burned her lungs.

The nurse poured a glass of water and handed it to her. "You nearly died from a knife wound. On top of that, you have a concussion. And if that wasn't enough, you nearly drowned and had some nasty river water in your lungs. You aren't going anywhere until we know you're one hundred percent."

Exhausted from another round of coughing, Zoe collapsed into the pillows, her chest burning.

The nurse gave Zoe an understanding pat on the arm. "Just get some rest, and you'll be out of here that much sooner."

As the nurse left, Zoe closed her eyes.

"I was all set to let you have it."

Zoe opened her eyes to find Daria walking up to the bed. "Daria."

"When you didn't show up for the funeral, I was really pretty angry. I couldn't believe you weren't there for me." She unbuttoned her black coat and slipped it off.

Draping her coat over the back of the chair, Daria leaned down and gave Zoe a cautious hug and a kiss on the cheek. "Then I saw Matt there, and he told me what happened. I'm so sorry, Zoe. There's just been so much."

"Don't apologize, Daria. I've been so caught up in this whole thing."

Daria sat down, dabbing at her tears. "Because I asked you to be. It wasn't very fair of me. I know how you are. I should have just trusted that if you could help, you would. I never thought for one moment about what it might do to you or what danger it might put you in."

"You didn't put me in danger, Daria. I rushed into that cabin, knowing the risks, and I chose to take them."

Daria reached out and clasped Zoe's hand. "This whole thing has been such a nightmare. All I could think about was my own loss. As if I were the only one grieving. There were other girls, other families."

"You're entitled, Daria."

Daria shook her head, twisting a tissue between her fingers. "How can you believe in Him, Zoe? After everything you've seen, everything you've been through. How can you believe in some wonderful God who loves us?"

Zoe saw JJ standing in the doorway, listening. *Help me explain this, Lord. Help me, because how does one put into words what You put in our hearts?*

"*Because* of what I've seen, Daria. After all the evil, I knew there had to be something else. Something better. Something more powerful. Marcus Tappan was obsessed with money and power. He chose to satisfy his own obsession with murder. You can't blame God for Tappan's choices."

Leaning against the wall, JJ spoke up. "If God loved those girls, why did He allow Marcus to kill them?"

Zoe shifted in the bed, trying to ease the ache. "So you think that He should have stepped in and stopped Marcus? Wouldn't that have been preventing Marcus from exercising his free will? If He did that, then God would have the right to stop you from doing something you want to do because someone else might not like it. How would you feel if He did that? You can't pick and choose, JJ. Either we have the right to do what we want or we don't."

Daria looked over her shoulder at JJ, then slowly stood up. "Hello, Josiah Johnson."

JJ nodded in her direction. "Daria. I'm sorry about your niece."

Daria merely nodded and picked up her coat. "I have to go. The family is getting together at Noreen's."

Slipping her coat on, she reached down and gave Zoe a kiss on the cheek. "I'll talk to you later, okay?"

"Give my love to them, will you?"

Daria nodded in response and, after giving JJ a cool look, left quickly.

"I guess she's a little mad at me." JJ pushed off the wall and took the chair Daria vacated so quickly.

"She's mad at God. Don't take it personally."

Stretching out his legs, JJ lifted one eyebrow. "I think she's a little mad at you, too. Her niece is dead and you're alive."

"Why did DeAnne die? Because Marcus chose to kill her. Why didn't God stop it? I don't know. But I know Him well enough to trust that He sees the bigger picture and lives will be impacted by this."

JJ snorted rudely. "Lives impacted? I'll say lives have been impacted. Families are devastated, a town is in fear, and friendships are being ripped apart. Doesn't sound like God to me."

"Can I tell you a story, JJ?"

"It's not one of those Bible stories, is it? A big flood and a big boat and two of every animal?"

Zoe laughed. "No. It's not that kind of story. It's about a man I met a few months ago. He had just graduated from college when his sixteen-year-old brother was killed in a car accident one Sunday afternoon. Because of that one accident, first his mother and father came to know the Lord. Then he did.

"Today, he's an evangelist, traveling around the country, visiting prisons with the gospel, and he's led thousands of men and women to the Lord. He's impacted thousands of lives. And it was all because of one car accident on one Sunday afternoon. If you were to ask him, he would tell you that because his brother died, thousands of broken lives have been made whole. Was it worth it? His family thinks so, and they're the ones who grieved and mourned and asked God why."

JJ stared at her for a moment. "You know why I don't like God?"

"Why?"

Standing up, he began to pace the room, his hands shoved deep in his pockets, his shoulders hunched as if expecting some blow from above. "All those rules. Thou shall and thou shall not. Ten Commandments and a hundred one rules on top of that. You could go crazy trying to keep it all straight."

Zoe reached back and swept her hair over her shoulder, shifting again against the pillows. "Can I ask you a question, Detective?"

"Sure. Are you okay? You look like you're in pain. Should I call the doctor?"

She waved off his concern. "I'm fine. I wanted to ask you how many laws there are on the books. You know. . .all the ones you have to enforce."

"I have no idea, to be honest. Quite a few."

"Society depends on the fact that rules and laws are not put in place to smother civilization; they are put in place in order to protect and serve the people."

JJ put his hands on the back of the chair and leaned forward. "So, you're telling me that God's rules are just put in place to protect people."

Zoe winked at him. "I always knew you were one smart detective. And the interesting part is this: If you check it out, you will find that most of man's laws are taken from the Bible. 'Thou shalt not kill. Thou shalt not steal.' God isn't trying to cramp your style, JJ. He's trying to make your life better."

"Does He happen to have anything in that book of His about catching killers?"

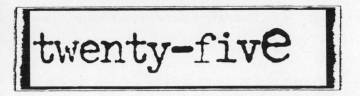

twenty-five

Zoe put the cap back on the red marker and set it aside, picking up the blue one.

"It's beautiful," Lanae told her, watching Zoe's every move.

Zoe reared back, tipping her head to look at the design she was doing on Lanae's cast. "It's different."

Lanae laughed. "I think it's very cool. Granted, I've never had a cast before, but I have never seen a mural on a cast."

Lanae was sitting up in bed, her casted leg hanging by the ankle. Zoe had pulled a chair up close to the bed and was busy creating a waterfall and tropical garden on the cast. Her shoulder was still bandaged and the stitches itched, but other than that, she felt practically as good as new.

"Zoe?"

"Hmmm?"

"They're saying on the news that they think Marcus drowned and the FBI is calling off the search. Do you think that he might be dead?"

Zoe lifted her head and looked over at Lanae. "No. He's not dead. But I don't want you to worry about him."

"But if he's still alive, what's to keep him from coming after one of us?"

Zoe snapped the cap on the colored marker. "You and Dana have a police officer stationed outside your doors. And I have JJ following me around like a puppy dog, making sure no one even breathes funny in my direction."

Lanae laughed.

"Besides," Zoe continued as she reached for a yellow marker, "I don't think you are even on his radar."

"So you don't think he was the one who tried to run me over?"

Zoe shook her head as she drew yellow flowers around the pool of water. "I don't think so. I could be wrong, but I just don't get the sense that he's after you. Maybe if you'd already proven that you were his sister and entitled to your share of the inheritance, then maybe."

"I don't want the money; you know that."

"I know." Zoe looked up from her drawing and smiled at the young woman who was quickly becoming a friend. "But that won't stop him."

The room door opened, and a nurse stuck her head in. "Miss Shefford? Could I talk to you for a moment?"

Zoe stood up, closing the marker and handing it to Lanae. "Be right back. No touching the masterpiece."

Outside in the corridor, the nurse explained. "Miss Tappan would very much like to meet Miss Oakley, but she's afraid Miss Oakley might not want that."

"I'll talk to Lanae. Give me a minute."

Zoe went back in the room to find Lanae angling her body to try and see the mural on her cast. She sat up as Zoe came in.

"Everything okay?"

"That depends on you. Dana would like to meet you. Would you mind if she came down?"

Lanae didn't answer right away but finally nodded. "You'll stay, won't you?"

Zoe looked at her watch. "Sure. I have time. Denise's funeral isn't until four."

❖   ❖   ❖

Dana wasn't sure what she expected, but Lanae didn't quite fit the bill. She was fragile looking with white blond hair and light brown eyes, high, chiseled cheekbones and full lips.

"You look like my aunt Margaret. I mean, when she was younger. In her pictures." Dana laughed nervously. "I guess I'm not doing so hot at this, am I?"

"I think you're doing fine. It's awkward, no matter how much we try to make it otherwise."

Dana rolled her wheelchair a little closer to the bed. "I like your cast. Pretty unusual."

"Zoe did it for me."

Dana glanced up at Zoe, offered a little smile, then looked back at Lanae. "I can't say that I was too happy to find out that you existed. I guess it was easier to think that you were a liar than to think that my father cheated on my mother."

"My mom was involved with him before he married your mother."

Dana nodded. "I know that now. It's hard to justify the anger I felt. Maybe it was finding out that I wasn't Daddy's *only* little girl."

"He never acknowledged me, Dana. I was never his little girl."

In spite of her desire to hate this woman, she found Lanae sweet, unpretentious, intelligent, and sensitive to her feelings. "I don't know why my father didn't want to know you. I think it was his loss."

Tears filled Lanae's eyes. "Thank you."

"What was your mother like?"

The tears spilled over now, running unchecked down Lanae's pale cheeks. "I don't really know. She was killed when I was still very young. I have few memories of her, and the ones I do have are blurry and unreliable."

"I'm sorry, Lanae." Dana reached out and took Lanae's hand. "You've been through so much."

Lanae shook her head. "My grandmother raised me, and she was wonderful. I never grew up feeling unloved or unwanted."

"I know that your attorney is arranging for paternity tests, but they really aren't necessary, Lanae. I have only to look at you and know that you are my sister."

Lanae started crying again and squeezed Dana's hand. "I didn't want the money. I still don't. I just wanted to know what happened to my mother and to know for sure who my father was."

"And now you know who your father was."

Lanae nodded.

Dana took a deep breath, trying to keep her own tears at bay. "But I have to tell you that I still can't believe Daddy killed her. I know it looks that way, but it's so hard for me to believe. Then again, I wouldn't have thought Marcus capable of murder, either, and look what he's done."

Suddenly the emotions were overwhelming. Bowing her head, Dana rested her forehead on the edge of the bed and gave way to the racking sobs that had been building for so long.

A moment later, she felt Lanae's hand stroking her hair, murmuring something softly reassuring and comforting.

He sat slumped in the front seat of the car and watched as the tall, leggy blond strolled out of the hospital and, after digging into her purse for her keys, walked toward the parking lot.

Finally.

The need to kill her had been building and building. It was all her fault. If it wasn't for her, he'd be sitting in his mansion, his cook serving him dinner, his Jag sitting out front all shined and gassed up for him to go out if he wanted, his lawyer and accountants bowing and scraping to make him happy.

Instead, he was dirty and wearing clothes he'd stolen from a Laundromat. And they were cheap. Probably Wal-Mart brands. Food? McDonald's rather than steak. He only had a few more dollars to last him. And he was reduced to driving this old, beat-up clunker he'd stolen from a used car lot that was closed for the week. A few more days, and it would be reported stolen.

But that was all the time he needed. He just had to get rid of the Shefford woman and wait for the cops to quit following Lewis around, and he'd be just fine. A shower, some clean clothes, then an airline ticket to Mexico.

❖　❖　❖

JJ turned up the radio and listened to a jaunty country tune, trying to kick himself out of a funk. Marcus Tappan's body hadn't been found, and today he was going to honor, then bury a comrade and friend.

He pulled up in Zoe's driveway and parked. And he was in love with a woman who swore she talked to God. And God talked back. She believed that God was all about love, and her eyes would light up when she talked about it, even when she was sitting in a hospital bed, recovering from a killer's attempt to end her life.

The woman was nothing if not a major aggravation.

Knocking on her door, he turned and looked around her neighborhood. In the middle of the day, it was quiet. Almost too quiet. He was going to have to talk Zoe into being careful. *Right.*

Zoe opened the door. Stared. Then pulled out a smile that lit up her eyes. "Wow."

"Wow, what?"

"You." She stepped out and pulled the door closed behind her. "I've never seen you in a uniform like that. With medals, white gloves, shiny shoes. Wow."

"It's standard for a police funeral." He shifted on his feet, starting to feel awkward as she walked around him, admiring. "It's just a uniform, Zoe."

"I've never seen you in uniform. You know, I've heard about women who have a thing for men in uniforms, and I've just never understood it." She jiggled her eyebrows. "Until now."

He glanced at his watch. "We have to get going. Think we could finish this in the car?"

They didn't, though. The conversation centered around the faltering investigation, Lanae and Dana meeting, and his speech at Denise's funeral. He didn't normally feel nervous about giving a speech, but funerals bothered him. There was something so final about them. It was all about good-bye. There were no second chances to change things, or to say things you always meant to say, or to take back things you shouldn't have said.

Zoe just thought funerals were merely the stepping from one part of life to another.

He wished, especially at times like this, that he could see things her way. How much easier all this would be if he knew he'd see Denise again someday. Or his parents when they died. Or Macy. What did come after this? Did Denise merely cease to exist? Or was there someplace like heaven—somewhere that housed her soul?

What if he died? Where would he go?

As he pulled into the funeral home and parked, the question suddenly seemed important.

twenty-siX

Friday, October 8—2:30 p.m.

Marcus knew opportunity when it came knocking. Or, in this case, came strolling through the parking lot of the hospital. Kieran Jennings.

Hunched down in his raincoat, he wove through the cars, coming up behind her. Deep in his pocket, he curled his fingers around the small revolver he'd stolen from the auto-parts store he'd broken into the night before. He'd been hoping for cash, but the owner had been smart enough not to leave more than the twenty-three dollars he found in the desk drawer. But he had found the gun under the counter next to the cash register. It was coming in handy.

"Kieran?"

She turned around, curiosity drawn across an automatic smile as she met his eyes. Then she slowly paled.

He exposed enough of the gun to let her know he had it. "I wouldn't scream or try to run if I were you. Wouldn't be smart."

"What do you want? Don't you realize the whole town is looking for you?"

"I heard the news. They think I'm dead." Smiling, he jerked his head toward the door to the emergency room. "Let's take a walk, shall we?"

When she didn't move, he ignored the fear on her face and took her arm, propelling her to move at his side. "Be a good girl, Kieran, and you may just live through this."

"Like Lori lived? And Pam? And DeAnne?"

He tightened his grip on her forearm and was pleased when she let out a little squeal in pain. "Don't mess with me, Kieran. I'm not in the mood."

Careful to keep his head bowed, he moved her through the emergency room and back to the elevators. When the doors opened, he pushed her inside. Unfortunately, three other people stepped into the elevator before the doors could close. Stepping to the rear, he kept Kieran in front of him, pressing the gun into her back as a reminder to keep her mouth shut.

A man and woman got off on the third floor, talking about their new grandbaby. The doors closed again and went up one more floor. The lone man got off, looking both ways before heading off to the right.

The doors closed, and Marcus heaved a sigh of relief. A few more minutes. Just a few more minutes.

The elevator doors opened, and he pushed Kieran forward. *Room five-ten. To the left.* He walked with quiet deliberation, as if he had all the right in the world to be walking down these halls and had done so many times before.

He stopped outside Dana's room and took another deep breath, trying not to laugh. With a smile, he pushed the door open and, keeping Kieran in front of him, stepped inside.

A nurse looked up from the bed she was making. The empty bed. "Can I help you?"

He nudged Kieran with the gun. She got the hint and spoke up in a trembling voice. "I was here to visit. . .Miss Tappan. A friend. She's a friend."

The nurse nodded as she smoothed the sheet. "She's down visiting her sister. Room two-fourteen."

❖ ❖ ❖

Zoe laughed as she tried to manage the chopsticks, dropping more back into the white carton than she was getting into her mouth. "Why did I let you talk me into this?"

Dana giggled. "Because you're an easy mark."

Lanae merely smiled as she maneuvered her chopsticks with the ease of a pro. "You know, if we're caught, they'll probably confiscate our food."

"You're the one who said you were dying for Chinese food," Zoe pointed out as she tried to get her chopsticks to stay together.

"Yeah, but I didn't think you'd actually smuggle all this in here. How in heaven's name did you get it past the nurses' station without them smelling all this scrumptious stuff?"

"I gave Nurse Nancy a couple of egg rolls."

Dana cracked up laughing, stretching her legs out to prop them up on the edge of Lanae's bed. "You're good."

"I know."

When the door opened, Zoe looked up. The smile on her face froze. And then vanished as she turned pale.

Dana looked back over her shoulder, then dropped her food to the floor. "Marcus!"

"Hey, will you look at this? Both my sisters in the same place at the same time. I mean, how much easier could you have made it for me?"

Zoe slowly came to her feet, her mind racing. "What are you doing here?"

Marcus slowly pulled the gun out of his pocket, pushing Kieran toward Dana. "Finishing what I started."

Dana screeched as Kieran fell into her. Marcus jerked his head at Zoe. "Sit down and stay quiet."

"Why? You're going to kill her no matter what I do."

Marcus tilted his head with a smirk. "True. But I can make it hurt her far more if you don't do what I tell you."

Zoe slowly sat back down. "You don't really think that you can walk in here, kill all of us, and walk out, do you?"

"I can do whatever I want. No one can stop me. Can't you see that? It's my destiny."

"No, it's your delusion."

Dana emitted a high-pitched squeak as he grabbed her arm and yanked her hard toward him. She lost her balance and fell hard to her knees at his feet.

"Don't mess with me, lady. I just want to know one thing from you."

"What's that? How long a prison sentence you're going to serve?"

Marcus glared at her. "What was all that rubbish about stuff in my house? What stuff were you talking about?"

"Let Dana go, and I'll tell you."

He put the gun to Dana's forehead. "Tell me or she's the first to go."

Zoe weighed her options. Marcus was a desperate man. He might very well pull that trigger in spite of the fact that it could bring a hoard of people running. "They found rope and a date-rape drug. And pictures of Dana's friends. The ones you killed. That's how they knew you were the one who killed them."

Marcus shook his head. "I never had any of that stuff in my house. Why would I do something so stupid? You're just trying to trap me, aren't you?"

Zoe swallowed hard as she tried to reach for something far

deeper inside than she had ever touched before. Peace began to flow over her. "I don't need to trap you, Marcus. The fact that you stabbed Dana. And tried to kill me. I don't need to know any more than that, do I? What they found or didn't find in your room is irrelevant to anyone except you. It means your friend betrayed you, doesn't it?"

"If he betrayed me, he's no friend."

"No. He was never your friend. He was just using you." Zoe felt the power building and could have almost laughed with the joy that filled her. "But you let him twist your own needs to suit him. He lied to you and used you, and now he's going to make you take the fall for all of it while he walks away with everything."

Marcus shook his head in denial, but she could see in his eyes that her words were impacting him. "Your father used him, so he used you. He hated your father, and he hates you. Where has he been these last few days, Marcus? Helping you get away? Protecting you? No. He's been hiding from you, hasn't he? He's been letting you run and hide like an animal while he continues to live in the lap of luxury. And if you got killed out there running from the police, well, all the better for him, right?"

Slowly the gun moved away from Dana's head as Marcus became consumed with the picture Zoe was painting.

"You wanted your father's love and respect, and you let him convince you that Dana had it all while you had nothing. But she didn't have it any more than you did. The only thing your father loved and respected was his money and his power."

Out of the corner of her eye, Zoe saw movement at the door behind Marcus.

"He was never your friend, Marcus. He planned this all along. With Dana dead and you in prison for murder, he could take control of everything, and you'd never hear from him again. He'd have everything, and you'd have nothing. Are you really going to let him get away with that?"

The truth dawned over his face with horror and resignation. "He planned all this? All along?"

"Yes, Marcus. I'm sorry. But he was just using you. There's time to turn this back on him, Marcus. It's not too late to make him pay for all this. But you have to let Dana go. It won't work if you hurt her."

Zoe nearly held her breath as Marcus just stood there and stared at her. *Come on, Marcus. Let her go. Please let her go.*

"He has to pay."

Zoe nodded. "I know. What he did to you was despicable. He has to pay, and you're the only one who can make sure that happens."

Slowly Marcus lowered his hand. Dana scrambled backward, getting as far away from her brother as she could in the small room.

Immediately Zoe pushed the table at the foot of the bed at Marcus. It slammed into him, knocking him backward as JJ grabbed Marcus's wrist and Matt put a gun to the back of Marcus's head. "Drop it. Now."

❖   ❖   ❖

4:15 p.m.

Zoe smiled at the duty officer as she passed by him on her way up the stairs. It was surprisingly quiet in the bull pen. Most of the detectives were away from their desks, and the few that were around were busy on phones.

She expected to find the conference room full and chaotically busy. Instead, only Barone was there, tapping away on his computer.

He smiled up at her. "Miss Shefford! How are you?"

"Better, thanks."

He stood up. "I heard about that move you made at the hospital. Quick thinking."

Zoe smiled. "Thank goodness Dana's nurse recognized Marcus and called for help. Where's JJ?"

"Down at interrogation."

"Tappan?"

He nodded. "His attorney just got here a few minutes ago, so pretty much everyone is down there to watch the fireworks."

She pointed to the door. "Is it okay if I go down there?"

Barone shrugged. "Sure. End of the hall, turn left. You should see a crowd."

Zoe laughed. "Thanks."

There was, indeed, a crowd standing in the hall. It looked suspiciously as if they were making bets. She looked around but didn't see JJ. Matt spotted her and waved her over. "Hey, Zoe. Are you feeling okay?"

"Yes, thanks. I'm fine. A little sore, but fine."

He led her to a door. "He's in here."

Matt reached for the door, and Zoe grabbed his hand. "If he's interrogating Marcus, I don't want to disturb him."

"Oh, no. This is the observation room. You'll be fine." Matt opened the door and waved her in.

JJ was standing in front of a two-way mirror, arms folded across his chest. He turned and looked in her direction. A warm smile crossed his face. "Hey, you."

"I wanted to see the grand finale if you didn't mind."

JJ pulled her into his arms and hugged her. "You deserve to see the curtain go down."

She looked through the mirror. Marcus was sitting in a nondescript gray metal chair, his feet resting on a matching table, a soda in his hand.

"Looks like he doesn't have a care in the world. How can he be so calm?"

JJ turned to look at Marcus. "In his mind, he was just a pawn and therefore not responsible for anything that happened. It's amazing to me sometimes how much people can convince themselves of in order to justify their actions."

Kieran took a deep breath as she stepped into her house. Immediately, her father came rushing out of the kitchen. "Kiki!" He swallowed her up in a bear hug tight enough to be uncomfortable. "Thank goodness you're all right. I just got off the phone with one of the detectives. Are you sure you're okay? I was going to drive down to the hospital, but they said you were on your way home."

She eased back out of his arms. "I'm fine, Dad. Really."

Suddenly Rachael came flying down the stairs, screaming in a high-pitched wail that hurt Kieran's ears. "Kieran! You're okay! How horrible for you! Are you sure you're okay?"

"I'm fine. I'm fine. Everyone can stop worrying now."

Her dad took her hand and pulled her toward the kitchen. "Come on. I made dinner. You need to eat and relax. Maybe take a nice, long, hot bath. Read a book."

Kieran stepped into the kitchen and stared in disbelief. "You made dinner?"

Her dad shrugged, looking a little sheepish. "Rachael helped me. It gave us a chance to talk. We both realize we've been a little unfair to you. You've always taken such good care of us that we've sort of taken that for granted."

"Taken you for granted," Rachael interjected as she pulled out a chair for Kieran. "Now, sit. Eat. Relax. We can do this."

Kieran shook her head, chuckling as she sank in the chair. "I don't believe this. You actually cooked."

"And I dusted," he said, lifting a casserole dish from the stove. "I'm not sure about the laundry, though. You may have to let Rachael handle that."

Kieran shook out her napkin. "I'm sure you could learn. I'm a good teacher."

The door to the observation room opened, and Donnie stepped in, closing the door behind him. "Morton's here."

JJ turned to Zoe. "Stay here. I'll be back in a few minutes."

Zoe nodded.

With his hand on the doorknob, Donnie grinned up at JJ. "You ready?"

"Do pigs fly?"

Donnie laughed. "This is going to be interesting."

He stepped out into the hall where Morton was waiting impatiently. "Mr. Morton. How kind of you to join us."

"I'm sorry it took so long, but I have other clients. Can I see Mr. Tappan now?"

"Of course." Donnie swung open the door to the interrogation room.

"I need to confer with my client for a few moments." Lewis Morton headed through the door. "And stay away from the two-way mirror. This is privileged."

Marcus Tappan launched out of his chair so fast, he surprised the officer watching him and slammed into Morton. Both men were knocked through the door and into the hall. Donnie grabbed for Marcus, who was on top of Morton, beating him in the face with his fists.

"You lied to me! You set this whole thing up and then framed me. You dirty double-crossing pig!"

"Get him off me! I have no idea what you're talking about. He's insane. He's insane! Can't you see that?"

Donnie hauled Marcus backward, pulling him into the interrogation room. He jerked him down into a chair and cuffed him to the ring on the table. "You sit down and zip it."

"I'll kill you, Morton! You hear me?"

Donnie leaned down close to Marcus's face. "I said, zip it."

JJ pushed Morton into a chair. "I don't think I've ever seen a client try to kill his attorney before the trial. Have you, Agent Bevere?"

Morton glared up at JJ. "He's insane. You saw that for yourself."

"Nice try, Counselor." Donnie turned a chair around and straddled it, folding his arms over the back. "Now, we have an interesting situation here. Marcus here says that you planned all the murders."

Morton jumped to his feet. "This is crazy!"

JJ shoved him back down. "Sit."

Donnie waited until he had Morton's attention again. "You know, we thought the same thing when we first heard Marcus's side of the story, but we thought, what the heck. It's worth checking out. And you know what we found?"

Morton appeared to shrink in his chair, slowly drawing into himself. "I have no idea, but I'm sure it was all his doing."

"He put your fingerprints on the pictures? I find that hard to believe. Oh. And there's one more small detail we can't quite figure out either, so we'd really like your help on this."

Donnie tugged on his ear as he stared at Morton. "Could you explain to us how your fingerprints ended up on the gun that killed Leona Oakley?"

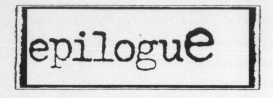

epilogue

October 14—3:00 p.m.

With the arrests of Marcus Tappan and Lewis Morton, Zoe watched as the town of Monroe heaved a sigh of relief. The police had determined an Alzheimer's patient, who lived in Lanae Oakley's apartment complex, was responsible for the hit-and-run accident that had landed Lanae in the hospital. Even so, there had been plenty of fuel for the gossip lovers and for the reporters, who had descended in force for the arraignment hearing and stayed for the memorial service the parents of the three girls had organized.

The press was packing up to leave now, but she knew it was temporary. They'd be back for the trial.

The families of the girls were still in shock and reeling from the grief. They huddled together, trying to comfort one another, yet unable to accept the comfort of others. It was too fresh. Too raw.

JJ had once again donned his dress uniform for the girls' memorial service. He stood next to Zoe, stiff and uncomfortable through the entire service. He stood silently with his head bowed and a faraway look in his eyes.

It wasn't until later, as they were leaving, that she noticed he was still far too quiet.

Taking his hand, she led him away from the crowds to walk through the gardens. "You want to tell me what's on your mind, Josiah?"

"Death."

She tucked her hand in the crook of his elbow. "It's all around us today. I suppose it would be hard to miss."

"What's after this, Zoe?"

"After the service? There's a—"

"No," he said, cutting her off. He turned to look at her. "I mean after death. We die and then what?"

"That depends, Josiah. If you belong to God, if you are one of His children, you go to heaven."

"One of His children. Following His rules. Letting Him have control."

"He's worth trusting, Josiah. He knows far more than we do."

JJ stared over her shoulder, then finally dropped his eyes to look into hers. "He really did tell you about all this, didn't He? About Tappan."

"I didn't always understand exactly what He was showing me, but yes. The longer I'm with Him, the more I get to know Him, the easier it will become to figure out what He's trying to tell me."

"And if I die without being His child, then it's hell, right?"

"That's what I believe, yes."

"I'm not sure I believe in hell, Zoe. But I think I believe in God."

Zoe felt her heart skip a beat. "It isn't believing in hell that's all that important right now, Josiah. It's understanding how much God loves you and how hard He's been trying to get your attention."

"About as hard as I've been trying to get your attention?"

Zoe laughed. "Oh, I think He was trying a whole lot harder than you were."

JJ lifted one eyebrow, then the corner of his mouth lifted in a crooked smile. "You know I'm crazy about you, right?"

"I know," she whispered softly.

"You're quitting this business, Zoe. No more."

Zoe's eyes narrowed suddenly as she stared up at him. "I beg your pardon?"

"You heard me. You can tell Cordette you're quitting."

Zoe punched him in the arm. "I will not! And if you think you can just tell me—"

His mouth came down on hers, cutting off her words, stealing her breath. She resisted for all of about ten seconds. Emotions surged through her, so big and so bright she expected them to explode around her like lightning in a summer storm. Wrapping her arms around his neck, she gave into the storm and surrendered to his kiss.

He lifted his mouth from hers a fraction of an inch. "You're not going to make this easy on me, are you?"

Zoe tipped back her head and laughed. "Not on your life, Josiah. Not on your life."

He grinned as he reached up and caressed her cheek. "Good."

About the Author

Wanda L. Dyson is a Christian counselor, author, and speaker. After fifteen years in marketing and advertising, she returned to her roots of writing stories. Her first book, *Abduction*, released in October 2003 to critical acclaim. Wanda and her daughter live on a 125-year-old farm in Maryland. Wanda can be contacted at www.WandaDyson.com.